Reviews of *The Curio*

'This is a very ambitious and dextr[ous...] with a rich collection of characte[rs...] impressive. So much to like, great plotting and Alex's drive and ambition is intriguing.'

Abi Morgan – BAFTA/Emmy winning screenwriter

'Adam Leigh may well have created a new genre: the fictional business memoir. If you've ever wanted to know what it's like to start a new venture from the ground up, then let this inventive novel show you.'

Jonathan Freedland – *Guardian* journalist & author

'I genuinely loved this book.'

Steve Parish – chairman Crystal Palace Football Club

'Adam Leigh takes us on a thrilling journey into the dark heart of start-up land, a place peopled with oddballs and outsized egos, where the relentless drive for growth at all costs means ethics are for losers. A great read.'

Rory Cellan-Jones – BBC journalist & broadcaster

'It's very believable, this book. Both emotionally and in its physical details. Adam Leigh has a way of making you feel you are part of his story, which is very satisfying.'

Daniel Finkelstein – *Times* journalist & broadcaster

'Pin-sharp writing, plausible, recognisable characters with credible motivations, great jokes, an intriguing and unusual subject, and plot turns that are sometimes poignant and often exciting. All of this brilliant stuff.'

The Jewish Chronicle

'I really enjoyed this book, particularly impressive for a first one! A very well written, innovative and ingenious novel – funny and clever.'

Arabella Weir – comedian & author,

Reviews of *Chicken Wars*

'A smart, darkly funny tale of love, destiny and the family ties that can occasionally threaten to throttle us.'
Sara Cox – BBC Radio 2 DJ & author

'Free-range comedy. Poultry in motion!'
Dan Patterson – co-creator, *Mock the Week*

'Humorous and heart-warming. A great holiday read.'
Deborah Joseph – editor-in-chief, *Glamour*

'I woke up my very cross partner at 3.00am laughing. Adam Leigh has done it again – taken a rather unappetising premise and made it un-put-downable.'
Jonathan Margolis – author & journalist

'Besides making me think hard about a chicken salad for supper, I laughed a great deal.'
Jenni Frazer – *Jewish News*

'Adam Leigh has done it again. He's gone and taken an unlikely premise and turned it into comedy gold. *Chicken Wars* is an ingeniously plotted and beautifully penned love letter to the Jewish community of Northwest London. It's also touching and very funny.'
Alex Pearl, author

'A charming and entertaining read that captures the essence of self-discovery, love, and the difficulties of balancing personal and professional life. Whether you're a fan of romantic comedies or simply looking for an engaging and heartwarming story, *Chicken Wars* is a book that will not disappoint.'
TheBookishHermit, blogger

'Adam Leigh's second novel, *Chicken Wars*, is a very funny and relatable story about a third-generation family business. I strongly recommend both of Adam Leigh's novels for humour, emotional warmth and fascinating glimpses of the commercial world.'
Paterson Loarn, author & blogger

The Pod Couple

Adam Leigh read English at university and spent the next thirty years in a career in advertising, enjoying lots of long lunches and producing the odd campaign for toilet paper or dog food. Adam has been married to his wonderful wife for over thirty years; she is his business partner and most uncritical fan. His three children are less forgiving.

Also by Adam Leigh

The Curious Rise of Alex Lazarus
Chicken Wars

www.adamleighwriter.com

The Pod Couple

A Love Story in Episodes

ADAM LEIGH

First published in Great Britain in 2025 by
Adam Leigh, in partnership with Whitefox Publishing

www.wearewhitefox.com

Copyright © Adam Leigh, 2025

EU GPSR Authorised Representative
LOGOS EUROPE, 9 rue Nicolas Poussin, 17000, LA ROCHELLE, France
E-mail: Contact@logoseurope.eu

ISBN 978-1-917523-28-8
Also available as an eBook
ISBN 978-1-917523-29-5

Adam Leigh asserts the moral right to be
identified as the author of this work.

All rights reserved. No part of this publication may be reproduced,
stored in a retrieval system or transmitted in any form or by any
means, electronic, mechanical, photocopying, recording or
otherwise, without prior written permission of the author.

This novel is entirely a work of fiction. The names, characters
and incidents portrayed in it are the work of the author's
imagination. Any resemblance to actual persons, living
or dead, events or localities is entirely coincidental.

While every effort has been made to trace the owners of copyright
material reproduced herein, the author would like to apologise
for any omissions and will be pleased to incorporate
missing acknowledgements in any future editions.

Designed and typeset by seagulls.net
Cover design by Shaun Patchett
Project management by Whitefox

*To Hannah, my better half
(Ask anyone)*

if this should be, i say if this should be—
you of my heart, send me a little word;
that i may go unto him, and take his hands,
saying, Accept all happiness from me.
Then shall i turn my face, and hear one bird
sing terribly afar in the lost lands

E.E. Cummings – 'it may not always be so'

PART 1
CHLOE

October 2018

The morning had begun badly because of the infuriatingly erratic Wi-Fi. For an ambitious production company trying to build a reputation for podcasts, this was not impressive and now they were over an hour late listening to the first recording. Huddled around a laptop, Chloe thought they looked like the French Resistance awaiting instructions for a mission. She couldn't bear the strained silence and felt compelled to break it with a feeble joke.

'Come on, chaps. You know what they say: *A watched digital file never downloads.*'

The silence remained unbroken, but Joe smiled, and their eyes met for an instant in mutual recognition of the bizarre concatenation of events that had brought them together again. For Chloe, it was completely unexpected, and Joe represented a former life from which she had long escaped. Indeed, the last three months of planning the podcast had been so intense she'd had little time to process their reunion, other than to contemplate the many ways things could still go wrong. It was like the melodramatic Victorian novels she loved – having run away from her past, she was now confronted by its consequences.

Joe's unease was clear. While he was her co-presenter, his demeanour was meek, suggesting he lived in constant fear of being fired. She knew his vulnerability was deep-rooted after the nomadic years of a bumpy career and thus he didn't want to put a foot wrong to jeopardise this opportunity. Seated between Chloe's agent, Mary, a woman for whom one expletive per sentence was rarely adequate, and Chrissie, the CEO of Listen Up Productions, he adopted a vow of silence as the safest way not to annoy anyone.

They had all worked so hard on the first series. While Chloe had a profile as a journalist and her new book was doing well, she still had to pull in favours to secure the calibre of guests needed to create interest in the podcast. Chrissie told her not to use up all her goodwill in one go, but Chloe's self-doubt prevented her believing the podcast would last beyond its first eight episodes, so she ignored the advice, contacting anyone famous she had ever met and begging as elegantly as she could.

After an interminable wait, their scruffy Californian producer, Kelly, gave a thumbs up to suggest everything was ready. Connecting his laptop to a wireless speaker, he nodded stiffly to each of Chrissie, Mary and the newly appointed advertising manager, Nicola. Chrissie produced a notebook and pen from her bag and Chloe prepared to have her homework criticised.

'Sorry, everyone,' Kelly began. 'Not helpful to have these glitches when we have so little time before going live.'

'Just play the fucking thing, will you, *beardy*,' Mary barked.

Unwilling to be cowed by the brusqueness of an agent who was not part of his creative team, Kelly paused to assert control.

'I will, of course. But first a word with Chloe and Joe.'

Chloe wondered what motivational cliché would now be delivered by their shamanic producer, who, in the few weeks they had worked together, loved delivering unsolicited motivational mantras. He spoke softly and sincerely.

'Well, good luck, you two. It's a very brave thing you are doing. You have put your hearts on the line and taken a big risk in working together. I am so pleased with what we have done in such a short time. Let's have a listen and see if everyone else agrees.'

They had argued for weeks about their theme tune and eventually agreed on a jazzy piano piece they found in a Japanese music library called 'New Beginnings'. To Chloe, it now sounded desperately inadequate at conveying the enormity of this creative undertaking, and self-doubt consumed her. Surely when relationships end, you move on without getting mired in the past? You certainly don't explore the subject with your first love and broadcast it to the world.

The music stopped and when she heard her presenting voice, it sounded like it belonged to a different, more confident person.

CHLOE: Welcome to the first episode of this new podcast, *Ex-Communicate*, with me, Chloe Adams, journalist and author.

JOE: And me, Joe Harris, ex stand-up, and writer of jokes of variable quality for other people.

July 2005

Chloe stared out of the window, hoping for a melancholic sunset to match her mood. A cloudy early summer's evening made this unlikely, so instead she called for backup. Despite it being her office party, her best friend, Emily, responded with the zeal of an emergency service and was en route in minutes, swiping a couple of half-full bottles from the open bar on her way out.

'The only way to stop you dithering,' Emily declared on arrival, 'is a rapid infusion of white wine.' Chloe did not question her advice and chugged a couple of glasses of warm Pinot Grigio without speaking, hoping her anxiety would be dissolved by the alcohol.

'To Dutch courage,' Emily said as they clinked glasses for the third time.

'To brave Vermeer, Van Gogh and Eddie Van Halen,' Chloe replied, needlessly showcasing the breadth of her cultural knowledge.

Emily looked at her quizzically.

'Are you nervous?'

'Does my shaking hand give it away?'

'That and talking *bollocks*. Calm down. You're doing the right thing.'

Emily had the bedside manner of a sadistic nurse, but it was what Chloe needed to prepare for the excision of Joe from her life. Now, there was nothing to do but wait. Starving and wine-woozy, Chloe retrieved a family-size pack of spicy crisps from Joe's hiding place of an unused saucepan, still with its price sticker. As she stuffed greedy mouthfuls, crumbs flecked her T-shirt and a pencil moustache of red paprika formed above her lip. She didn't care if she looked a sorry mess. It might lessen the blow.

* * *

'He has no idea what's coming, does he?' Emily asked an hour later as they sat, knees touching, on the battered leather sofa, drinking coffee so that Chloe could sober up and sound convincing when Joe arrived.

'Nope,' Chloe replied, staring into her cup, 'he's going to come home frisky and completely oblivious.'

Joe always hoped that an amenable night in the pub would end with her relenting to his daily request for sex, although if he had drunk more than a thimble of booze, he was likely to fall asleep, half-undressed, in the time it took her to brush her teeth. His foghorn snoring would then keep her awake and the night would be spent working out the best way to commit murder and dispose of the body.

Emily put her mug down on the threadbare carpet.

'It's bizarre. When he left this evening, he was unaware of the slightest kink in your relationship.'

'Well, that's your view, Em. These days I find it hard to distinguish Joe's emotions. I can never tell if he's moved by something or just has trapped wind.'

She had discussed with Emily for weeks how to annul her six-year relationship, as if her frustrated life with Joe in a dingy Kilburn flat required the kind of love stratagems that would grace a Jane Austen novel. It occurred to her that if her heroine Jane had written about their relationship, she would have called the book *Delusions and Delusional*, because Joe thought everything was fine while she fantasised about a swarthy, stubbly stranger not afraid to cry in front of her.

They lapsed into a maudlin silence, and Chloe stood up to pace the length of the small rug that she and Joe had bought on their first trip abroad together, to Marrakesh.

'I've never had to go through a break-up. It's torment.'

'Certainly, for me. Could you keep still? You're making me queasy.'

Chloe sat down but jiggled her leg instead.

'I've only had one relationship and that's Joe. Look how far we've come!'

'What, from Freshers' Week in Leeds to a grotty flat in Kilburn? Oh, the glamour.'

Chloe looked at her surroundings. It was a shithole. Patches of fetid damp spread across the bedroom walls like the oil slick of disappointment that had enveloped her.

'I love Joe. I really do.'

'I know, sweetheart,' Emily replied, patting Chloe's knee to stop it vibrating like a woodpecker on steroids.

'He's my best friend, and so supportive of all my journalist stress.'

She just wasn't convinced that was enough. London twinkled with the opportunity to become feted in artistic, cultural and political circles, and her ambition to be part of a conversation was all-consuming.

'I thought I was your best friend?' Emily said mockingly.

'You are too. Anyone can apply, so long as you tell me I'm fabulous and don't complain about my literary references.'

* * *

Her career was beginning to move ahead of his. It was amazing that she was now writing celebrity interviews for national newspapers, albeit only when the proper journalists were on holiday, or the celebrity was minor. (The last one was *actually* a minor – a disabled ten-year-old girl with a charity hit single.)

They should never have met, given she only chose Leeds University on the rebound from the crushing disappointment of Oxbridge rejection. Downing College Cambridge was where she thought she belonged and from the moment she applied, she buried her head in arcane literature while curating a wardrobe for her future studies that made her look like she was auditioning for a costume drama. Six months later, having failed to persuade them of her brilliance, she found herself at a night club surrounded by hordes of very nice people not interested in intellectual discourse but rather finding the cheapest beer available and somewhere quiet to throw up at the end of the evening.

Her anxiety was debilitating, and she was about to leave the overcrowded venue to return alone to her room when Joe emerged from an enormous cloud of dry ice that had just belched from the dance floor. Spotting her alone at the bar, he sidled up hesitantly.

'So, you're struggling to make any friends tonight as well?'

She bent back her ears to indicate she could not hear him.

'I said, are you struggling to make any friends?' he persisted.

She shook her head, suggesting she was still confused. Joe shouted even more loudly.

'I said, YOU HAVE GOT NO FRIENDS.'

The pounding music briefly quietened, and his last comment was clearly audible to other people at the bar, who smirked at them. Chloe remained composed.

'Well, there's no need to be unpleasant.'

'Sorry, I just wanted to say hello.'

'Go on then.'

'Go on what?'

'Say hello.'

'Hello.'

'Not much of a conversationalist, are you?'

Why was she being horrible? She had hitherto enjoyed so little male attention. At school, she wandered lonely as a geek to the school library, pretending that work filled the gaping hole created by her social exclusion. Hiding behind her wit, she would never give an unironic answer. Sadly, being the mistress of a *bon mot* didn't get her invited to many parties.

'I'm Joe,' he said, extending his hand formally.

'Chloe. Is this an interview?'

'If you like. I'd like to get to know you.'

'I'd like that,' she replied, softening.

'What brings you to Leeds?'

'My dad's car. He's a vicar.' She had no idea why she added the second bit of information. Being a vicar's daughter hardly made her cool in front of this cute boy, who had a clump of mad curly hair and a facial growth that could not legally be described as a beard. Nevertheless, even in the murky light, she liked his kind green eyes – a phrase she had read many times in books and was delighted to apply to her current situation.

'So do you believe in God and go to church a lot then?' Joe asked earnestly. It was a reasonable question given she was the one who had brought up religion, but the adrenaline surge of excitement made her want to move the conversation on quickly.

'Nope, don't believe in God – not since my mum died of leukaemia when I was twelve. Sort of made me a bit of a nihilist.' While the statement was entirely true, she couldn't believe that she was making the awkwardness of this encounter worse. Joe now looked bemused, and his mouth moved several times without his brain providing the appropriate response. Eventually, he leant towards her so that she could hear him over the noise.

'I am so sorry. That must be truly awful. Shall we talk about something else? Tell me about yourself.' Chloe's heart was pounding as she inhaled the aftershave/body spray/shower gel combination he was sporting. He wasn't like anyone else she had met in the last few days. There was something substantial about him; someone you could trust to be loyal.

'There's not much to know,' she replied. 'I'm just getting going with my life. My head is full of ideas, but I have no one to share them with.'

They chatted further, and with each question he moved a little closer so that their legs were touching. She didn't mind, and soon they were kissing with the fervour of two young people grateful for the reciprocity of desire.

* * *

'I can hear him outside,' Chloe whispered. It was a warm evening, and the window was open. It sounded like Joe was singing his new favourite song, 'Mr. Brightside', and forgetting the lyrics. Her heart beat arrhythmically in anticipation of explaining why she wanted to leave him, both as his girlfriend and in the real sense of taking her packed suitcases to Emily's flat, which would become her temporary home. She had never broken someone's heart before, and it was horrible.

They had thrown themselves into all aspects of student life with the security of their stable relationship as the foundation for their happiness. On graduation, they decided to move to London and live together, which in retrospect was a decision taken without either asking if what they really needed was distance to validate their long-term potential. Now, three years later, they had settled into their professional lives with different levels of enthusiasm. Chloe had scrapped her way through any journalistic assignment she could find to become a junior features writer for a Sunday supplement, whereas Joe was propelled by inertia (her favourite description of him) to become a grumpy history teacher who did even grumpier stand-up.

She loved him and he was the first man who loved her. He made her laugh, sometimes so much she'd get hiccups. He was gentle and compassionate with an ego that didn't need watering, let alone stroking. She adored his parents, particularly his exuberant and forthright mum, who sort of filled the gap, without trying, left by her own mother's passing. They liked the same books, watched the same films, and shared the same taste in soppy acoustic songs about the complexity of love and dead pets. And their lovemaking, not that it was dissected or reviewed, was regular, passionate and uncomplicated. She was about to give this all up because of a hunch there was something more spiritually rewarding beyond the cosy confines of their interdependence.

'Right,' Emily declared. 'I'd better make myself scarce.'

Neither of them had thought through the logistics of the situation and there was no time for Emily to run out and do a few laps of the block.

'Get in the bathroom, and you'd better turn the taps on so you don't hear anything.'

'Are you planning to shoot him?'

Chloe didn't smile and nudged her towards the tiny bathroom. Emily turned the shower on quickly and didn't move her arm away in time, so that it was soaked. She then turned on the sink taps as the front door opened and a tipsy Joe entered. He locked eyes with Emily, just as she shut the bathroom door.

'Why is Emily having a shower in our flat?' he asked.

The sound of running water after several glasses of wine made Chloe desperate to pee, and consequently she gabbled like a nervous child in a school play.

'I'm sorry, Joe … this isn't working, and I think we should split up. I need to see what's out there and I'm just not sure you understand my needs. I love you. You are a wonderful human being. It's just, that may not be enough.'

His face remained impassive, which, while a justifiable processing reaction, was a reminder that his expression was often inscrutable. She couldn't bear his lack of emoting.

'Say something, please, Joe. I'm sorry if this has come out of the blue, but it's been building for me for some time.'

'What do you want me to say?'

His response was frustrating. She'd made the hardest choice of her young life and would have welcomed a clue as to how this made him feel.

'Well, for a start, didn't you realise I was unhappy?'

'Honestly, Chloe, you bombard me with so many of your thoughts and feelings every day that sometimes I feel the best thing to do is be Switzerland and not have an opinion.'

'I'm sorry, but neutrality is not sexy. And there's only so much chocolate I can eat.'

'Do you think this is funny? I pop out for a couple of hours and you and Emily plot my demise. Tell me what I'm doing wrong, and I'll try to improve. I'll read a book or go on a course. Anything for you to stay. Talking of which, how am I going to pay the rent on my own? Homeless and single. Could it get any worse?'

His desperation grew with each heartbreaking entreaty, and she wanted to gather him in her arms and forget the whole thing. But the plan was to try a new life and what it required was a forceful communication of her needs that would leave him in no doubt of her decision. Like a sadistic town crier, she shouted out the cruel speech she had rehearsed.

'Joe, you are clueless. We talk all the time, yet you are incapable of understanding what I'm saying. Haven't you guessed, I want to go out, not spend quiet Saturday nights watching a DVD and having a shitty curry? That resigned look on my face every time you asked if I wanted the biryani or rogan josh. Did you think it was because I was worried I'd ordered wrong? You are so homely, and that's not meant to be an insult, but right now I don't want to spend a minute more here, listening to your problems teaching Tudor history to delinquent children. Maybe this sounds arrogant, it's just I've outgrown you and I don't think we can make each other happy.'

It sounded much less cruel in her head, and she certainly hadn't planned to use the word 'outgrown', which suggested she thought she was morally superior. It may have been the root of why she was ending her relationship, but it wasn't something to openly admit when destroying a lovely human being. Her cheeks flushed with unwelcome shame.

Joe looked like he was going to speak, but instead his exhausted face now collapsed under the weight of an enormous sigh. Shaking his head, searching for a reason to change her mind, he eventually spoke in a timid whisper.

'I don't think there's anything I can say to stop you going, is there? I always knew you'd tell me I was holding you back somehow. You think there's fame and glory awaiting you that you'll never find with someone like me who loves you quietly and just wants to stay together, irrespective of what we achieve.'

As an aspiring writer, she was impressed by his ability to produce such a zinger in response and flinched with self-loathing that she had caused him pain. After all, he had done nothing wrong other than want to live a quiet, unanalysed life, which was fine when they were trying to gain a foothold in the world but now threatened to immerse her in suburban mediocrity.

She desperately wanted to kiss him goodbye, a coda to a hitherto loving relationship and a final reminder of his familiar smell, which had once been so comforting. But no, that would be unfair.

She had to be true to the explanation she had given and its irrevocable consequences for her freedom. Instead, she got up and shouted through the bathroom wall to Emily, asking her to turn off the taps and help her with the bags. They struggled to carry two overstuffed suitcases through the open front door as Joe, paralysed by the pathos of his situation, watched despondently.

Within minutes, she was gone.

'THE MERRY WAR'
The Times, November 2008

At last.

No more being sent hither and thither to interview (faded) rock stars, (retired) footballers and (resting) actors. Adios long car journeys for thirty awkward minutes with a monosyllabic C-lister deigning to meet me at the behest of their publicist. Never again will I be trapped alone with a lascivious Tory MP (remarkably still in the Commons) asking me to 'experience his stately pile while inspecting the ancestral sword'. After six years of pandering to the egos of the not-so-good and certainly-not-that-great, I have been given my shot at freedom with this new weekly column.

It began inauspiciously when I was corralled into my lovely editor's office and subjected to a conversation that would have made our Head of HR spontaneously combust. (Not that I will push the matter because in our alpha male and attitudinally antediluvian broadsheet, HR might as well stand for 'Hardly Recognised'.)

Here's my verbatim(ish) recollection of our dialogue.

'Chloe, you're always dating, aren't you?'

'No more than most.'

'Not what I heard.'

'Who did you hear that from?'

'Do you want the list alphabetically?'

'Why is it any of your business?'

'Because we need a millennial dating column.'

'What do you mean?'

'You know the drill. Publishable sex references. Your continual humiliation and enduring loneliness. A thousand words a week. Make sure it's funny.'

I had to look up if I was a millennial. Technically, yes, as I was born in 1981, but the joke is on my dopey Baby Boomer editor because, in truth, I am from a completely different age. Circa Nineteenth Century, if I had to give it a label.

My friends mock my romanticism, which expects my soul to intertwine with the soul of my one true love. They tell me that I am pretentious and look to literature to understand the dilemmas of love, rather than OkCupid or other new dating sites that promise eternal happiness.

I suppose they have a point.

I am calling the column 'Merry War' because it refers to my literary heroine, Beatrice, from arguably the greatest romcom in history, *Much Ado About Nothing*, who was always sparring with Benedick to mask the depth of her feelings. Watch the film with Kenneth Branagh, you'll get the picture. In Act 4 Scene 1, there is the following exchange:

Beatrice: You have stay'd me in a happy hour, I was about to protest I lov'd you.

Benedick: And do it with all thy heart.

Beatrice: I love you with so much of my heart that none is left to protest.

How I would have loved such a declaration on my last date with a surveyor called Greg, who was wearing sports shorts and proudly told me that he hates books. I want a Benedick – a person of substance who will mock me and I will mock right back. I found love once and then ran away because I wondered if something else wonderful and unexpected would turn my life from monochrome to technicolour. My quest is ongoing.

At this point, you might as well know that my favourite poet is Thomas Hardy. I love the moody bugger. Not for his novels.

(Too many yokels conversing in unintelligible dialect and descriptions of limestone topography.) His poetry sparked my romantic engine to life. For my eighteenth birthday, my father gave me an ancient volume he found by chance in an antique shop. Those elegiac reflections on the nature of lost love were exquisite, the most moving of which were written after the death of his estranged first wife. The painful verse made me aspire to a future relationship that would not dissolve into remorse and recrimination. This is my favourite line, in case you were interested.

I should have kissed her if the rain
Had lasted a minute more.

I have thereafter wanted to avoid such soggy regret as the swell of bittersweet emotion his poetry evokes for me. I told you my friends think I am pseud and I bet my editor is now having serious regrets too. But don't worry, the GCSE literature lesson is over. From now on, we embark on the practical journey to find a partner and the unexpected directions it will take me. For good taste and legal reasons, names, dates and outcomes might need to be changed. But not the core of each encounter and emotional union. I am going to share everything with you until I don't need to anymore. You are about to find out how rubbish I am at relationships, which I suppose makes me hopeless at being a hopeless romantic.

So, to the love of my life, wherever you are, stop what you are doing. I am going to track you down.

* * *

'THE MERRY WAR IS OVER'
The Times, August 2013

I am in all sorts of trouble. For the record, I absolutely love working for *The Times*. I have grafted so hard to get this column in the magazine every Saturday, scratching my way to the top with the ruthless cunning of Medea. (Look it up on Wiki. She's a psycho.) Any rivals to my progression have been undermined, back-stabbed and discredited without the slightest concern for their emotional well-being, mental health or prosperity. I have schmoozed those who can help me progress (aka my lengthy Christmas-party chat with our immortal Australian proprietor, one of the cutest octogenarian billionaires I know) and ignored those who provide no assistance to my relentless pursuit of success. I file my copy with the reliability of Big Ben's chimes and after the years of toil can boast a legion of adoring social media followers who assuage my embarrassing need to be liked by strangers.

However, this golden ascent to journalistic immortality may be about to evaporate like morning dew on a summer's day. You see, I am getting married next weekend and will therefore need something different to rail against now that I have found true emotional happiness. A lifetime of crimson sunsets staring into the eyes of my life partner beckons.

Yup, at 3 p.m. on Saturday, in my wonderful father's church in quaint West Buckinghamshire (all right, it's in Reading, but why demean the occasion?), I will wed my French-born fiancé, whose name I will **not** be taking because frankly Chloe Dubois would make me sound like a chorus girl at the Moulin Rouge. The planning has been meticulous, although we are still struggling with the logistical challenge of how my father, Malcolm, can walk me down the aisle and then pop on his cassock and conduct the service without it looking like we couldn't afford a proper vicar.

For the last five years, I have been writing about my quest for a meaningful relationship and what makes us compatible with another soul, especially if you have watched them pee an inelegant map of Africa on their khaki chinos.

I told you about the men who were kind but dull and those who were intoxicating, quixotic and feckless. I lamented the disappointments of incompatibility, the misalignment of libido and the incongruity of my need for affirmation from individuals who saw affection as a peck on the cheek on their way out.

My aim was never to denigrate those individuals who bizarrely did not want to be my life partner. They were fundamentally a cohort of gorgeous individuals for whom I was often a vulnerable and restless narcissist, character traits I'd recommend redacting from your dating profile if you want to meet a mensch. And surely, this is what we all look for in our search for a life partner? Relationships need to be rooted in 'adjacent and conflicting emotions to produce equanimity', as any decent fortune cookie will tell you.

Anyway, 'mensch' is used to suggest a bona fide good 'un. It's from the German word for 'person', implying an individual rounded with all the necessary attributes for a seat at the top table in Heaven, and I don't mean the drag club off Tottenham Court Road.

Enter stage left D'Artagnan Dubois, the musketeer who won my heart two years ago. His name is David. He's a 34-year-old balding, specky asthmatic and, despite his French surname, is from Woking. But he's lovelier than a meadow in blossom and has granted me this one opportunity to provide some biographical detail. Allow me, therefore, to overshare my pride in having bagged this complete mensch package.

David is a successful creative director in advertising who has just started directing commercials and will one day, no doubt, take me to the Oscars to watch him in tears when he thanks me in his acceptance speech for 'Best Picture'. He is funny, cute in a boy-next-door-sense (so long as you don't live next door to Wayne Rooney), and empathetic in his management of my insecurities about my writing, job, friends, dress sense, singing voice, shape of my feet and death of liberal democracy. He wants me to flourish, and to spend unlimited time by my side. We revel in each other's successes. We are egregiously smug about our enduring happiness.

Which means this column has no future. No one will want to read about a happy marriage. As we become the sum of our loving parts, why will my immutable contentment be of any interest to you? Nothing is going to happen worth commenting on in our lives as we build a great home for our imminent brood of catalogue model progeny. It's just not that considerate to extol our good fortune in finding each other to people who may not be as lucky.

So, it's au revoir to my unsolicited life lessons now that I have learnt the most important one myself. I'm not sure I agree with that ridiculous line at the end of *Les Misérables* when they warble 'to love another person is to see the face of God'. If that were true, my deity has the scrunched-up smile of a weasel and a few acne pockmarks. Nevertheless, I couldn't love him more, and thank you Eros, Cupid, Aphrodite for providentially delivering him to me.

Fear not, I am still on staff at this wonderful newspaper. (After all, I told Rupert after my fifth G&T at the party that he was the greatest media magnate I had ever met and asked how many kangaroos he had.) I hope everyone reading this can enjoy that glow of fulfilment I now have from anticipating my life with David.

Now, if you will excuse me, I have a trousseau to prepare. I haven't got a clue what that is but, like my future marriage, mine is inevitably going to be the trousseau of all trousseaus.

October 2016

She had been awake for hours, listening to the autumnal squall. Outside, branches rattled the wooden frames of her rotting casement windows and each gust produced a draught the duvet could only partially repel. Scrunched up against the wall of her bedroom, she missed the warmth of David's body pressed next to her, Instead, he was fast asleep next door, and it saddened her that they were forced to be in different rooms.

He'd abandoned Chloe and their two-year-old twins in the middle of the night so that he could rest properly, leaving her with the overtired and wide-awake toddlers. Alice nestled in the crook of her numb arm and snored like a pensioner, while Mikey crawled over her head. The pungent stench of his recently filled nappy made her want to retch.

The bin men were clattering up the street, disturbing the neighbourhood in retaliation for their own early start. Chloe remembered less debilitating jet lag, her mind clouded by exhaustion and her limbs pinioned to the mattress by her children. Another day of chaos in which her catatonic state would make it impossible to speak in full sentences, let alone write a book.

The loud ping of an incoming text woke Alice, who began to wail in fury, perhaps at her inconsiderate mother's need to be in constant communication with her friends. Chloe somehow managed to retrieve her phone from the bedside table to look at the message. No sensible friend would be up that early, so it had to be serious. It was indeed the worst news a working mother could ever receive.

Throwing up. Feel shit. Must be last night's meal. Sorry not coming x

Jo the nanny was calling in sick.

* * *

Chloe came back into the kitchen from a three-minute shower, her hair still wet and frizzy. She was resigned to looking a mess, given that, at present, a meticulous beauty regime was for supermodels and the unemployed only. How many consecutive days had she worn the joggers and hoodie? Two, three, a week? Her wardrobe choices these days were a blur. Fortunately, the stain count was low, and it would do. Besides, David constantly told her she was beautiful, but she worried the compliment was an increasing challenge with each scruffy outfit she donned.

David was feeding the twins their breakfast, making funny faces, which were met with the hysterical laughter of the easily impressed. His parenting skills were strong, although today praise was hard to find as the childcare burden was about to fall on Chloe again with the force of a boulder dropped from a skyscraper.

'Here comes the 7.48 from Maidenhead,' he shouted, shovelling the last toast soldier into Mikey's Marmite-smeared mouth. 'Apologies for the late running of this service as Mummy the train driver was a bit tardy getting breakfast ready this morning.'

'You are funny, David. Amazing what an uninterrupted night's sleep can achieve.' Sensing her upset, David encircled her waist and pulled her towards him, toast soldier in hand, making *choo-choo* sounds as he moved it towards her mouth.

'If that Marmite goes near me, I will castrate you with a spoon,' she said, trying not to laugh.

The twins squealed in delight and Alice, more advanced in speech than her brother, shouted, '*Cstrate mrmite. Cstrate mrmite.*'

'Honestly, Chloe, what sort of influence are you trying to be on our children? And your father a vicar and all.'

Chloe took the toast from David's hand and smiled. He leant towards her and kissed her softly on the lips as she encircled his neck with her free hand. The kiss lingered and when he separated from her, his cheek was smeared in buttery Marmite.

'Now you can smell of rancid yeast all day, which I think is sufficient penance for you abandoning the marital bed for a decent night's kip.'

'You know I don't abandon you lightly, and I suppose it's no consolation to you that the mattress is bloody uncomfortable in the spare room. My back is terrible this morning.'

'Pathetic attempt to claim the moral high ground. I am looking down on you from so high, I've got a crick in my neck.'

Chloe moved away to distract herself from her frustration. It was time to begin her morning ritual of coffee preparation, and she manically scooped coffee into a large cafetière. Her body had craved caffeine for hours, and she had every intention of drinking the eight-cup pot, with a straw if necessary.

Having filled the cafetière with too much coffee, she was unable to push the plunger down and resorted to leaning on it, her body weight causing a temporary vacuum, culminating in hot black liquid ejaculating over the entire work surface and splattering the cream blinds several feet away. She swore and swore again, a profane loop of frustration. David said nothing, grabbed a cloth and gently wiped her hands. Even the twins sensed the tension and graduated from hyena-like giggling to fearful whimpers.

Minutes passed in silence as they cleared up the hot coffee. Chloe managed to pour herself a large mug from what remained in the pot and took a couple of restorative breaths, as if finishing a yoga lesson. She picked up from David's complaint of back-ache.

'I'd like to be sympathetic, darling, but it's the third time you've done this to me in a week. Right now, I'm thinking of briefing my divorce lawyer and making sure you get custody.'

David struggled sometimes to differentiate Chloe's banter from the genuineness of her emotions, and this was one of those moments. For him, the need for a proper night's sleep was self-evident and he was confused as to why she was making this difficult.

'You know what an important week this is for me. To tell the truth, sleep is tricky whatever I do, my mind is racing so much. Tomorrow is going to be the biggest day in my professional career. It's my future. Our future.'

Chloe bristled at her inclusion in his statement. Of course she knew that his meeting with the producers of the first film he was going to direct was enormous. He had worked for two years for this moment of sign-off for the romcom that was going to propel him into a new world of fame. She had listened to every script problem, casting issue and directorial interpretation and patiently absorbed his anxiety for the vagaries of trying to get a film made. She'd done a great job as his muse, therapist, script doctor, wardrobe consultant, location finder and all-round smiling cheerleader.

It's just that David's pursuit of his creative dream was a vortex of self-interest that pulled everything towards its core and left her denuded of the energy needed to pursue her own. She was in danger of saying something hurtful in this state of exhausted frustration, unable to process his concept of co-parenting in which '*co*' basically meant her.

David lapsed into silence as he cleaned the twins' faces with baby wipes and released them from their high chairs so he could finish clearing up their breakfast. As he spritzed disinfectant on the high chairs, he looked at Chloe sympathetically.

'I know this is frustrating for you and you want to write your book. Doesn't a good relationship require that sometimes you sacrifice your needs temporarily? Mine are not more important, just a bit more pressing.'

'Sacrifice or suspend? There's a big difference.'

'Dare I say it, and for fear of you throwing more coffee at me, you may be overreacting. I'm just asking for a little understanding because I'm further down the track with my project than you are with your book.'

His attempt at reasonableness made it worse and she wondered if she was being unfair anticipating a dynamic in their marriage yet to emerge. He always claimed their creative aspirations were equal, yet a fear was growing like Japanese knotweed that her future achievements, no matter how great, would have to fall in line with whatever production schedule David had.

Why was she so upset with this perceived imbalance in the relationship? After all, his prosperity as a commercials and music video director had paid for Jo the nanny, allowing Chloe space to write a fortnightly column and plan her book. She should be grateful. David was universally acknowledged to be a kind and loving husband. (Indeed, Emily, still single, told her most weeks she would steal him without a second thought if she carried on complaining.) She just worried his solipsism required him to be the more successful creative force in the marriage.

The twins, fuelled by food, were now frenetically running around in circles and she knew that nausea and tears were inevitable. If not theirs, most certainly hers. The day required a resilience that no amount of black coffee and chocolate could stimulate. Her only option for respite now was to turn to God for a bit of assistance.

She phoned her father.

* * *

'I'm not sure that even on a good miracle day, Jesus could help you. I can nip next door, unlock the church and have a quick pray, but childcare isn't something that just arrives from nowhere.'

Chloe wasn't ready to admit defeat.

'Not nowhere, Dad, you pootle up the A40 in the trusty Astra and arrive here in an hour. It's not like you have any fetes or christenings on a Wednesday.'

'Nice try, but I told you, I have my bridge lesson with Sally and then we're going out for a lovely lunch in Marlow.'

Chloe watched the twins standing next to their toy kitchen and serving each other plastic vegetables. They were adorable, it was lovely and yes, she was blessed given all the misery in the world, blah blah blah. However, right now what she needed was for her father to give up his plans for the day so she could get on with hers.

She tried one last time.

'Bridge is for old losers who don't like conversation or can't play sport anymore. You are not yet seventy. You need to chase a couple of psychotic toddlers round a small, impractical house for a few hours and feel young.'

'Honestly, Chloe. I know you're my only child who I love more than Christmas, but *piss off*, there's a good girl. My word, how my language degenerates when I'm in your presence. Why is that?'

'Guilt, I should think, for putting your love affair ahead of my immediate needs. What's Sally got that I haven't?'

'A much less demanding temperament and grandchildren who live in Spain. Those are two big advantages.'

Her babysitting entreaties were futile. What she wanted was comfortable paternal reassurance, the blanket of unconditional approval that only he could provide.

'All right, I will graciously allow you to slip into oblivion playing bridge and doing crosswords. It's not a good look, but then again, since you wear a dog collar most of the time, what do you know about fashion? Can we just chat? Give me a second while I heat up my coffee so we can have a bit of a chinwag.'

She popped her mug in the microwave and waited thirty seconds, enough time for her to lament the unreasonableness of her behaviour. Her father had been a widower for over twenty years, single and dedicated to two things: his congregation and his daughter. She would never be able to thank him sufficiently for his devotion.

The grief of Chloe's mother's death was a constant in both their lives, a low-lying mist not thick enough to prevent them functioning, yet always obscuring their horizon. Chloe had been young enough to move forward, but Malcolm subjugated his happiness to helping others find theirs. While sometimes bemused by the noisy drama of his daughter's turbulent emotions, he knew non-judgemental listening was the most sensible strategy to deploy. This could be challenging when she chronicled her dating life in a weekly column describing behaviour that, theologically speaking, merited eternal damnation.

After he walked Chloe into his church and performed her wedding service, the responsibility for her well-being loosened and for the first time since his wife Alice's passing, he contemplated an alternative existence with love for another partner at its core. It did not take long for him to snag Sally, a friend of a friend, divorced, lonely and readily available, the type of companion he consistently eschewed when raising his daughter.

Chloe confronted this relationship with a mixture of jealousy and affection. Malcolm had been on call for her like an overworked junior doctor and now his availability was timetabled like an in-demand Harley Street consultant. While thrilled for this new chapter in his life, she selfishly reacted to his distracted focus with a nostalgia for when he was too sad to do anything other than dote on her.

Coffee in hand, she sat on a bar stool. The children were still distracted in their culinary play world, and she hoped for some of the reassurance that David was struggling to provide.

'OK, Dad, sorry about that. If you're going to abandon me, I'm going to need intravenous caffeine to give me strength. Now, let me start with a little bit of a Thomas Hardy update. I've found a way to shoehorn your favourite poems into my book to show how relationships are built on foundations of regret. What do you think about that? Could be very interesting.'

Malcolm didn't reply, and Chloe could hear Sally calling in the background. Her father mumbled a response that was much louder than he realised.

'I'll be with you in a minute. I just need to get Chloe off the phone.'

'I heard that, Dad, your stage whisper needs a lot of work. Go, if you need to, you don't need to listen to my writing nonsense.'

She hadn't wanted to sound like a hurt fourteen-year-old but had clearly failed as her father replied in the soothing voice he reserved for the bereaved.

'Darling, don't be upset. I told you we had a lesson this morning, and I'm now rather late. Please don't take it personally, I'd tell the Archbishop of Canterbury where to stick his mitre if he called now. Sally hates missing the start of the lesson and frankly, however unstable you are, she's much scarier than you when angry.'

'I'm sorry, Dad. You go and join the old biddies for a fuddy-duddy game of cards. I'll look after Alice and Mikey, and it won't be your fault that you grow up a stranger to them.'

Malcolm laughed. Chloe loved his phlegmy cackle, which suggested the warmth of Santa Claus and the wisdom of the ages.

'Thank you for allowing me to do what I want, it's most unexpectedly kind of you. I'll call you tomorrow. You'll be fine. Of all my children, you are by far the best mother.'

With that, he hung up. He was of the generation who never concluded a conversation by saying *I love you*. Chloe craved those words of parental support but hated her visceral need for her father's love to offset the inadequacies of David's. Though her husband validated their marriage through many compliments, she was beginning to realise his ambition was like a mistress demanding his attention and with whom she'd have to compete.

June 2017

The first thing that struck Chloe about her new agent, Mary Read, was that she looked fifteen and there was no way she could work with someone who'd probably just had her braces removed. The only evidence of adulthood was the tattoo on her wrist, which Chloe noticed when they shook hands. The words *Shake It Off* were written in a spidery script. Anyone that was prepared to engrave the philosophy of Taylor Swift on her body was not to be trusted.

She had been lucky enough to be represented by Norman Collins from Norman Collins & Associates for over ten years and he had provided her with the support essential to counter her debilitating self-doubt. Twice a year, they would meet for a three-hour lunch at Langan's Brasserie in Mayfair, a chance to discuss her work while testing the resilience of her stomach to a bacchanalian onslaught that would have floored Hercules. Three courses of creamy French cooking washed down with G&Ts, several bottles of Sancerre, brandy to finish – she was always relieved not to pass out on the Tube home. Yet she looked forward to these conversations for weeks and would bask in the glow of his encouragement.

She knew Langan's had been a big deal in the 1980s and wondered if the same was true for Norman. His vibe was more merchant banker than promoter of diverse literary talent and he always dressed the same: an impeccable three-piece suit with a gold watch fob and Hermès pocket square and an antique pince-nez perched precariously on a bulbous nose, criss-crossed with red blood vessels like a badly planned Tube map. An avowed tech-hater, he would still make most calls on a landline and favoured a handwritten missive over email correspondence.

At their last lunch, a couple of weeks previously, she had been blindsided when he casually announced, his spoon hovering over a four-chocolate fondant dessert, that he was dropping her from his list. The explanation sounded so reasonable – at seventy-one, he was trying to slow down and focus on a handful of clients for whom he could make a real difference. Chloe was sufficiently established in reputation to allow him to make this change and besides, his new young agent, Mary, would bring 'a fresh cultural alignment' to her work that would benefit her enormously.

The perceived rejection confirmed her career was waning. Ambition, which impelled so many creative projects, had become dulled by the challenges of working motherhood and a husband refusing to adjust the trajectory of his own career aspirations. For Norman, this meant he no longer needed to sit in an expensive restaurant with her for three turgid hours, being polite. His expertise could be subcontracted to an enthusiastic junior.

And Mary was certainly enthusiastic.

She had opened the door to the wood-panelled meeting room in Norman's Kensington office with such force that the Victorian watercolours almost fell off the wall. Chloe had not even taken her coat off when Mary launched into an outpouring of gratitude for the opportunity of representing this new client. What Chloe did not expect was Mary's gravelly Burnley accent, and her constant swearing, so different from Norman, whose greatest criticism of authors was gratuitous profanity.

'Fuck me, Chloe, I couldn't believe it when Norman told me that I was getting my first list, and you were going to be my big name. I fucking loved your weekend column in *The Times*. I was properly gutted when you went and got married. Anyway, I won't let you down. We are going to do great things together. And just because I look like a Year 10 Hermione Granger, don't be fooled.

I am twenty-seven and have had to put up with more *shit* than most people, let me tell you. I'll fight for you like a demented mother on crack trying to keep her kids out of care.'

Chloe thought she was hallucinating. This was not like a conversation with ever-polite Norman, who dispensed advice like an avuncular Oxford don from one project to the next. Mary was not just from a different generation, she was from an altogether different universe. One in which talking very loudly without interruption was the social norm. She had evidently prepared a précis of her life intended to win over her new reluctant client and was not going to stop until she had done so.

'My grandmother raised me because my parents couldn't be arsed. My dad was so unstable he made Liam Gallagher look like a Buddhist monk and my feckless mother preferred hooking up with even dodgier blokes to looking after me. I was a freak in my family because I read books, so I was largely ignored. Our local librarian was more of a parent to me than those fuckers.'

Chloe nodded. It was a million miles away from her own upbringing, in which her father was a constant comfort blanket of love. Mary did not want to be interrupted.

'Do you know I went to Leeds like you? Same course. First member of my family to go to university. I got a first like you too, and no one from the family came to my graduation. It only made me stronger and more determined. So, I arrived in London and knew that I wanted to be in publishing, but quickly found out that all the good jobs went to the Oxbridge wankers with privilege oozing from every spa-pampered pore.'

'I hate spas, if that helps.' Chloe wanted to say something supportive, and this was the best she could do. Mary looked at her quizzically.

'Good to know, although I wasn't thinking of going to one with you. Anyway, I spent the next eighteen months working at Nando's before I eventually managed to persuade Norman to give me a shot at being his assistant and he fell in love with me immediately. He told me I have rare commercial judgement and a contemporary cultural perspective that the business needs. He's letting me modernise the agency without even learning how to turn on his computer. You know he never married and has lived only for this agency and his clients. I am not going to let him down, especially as I've got shares in it, can you believe. And now he's given me some of his favourite clients.'

Chloe was touched by this story and her disappointment began to crumble like a sandcastle at high tide. She had assumed that in moving her to his protégé, he thought she was useless. It was the opposite, and Norman was giving her new impetus. If Mary could find new opportunities for her to grow readership and awareness, it was going to be good business for everyone.

It didn't take long for Mary's assertiveness to become hardwired in their relationship. Chloe had assumed that her previous conversations with Norman on the book counted for something. Mary's opinions, however, were her own and not to be challenged.

'Well, the title is going to have to change,' she barked.

Chloe put down her third cup of tepid coffee and tried not to look disappointed.

'I love the title. Do you know how long it took to come up with?'

'Don't care. It's *shit*.'

Mary's initial Orphan Annie charm offensive was clearly an act. She was much more Miss Hannigan.

'Tell me what it's about,' Mary continued, as if talking to the class dunce.

'Relationships. Why they fail and how the lives of the couples have been affected by separation. It looks at famous break-ups, historical and contemporary, and asks both what we can learn from relationships that don't work and how love changes as a consequence.'

'And now tell me why you think "The Failings of Love" is such a good title. I mean, I'm trying to get a bidding war going, not a fucking bidding minor skirmish. Why is anyone going to get excited by a book that sounds so negative?'

Mary's confidence was prodigious. She seemed to be suggesting publishers were going to fight for Chloe's new book. Was that realistic? Her first two books, a collection of her journalism and a coming-of-age novel, had done well enough to keep the publishers happy, but had hardly threatened the top of the bestseller charts.

Yet Mary believed that this study of historical couples (from Mark Antony and Cleopatra to Napoleon and Josephine), along with interviews with contemporary well-known former couples, gave a refreshing angle on the alchemy of attraction and the impact of heartbreak. And the conversations with rock stars, actors, politicians, writers and celebs gave the book its wide appeal. Chloe's prose was crisp, emotional, insightful and extremely witty. The title was the only outstanding issue.

'I don't have a readily available alternative to hand. I'll have a think.'

'Take a day and come back with your best effort. You shouldn't need longer than that.'

'Thanks for the generous deadline,' Chloe said, but Mary didn't care.

'Being comfortable is not the way to get things right. Get some fire in your belly. You strike me as someone who has never really known hardship or benefited from true suffering.'

'Does my mother's death when I was twelve qualify? That hurt a fair bit, from memory.'

The meeting was moving in such an unexpected direction. Mary's arrogance was refreshingly irresistible and instead of apologising, she wanted the last word.

'Your dead mother only counts if you were so poor as a consequence you had to scramble in the bins for food to eat.'

Chloe considered taking offence, Lord knows she had reason, but couldn't help smiling at Mary's brazenness. Instead of storming out or complaining to Norman, she got up, walked briskly towards Mary, and encircled her tiny frame in a lingering hug.

'You are totally fearless, aren't you! You're going to make me so much more successful than Norman would.' She was a few inches taller and addressed these words to the top of Mary's head.

'Finally, you get me, Chloe. I'm like Lara Croft with the balls of Tyson Fury. We're going to shake things up big time, I'll tell you that for nothing. Well, not nothing – fifteen per cent of everything you earn anyway. Now, one more thing before you grab me again in a non-consensual hug.'

Chloe sat down and turned from side to side in the tatty swivel chair as if moving to imaginary music.

'Do you not want me to use the word "and"? Or should I write some of it in Italian?'

Mary shook her head dismissively.

'A podcast.'

'A podcast?'

'I can say it as many times as you want, you deaf bitch. We're going to do a podcast about ex-relationships just after the book comes out. The medium is exploding, and you'll be a brilliant presenter. You're very funny, even if you talk like a first-year student with a thesaurus stuck up her arse.'

By now, Chloe was impervious to the insults, realising they were going to be the price she paid for success with Mary.

'And you think this is commercially viable? Will people be interested?'

'Are you kidding? If we get the right guests and you persuade them to talk, it'll have a cult following. There'll be live shows, books and merchandise within a couple of years, mark my words. You're going to be famous. That *is* what you want, isn't it?' Mary emphasised the point by putting her hands on Chloe's shoulders to hold her in place until she assented.

'The occasional request for a selfie and a few movie première invites would be nice, I suppose.'

'Oh, I think we can do much better than that,' Mary replied, clearly anticipating future world domination.

July 2017

She had half an hour until she had to pick the kids up from nursery and ordered a second coffee from the excessively tattooed barista with the beard of a druid. Nanny Jo had been an affordable luxury when David was directing lucrative commercials, but the modest budget and all-consuming nature of his first Netflix movie had made them reconsider their short-term disposable income and opt for cheaper childcare. Inevitably, with this new arrangement, the responsibility for drop-off and pick-up was firmly hers as David threw himself into his directorial debut like their future prosperity depended entirely on its critical success.

She hoped it would be successful, despite its unlikely premise. A romcom called *Chicken Wars*, it was the unusual tale of a kosher butcher falling in love with a vegan café owner and not quite telling the truth about his profession for fear of ending the relationship. She had worked with David (not that he'd admit to their collaboration) on adapting the script from the original novel. The source material wasn't up to much, in her opinion, and hopefully the film would be miles better than the book.

Uncontactable on location for several days, he was due home later and would expect her rapt attention as he recapped his on-set struggles. David could not focus on anything other than the film, which he saw as a ticket to their future life in an ultra-chic hacienda in the Hollywood Hills. With no space to listen to her writing anxieties, he prioritised the kids in what little free time he had. All she wanted was to tell him about her work, and her resentment bubbled like soup in a pan.

She watched a couple snuggling on a sofa in the corner of the coffee shop, the woman's leg draped over her boyfriend as if they were watching television in their living room. Her head rested on his shoulder and every few seconds they would dissolve into a languid kiss. There was something so exquisite for Chloe about that period of self-discovery with a lover, in which every new revelation becomes another piece of a giant jigsaw forming a picture of their compatibility. When she first met David, they spent most of their early time talking about their shared passion for films, books and the arts and their aspiration to create something worthwhile themselves. Maybe in reading poems aloud and quoting from obscure films, they forgot to compile the more basic questionnaire about their character traits and run them through the computer to see if they were likely to cause future conflict?

For years, she'd blocked out the cruelty of how she abandoned Joe. But as she watched these strangers canoodle, it made her relive what it had been like with him. Of course, it was very different to this smartly dressed twosome in their thirties. Back then, she and Joe were hesitant butterflies emerging from the awkward chrysalis of their teenage years. Kids learning on the job, their love growing with each term they shared until they graduated from university, both as students and as a couple, and found themselves living together way before their friends did. She didn't remember her heart racing with longing each time he left her to go to play football on a Sunday morning. At the same time, he was always there, her greatest champion when she had self-doubt about an essay or a bad performance on stage.

Her nostalgia made her want to chat to Emily, who she hadn't spoken to for ages as it was always so hard to find a convenient time to catch her in New York where she worked. When they did speak, Emily would complain about the intensity of her schedule as a marketing director for a global skincare brand in which meetings were 'wall-to-wall', 'back-to-back' and 'end-to-end'. Chloe once joked that it must be physically challenging with such an unusual seating arrangement.

How she missed the proximity of her closest friend, who had been away for four years. Emily lived in a small brownstone apartment in Brooklyn and was flourishing professionally but sounded lonely when she described to Chloe her constant and unsuccessful dating effort to find a reliable partner. Their relationship increasingly relied on the muscle memory of former closeness and was thwarted by the inevitable challenges of being so far apart from one another, not just in geography but in lifestyle.

Chloe stopped watching the man rummage in his lover's top as if he was looking for lost keys and called Emily. She sounded irritated.

'And to what problem do I owe the pleasure this morning? You'll need to be quick. My day is full of meetings about how to communicate skin hydration with two types of hyaluronic acid to smooth facial fine lines.'

'Very scientific. I get by on home-brew moisturiser: one part feta to three parts peanut butter. I haven't had a spot for ages, although I do get followed by dogs a lot.'

'Hysterical, but I haven't got time for this. What's the crisis?'

'No crisis, I just wanted to chat about stuff with someone who understands me.'

'David not returning your calls again?'

'He's shooting on location in an abattoir.'

'An abattoir? I thought you told me it was a romcom.'

'A long story for another time.'

'I'll book the day off.'

Emily's clipped comments reminded Chloe how unwise it was to expect much warmth and wisdom while she was at work. Chloe now regretted calling but hated silence even more, so carried on jabbering.

'I just wanted to tell you that my new agent, Mary, who looks like she's on work experience, turns out to be this mesmerising woman who has so many ideas for how to make my new book huge.'

'Like?'

'We're going to do a podcast about relationships, and she's convinced it'll be bigger than the book. She said she's going to make me famous, and we've been meeting production companies to discuss the project.'

'I thought profile didn't matter after you stopped writing about your sex life every week.'

'I wasn't famous,' Chloe protested.

'You were certainly infamous.' The sound of clacking keys suggested that Emily was doing something else as she spoke.

'Look, I just want to share my writing with as wide an audience as possible,' Chloe said meekly. 'I've worked so hard on this book. And a podcast will stretch me.'

'How's David going to react?'

Freakishly, at that moment, Chloe's call waiting alerted her to an incoming call from him.

'Weird, he's on the other line. He can wait. To answer your question, he wants me to pop out another baby or two. Three kids minimum are apparently essential for the correct image to get him the big family films he wants to direct. I mean, a child would be nice, I suppose, I just don't know if I want another.'

Emily's voice became a growl.

'You know, you are such a *dick* sometimes, Chloe. Do you ever listen to yourself?'

Chloe didn't know what she'd said wrong as Emily's rant gathered momentum.

'You amaze me – you just don't think what life is like for anyone else. You glibly tell me that maybe you'll have a baby, like you're booking a holiday. I'm on my own, in a different country, away from my family. Away from my best friend, who apparently can't appreciate the basic detail of my life I try to share with her whenever she finds a minute to call me and not talk about herself.'

Chloe knew her face had reddened with shame.

'Forgive me. I don't want to dump on you, but the Samaritans have stopped taking my calls.' Humour was not such a sensible idea, and Emily ignored her.

'It's not that you're trying to hurt me. It's just that you've lost empathy for a life that's not structured the same as yours. And from my perspective, yours looks pretty good next to mine. New York is filthy. The men are awful.'

Chloe didn't want to say the wrong thing and upset her further.

'Can we speak when you get back from work?' she pleaded. 'I'll wait up if I need to.'

'You can't try to fix everything when you want. I'll ring you as soon as I can.'

Emily sounded more distant than the ocean between them as she ended the call with abrupt displeasure. She'd got it all wrong and Chloe wondered how she would ever manage to balance the desire for recognition with the need to be loved by everyone she cared for. Packing her bag, she saw David had left a message. He sounded flustered and distant as he explained that they needed to shoot for another day, and he wouldn't be home.

Chloe wanted to be a good person, it was just that her decent attributes were often undermined by the unrelenting quest for praise, validation and affection. As she walked to the door, she glanced over her shoulder to see if the couple were now having full-blown sex on the farmhouse table. To her disappointment, they sat apart, and the woman was now pointing angrily at him like she'd just identified him in a police line-up.

April 2018

'What on earth does *Shagabala* mean?' Malcolm asked.

Dandy Dan the entertainer was shouting the word in a variety of silly voices and Alice and Mikey were laughing as if he was the funniest person alive rather than a middle-aged man dressed like a colour-blind clown. Chloe looked harassed as she laid out big bowls of crisps on the dining-room table in anticipation of the imminent onslaught of twenty-five hungry four-year-olds.

'Who cares, I'm just glad he showed up on time,' she replied, irritated that the group of mothers in the corner of the room were more interested in chatting to one another rather than helping her. At such moments, she resented the extent of her parenting duties, accentuated by David's current inability to share the load. It was even worse today because he still hadn't arrived home from the first screening of his film. For weeks, this production milestone had hung over them ominously and she had done everything to prepare for the birthday on her own, from present buying to balloon blowing. Malcolm, as ever, proved her saviour, managing to charm kids and parents alike in his assumed role of co-host.

Chloe saw the day in practical terms, given the twins were unlikely to recall any of this effort when they were adults. She was, however, trying to prove to Sharon Robinson, a mother she hardly knew but instantly hated, that she loved her children and was not an ego maniac writer focused only on herself. When Sharon appeared at the door with her revolting daughter Ivy (so called because she was clearly poisonous), her criticism was immediate.

'Oh, it's Dandy Dan. He's a far less popular choice than the other entertainers he works with, Silly Sally or Dopey Dolly. You should have booked it earlier. I hope the kids aren't too disappointed.'

Chloe smiled feebly and said nothing to Shithead Sharon, knowing she was in for an afternoon of not-so-silent judgement. *Focus on the children*, she reminded herself as she took Sharon's coat, contemplating if she should leave a messy jam sandwich in the pocket as her going-home present.

After forty-five minutes of Dandy Dan's grating songs, appalling magic and impromptu disco competition, the children divided into two cohorts – feral or crying with hunger. Chloe was by now being helped by several parents with the final teatime preparation. She was proud of the spread and wondered if Sharon would be fooled into thinking she had iced the twins' names on the cupcakes herself – unlikely, given the name of the baker was embossed on the paper doilies. If necessary, she would point out to Sharon that she had cut the cucumber, carrots and fresh fruit and it had taken ages.

Dandy Dan switched off the music and shouted, 'OK, kiddy plop plops, time to stuff your faces with all you can eat.' Chloe wondered if he had children of his own or had ever read an article about healthy eating if that was his call to the table, but then realised she was about to encourage them to ingest a plantation's worth of sugar with little restraint. The children swarmed to the table, shoving each other, and screaming, as if deranged by hunger. At least there was only half an hour to go.

Dandy Dan was in the garden smoking a roll-up, so Malcolm took it upon himself to provide some distraction and respite during tea. Chloe marvelled at how he had absorbed the song lyrics from the TV programmes he watched with his grandchildren far better than she was able to and he belted out a medley of complete bangers. She was filled with uncomplicated love for his kindness.

As they were clearing the table, she realised David had slipped into the room and gone to the twins, whose faces brightened at his arrival. He tried hard to smile but his features seemed to be congealed with sadness and Chloe could see his thoughts were elsewhere.

* * *

'You have abused an exceptionally kind pensioner,' Malcolm declared as he put on his coat. 'You know, if this carries on, I may change my number.'

'Sorry, Dad,' she replied, hugging him tightly. 'I don't mind knackering you out if it guarantees you sing "The Wheels on the Bus" for forty minutes straight.'

He had stayed for a couple of hours to help her clear up the mess, although the bigger challenge was calming down the overheated twins, who insisted on opening all their presents – the living room resembled a Toys R Us store before Christmas. Malcolm, horrified by the material excess of the birthday celebrations, tried to explain to them the Christian value of selflessness. However, reciting Luke 12:15 – *Be on your guard against all kinds of greed; life does not consist in an abundance of possessions* – did little to stop them hyperventilating each time they tore into the wrapping paper of another gift.

A rip tide of exhaustion swamped Chloe and even though the twins were finally asleep, she now had to confront the challenge of David, who had disappeared to the study the moment the party guests left. She heard him ranting on the phone in anger and frustration. Things must have been going badly because he didn't even find time to pop up and kiss the children goodnight.

She sat in the kitchen with a glass of white wine and a plateful of leftover finger-sized sandwiches for dinner. The day had been so full on that she'd not had time to keep up with her emails and was daunted to see at least thirty unread messages about the progress of her book's publication. As she waded through them, she realised momentum was building much faster than she'd anticipated. How unfortunate that her book and David's film were coming out at similar times, and they were going to experience their launches in quasi competition with one another. Different reviewers and audiences notwithstanding, the need for recognition burned with equal intensity in both of them.

Her weariness was quickly replaced by mounting excitement. First, the cover quotes were arriving from an array of journalists and writers. Their alacrity at reviewing the book in its pre-publication stage showed she had a network of supporters willing to heap praise on her in a way that would certainly help her attract new readers. Two consecutive emails contained perfect future marketing material: *First-rate. Brilliantly witty and wise*, said a well-known novelist she hardly knew. *Chloe Adams has expertly and intelligently shown us why the failure of a relationship can be the start of a happier life. If only I knew this when my wife dumped me*, gushed a misanthropic and alcoholic ex-colleague, who nevertheless had a significant following of fans.

Her publicist had gone into overdrive: book tours, blog tours and launch events were scheduled on a complex multicoloured spreadsheet that looked like the timing plan to build a shopping centre. She was thrilled by the volume of opportunities created for her, at the same time aware she needed a childcare solution that allowed her to be in Manchester one day and Exeter the next. She'd not fully thought through the logistics and unless she could find a temporary nanny, the launch would require a lookalike to stand in for her.

There were also lots of media appearances planned, with a day of radio interviews, profiles in a couple of weekend newspapers and some TV too. She was so excited to be able to develop her broadcast skills, and the subject of the book afforded her an expertise that would hopefully generate many future opportunities to be erudite on national media.

The final email was from Mary, who had been in a meeting with the production company for the proposed podcast she had been pushing for months with rhapsodic enthusiasm. Its form and structure were beginning to take shape and a tentative launch date three months after the book publication was nearly agreed. Mary was irritated that Chloe had missed the meeting because of the kids' birthday party, which she deemed a pathetic excuse. Nevertheless, the conversation had been successful, and the email was succinct in its positivity.

This podcast is going to be bigger than a porn star's todger.

Chloe was about to reply, contemplating the appropriate simile required to converse with her agent, when David emerged from his creative purdah in search of food and consolation.

'Why are you smiling like you've just won the lottery?' he asked testily.

'Oh, just something about the book from Mary. It can wait. I want to hear about you. You look like you've had better days.'

His vulnerability was obvious as he walked towards her, shoulders stooped and his face ashen.

'Would you like a hug?' she said, as if he were a child who had just fallen off the swings in the park and was having a good cry. He froze.

'I'd prefer something to eat. I haven't had anything all day. What's on offer?'

'Well, the dinner special is peanut butter sarnies, with some chocolate buttons and Hula Hoops, and to drink we're serving the Capri Sun, Fruits of the Forest, which is an impudent little juice with a plum and oaky finish.'

She got out some bread and started to mash an avocado vigorously. He watched her distractedly. The elephant in the room was becoming a herd, the longer she continued to avoid the question she needed to ask. As she added tomatoes and mozzarella to his sandwich, she could hold back no longer.

'What happened, David, at the screening? Was it that disastrous?'

Given his funereal body language suggested that must have been the case, she was pleasantly surprised by his answer.

'Not terrible at all. People quite liked it.'

'That's great. Then why have you been acting like you were lynched by an angry mob of critics?'

'You didn't listen properly to what I said.'

She was confused.

'What do you mean? People like it. That's great.'

'I said *quite* liked it.'

'I don't follow you?'

'It's not that complicated. *Quite* is the worst word you can ever encounter in response to your work. It's about sixty per cent towards excellence.'

He got up and started to pace small circles, carrying on before she could say anything.

'*Quite!* Who aspires to achieving *quiteness*? It's like being "nice" or "sensible" or "decent". *Quite* is the enemy of good.'

'Thank you, Master Yoda.'

She regretted it the moment it came out of her mouth. Sometimes the knee-jerk requirement to be witty clouded her reason and right now David wanted to be able to express himself, unconstrained by her attempts at humour. She knew immediately this half-slight had catalysed a chemical process in her husband that she had seen several times before and which produced an eruption of anger that was both cruel and personal.

He stared at her with incredulity and then swept the sandwich plate she had been preparing on to the floor. While Chloe was worried about what was to come next, she did think his physicality rather camp. Not the time to tell him that the gesture was more flounce than fury.

'So *fucking* typical of you, Chloe. Mock. Mock. Mock. I want your support, not your smug, patronising superiority. You're so pleased with yourself because you've written a book and are having a fancy launch with lots of very clever people who'll compliment you on the wryness of your writing. All I wanted to know was that I could produce something funny and popular. And I've found out today that it's just OK, nothing more. I come home exhausted, and you're too busy to ask me how it went, so I have to wait. In fact, you don't even pop your head round the door to check in on me. Then when, finally, I try to tell you, you don't listen. You just make a *shit* joke because you always want to be cleverer than me.'

Chloe fell into a chair, blasted by the gust of his anger. Disturbed by all the shouting, Mikey began to wail and was soon joined by his sister's shrieking in their shared bedroom. As their screaming intensified, Chloe trudged upstairs in silence. Not that she could think of what to say.

* * *

Sleep was frustratingly elusive. She was desperate to avoid further conversation, yet her exhaustion was not enough to stop her mind racing. The despair of her unhappiness co-existed with a need for reconciliation with David.

Was she to blame? Then again, isn't that what abuse victims always say? He'd screamed at her when her crime was simply sarcasm. That was horrible. Should she be more intuitive to his needs or was he just a narcissist? Back and forth she went in her head, catastrophising the end of her marriage and the next minute trying to celebrate its strength. After all, she loved David. She loved her children. She loved the life they had created. Surely there was room for both their egos to co-exist.

She wanted to have the conversation in the morning, when the darkness of his attack would be replaced by some sunshine and blue sky. Yet the more she tried to sleep, the faster her heart fluttered with anxiety.

According to the red digital glow of her bedside clock, it was 1.38 a.m. when David came into the bedroom, and she felt the weight of his presence as he sat on the edge of the bed next to her feet. In the silence, she feigned sleep with some shallow breathing but knew it sounded unconvincing.

'I know you're awake, Chloe.'

'No, I'm fast asleep. I'm only talking because I'm very good at multitasking.'

She'd had enough misery for one evening so made the conciliatory gesture of a joke.

'I am so sorry, my darling. I am so sorry,' David said softly.

'And?'

'And what?'

'What are you sorry for?'

He paused to make sure he said the right thing.

'For being nasty and saying some terrible things.'

Chloe couldn't take any more childcare and marital misery. Sensible conversation would have to wait for the morning. Instead, she reached for his hand, and they interlocked fingers in reassuring silence. Eventually, she spoke.

'David, we can't do this to each other.'

'I know. I know. I was just so upset about the screening.'

'Surely you can do some work on the film and make it great?

It can't be that far off? We didn't talk about it because you were too busy throwing my food on the floor.'

'I haven't a clue what to do and that became clear to everyone on the calls this evening. I panicked and I'm sure they've lost confidence in me.'

'Their confidence isn't lost, just temporarily misplaced.'

'And you accused me of sounding like Yoda. Anyway, enough talking for one evening, let's go to sleep. Maybe you can just hold me for a while, and we can forget what's just happened?'

As he disappeared into the bathroom, Chloe felt the relief of their renewed affection. How strange to encounter these conflicting emotions in such a short space of time. Yet David had said things that evening that, while supercharged by frustration, were clearly rooted in genuine sentiment. There was no point in trying to over-analyse the situation. It seemed best to focus on her work and let David do the same. At some point, they would reconnect.

By the time David got into bed, she was snoring and oblivious to his attempt to wrap her in his arms.

May 2018

At 3 p.m. Chloe got a phone call from Kathy, an assistant producer at BBC Radio 5 Live, who briefed her without drawing breath.

'Your presenter Matt Simpson is a stand-in today because no one wanted to work on a bank holiday although we had intended doing a feature on what makes relationships work with you and a couples' therapist, but the therapist has had a personal crisis of some sort and so can't come in and that made us have a bit of a rethink in the office this morning and we decided, because of the nature of the book, which is basically an examination of failed relationships, we'd turn the segment into a sort of discussion on why people write books about emotional subjects that are often very personal, so we looked at the bestseller list and tried to get in another non-fiction author to cover the subject, however it was completely impossible to get anyone with a profile at such short notice, so let me tell you we were stumped until Tom our enthusiastic intern mentioned this book he'd been given and read the first thirty pages which were funny and then we watched some old bits of the guy on YouTube doing stand-up and we called him this morning and he is going to join you, so all you have to do is answer Matt's questions which will be mainly about your book but it would be useful if you could engage with the other guy too as these things are always more successful if there's some chemistry between you both, er ... now let me enter you through into the conference line waiting room where he already is and you can chat to him for a few minutes before going on air ...'

PART 2
JOE

November 2018

Nicola Baker, Listen Up's advertising and sponsorship manager, had only been in the company a few weeks and was proving tenacious in finding commercial partners for the podcast. Joe liked her twenty-seven-year-old energy and charm and the fact that she was always smartly dressed, in contrast to everyone else's shabbiness. Standing next to her by the gleaming new chrome coffee machine, he tried to conceal his nervousness.

'How do you take your coffee, Joe? This is going to be the only time I make you one.'

'Black no sugar.'

'You must be relieved how well that went,' Nicola said as she took out some instant coffee and switched the kettle on. Clearly, Joe was not worth the faff of the posh machine.

The entire production and management team had loved the first episode, and the collective praise banished the memory of the Wi-Fi problems that had kept them all waiting. It helped that Chloe had secured guests who were such a major PR coup, and as he listened to the recording, he was impressed by how natural they sounded together. Even Chloe's terrifying agent, Mary, who had largely ignored him since coming up with the idea for his inclusion, had congratulated him like he was some sort of broadcasting savant.

'It's a huge relief. We're lucky to have Kelly as producer, even if he dresses like Dennis Hopper in *Easy Rider*.'

Nicola looked blankly at him.

'What's *Easy Rider*?'

'A masterpiece of seventies' cinema about social liberation.'

It sounded ridiculous as it came out of his mouth. Having never worked in an office before, chatting with colleagues was a new experience and he would clearly need some practice. He just wanted to be accepted as competent and a valued member of the team after so many years without support around him.

They took their coffee and entered the meeting room where Chloe had been working on scripts. She was in no mood for chatting.

'Can we be quick? I have to pick up the kids.' It was the third day in a row Joe had heard her say this.

Nicola nodded.

'I want to discuss the ad for the next episode. I have the final draft and I'd like to do a quick read-through.'

She handed them both a sheet of paper and Joe quickly read the revised text to see if she had incorporated any of his suggestions. He was very uncomfortable with this aspect of the job, the requirement to directly promote products and services that were so alien to his lifestyle. There was no choice, however, and each time he tried to shape the ads, he was told that his ideas were not acceptable as they mocked the product rather than attempted to promote its benefits.

Chloe was much less diffident and understood the importance of advertising to their future prosperity. She put on her glasses to signal she was ready and started to read.

'*Do you like fish, Joe?*'

'*No, but I've seen* Finding Nemo *twice, if that counts.*'

Chloe banged the table.

'Can you please stick to the script, Joe, or we'll be here forever. Just read it properly.'

'Sorry, Chloe. Just calling on the comedy muse.'

'Pop round to see her on your own time.'

Nicola smiled at her in sympathy and Chloe continued.

'*Do you like fish, Joe?*'

'I'm not a massive fan.'

'Because the Omega 3 in fish is crucial to aid your brain function and if you want to concentrate more, you might want to take a supplement like I do.'

How desperately he wanted to make a joke about his brain being his second most effective organ. He looked at Chloe to see if she was as pained by the awfulness of these opening lines as he was, but her eyes were focused on the script. There was no choice other than to do as he was told.

'And what do you recommend?'

'I've been taking Alaskan Fish Boost tablets for a few months, and I really think my concentration has improved.'

'Are you sure?'

'Well, as a busy mum, writer and journalist, I'm managing to get more work done these days.'

'And you're sure it has something to do with the Omega 3?'

'I'm glad you asked. The long-chain fatty acids EPA and DHA are important to your overall health and contribute to the maintenance of normal vision and brain function.'

'How many tablets do I need to take?'

'Just one with each meal. They're really easy to swallow.'

'And what sort of fish are you talking about?'

'The oils are sourced from the Alaskan seas from a range of different oily fish, depending on the season and availability, and they're not farmed.'

By now, Joe would rather have read the Shipping Forecast than discuss the provenance of Alaskan fish, whereas Chloe was giving it her all, as if on stage performing *Hedda Gabler*. He admired her discipline, seeing it as another example of a maturity he struggled to attain. Distracted, he lost his place in the script and Nicola waved at him like an angry orchestra conductor to get him back on track. He carried on with words he had never uttered before.

'Sustainability is so important.'

'It is, you can take them knowing they've been ethically sourced. It's win-win.'

'Yes. Yes.'

'One "yes" only, please, Joe. It's not hard,' said Nicola, tutting.

'And the other great thing is that they're delivered straight to your door. Find out more online at www.alaskanfishboom.com and make your first order. You'll thank me, Joe, in a month.'

'Why is that?'

'Because with all the boosted brain power and improved cognitive function, maybe you'll find a date.'

Nicola motioned with her arms the end of the reading and checked her smartwatch to confirm the timing. Joe started a sarcastic slow handclap.

'That punchline was hysterical. Some of the audience will need medical attention because their sides will have split. Honestly, could you make it sound any more like it was written by a computer?'

Nicola dismissed him with a frown.

'Not your job to comment. You're just here to do as you're told.'

For someone quite a lot younger, she wasn't showing Joe much respect. He contemplated getting angry, but it wasn't really in his nature and, besides, Chloe had returned to annotating her notes. As far as she was concerned, there was nothing more to discuss.

'Don't listen to him, Nicola, he's just grumpy because he forgot to take his fish oil tablet.'

'Thanks, Chloe, it's great to be working with at least one professional. Right, I'll nip off and agree the final script with the client. Joe, please read the words as written, even if they're a series of insults about your mother. Next up is a protein shake that gives you a ripped body. You'll really need to show us your acting skills with that one.'

After she left, Chloe stopped writing and stared at Joe for an unnaturally long time. He could only read basic facial expressions – anger, laughter or bewilderment – and she seemed to be manifesting all three. In the ensuing silence of her fixed gaze, he wondered what she really thought about him now, confused by his own unsettling feelings of affection and fear.

To his surprise, she leant towards him and kissed him inconsequentially on the cheek, as if saying goodbye to a casual acquaintance.

'Who'd have ever thought we'd be working together like this. So, tell me, Joe. Am I forgiven?'

July 2005

Suddenly, a tiny flat in which they constantly bumped into each other felt like a cavernous aircraft hangar without the planes. Joe even managed to zone out from the Italian family in the flat below with the screaming toddler engaged in a daily battle of potty training. He was focused exclusively on his own pain.

Why did Chloe need a wingman to dump him? He'd never liked Emily from the moment she and Chloe appeared together in an all-female *Macbeth* in their second term. She had played Lady Macbeth to Chloe's Macbeth and their performances were full of edge and menace, which he should have taken as a future warning. His anger calcified at their constant need to declaim they were *best friends*. Chloe seemed to operate some sort of friendship league table, with the possibility of promotion or relegation. She was always in need of validation – of her wit, her writing, and the possibility that one day she was going to be phenomenally successful. No time any more for dorks like him.

You never know what's around the corner, he mused. His philosophy was quite basic, questioning the cruelty of a universe in which he had returned home the previous evening anticipating a shag, only to have its possibility permanently removed from his life. The irony was that he got dumped after coming back from a drink with Tom, his best friend from university, in which they had discussed how lucky he was to have Chloe.

It had been an appropriately awful day at the grotty school in Paddington where he had the misfortune to work. His classes on the Tudors were met with indifference by pupils who thought that the expression 'history repeating itself' was when you were caught in possession of Class A drugs by the police more than once. Year 8 had been a particularly unpleasant lowlight that morning. Kieran Simpson, somewhere in the evolutionary scale between a moron and a sociopath, took enormous pleasure in shouting *did she give head before she lost hers?* when Joe tried to explain the nuances of Anne Boleyn's marriage. He hated teaching and worried that if a child didn't kill him, the profession would.

He felt alone but not entirely surprised she had gone. While vaguely aware of her unhappiness, he hadn't expected her to act so decisively. Living in the moment with Chloe had proved increasingly tricky as each moment had to be filled with the endless analysis of her feelings. While he was always delighted to discuss the contradictions of the world, she wanted to chat about how she was going to shape it with her achievements. And if he misinterpreted one of her emotional outbursts, he was castigated mercilessly. If only she came with an instruction manual.

A full vodka bottle was now half empty. Maybe the alcohol had evaporated, like his hopes of future happiness. Nope, he'd drunk it, as the room was spinning, and he struggled not to regurgitate the pizza he had shoved in his mouth like a man breaking a hunger strike. He wondered if the four cheeses would come up the same colour.

It had seemed a good idea to call her father when he got back from school. He always liked Joe, plus, as a man of God, he was specially trained to bring comfort to the needy. It was so unfair – Joe had been making such good progress to be fully integrated into their tiny but unbreakable father-daughter family unit. Surely common sense would prevail, and he'd be granted a bit of relationship absolution?

Reverend Malcolm was no use. He had already spoken to Chloe and had unsurprisingly taken her side in the schism. Listening patiently to Joe's protestation that her ending of the relationship was short-sighted, he occasionally chipped in some cursory consolation that made him sound like a trainee couples' therapist. By the fourth time he said *I'm so sorry you feel like this* or *how hard for you this must be*, Joe's atheism was burning stronger than ever.

There was no one else to turn to now and nor did he have the energy to plead his case, semi-drunk, to an indifferent third party, even if he could find one willing to listen. If this was heartbreak, it was worse than stubbing your toe or sunburn on your shoulders. He just wanted the door to open and a contrite Chloe to walk through with a beautiful smile of love, a bunch of flowers and a commitment to respect the happiness of their past for years into the future.

Why did she have to ruin his life?

July 2010

Ten-year-old Sasha Vinogradov looked more bored than usual, squinting in the bright summer sunshine as he stared out of the window of the opulent townhouse in Belgravia. Another pointless afternoon for Joe, who had been tutoring Sasha in maths and English for six months for £150 per hour. Having given up on full-time teaching and committed to trying stand-up, he needed to make money as quickly as possible. He didn't want to share his financial challenges with either of his parents, who would tell him in a well-meaning but critical fashion that drifting was something you did on a lilo in the pool on holiday. It was not a strategy for life.

Still, needs must, and on a good week he would eke out four lucrative hours with Sasha, whose apathy would increase like an expanding universe with each lesson he was forced to sit through. Joe understood you shouldn't call a child 'thick' these days, but for Sasha it was the closest description he could find, apart from 'evil little psycho'.

Sasha's mother, Irina, took things more seriously and believed his forthcoming Westminster School exams were crucial for his future place in the high echelons of British society. The billions of dollars his oligarch father, Oleg, had plundered from the Russian people would also come in helpful, and Joe knew his tuition was unnecessary as the only chance of Sasha's progress was the endowment of an enormous new library.

'I was hoping you'd write a bit more than this for your composition. You've only managed three lines, instead of a whole page like I asked you.' Joe tried to look disappointed rather than indifferent.

What Sasha had written proved that excessive money does not guarantee a contented upbringing. The exercise was to write about 'A Happy Place' and Sasha described the family villa in St Tropez by saying: *My house in France has 23 bedrooms and I don't know how many bathrooms.* More poignantly, he explained that the villa was *where I sometimes see my father although not very often.* Clearly estranged, Oleg was probably on the run, having double-crossed President Putin, or simply preferred hanging out with his mistresses and children from previous marriages. Joe didn't want to learn too much about this powerful and miserable family, fearing that too many questions might result in being clubbed with a balalaika by Oleg's KGB mates round the back of his flat.

'My mother really likes you,' Sasha announced randomly.

'Can we stick to the work, please. Now, how could you have expanded on what you wrote?'

'She wants you to come with us to the villa this summer to tutor me.' The boy had become animated in a way that had never happened before.

'That's very nice, but we'll be having a break in your lessons when you go away. We've discussed this.'

'She is unhappy and cries a lot. My father doesn't speak to her. He's much older than her, you know. I have three brothers in Russia. I never see them.'

Joe was entering uncharted teaching waters with these confessional facts. Normally, they spent their time in truculent silence, with Sasha frustrated at having to work instead of playing *FIFA* on his PlayStation. He seemed more vulnerable than usual and wanted to talk freely, not made easy by them sitting on either side of a dining-room table large enough for an imperial banquet. Joe tried again to get the lesson on track.

'What are some of the other descriptions you could have included in your writing?'

'Do you want me to say what the guest bedroom looks like?'

'If you like, but only if you use at least three adjectives.'

Before Sasha could respond, the solid oak doors slid open and Irina fell into the room as if she had been listening on the other side. An actress before meeting Oleg, she was a short woman, who struggled to smile due to the chemical-induced tautness of her face. Wearing a tight shocking-pink dress and dagger-sharp high heels, she seemed overdressed for a Thursday afternoon at home.

'How is it going?' she asked.

Normally, they would spend ten earnest minutes at the end of each lesson assessing Sasha's progress, and Joe was adept at giving constructive feedback that obscured the fact Irina's child was a moron. It was unusual for her to engage with Joe mid-session and her cheeriness seemed forced.

'I told Joe your idea about coming with us to France?' Sasha bellowed.

OMG he was telling the truth. Despite the air-conditioning, Joe could feel islands of sweat forming across his khaki T-shirt.

'Come now, *Sashenka*. It's not for you to invite him,' Irina replied gently.

'But Mama, you said you were going to ask him. You promised. You promised.'

'Ask him what?'

Joe wanted to remind them he was still in the room, although they were unflustered by his presence. Irina sat down next to Sasha, and they faced Joe like an interview panel across the table. Shifting from buttock to buttock, Irina was fidgeting like a guilty person about to confess a crime.

'Sorry to interrupt you. I know how crucial it is to you to have Sasha's complete concentration during your lessons.'

'Not always easy to get that, eh, Sasha?'

No one smiled.

'I hope you don't mind me asking. Would you consider coming to the villa in France with us for a couple of weeks next month? I have thought about it, and it would be an excellent way to focus Sasha. Maybe you can spend time teaching him some general knowledge too. Go for walks, that sort of thing. Explain how the world works. I'd double your hourly rate. Six hours a day, minimum.'

Joe was weak at mental arithmetic, but still calculated she was offering him enough to pay his mortgage for a year. It was very tempting. He imagined himself like an idealistic tutor found in a classic Russian novel, imparting spiritual wisdom to a young charge while teaching him the names of flowers. Not to mention the enormous wads of cash at the end.

Irina wasn't finished, however. There was something coquettish about her expression: olive eyes turned downwards, cheeks flushed and eyelids fluttering like the wings of a bee. It was a decidedly manipulative performance, and her voice dropped in volume as she got to the nub of her request.

'Also, it would be nice for me to have the company. You see, we don't really see Oleg anymore and it can be very hard to be alone in the villa with just me, Sasha and the staff. You seem a good listener and I'd love to get to know you. Hopefully, you will not find me too dull. Our villa has wonderful views, it's so relaxing at the end of the day watching the sunset with a glass of wine. Can I tempt you, Joe?'

He had no idea whether her crooked smile was imploring, inviting or threatening. How things had moved on in five minutes, from a dull lesson to a suggestive invitation from a lonely woman with a rather large holiday home. Previously, such an offer might have made him rush out to buy a linen safari suit and new Speedos. Now it terrified him, and not just because he was being propositioned by the unhappy wife of a powerful man who probably killed puppies for sport. What scared Joe was the haphazard trajectory of his life; five years on from Chloe and for want of anything better, he was heading down emotional cul-de-sacs. This highly lucrative proposal was yet another illustration he was cut adrift from any prospect of long-term happiness.

Too embarrassed to look at Irina, his eyes flitted around, taking in the valuable paintings, sculptures and antiques, some modern and abstract, others looking like they were once owned by Marie Antoinette. They didn't belong together in the same room, like he didn't with Sasha and Irina, these unhappy people with values he despised. He had to extricate himself from this venality while sounding sufficiently disappointed to avoid causing offence.

'I'm so sorry, Irina. You should have given me more notice, I have loads of commitments this summer. I hope that's OK for you and we pick up again when you get back.'

Irina's expression was now blank and without a trace of warmth, the invitation of affection rescinded as quickly as it had been offered. Her son did not react as calmly and he threw his exercise books furiously to the floor, stomped on them a couple of times and ran out of the room. Joe suspected his services would no longer be required.

'It was just a suggestion,' Irina said flatly. 'The lesson is finished, and we will be in touch. Goodbye.'

She got up and followed her son without looking back. The exercise book lay open, with the dusty imprint of Sasha's sneaker on a page of long-division questions he had not been able to answer. Joe walked briskly to the front door and let himself out. The relief this job was over was immediate, as was the anxiety that he might need witness protection from now on.

January 2015

The green room in The Chuckle Club, Waterloo was in essence a dimly lit storage cupboard with boxes of crisps, empty beer barrels and the detritus of a poorly run bar. For the nervy performers, however, it was the only place available for them to change and prepare.

Joe sat on a broken chair, twirling a pen as if waiting for one last injection of inspiration to hone this new set of material. He stared at the personalised Moleskine notebook Grace had given him for his birthday the previous year. She had thoughtfully embossed its cover with the words 'New Gags Please' and he wondered if the pages of his illegible doctor-prescription handwriting were in any way funny. They'd better be, because he was up next.

Given he had a fifteen-minute slot to entertain a fullish Tuesday night crowd, his mood was unpropitiously sombre, a debilitating mix of sadness and introspection that did not bode well for an energised performance. He had never been into drugs and the inhaler nasal stick he carried at all times for his congested sinuses was not going to give him much of a pre-show rush.

Grace was sitting dutifully in the audience, his most vocal cheerleader. She had heard the routine many times and encouraged him throughout its gestation that each line was funny. He marvelled at her patience. Three years on from meeting, she seemed undiminished in her belief he was worth the effort and endured his ranting at still having to teach because of the meagre living he made as a comedy writer and performer. As he railed about his struggles to get bigger and better gigs, she found different ways of helping him believe he would break through. What made him carry on was unclear, given how melancholic his lack of progress made him, and he knew her loyalty deserved better.

They led such different lives. He wrote gags during the day, while she was a senior social worker for Ealing Children's Integrated Response Service. His biggest challenge was to nail three successive punchlines per paragraph of meaningless stand-up. She was dealing with the unimaginable pain of protecting children from fractured and violent families. That day, she had left the house at 7 a.m., driving for two hours to deal with a fostering emergency, and now was required to validate his trite comic material until the early hours.

It wasn't just the guilt of making her stay up, though, that was causing this introspection. He couldn't understand why he didn't love her with the same fervour she seemed to have for him. His mother had recently castigated him for not committing properly to Grace, reminding him that a relationship without progression was the ultimate act of cruelty. And she should know, given she walked out on his father after thirty years of marriage because her love had evaporated.

As he climbed the stairs to the stage, he considered the promise his mother had extracted from him to talk to Grace properly. Living together was clearly not enough for her, but perhaps it was all he could commit to now. He couldn't reveal his true emotions for fear of destroying everything: his heart was filled with admiration and fondness, but not a whole lot more. Her name summed up the problem. *Grace* was a perfect articulation of her kindness. It described her dignity in trying to guarantee their future. *Grace* should surely be something God-given and wonderful, so why did he still feel something was missing?

And was it wrong to share his indecision with two hundred strangers for a few easy laughs?

* * *

Good evening, everyone. Great to be here. I can honestly say that playing The Chuckle Club has been my dream ever since The Comedy Store stopped returning my calls. Still, lovely to be here to try out some new material.

This is my first time performing it, so in the unlikely event it is unfunny, please send me constructive feedback – and if you want to rewrite anything, all suggestions gladly received. I know I make stand-up look effortless, but it isn't, you know.

Anyway, can we start by giving a big shout out to my girlfriend, who is here supporting me tonight. Yep, that's her, the lovely woman at the back there looking mortified, who wishes she'd never met me when she took up teaching. Thank you, Miss Allen, I'd never have got that Geography GCSE if it wasn't for you.

Of course, I'm joking, I'm the teacher and she'd never hit on a child given she's actually a social worker and her bosses frown on that sort of thing. We're just your average urban couple with not enough money to cover all the streaming subscriptions we need to keep ourselves entertained because we can't afford to go out. Our flat is so small that when I tried to swing our cat recently, I accidentally bashed its brains out on the wall.

What I want to talk about tonight is relationships and how unfathomably complicated I find them.

You see, things are getting a bit serious for me.

I'm thirty-four and most of my friends are married now, but for some reason I'm not. You'd think my elaborate skincare regime, aversion to vegan food and collection of *Spider-Man* comics would make me quite the catch.

Consider the facts.

I'm a serial monogamist, which should count for something – and no, that does not mean I only eat Shreddies. I try to be a model boyfriend, although so far none of the big fashion houses have offered me any catwalk work.

To tell the truth, Grace is pissed with me because I recently discovered in the paper that my ex-girlfriend and first love was getting married, and this made me grumpy. She's a journalist who writes a column about her love life, which has not been helpful to me in forgetting her, although I have enjoyed reading her pieces when she's been dumped and was completely broken and destitute. You can see, I've moved on.

I'm over that awful moment when she walked out on me nine years ago because I was somehow holding her back. Well, I was when she tried to leave the flat, but she was too strong for me.

It was a tough time.

I got evicted because I couldn't afford the rent and had to move back in with my mum. And then, ladies and gentlemen, I met my wonderful girlfriend. If she wasn't hiding under her coat and hoping for a fire drill, you'd see for yourself. As I said, she's a social worker. Imagine the perks that come with that job. If I want to foster a child on a whim, she can get me one in days. Maybe even siblings.

After I split from my journalist first love, I suppose I had a few lost years. I could commit to very little other than an occasional tennis game and turning up to my grandmother's funeral. (Although I was late for that one and had to sprint to catch up with the coffin on the way to the graveside. Luckily, the tennis had made me quite fit.)

So, when I saw that my ex was getting married, I was OK. She'd always wanted to be in a happy relationship that she could write about for the nation to read over their cornflakes.

You get curious, don't you, about what 'the one' looks like for someone for whom you once thought you were 'the one'. Clearly,

I was not 'the one'. I was probably not even 'the two' or 'the three'. I decided to look him up and see if the upgrade had better features and settings than I did.

You can decide for yourself.

Does anyone in tonight work in advertising? Maybe you know him, as he's apparently the creative director of some cool agency in Shoreditch with an office that looks like the set of a Mad Max film and is filled with more wankers than a boys' dorm at boarding school at lights-out.

I checked out his LinkedIn profile and he's bloody earnest. I'll tell you that. Do you want to hear his creative mantra?

Only creative anarchists can grow the commercial mainstream.

Who among us hasn't said that at some time in our life? I say well done to my ex, therefore, for finally bagging a genuine anarchist after all these years. I'm sure you'll be very happy, but you may want to check how he stacks the dishwasher. Anarchists always mix up the cutlery.

Am I coming across as bitter? I hope not.

I wish them and their future anarchist children, Baader and Meinhof, only good things. I'm happy for her so long as my audience keeps laughing at the fact that she married a bloke who once won an award for an advert for recycled toilet paper.

And to my lovely girlfriend. What can I say for the last three years of companionship, laughter, affection, kindness and gravity-defying sex other than … you're welcome.

* * *

Grace just wanted to sleep. She ached with weariness and now had to endure Joe's rant. Propped up in their bed, refusing to turn off the light, he conducted a post-performance analysis of his set, which had been met with polite and affectionate tittering but lacked the viral energy of infectious laughter. He had explained to her once that comedians use the language of violence to describe their success.

I killed them tonight.

I knocked them dead.

At best, he had caused a slight flesh wound. He couldn't be sure if it wasn't funny enough or simply that his performance had lacked timing and panache. Recently, he'd begun to wonder if he was not talented enough on-stage to merit persisting. Maybe he should stick to writing? Or was that a ludicrously misguided aspiration, given he was still struggling for meaningful recognition? Could this ever be a proper career for him, rather than an exhausting sideline generating little reward?

'I just don't know. I just don't know.' He shouted as if he was still in front of a large audience. 'I thought it would go better. Oh *fuck*, what am I doing?'

'I can't talk about this now,' Grace said.

'You're not upset about the jokes about Chloe? It's not as if you haven't heard it before.'

Perhaps that was the problem. He'd been honing his set for a year and Chloe was central to its humour. Grace turned her back to him and tucked her knees into her chest in a gesture that suggested the need for self-preservation. Joe kept on talking, prodding for a truth neither had been willing to articulate.

'I can't carry on with this if this is as good as it's going to get,' he said tentatively.

She replied after a few lonely seconds. 'Are you talking about your stand-up or *us*?'

Joe took a second to process her response, wrapped up as he was in his own frustration.

'Perhaps both.'

He tried to stroke her back, but she flinched. She spoke with resignation.

'It was pretty humiliating to sit in the audience as the butt of your jokes when what you were really saying, I realised, is that I am not "the one".'

He didn't know how to contradict her and lay down in the bed, listening to the early-morning whoosh of the occasional car as it passed outside their small flat next to a dual carriageway. Grace was his first enduring relationship after Chloe, and he had sabotaged it by revealing his uncertainty in his stand-up. He may not have slayed them in the aisles a few hours before, but he had most definitely killed the vibe in the bedroom now.

Contemplating the inevitable uncertainty of the next few months, he gave the duvet a little tug to provide him some warmth. Grace tugged it back sharply and his leg lay exposed to the chill of their draughty bedroom. Neither of them could sleep.

May 2017

The couple stood under a chuppah, a canopy covered with prayer shawls and decorated with an over-the-top floral display seen normally at a royal wedding. After a dramatic pause, the groom stomped his foot on a glass wrapped in a white napkin, everyone shouted '*mazeltov*', and the klezmer trio burst into rhapsodic melody. As the guests clapped in time to the music, the two families hugged one another, and the newly married couple kissed gingerly, conscious of the layers of bridal make-up that could be unwittingly smudged if things got too frisky.

This was Joe's first Jewish wedding and a link with family traditions he had no idea existed. He turned to his father and shouted over the celebratory din.

'I can't believe you kept me away from all this, growing up.'

'It's as unfamiliar to me as it is to you.'

Indeed, Michael Harris had known very little about his religion. His own father was an orthodox Jew who scandalised the family by marrying an Irish Catholic in the early 1950s. Michael had brought up Joe and his younger sister, Amy, in a state of blissful atheism, punctuated only by family gatherings at which Jewish aunts and uncles welcomed them to north-west London as if they were visitors from abroad.

Ella, Joe's second cousin once removed, was getting married, and he marvelled at the intricacy of the celebration she had clearly been planning since her bat mitzvah twenty years previously. That was the last Jewish event Joe had attended, and he enjoyed this ceremony much more. The love of the couple for each other was palpable and Joe was delighted for Ella, of whom he was very fond.

Normally, he didn't like the formality of a lavish wedding and the five-star hotel banqueting suite in central London, decorated to ensure seamless colour co-ordination of food and apparel, could not be described as low key. Nevertheless, Joe refused to be a curmudgeon and wore a rictus smile of enthusiasm that would get him through the next nine hours of the party.

It was going to be a very long evening, and he hardly knew anyone. He was therefore going to have to make endless conversation with his father's partner, Debbie, which was a far greater ordeal than being single in a room full of happy young couples.

* * *

If the meek do inherit the earth, Joe had joked to his sister, then Debbie was going to take possession of at least a couple of continents. It wasn't that she didn't speak, but rather that when she did, it was so banal. For sure, she was a nice person, who made his father happy; it's just he couldn't understand how Michael could withstand dinner after dinner discussing the mundane in minutiae.

Joe was in agony, trying to keep up conversation while hoping that an unknown allergic reaction to the diverse array of canapés he had consumed would provide a means of escape. The reception was dragging into its third hour and no sign of a call to dinner. Joe had been on shorter holidays, and it was worse because he had found himself trapped with no visible means of escape.

Debbie was commenting on how clever the caterers were to create an array of dishes in miniature, as if a dollop of risotto on a spoon was the most remarkable discovery since Edison's light bulb. Michael was silent as she wittered on, and Joe wondered if he was having buyer's remorse. Once an urbane lawyer, when Joe's mother left him he had crumpled into a melancholic state of low self-esteem and high self-pity. Joe and his sister looked after him, which was not always easy as waves of despair washed over him. They were thrilled when he finally emerged with Debbie in tow, a widow and former colleague, ten years younger and utterly devoted to him. It was just such a shame she was so dreary.

He knew he'd have to wait until dinner provided a means of escape. Besides, his father seemed troubled and the familiar drag of responsibility made him stay put.

'What is it, Dad? You look like you're going to punch a waiter.'

Michael knocked back the dregs of his champagne and ran his hand across his head, which Joe knew to be the most common indication of his anxiety.

'How's your mother?' Michael spat out bitterly. 'Is Jane still making her happy?'

Yet again, all he wanted to talk about was his ex-wife, Helen, and her soon-to-be wife. Debbie grimaced and touched his arm in admonishment, but Michael stared at his son as if she wasn't there.

'Is now really the time?' Joe asked, trying not to sound irritated.

'It's the perfect time. We're at a wedding, and I want to talk about my ex-wife's imminent wedding to another woman, if you don't mind.'

His father's hand was trembling. The explosiveness of his reaction had been superseded by intense sadness.

'What do you want to know?' Joe asked gently.

'Is she happy?'

Joe knew the question was really, *why did she leave me for another woman?* He had been asked the same thing so many times by his father that he had nothing new to contribute. Helen had told her children she felt trapped by the overpowering intensity of Michael's devotion. She stopped enjoying his company and while she could not explain why, she knew somehow that she was leading the wrong life. Happy as she was as a mother and a doctor, her marriage to Michael, she would tell them, was like *living your life in a giant maze, lost, and continually arriving at dead ends. And that was on a good day.*

'We can't do this again. Surely you understand by now,' Joe implored. There was no way he was going through it all again.

Helen had left the family home and cut off contact with them all for a year, telling Joe and Amy she was living with an old school friend, Jane. One day, Helen invited them to her new flat and explained in excruciating detail that she had never enjoyed sex with their father, and now that Jane was her lover all was clear and she had *more climaxes than a good spy thriller.* Joe got very drunk that night in an attempt to black out the memory of his mother's new sapphic euphoria and her convert's need to outline it in detail.

In the intervening years, Joe had been forced to examine the carcass of his parents' relationship with his distraught father, for whom rejection was amplified by his shame. For Joe, his father's cloying pain made him more convinced that long-term contentment in couples was the exception rather than the norm. Michael's anguish had returned a few weeks back when he found out that Helen and Jane intended to marry in a small ceremony in front of their respective children.

Joe was saved from having to say anything further. A tearful Debbie had run off to consider if her future was ever going to be free of Michael's unhappy past. Michael looked at Joe wistfully and then pushed through the throng of guests in search of Debbie, presumably to apologise as sincerely as he could. She had a low bar of expectation and Joe reckoned she'd be giggling away, discussing how the napkins had been folded, within half an hour.

He stared at his message-free phone, pretending to answer a long list of imaginary texts, hoping that somehow the evening would get better. Eventually, a toast-master, dressed like he was attending a military ball, appeared from nowhere to shout into a microphone that dinner was at last served. The doors swung open to the ballroom and an eighteen-piece band kicked off the opening bars of the Black Eyed Peas classic party song 'I Gotta Feeling'. Joe made his way to his table, alone.

* * *

'So why have you been put on the waifs and strays table with me?' asked the elegant woman in the emerald dress next to Joe.

Joe had thought the same thing as he introduced himself to each person before sitting down. There was the groom's childhood German au pair, an eccentric cousin of Ella's who lived on a croft near Aberdeen with his wife, dressed as if she had just milked a cow, Ella's former piano teacher, a child psychologist who had treated one of the newly-weds, but would not say which one, and some friends from Amsterdam they had met travelling.

'I reckon that's why we're so far from the dance floor. We must be a social experiment,' he whispered conspiratorially.

'Speak for yourself. I'm livid and will sue for wrongful table planning. I'm Laura, by the way, Ella's first boss.'

'Joe.'

'And what brings you to my table next to the toilets, Joe?'

'Ella's my cousin and I'm a sucker for an all-day wedding.'

They shook hands in what seemed a very formal gesture. Joe sensed the former au pair on his left was staring at him, trying to join in the conversation, and he turned his back on her, pretending not to notice. He wanted to give Laura his full attention.

'Are you on your own? It seems everyone else in this room is a couple.' She was staring at him with a disconcerting intensity given they had just met.

'I am not alone, thank you very much. I have just spent two hours in conversation with my father and his girlfriend, Debbie, over there. Dad got a bit miserable about my mum, who left him years ago, and Debbie got the hump and stormed off. It was hardly entertaining, but it passed the time.'

Laura took a sip of the white wine that a waiter had just poured and said nothing for a second.

'Well, let's see how entertaining you can be then. I can't wait to hear more about your father's love life.'

'Only if you tell me what brings you here tonight, Norma No Mates?'

'Since you ask it as if it's a crime, you should know I'm a single mum of a very challenging teenage son. So quite frankly, I'd take a night out on my own at a wrestling match or a wake. Does that answer your question?'

Joe worried he'd caused offence quicker than usual and she'd abandon him for the heavily bearded crofter on her right. Before he could make amends, the toast-master asked for silence to welcome in the happy couple. The multicoloured spotlights swirled manically until one yellow beam lit up the entrance and Ella and her new husband, Daniel, threaded their way through the tightly packed tables hand in hand.

The couple's walk-in music was Maroon 5's 'Moves like Jagger' and Joe thought that Mick would not be happy, given the groom's out-of-time gyrations looked like a cross between back spasm and a goose-step. As they reached the top table, the band launched into a traditional Jewish song, heralding a set of hora dancing, and a chaotic mob of several hundred people followed the newly-weds on to the dance floor. Separate circles of men and women were formed as strangers held hands and moved in different directions. Everyone had clearly done this before; they just hadn't quite mastered the choreography.

Laura enthusiastically ran to join the women, leaving Joe compelled to fall in with the group of mainly young men behaving as if they were in some sort of *shtetl* mosh pit, bouncing into each other, hot, sweaty and exuberant. At one stage, Daniel lay across a tablecloth held by about twenty men and was tossed high in the air, nearly hitting his head on a huge crystal chandelier. Meanwhile, the women undertook some sort of mass line dance in which many of them didn't know the steps while others performed the routines with the earnestness of a *Strictly* contestant.

Joe found the celebration unfathomably moving. He couldn't see himself in a relationship worthy of such attention and collective happiness. And yet he remembered being with Chloe and thinking that despite his lack of a concrete plan, there would eventually be an acknowledgement that their love for one another was a thing of beauty. Something low key and barefoot in the Seychelles; him in a white linen suit, Chloe in some sort of billowing dress, flowers in her hair. And a horse. How else was he going to gallop off into the sunset?

When the dancing finished, his hope that he would be able to reprise the Nora Ephronesque banter with Laura was shattered by the endless speeches. Ella's father welcomed them. Daniel's father thanked Ella's father for welcoming them. Three of Ella's bridesmaids (there were about twelve, in lilac dresses) reminisced affectionately about her promiscuity at university. Daniel's two best men reflected that given his nerdiness, it was miraculous he had even kissed a girl, let alone married one. Daniel thanked everyone for coming and concluded sweetly by saying that Ella's love for him proved *God did not just move in mysterious ways; he was also a very generous champion for the underdog, because the only explanation for today is divine intervention.*

Joe listened to them and thought there must be something wrong because he had never experienced such intimacy with anyone since Chloe. Meanwhile, instead of talking to Laura, he could not escape the overzealous attention of his other neighbour, Ingrid, who mistook him for a priest in the confessional. It turned out that since her days as an au pair, she had married a doctor and endured many years of his infidelities as she raised the children. Joe longed for rescue. Even Dull Debbie and a discussion about flower arranging would have been preferable, especially as Ingrid wanted to ask if pornography was the key to spice up a middle-aged marriage.

Eventually, the dancing started again. Ingrid's departure to the loo gave Joe a brief window to suggest to Laura they got a drink at the bar, and they fled the table, like a crime scene. Clinking whisky glasses in a quiet corner, they compared their dinner conversations.

'How did you get on with beardy?' he asked.

'Farming subsidies. All he wanted to talk about is why leaving the EU is a disaster for sugar beet. And you?'

'Dildos and their role in saving her marriage. I win, I think.'

'You probably do, and I hope you were helpful. We'll have to make up for lost time. I don't even know what you do. I'm guessing it's something impressive. Human rights lawyer or orthodontic surgeon to the rich and famous. Am I close?'

'Not remotely. I'm an ex-teacher, failed stand-up and comedy writer. I write for radio shows, some jokes for a few stand-up comedians, and supplement it with a bit of copywriting and journalism. I'm writing a book as well.'

'What's it about?'

'About three hundred and fifty pages, but I may edit it further.'

'I can see why you gave up the stand-up!' She touched Joe's arm lightly and he wondered where the conversation was heading.

'Funnily enough, the book is about my life as a stand-up. I wasn't terrible, I just didn't want it enough to get the big breakthrough. And it would have been nice if the audience laughed occasionally too. So, for someone who has achieved nothing, I have rather grandly written a memoir.'

'And are you still single?' Laura asked, clearly more interested in his status than his life story.

'Yup. Ever since I chased a lovely person away. I have a problem expressing my feelings. That was the official version anyway, but I think I just couldn't fall in love with her. Odd, because she was amazing – a social worker who used to deal with all sorts of losers. She couldn't crack me though.'

Joe realised he must have drunk a microbrewery dry over the last few hours because his thoughts were pouring out unchecked, like a torture victim confessing everything to stop the suffering. Laura got her phone out of her bag, perhaps to order an Uber. The prospect of her leaving made him panic-ask his next question.

'Are you a single, single mum? What's your shtick?'

'I prefer to call it my actual life, rather than my shtick. It makes me sound a better person.'

Joe nodded, feeling slightly embarrassed by his decision to use the word 'shtick' for the first time in his life.

'Yes, I'm single too, and not really looking for a relationship. I'd like a bit of fun, if that's not too much to ask. I have my own PR business, which is doing very well, and a son who is not. He's just been diagnosed with severe ADHD.'

'Is his dad not on the scene?' It seemed an easier question for Joe to ask as he couldn't remember all the differences between ADHD and autism and now was not the time to look even more stupid.

'All you need to know is I got to thirty-five alone and wanted a child. I didn't have a man in my life but took matters into my own hands.'

Joe was confused.

'How old is your son?'

'He's thirteen.'

'But that makes you forty-eight?'

'Forty-nine.'

'Wow' was the best he could muster in response. She was twelve years older than him.

'Wow, what? Wow, I look incredible for my age or wow, you like my shoes?'

His next answer was crucial. The fact she was older and at such a different stage in life was disproportionately enticing and the prospect of a one-dimensional relationship was a notch up from nirvana after not being able to properly love Grace.

'Wow, I think you're amazing. Wow, I'd like to see you again. Wow, this wedding has turned out better than when it began about four days ago.'

Things were moving fast. Kissing him lightly on the lips, she entwined her fingers in his as if they were going to get up and go for a walk.

'I was hoping you were going to say that. You're perfect material for the sort of relationship I need now.'

'And what is that?' he asked enthusiastically.

'Imagine a scale of *1 to 10* where *1* is a purely physical coupling and *10* is the full shebang – emotion-discussing, parent-meeting, friend-sharing, toilet-door-open-when-you-pee sort of thing. What are you looking for in your life, right now?'

Was it a trick question? He desperately wanted to say *1* but worried if he answered with a low number, he would come across as an emotion-free bloke only after one thing. However, if he went high, he would probably scare her off as someone looking for a life partner and fifty per cent of her wealth.

'*3* … ?' he said very slowly, to allow for the possibility of changing it to a *7* if he saw her frown.

'Shame, I'm a *2,*' she replied, enjoying his discomfort.

She handed him her phone for his number and he typed in his details, trying not to smirk.

'So, when are you around this week?' he asked, kissing her hand. 'Because apart from my full body wax, my diary is pretty free.'

November 2017

Joe's first trip to New York was not the romantic escape he had hoped for. He'd always imagined exploring smoky jazz and comedy clubs with a lover and strolling the streets, looking hip, as eddies of steam rose from subway grilles and swirled around his feet. That was not going to happen now. Of course, the real irony of the trip was that it was provided free by Laura, making him some sort of amoral jet-setting gigolo dependent on the charity of his older lover. Maybe at thirty-seven that's all he was – an opportunistic freeloader.

Their relationship had chugged on at a steady pace since they met, without much danger of getting anywhere, driven by routine and very little commitment. They would meet as often as she could get overnight childcare for her son, Alfie, have dinner or see a film, and finish the evening most enjoyably in bed at his grim flat in Tooting. She'd never complain or pass judgement at how he lived and would leave happily the next morning, promising to text as soon as she knew her schedule.

When they were together, things bumbled along easily enough on general topics with no mention whatsoever of their emotions. Joe came to understand that inane dinner banter was as far as it was going to get and every time he enquired about Alfie, Laura changed the subject.

The casualness of the relationship suited her. She had a very successful business and plenty of friends to whom she had no intention of introducing him. When they were together, she was passionate, enthusiastic and entertaining. When they were apart, she could have lived a completely different life as an international jewel thief or active member of the *illuminati* for all he knew.

As it happened, she had a very successful PR business and did a lot of work in New York, so when she suggested he join her on a four-day trip, he was reminded that in many ways he was on to a very good thing and should not complain. He would fly on a business class companion voucher followed by a stay in the Standard High Line hotel, so far out of his price range that he would not have considered a beer in its bar without her. In return for this and lots of New York sex, he'd remember to ask '*how ya doing*' at climactic moments and try to act grown up.

He became hyperactive with excitement the moment he entered the Club World lounge at Heathrow. As Laura answered emails, he ran around filling plates with food he didn't necessarily want, wondering how best to maximise the free booze available. On the plane, he behaved as if his flat-bed seat was mankind's greatest achievement, testing its functionality by lying at every conceivable angle. Each meal was consumed with the enthusiasm of a child on a first trip to McDonalds, and he flicked through movies as if the concept of streamed entertainment was completely new to him.

Unfortunately, Laura, who had started to sneeze in the terminal, turned a pallid grey as she shivered under her blanket. Unable to sleep, her limbs ached at the joints, and she endured the flight through a cocktail of paracetamol and ibuprofen taken as often as possible. By the time they got to the hotel, her normal bonhomie was replaced by self-pity and all the symptoms of full-blown flu.

Joe was solicitous and helped her get into bed before going out for dinner to stay up late and minimise jet lag. She was fast asleep when he got back to the room, sweat glistening on her feverish forehead and snoring with a phlegmy rasp. He crawled under the duvet, relieved that the bed was at least a super king, and rolled her over gingerly to the other side as if handling radioactive waste. He turned his back and listened to the night-time sirens of the city, feeling sorry for himself because romance was not going to be on the agenda for the rest of the trip.

In the morning, she awoke drenched in sweat and tearful. She had several very important meetings over the next few days with prospective clients and somehow would have to find the strength to make her presentations without passing out. Joe felt he was in a room with a stranger. She didn't want to talk, nor did she want to listen to any advice he tried to give her about rescheduling. He refilled her water bottle, popped out a couple more paracetamols from their packet and put a pile of tissues in her bag.

How quickly things change.

He'd looked forward to being with his attractive, carefree lover, who thought he was sexy – frankly ridiculous given he had no abs and was wearing boxer shorts nearing their third decade. Now he was little more than a front-line healthcare worker, unable to think of anything helpful to say.

Joe smiled at the thought that he had fully expected to rub Laura's chest a lot on the trip, but not with decongestant. Unfortunately, he couldn't help repeating the line to her as he opened the door to the cab taking her to the meeting. She said nothing, but her puffy and watery eyes couldn't hide her disappointment.

* * *

Joe planned to do as much sightseeing as possible and began the morning in Central Park. The leaves on the trees were turning deep red and gold and the steel Manhattan skyline glistened against the clear blue sky in the autumn sunshine. So why did he feel so sad and lonely in such a spectacular setting? Maybe it was the procession of couples strolling hand in hand past him, revelling in its romantic possibilities. He walked up to the line of horse-drawn carriages at the park's entrance and wondered if it would be a special experience to snuggle under a blanket with someone you loved, enjoying a ride to the sound of clopping hooves. Judging by the decrepit state of the horses and the scruffiness of their liveried drivers, a nasty rash from the filthy seats was the more probable outcome.

Following Google Maps, he walked to Katz's on the Lower East Side to experience a traditional NY deli. He could tell from the website it was touristy since it boasted that the famous orgasm scene from *When Harry Met Sally* was filmed there, confirmed by a sign suspended over the very table where it was shot. He didn't care if it was naff and his stomach rumbled as he watched waiters carrying wedding-cake-sized sandwiches, deftly weaving between the throng of customers.

He was shown to a small table where an older woman, dressed in a leopard-print trouser suit that made her look like she was on safari, was slowly sipping chicken and noodle soup in a bowl with floating dumplings. Joe remembered from his distant Jewish family that these were called *knaidlach* and achieved that rare culinary feat of being stodgy and delicious simultaneously. He couldn't help noticing the woman's liver-spotted hands were bejewelled with several rings with diamonds the size of conkers.

'Do you mind if I sit down?' he shouted over the din of clanking cutlery and plates.

'Of course not. I'd be delighted to have some company,' she replied, putting her spoon down. She inclined her head inquisitively.

'You're English?'

'Afraid so.'

'Don't apologise. I love the Queen and your breakfast tea.'

'And I suppose I should thank you for bailing us out in the last war?'

'My father was stationed in England. In a place called Bournemouth. Do you know it?' she asked.

'Of course. There were some massive battles down there with the Germans. Mainly because they put their towels on all the deckchairs.'

She missed the joke, and they spent the next ten minutes having a strained conversation about why he was in the city. In particular, she struggled to understand his relationship with Laura and shook her head a lot when he tried to justify why it suited him not to have a commitment at this stage of his life. When she got up to leave, she pointed her finger at him accusingly and gave some unsolicited advice.

'Don't be such a schmuck. Just because you once got hurt doesn't mean you should now date your mother.'

He spent the afternoon on a walking tour of the Lower East Side and by 6 p.m. decided it was time to check in on Laura so headed back to the hotel. She was having a hot bath, trying to wash off the sweat of her feverish day, and he sat on the toilet and chatted to her as she soaked. It felt a bit intrusive given it never happened in his flat, where the mould in the bathroom was probably contagious. Past caring, she was more worried about how she was going to get home if she was this ill. He wrapped her in a towel as she got out of the bath, steadying her as she wobbled with wooziness.

When she was back in bed, he convinced her to order some soup to at least give her a bit of energy. She dozed until it arrived and then he attempted to cajole her to drink it, but she managed only a few reluctant mouthfuls. There was little further conversation. She apologised for ruining the trip and Joe mumbled something about it not mattering, hoping she felt better the next day. He asked housekeeping for an extra duvet and pillow, realising that the sofa was preferable to a second night in a germ-filled bed. After a quick shower, he left Laura asleep and wandered down to the hotel bar for a drink with his book.

* * *

Joe had been staring at Emily for at least half an hour. A couple of tables away in The Rooftop Bar, she was at the tail end of what looked like a very miserable date. It was Thursday night, and the room was rammed with beautiful young people. Joe wondered if the undercover fashion police might eject him as no one else was dressed in tatty jeans and a grey sweatshirt that was once blue.

Emily and her date were nursing cocktails and chatting in a very disconnected fashion. The man was extremely tall and waved his arms as he spoke, like he was directing traffic. Joe could tell that her answers were curt. Eventually, the man got up to leave and she seemed unwilling to get out of her chair, most likely because the disparity in their height would have meant she had to say goodbye to his groin. She sat for a couple of minutes nursing the dregs of her cocktail, staring out of the window, until Joe decided that it was all right to approach her.

'Emily? It is Emily, isn't it? Do you remember me?'

She looked bemused for a second and couldn't place him. Joe thought she looked disappointed when she realised who it was.

'*Joe Harris?* What on earth are you doing here? Please tell me you haven't been watching me.'

'Erm, only for a few minutes. I caught the end of your date with the Harlem Globetrotter.'

'He was six foot seven. I'm five foot three. It could never have worked. It didn't help that he was in insurance and the only person I know in New York who voted for Trump. I thought dating algorithms were meant to prevent that sort of thing happening.'

Joe was resting one hand on the chair next to her, holding his book in the other, which he had brought with him from his table. He could not have appeared more awkward. She looked at him quizzically.

'*Anna Karenina?* Are you seriously reading Tolstoy in a bar? That's a first. You'd better sit down and explain.'

The room was very noisy and he had to pull the chair close to hear her.

'To be honest, it's very boring and I'm not making much headway.'

'Too many passages about wheat and the existence of God?'

'Far too many. Plus, I know she gets hit by a train at the end. I might give up, it's just one of those books I always thought I should get through. I wasn't expecting to have so much time to read on this trip.'

A waitress walked past them, and Joe waved furiously at her like he was hailing a cab in the rain.

'Would you join me for a drink, Emily?' It sounded a very formal offer and to his relief, she smiled.

'That would be lovely.'

She turned to the waitress and ordered a beer, and he did the same, thankful not to have to confront the complexity of a fourteen-page cocktail menu. He showed the waitress his key card and charged the drinks to his room.

'Are you staying here? I hear it's fab, but the rooms are a bit small.' She seemed to be looking at him differently now that she realised he could afford a $500 room in New York. He may have been mistaken and she was just squinting in the darkness of the bar. He tried to sound nonchalant.

'It's lovely. Unfortunately, my girlfriend is sick in bed, so the trip's not going quite as planned.'

He couldn't detect a reaction when he mentioned Laura, but he did feel guilty that he had infringed the Trade Descriptions Act referring to her that way. Still, he could hardly use the more accurate phrase 'Sugar Mummy'.

'So, who's your girlfriend then, Joe? We have a lot to catch up on. How long has it been since we last saw each other?'

'Twelve years, two months, three weeks, four days.'

'You're kidding? How can you know that?'

'I don't. I made it up, but I think it was 2005 when I last saw you. From memory, you hid in the bathroom while I got dumped by Chloe.'

She smiled.

'Sorry about that. I remember that we planned it all but forgot where I should go. Anyway, no hard feelings, I hope.'

Joe didn't answer because he couldn't think about that evening without wondering what life would have been like if it hadn't happened. The silence was punctuated by the arrival of their beers, and they clinked glasses, both succumbing to the rising tide of nostalgia. Emily spoke first.

'You haven't told me about your girlfriend. Who? How long? Will I need to buy a hat for the wedding?'

'She's called Laura. She has her own PR agency. It's been about six months.'

Emily's face crinkled.

'Does she specialise in Health and Beauty?'

'I think so?'

Emily got out her phone and frantically checked her diary.

'She's not called Laura Simons, is she?'

Joe was getting very worried now. He didn't remember Emily being psychic.

'Yes, how do you know?'

'I'm meant to be meeting her tomorrow morning as she's trying to pitch to me. I got a message before I came that she wasn't well and may have to cancel.'

For a second, neither of them could think what to say next given the enormity of the coincidence. Two coincidences, in fact, if you included them running into each other in the first place. Emily sipped her beer contemplatively, clearly weighing up her next question.

'Do you mind if I ask you something personal?'

'I feel like you're going to anyway.'

'All right then, is Laura a bit older than you? I was looking at her profile today.'

'Twelve years. What of it?' Joe sounded defensive and didn't help himself by folding his arms as he spoke. It was something to celebrate, not apologise for.

'Sorry, just trying to match you up in my mind, which of course is something I have no right to do. Well, certainly not to admit it to you, anyway.'

Suddenly, Joe couldn't be bothered to pretend. It was the second time in the day he'd had to apologise for the relationship.

'To tell you the truth, Emily, it's weird. She's brought me on a business trip to keep her company. I'd say it's a bit of a stretch to call her a girlfriend. She's a friend with benefits that are apparently tax deductible.'

'Does she give you cash in the morning and tell you to buy something pretty? Oh, I'm sorry, I shouldn't have said that.'

'She'd be bloody angry if I came back dressed like this. I think she could get a better escort than a failed stand-up comic barely making a living as a writer.'

'That's a lot to unpick. We clearly have some catching up to do.'

'Well, that's fine by me. There's an elderly lady with flu in my room so I'm in no rush.'

* * *

Three hours later, they were still updating each other on their respective journeys. Emily told Joe about her career and the lifestyle its success afforded, travelling, and thriving in a corporate environment that blended job security with creativity. It was an alien world to Joe. He'd been booked a couple of times in the past to perform stand-up at company events and awards ceremonies. He never tried to understand the business, focusing rather on how he could mock the name of a silly product or marketing strategy that he'd looked up on their website.

Joe's peripatetic career in performing and writing sounded to Emily a terrifyingly precarious existence. She wasn't a huge fan of live comedy so hadn't come across any of his work. In fact, it seemed to Joe that she had given him very little thought since she last saw him, and he represented a student existence long forgotten. How she had changed. He recollected her hanging around campus, when she was either a Goth or an emo (he couldn't recall, but knew black lipstick was involved), and now she was immaculate. Straightened hair, perfect make-up, skinny jeans, a cream silk blouse with a hint of cleavage. He didn't remember her being this pretty.

She was fascinated by his book, however, as an English graduate who loved reading. Joe was flattered, suffering as he did from huge imposter syndrome and believing a writer was someone who sat down and wrote rather than sat down and scrolled through his phone for football stories. He was nevertheless excited about the spring publication of *Sit Down if You're No Good at Stand Up*, his memoir to both performance and relationship failure.

Joe became animated when he told Emily his publisher had high hopes for the book's success. He described his recent first meeting with his super posh publicist Charlotte Erskine-Hill, who was supposedly well regarded and was going to do great things with the book. He had his doubts as she usually worked on award-winning literary fiction and his was likely to be neither. She told him at the meeting that her plans were *a bit mad*, which she qualified by saying *in a Henley Regatta sort of way*. He hadn't a clue what she was talking about, and Emily laughed when he showed her Charlotte's gratuitously French email signature, *Milles baisers.*

'That's a lot of kisses on each cheek. You'll be there for hours next time you see her.'

'I think she likes the novelty of working with someone as disappointing as me. If she can make me famous, she can take on anyone in the future.'

It was nearing midnight, and they still hadn't mentioned the person who had brought them together in the first place. Joe tried to look nonchalant as he asked the question. 'So, are you still in touch with Chloe?'

Emily answered hesitantly.

'Yes, we're still supposedly best friends.'

'*Supposedly?*'

'It's complicated.'

'Are you on a break?'

'Kind of. I'm a bit pissed off with her, to tell the truth.'

'Well, I'm not sure I've forgiven her either, if that's any consolation.'

'None. Don't be pathetic, Joe. You should be over her now. Is that why you wrote your book, as a very late attempt at catharsis?'

'No. She's in it, sort of, but I've focused on my very many dating disasters thereafter. I did include a bit in my routine a few years back about Chloe, when I saw she was getting married. You can look it up on YouTube if you're interested. Is she still with that bloke Daniel?'

'David. But of course, you knew his name, didn't you?'

'Maybe,' he replied sheepishly.

'She's very happy, with gorgeous twins who are my godchildren.'

Joe knew that his expression had changed at the news but didn't know why Chloe's family should have that effect.

'You're looking sad,' Emily said, confirming he didn't have much of a poker face. 'You can't have expected that she'd remain celibate and childless on the off-chance you got back together?'

He was being ridiculous and so flipped the conversation back to the state of her relationship with Chloe.

'OK, spill the beans. What's happened with you two? I'm happy to share the cost of an assassin if you want her bumped off.'

'It's nothing.'

'No, it's something. You've clenched your fist and not even noticed. Either you're going to punch me, or Chloe has really upset you.'

'She hasn't. It's just I'm struggling with her.'

'What do you mean?'

'She's still lovely and funny. It's just I'm working flat out in a job, no partner and not the future I imagined. Every time I speak to her, she tries to ask the right questions, but her need to be the perfect wife and mother who everyone loves tends to dominate our conversations. At least, that's the way it seems to me.'

Joe put his hand on Emily's shoulder.

'Do you know what, my old friend who never used to like me?'

'Enlighten me.'

'You and I need to spend a lot less time thinking about Chloe.'

'You go first and show me how it's done.' She briefly stroked his cheek and they sat, not speaking, until Emily looked at him with a half-smile and unmistakable intent.

'I don't suppose you want to jump in a cab and come back to my flat?'

He was neither surprised nor disappointed.

'Is that a good idea?' he asked as he requested the bill from the waitress by writing with an imaginary pen on the palm of his hand.

'I promise to give your friend Laura some business if she makes it to the meeting tomorrow.'

Despite the late hour and the beers, Joe felt clear-headed in his actions and tried not to think about his amorality in abusing Laura's largesse like this. His behaviour was shocking, but that was something he'd consider tomorrow when he snuck back to the hotel, hopefully before Laura woke up. As he guided Emily towards the door, he wondered if it would be poor form to send a selfie to Chloe.

May 2018

He decided on a long walk to stave off the surge of loneliness. Bloody Bank Holiday Monday: an extra day off for all the happy people and a further reminder that he was a single man without any arrangements. Apart from a brief cup of coffee with his sister, he'd done nothing meaningful all weekend.

While not a particular nature lover, he tried to appreciate the vibrant late-spring colour – a reminder that however bleak things became, renewal was inevitable. The bloom on branches, dry and dead a few months previously, seemed an appropriate metaphor for the gloominess he had to overcome.

Battersea Park was busy, even in the early morning. Parents, resentful at their curtailed lie-ins, dragged recalcitrant toddlers by the hand to already overcrowded playgrounds. Like them, Joe sipped from his coffee cup, hoping that caffeine would somehow revive his waning spirits.

Dogs ran towards him, their owners engaged in banal conversation with one another, and he bristled at their passion for pets, who seemed to be on the whole shrunken versions of the Alsatians, Dalmatians and Labradors he remembered as a child. Now they were all bred in miniature, with tiny legs and bourgeois names. No more Fidos, Rexes and Sheps. Just a plethora of middle-class voices shouting *Here, Jessie. Fetch, Freddy. Come to Mummy, Molly.* Was there a word for the canine misanthropy all those yapping *cockapoodleschnauzerspaniels* engendered?

Eventually, Joe found a bench overlooking a bed of purple rhododendrons and sat for a moment to ponder his situation. Work was a massive struggle. Although he had plenty of writing gigs, a new satire radio programme and a high-profile stand-up comedian as his latest projects, the money was appalling. He'd even had to start tutoring again, although he made a point of ignoring the scions of oligarchs for his peace of mind.

Meanwhile, he was floundering to find emotional happiness. Laura had cooled considerably, and their dates these days were sporadic and largely sex focused. She was not quite ready to let go of their flimsy connection, but she was certainly unwilling to invest anything more than the cost of dinner and an Uber home. He wondered if it had anything to do with him sleeping with Emily that night, but then how could she have known about it given she was poleaxed by flu at the time.

Emily.

Now, that had been a surprise for them both, given they had never really liked each other when he was with Chloe. While their evening in New York had been somewhat magical in its unexpectedness, there was still something awry. The shadow of Chloe hung over them from the minute they got in the cab to her flat, even if, like Voldemort, her name was not mentioned aloud. As he snuck back to the hotel at 5 a.m., he was overwhelmed by confusion. They seemed to have a connection, but was this just mutual resentment of Chloe? They owed her nothing. Nevertheless, there was an awareness in their subsequent FaceTime calls that the growing affection between them evolved from anger at a third person rather than compatibility.

To begin with, they chatted a lot. Emily came home for Christmas, and they met up a couple of times, spending the night together entwined under his duvet, trying to avoid the draughts and antiquated heating of his depressing flat. When she returned to the US, they reached an agreement that while they liked each other more than either would have believed possible, the logistics of their different lives made it unwise for them to continue. He came off the call sad at his inability to behave like other people. What sort of future was there if each time he started a relationship, it was tethered to a particular set of intractable problems that no amount of passion could overcome?

* * *

Joe walked the perimeter of the park several times, working up a moderate sweat in the muggy haze of the morning. Killing time was killing his soul, he reflected. Then he reflected that only a pretentious *twat* would talk about a soul being killed. There was no such thing as a soul. There were only your actions. And his were so unimpressive. Which was why, evidently, he was walking alone in a park, trapped by his thoughts. Solitude was awful. So was company if you didn't like the person or, more pertinently, didn't like yourself.

Aaargh. *Make it stop*, he shouted aloud, and a couple of teenage girls giggled at his weirdness as they passed him on the path. He recalled how, when she left him, Chloe had accused him of being incapable of expressing his emotions. He still didn't know how to summarise their complexity. Surely he should know what he wanted now? And how ironic that this peak cluelessness coincided with the publication of his book about why his mediocre stand-up career had dented any chance of a proper relationship.

What was really pulling him down (apart from having no one in his life, not enough friends and no money) was the muted response since its launch six weeks ago. He had pinned enormous hope that it would begin a new chapter of recognition, a springboard to a brighter writing future. Unfortunately, like so much else he had done in his career, it was only moderately successful and unlikely to lead anywhere. Frankly, this was utterly galling, as the book was excellent and he deserved more than a lukewarm reception.

His publicist, Charlotte, had used all her Cheltenham Ladies' College energy to arrange a few appearances in smaller bookshops and events. (Who knew that Solihull had a literary festival?) Media interest, however, had been decidedly regional rather than national. He had done several local radio interviews, which followed on from the stories about escaped sheep and sightings of Ed Sheeran at a local chippy. He had spoken live to a station for the half million British expats on the Costa del Sol. He didn't want to be ungrateful, but he was certain that very few were missing pool time at their Fuengirola villas to listen to him.

Besides, what did bullion van robbers know about books.

This memoir had required enormous effort and the response had been underwhelming. He'd tried to supplement the publicity with an active social media campaign of witty tweets and posts, yet his following was still smaller than the population of a ghost town. Indeed, the reading public clearly liked different genres. If he'd written a murder mystery sci-fi historical romance about Sir Lancelot and a sassy barmaid, he'd be raking in millions. A washed-up comic telling the world about why he was so mediocre was not exactly a page turner.

* * *

'Darling. Darling. Drop everything, I have simply divine news. Where are you now?'

Joe didn't look who was calling when he answered and was momentarily confused by the plummy voice sounding like a débutante announcing her engagement. Then he realised it was Charlotte.

'I've just got home from a long walk with some friends,' he replied, embellishing his morning through the addition of imaginary friends.

'And what are you doing this afternoon at about three fifteen?'

'Splitting the atom. Why?'

'Très drôle, mon cheri. However, despite it being bank holiday, I have a frightfully delightful opportunity for you to appear on national radio. National, darling. Not Radio Northampton like last time.'

'What do you mean?'

'Radio 5 Live are doing a segment about books on relationships and one of the authors they booked has dropped out. They'd like you to step in. How marvellous is that?'

'So, I'm a sub then?'

'Less a sub, more of an upgrade.'

'Charlotte, it's very nice of you to fawn on me like this, but if they didn't want me, they'll probably give the others more airtime.'

'It's only one other person. And why would they do that?'

Joe looked at the detritus of his filthy kitchen with two days of dirty plates piling up on the ancient Formica worktop.

'I don't know if I'm up to wowing the nation. Who listens to the radio on a public holiday anyway?'

Charlotte couldn't conceal her irritation any longer. After all, she'd taken time away from her two children to secure this opportunity for this increasingly unimpressive client. She snapped back tetchily.

'Stop feeling sorry for yourself. Millions of people are listening. I've put up with your whingeing for months about how disappointed you are that no one is paying you any attention. Go out there, be funny.'

He quickly realised she was right. Empowered by her energy, Joe made an indistinct thumbs-up sign to his empty flat, realising that of course he was going to be awesome.

'Sorry, Charlotte, what was I thinking? Let's do this and I won't let you down.'

'That's more like it, darling. A bit of gumption is what you need.'

He was beginning to feel better as he remembered that he hadn't done a national interview yet and realised that this could stimulate his flagging book sales.

'Who am I on with? I hope she won't mind me muscling in.'

'She'll be thrilled to be with someone as funny as you. Her name's Chloe Adams. *Maybe you've heard of her?*'

PART 3
PODCASTING

Bank Holiday Monday, May 2018
Radio 5 Live. 3.15 p.m.

MATT: More news and sport coming up in fifteen minutes this Bank Holiday Monday. But now we're going to move on to talking books. I'm joined on the line by the journalist Chloe Adams, who has just published her new book *Ex-Communicate*, a history of broken relationships and what they tell us. For years she chronicled her own dating progress in her column 'Chloe's Merry War'.

CHLOE: Hi, Matt.

MATT: I'm also joined by Joe Harris, a former stand-up comedian who has just written his memoir, *Sit Down if You're No Good at Stand Up*, an honest account of why, to his mind, he failed and the impact it had on his ability to find relationship happiness. Let me start with you, Joe. Were you really such a rubbish comedian?

JOE: Afternoon, thanks for having me on. 'Rubbish' is a bit strong – although it was a word I heard a fair bit from hecklers. Let's just say, I did it for over ten years, played some big venues, was even on TV a few times, I just couldn't get any momentum to make it feel worthwhile.

MATT: And this is why you're still single? I'm struggling to find the link. I'm sorry, I haven't had the chance to read the book yet, so perhaps you can elaborate?

JOE: I'm not saying a stand-up is some sort of celibate monk. I think in my case the need to be funny has somehow become entwined with my self-esteem. And, full disclosure, when I didn't feel good about myself, I wasn't suitable boyfriend material. So, I wanted to write about the hardships of comedy and how if I thought I wasn't killing it on stage, I couldn't function emotionally, and …

CHLOE: … Oh, sorry for interrupting, but come on, Joe, surely that's not why you're single. You were funny most of the time, if memory serves me correctly.

MATT: Err … sorry, do you two know each other?

JOE: Just a bit.

CHLOE: We hadn't seen each other for thirteen years until we met on a phone line about ten minutes ago.

MATT: You're kidding.

CHLOE: No, we're not.

JOE: Hi, Chloe. Long time no see.

CHLOE: Hello, Joe. This is awkward.

MATT: Why is it awkward?

JOE: It might have something to do with the fact that the last time I saw her, she dumped me because I didn't understand her emotions. Thanks for writing a book to clarify them for me.

CHLOE: I was sort of hoping you may have moved on when I moved out. Now, Matt, surely it's not a coincidence we're here together.

JOE: Hmmm ... I'm beginning to wonder if one of Matt's talented researchers found an old clip of me on YouTube when I may have done a little bit of a routine on your engagement. Maybe that's why I'm the last-minute mystery substitution for this slot.

CHLOE: Yep, saw that video and wasn't too impressed. Nor was my husband, David. He calls you 'Jilted Joe' now.

JOE: All's fair game when you're trying to get a laugh. Anyway, since we're here, shall we plug our books? I don't know about you, but I need to sell a few. Matt, feel free to jump in whenever you want and ask us some questions.

MATT: Good point, I'm afraid I got a bit engrossed in the excellent banter. I promise I didn't know about you two, although my producer is now making weird faces at me through the glass that suggest you've been set up. Obviously, they didn't want to tell me too. Let's press on with my first question to you, Chloe, which now perhaps has added significance. What is so interesting about ex-relationships and why have you written about people splitting up rather than staying together?

CHLOE: I'm sure Joe and I can be civil, so long as he respects the restraining order.

MATT: The book, please, Chloe.

CHLOE: I remember studying Napoleon at school and one thing struck me as incredible. His love for Josephine was very real, but when she was unable to give him an heir, he told her at dinner that he'd made a list of eligible princesses, and for the good of France they needed to get divorced. Two months later, they had an annulment ceremony at which they read solemn vows of devotion to each other, sort of a wedding in reverse. It made me think that sometimes relationships can end for reasons that transcend the love in them, as if for a higher cause. Then I looked at other famous couples to understand if sometimes things work out better when a relationship ends, despite the pain. Do you need to experience short-term pain to find a more enduring happiness? And perhaps you stay in love with the person you've left behind even as you find love elsewhere.

MATT: Well, Joe, that seems to be a question to ask you, given your book is about how you haven't found permanent love. Would that have anything to do with Chloe?

JOE: Of course not. My book is about how professional dreams have impacted my ability to have a personal life. Nothing to do with being dumped out of the blue by my first love. And Chloe, Napoleon, really? I was the one who studied history at university. I don't remember you ever mentioning Napoleon to me.

CHLOE: Only in relation to some of your complexes. I think, Matt, you are trying to link our books to the brief biographical evidence your researcher has dug out on us. Clearly, we've written about things that have little to do with each other. For example, there's a chapter in mine about the real relationship of Mark Antony and Cleopatra and I am definitely not an exotic queen, and I'm pretty certain that unless Joe has a new gym routine, he is no warrior.

JOE: We did once go to Sharm El-Sheik on holiday together though.

CHLOE: Yes, and you got dehydrated. Look, my book and new podcast in the autumn has a core thought at its heart.

MATT: And that is?

CHLOE: My contention that relationships are in decline from the moment they begin. Passion wanes. Routine prevails. Sometimes, the foundations of love are built out of a type of concrete that can crumble over time. But that doesn't have to be a bad thing. If you look at great 'affaires de coeur' that have not survived, the individuals have benefited from the suffering in a way that staying together in a state of inertia will not do.

JOE: I hope David isn't showing any signs of inertness.

CHLOE: Thank you, Joe. He is perfectly 'nert', last time I checked.

MATT: It's a bit of a bleak view, isn't it, though, Chloe? Is that what you really think?

JOE: The thing is, Matt, she's always loved a grand statement, regardless of whether she believed it or it just sounded like something a French philosopher might spout in a Parisian café.

CHLOE: Says the man who expresses his emotions to strangers through jokes.

JOE: OK, let's call a truce. What was that Shakespeare line you loved? 'Thou hast frighted the word out of his right sense, so forcible is thy wit.'

CHLOE: Wow, I can't believe you remember this.

JOE: I remember all your favourite plays and books. See, I was listening.

CHLOE: I'm touched, Joe, and ...

MATT: Sorry to interrupt, Chloe, I'm afraid I must stop you as we've run out of time. Well, that was certainly unexpected and extremely entertaining, if you don't mind me saying. Thank you so much for joining us and revealing a little bit more than you probably both expected. OK, everyone, I suggest you all go out and buy Chloe Adams's book *Ex-Communicate* and Joe Harris's *Sit Down if You're No Good at Stand Up*, because quite frankly they need a bit of good fortune after enduring the ordeal of appearing together. Now, after the news and sport with Peter, we'll be changing the subject somewhat when we discuss the growth of electric cars and the government's plans for us all to buy them.

June 2018

Locking the bathroom door before the family was awake, Chloe sat on the edge of the bath downloading Joe's book. The covert op was necessary because reading it in front of David might be seen by him as an act of disloyalty with the imminent release of his film. Indeed, despite significant re-editing, he was paralysed with self-doubt, and it was her job to bolster his confidence as sincerely as possible without being distracted.

David had been too immersed in his work to listen to her radio interview, and she thought it best not to unsettle him with a funny anecdote about her unexpected on-air banter with a former lover. It would be disastrous. He'd never been comfortable dealing with Chloe's former love life, a source of never-ending insecurity for him as it was freely available online. While he had been in several longish relationships of his own, he was spooked by the ghosts of her lovers, who in his mind could do more press-ups than him. She consistently reassured him that what she wrote was amplified for comic effect.

Joe was the biggest challenge to his self-esteem. By nature sentimental, David believed first loves were different to other relationships, and since Joe and Chloe had grown up together, there was a part of her that was forever his. Most of the time it didn't matter, but any reminder of Joe was deeply unsettling for him. Recently, at a Sunday lunch, Malcolm had mused wistfully, *whatever happened to lovely Joe?* David had announced that he was a useless stand-up with a rarely visited YouTube channel, while Chloe fussed over the twins without replying.

She was reeling from meeting Joe on air. Over the years she had stalked him a little on social media and had built a vague perception of his life, without much detail. Now her curiosity had grown like bacteria in a Petri dish, and she was desperate to find out more. She had watched some of his stand-up and was both flattered to feature in routines and irritated to be the butt of his jokes. He had every right to be cross, of course, but it pained her to think that her impetuosity soured his view of her now.

She dropped the twins at nursery, almost throwing them out of a moving car, so impatient was she to begin the book. Back home, she prepared a large pot of coffee, spread an entire pack of biscuits on a plate and muted her phone, her heart beating faster than usual. It was hardly a treasure map to hidden gold, so why this giddy feeling?

Eight Hobnobs and a litre of coffee later, she finished the memoir, extremely disappointed to discover she was not a major plot line. Even worse, when she did appear, it was as Candice, a deliberately naff pseudonym surely intended to irritate her. The narrative began with the aftermath of her departure in 2005, with the words: *So I turned once more to comedy when my relationship turned tragic.* Occasionally, he would reference *the wondrous fun of life with Candice* in nostalgic terms that made it seem like they were living in a bucolic thatched cottage with a wishing well. Not quite how she remembered their squalid flat and penniless existence together.

Despite her vague characterisation, she laughed out loud frequently. His description of dying on his feet with new material and then getting in his car to drive all night to the next venue was an impressive demonstration of resilience. (The routine about why vegans have bad complexions was truly excruciating.) He counterbalanced the development of each stand-up set with an explanation of how his relationship at the time failed, linking the comedy to the specific reason why another partner left him. He described Grace, whose name he didn't change, with genuine affection, ashamed that she had to endure trite jokes about Candice when all she wanted was some unconditional love.

While she didn't know the person Joe had become, she recognised his self-deprecating wit. His true emotions, however, were still opaque, and the relationship revelations entertaining but superficial. Was it her fault he had become a stagnant person? In the past, she had imagined bumping into him on the street, in a restaurant or at a party. They would flirt harmlessly with affectionate nostalgia, like a couple in a Noël Coward play, secure in the stability of their current relationships. Their encounter on the radio had been sardonic and bitchy.

A bigger challenge arose when Mary declared by text later that day her conviction that Joe should be her co-host on the podcast. The barrage of emails that followed were worse than Chinese water torture. Not a *drip, drip, drip* (there was nothing drippy about Mary) but rather *splash, splash, splash*: a relentless deluge of communication like a bucket of icy water poured over Chloe's head every hour. All she had ever wanted was to be well respected for her writing talent. A podcast was different, apparently. Global fame could be earned in months by a successful format and presenters catapulted to ridiculous levels of popularity. Mary was convinced that Chloe was on the cusp of a shift in fortune.

Her agent had few qualms employing an array of inappropriate expressions to bludgeon Chloe into agreement, including the observation that *even Stevie Wonder in a fucking balaclava could see I'm right. You arseholes were hilarious together.*

She went on to explain that what the podcast needed was tension and conflict to make its subject matter (the end of relationships) more credible, and she was convinced Joe's status as a funny loser would make him the ideal foil to Chloe's intellectual brilliance.

It wasn't such a daft suggestion when Chloe looked back on what had happened. Before the interview, she was too shocked to do more than ask Joe why he was there. By the time they went on air, she was furious that her limelight was diminished by this unwelcome reunion. Suddenly, she needed to be cleverer and funnier, recalling many drunken evenings in pubs when they tried to outperform the other in front of a group of friends. It was a reminder that she was the queen of banter.

As the siege of emails, voice notes and texts proliferated, Chloe rebuffed Mary with increasingly spurious reasons: *she didn't want to split the revenue, she hated the way Joe had talked about her, the chemistry of that one-off interview could not be repeated.* Yet, her reticence was not about working with Joe. It was simply that David's emotional fragility would most likely shatter if she hooked up with her ex, even if it was only in a professional capacity. Putting Joe down in public would be easy and two presenters created greater interest, which would lead to a bigger audience and more money. Mary's suggestion made sense, despite being totally mad.

* * *

Charlotte called Joe the day after the interview to congratulate him on being so funny and creating a moment of 'car crash radio' that would be talked about for some time. Indeed, the BBC Radio 5 Live Twitter feed had buzzed with a spiky debate on their conversation, opinion divided as to who had fared best. Joe trended well with women, who accused Chloe of being 'stuck-up'. As he read the threads, Joe's smugness was tinged with a smidgen of sympathy for Chloe, whose on-air confidence evinced such blatant sexism. There had even been a small spike for his online book sales after the interview, although, given the low base, the uplift was going to make little difference to the negligible royalties he was earning.

His interest was piqued, and he needed to find out more about her, even though he'd read most of what she'd written over the years.

He knew it wasn't a good idea to confront their past, but nevertheless downloaded her book and was up most of the night searching for an explanation as to what had happened to him.

No such luck. There wasn't a scintilla of personal revelation, just beautifully crafted prose that did little to shed light on her actions. While the historical portraits were well researched, what use was an analysis of why Charles Dickens dumped his wife, Catherine, in explaining Chloe's brutal abandonment of him in 2005? The interviews with contemporary couples were equally unhelpful because none of the scenarios were analogous to his circumstances, and who wants to read ten pages of some poor sod lamenting their heartbreak. Chloe's conclusions were based on the premise she outlined on the radio, which he thought nonsense. Indeed, if relationships are in decline from the moment they begin, her poor husband was going to be in for a bumpy ride.

Like Chloe, he had imagined a variety of scenarios in which they ran into each other, all of them ending in his triumph. In his favourite one, he would be smooching in a restaurant with an Audrey Hepburn lookalike, celebrating her recent Nobel Prize win. Chloe would be alone on the next table reading a self-help book on relationships, well into her second bottle of Pinot Grigio, her best friend these days. They would walk over for a chat, the Audrey H doppelganger stroking his arm sensually as she explained to Chloe how she'd developed a technique for bringing sustainable energy to developing countries by heating milk and carrots together. Chloe would slur the odd word and as they walked away from the table, Joe's partner would whisper, *well, she certainly didn't look like I imagined*.

After the interview, his thoughts were conflicted. Their on-air banter reminded him of both the excitement of being with someone sharp-witted like Chloe and his anger at being rejected. It was crazy. She was married, she was a mother, and he was a part of her adolescence rather than her adult life. So why, for all those years, did he evaluate every subsequent relationship against a Chloe scorecard: was she as funny, was she as pretty, did she share the same cultural tastes?

His mother had often told him that splitting with Chloe had destroyed his capability to find a soul mate, or even a soul nodding acquaintance. He protested that he was not meeting the right person and pointed out a succession of long-term relationships he had worked hard to build. It was an unconvincing argument given these women always left him after making a doomed effort to secure his undivided attention. The spectre of Chloe could not be exorcised.

Joe was scared by his failure to commit. He was always affectionate, loving and kind, but that was not enough to make him trust others. And so he floated from casual dalliance to brief cohabitation with a cohort of lovely partners who were all destined to find happiness elsewhere. His superpower was convincing women not to settle, for which they would all in time be very grateful to him. Meanwhile, he plodded on in a state of unsatisfactory relationship inertia. Lots of liaisons. Very little heartbreak.

He was ready to meet Chloe again now, but this time not in front of millions of radio listeners. There was no statute of limitations on what she had done, and he wanted to explain calmly the very real emotional pain that had crippled him after she left and for her in turn to say sorry. Actually, he wanted a full-on signed grovelling apology, which he'd then release to the newspapers. She could choose the titles as he didn't want to seem unreasonable.

A week or so later, he received an email out of the blue from someone called Mary, inviting him to a meeting to discuss working with Chloe on her podcast. He wondered if he was being scammed by a bored Russian hacker, as the prospect of presenting a podcast on relationships was preposterous and this could only be a wind-up.

Asking Joe for emotional advice was like asking a priest to explain the principles of tantric sex. For a few days he ignored her, but this did not seem to deter the woman from bombarding him daily. Her tone was less of a suggestion and more of an edict, signing off with the assertion that *only an absolute twat would not want a meeting after that shitshow*.

Mary proposed he and Chloe meet at her office to get reacquainted and see if they could work together. While the chance to ask Chloe awkward questions was appealing, now that the opportunity presented itself he was terrified that such an encounter might end unhappily. He wasn't brave enough to hear what Chloe had to say so he responded with a series of polite rebuttals. These just seemed to make Mary more persistent, and it was clear it would be hard to withstand the onslaught forever.

As the messages grew more threatening, Joe realised that he could carry on as a passive bystander in his own life or show some maturity for once and confront an awkward situation with the hope of a more positive outcome. Plus, this could be the vitamin boost his flagging career needed. A new creative opportunity was being offered to him (and free lunch) and all he had to do was accept the possibility of experiencing personal rejection once more. He texted Mary and a date was fixed, leaving him only one important question to consider further.

Stubble or clean-shaven?

July 2018

At breakfast, Chloe scanned the paper and saw it was Mick Jagger's seventy-fifth birthday. She knew from assiduous reading of celebrity gossip that he had become a father again at seventy-three, with his partner forty-four years younger than him. She didn't get his appeal and thought his face looked like a craggy cliff face eroded by the sea. It didn't seem to hold him back, however, from continuous relationships with beautiful women and when he sang that he couldn't *get no satisfaction*, he was probably lying.

En route to town, she tried to understand her resentment for a rock legend she had never met and whose music she loved. The walk was only ten minutes to Chiswick Park Station, but she was wilting in thirty-degree heat. What an idiot she was to take the Tube on one of the hottest days of the year, and the carefully curated look she had planned for Joe was in danger of being ruined by her summer dress now being superglued to her clammy skin.

That's why she was pissed off with Sir Mick. It was effortless for him staying young in body, mind and relationship, and it didn't matter that some of his grandchildren were older than his children since he was still having plenty of fun with his *jumping jack flash*. She had begun the day intent on showing her ex-boyfriend how good she looked, and now, melting in the sunshine, she was resentful that men could improve in their attractiveness with age, irrespective of their moral worth.

Her frustration grew, causing her to walk faster and sweat even more. Her thoughts wandered to a section in her book where she referenced a famous academic study of a hundred thousand people that showed men were twice as likely to claim they fell in love at first sight and say *I love you* before their female partner. According to anthropologists, evolution made women more reticent to jump into relationships with less than optimal mates and miss out on better opportunities that could increase their chances of healthy offspring. Not the same for men, who casually flit between encounters, each of which could potentially lead to a sprog at any age. No wonder they were happy to blurt out declarations of love without a care.

By the time she entered the station, she had worked herself into a state of despair at this perceived unfairness. Women had to work so much harder to find emotional equilibrium, while men could do what they liked until they were geriatric. The rumble of an arriving train made her run down to the platform to avoid being late. As the doors opened, the heat hit her like the blast of air from a demented hairdryer. Slumping into a seat, she tried to calm down, realising her railing against the iniquities of ageing was just an attempt at distraction. How on earth could Joe have this effect after so many years?

When she arrived first at her agent's office, Mary did little to bolster her self-esteem.

'Fuck me, darling, you could have tried to look nice. We want to snag him, not scare him off.'

After thirty minutes in a sauna masquerading as a Tube train, Chloe was not in the mood for Mary's bluntness.

'Do you have many female friends, or any friends at all? Sometimes, a bit of respect would be a nice change.'

'All right, J.K. Rowling, calm down, I was only joking. Don't be so sensitive. I know you're worried about meeting Joe, but rest assured, we are in charge. I've spoken with his agent and he's not particularly on the ball. Let's just say this won't be the first time you've screwed him.'

Chloe grimaced at the prospect of the meeting if it was going to be punctuated by comments like this. Granted, Mary had proven herself brilliant in negotiation, but today wasn't really about the money. She wanted emotional rather than commercial support, unlikely to be forthcoming from this woman who thought that only weaklings and the infirm had feelings.

Mary's drive was not unreasonable given how much work she'd done to make the podcast happen, and most of the details had nearly been finalised – from selecting a production company to negotiating its distribution. Chloe had loved the process, leading discussions on the exact format and drafting a tentative guest list for the first series. Mary had done a great job to secure Chloe both a presenting fee and, unusually, a small share of advertising revenue.

The plan was to meet in the office for a few minutes and then go for lunch to get reacquainted. As Mary went to fetch Joe, Chloe suddenly wished she was home playing with the twins. A minute or so later, Mary entered with a nervous-looking Joe. She had forgotten the blueness of his eyes, the warmth of his smile and the tight curls of his hair, now elegantly speckled with grey. The *bastard* had aged well.

Chloe stood awkwardly by the desk and walked towards him as he entered. He leant forward to kiss her on the cheek and she placed a light hand on his shoulder, inclining her head towards him. She couldn't be sure, but sensed he was inhaling her perfume, and the familiarity of his proximity unnerved her. Any poignancy in this moment was obliterated by Mary, who decided to break the ice with customary indelicacy.

'I'll leave you frisky lovebirds to it. There's no introduction needed to the first person you ever shagged.'

* * *

'I think we only ate in a restaurant like this when my parents took us out for my birthday,' Joe observed as he absorbed the grandeur of The Wolseley. Despite the Saharan weather outside, its marble columns, mosaic floor and vaulted ceiling made it pleasantly cool.

'And how are they these days?' Chloe replied, shouting over the clanking cutlery and crockery of the busy lunchtime trade.

'Divorced. Oh, and Mum is married to a woman now.'

'You're kidding?'

About to take a bite of her breadstick, the revelation made Chloe drop it on the starched white linen tablecloth.

'Nope. Dump me and you're going to miss some meaty dramas, I'm afraid.'

'I'm not entirely surprised they split. Your mum always looked a bit bored around your dad. Is that unfair?' Joe was amazed Chloe had detected the future schism between his parents when he had been so oblivious.

'Maybe he's not as interesting as I thought. You should meet his new partner, Debbie. She's Olympic level dull. As for Mum, I'd need the rest of the meal to tell you about her new life with Jane. They're like hormonal teenagers.'

'Is that difficult for you?'

'Only when she insists on giving me a post-match report on their love life. No child should have to go through that.'

The waiter, unctuous and immaculate in a dark suit, arrived to take their order. Chloe ordered the salade niçoise and Joe, barely glancing at the menu, ordered the veal Milanese and fries. Asked if he had any allergies, he was in such a hurry to get rid of the waiter that he didn't even make his favourite joke about hay fever and bullies. When they were alone, Chloe placed her elbows on the table and rested her face in her hands.

'Oh, go on, tell me about Helen. I'm fascinated.'

'I am not prepared to relive the trauma with you.'

'Spoilsport. I can keep a secret, if you're worried.'

'Nope, I need to respect the sanctity of Mum's antics in the bedroom. Changing the subject, how is Reverend Malcolm? I always loved your dad.'

'Guess what, he's got a new girlfriend too.'

'That's great. Or is she an atheist?'

'Catholic, actually, but Dad doesn't seem to mind. She's a very nice ex-headmistress who can stare you down and make you feel like a naughty child.'

'Still a Daddy's girl then?'

'He's everything to me.'

'Isn't that what your husband should be?' he asked provocatively.

Chloe picked up her fork and pointed at him.

'So, we're doing this before the food arrives?'

'Doing what?'

'The bit where you ask what I see in him and why we got married. Is it because you're short of material for your next set? Oh wait, you couldn't make a living and had to give up stand-up. I read your book, you know.'

'And I read yours, in which you explain all relationships are destined to fail. Bit of a bummer for your marriage then?'

'That's not quite my argument,' Chloe said, and made the 'time out' signal with her hands. 'Let's call it quits for now, before we say something vindictive. I'm sorry for that last comment, it was uncalled for. I guess I'm nervous.'

'Why are we here, Chloe?'

'The Wolseley? Mary booked it for us.'

'Very amusing, you know what I mean. Why do you want me on your podcast? We're already bickering, and I haven't forgiven you for breaking my heart.'

Another waiter arrived with their bottle of rosé, and they were silent while he opened it and poured some for Joe to try. He had no knowledge of wine, but he nodded earnestly.

'I think it's because we're bickering that Mary thought it such a good idea to connect us. Much as I hate to admit it, there's a logic to having two people present a show about relationships who were in one together,' Chloe said.

'I'm hardly the ideal choice. And how do you know I'd be any good at it?'

'Just because you're incapable of being a happy couple doesn't mean you won't be funny talking about love. That's the theory.'

'I'm very good at relationships. Well, certainly getting them started. Keeping them going is proving much trickier.'

'I rest my case. Seriously, though, I wouldn't be here if I didn't think it an interesting idea. And what's the big deal about us being co-workers? We were always funny together, so why couldn't we be again?'

Chloe downed her wine like an athlete rehydrating after exercise. Her positivity about working together was complicated by butterflies in her stomach. Years had passed without her giving Joe too much thought and now, their knees practically touching under the table, she succumbed to a cocktail of nostalgia and confusion.

'You're happily married then?' he asked.

'Sorry to disappoint you, but very,' she said with deliberate forcefulness.

'And he doesn't mind us possibly working together?'

'Why should David mind? It's my job, nothing else. Does your girlfriend mind?'

'Ah, nice try to find out my status. My private life will remain private.'

'So, you're single then.'

Joe could tell she was uneasy. Refusing to hold his gaze, it was a dichotomous situation he would never have expected. He was making her grovel for what she did, a power he had long craved, but was also reminded of all the things he had loved about her – from the perfection of her cupid's bow to her gap-toothed smile and dimples. It was much harder to be with her than he had expected, and he drank some iced water, hoping it might freeze his brain and prevent him saying something irreversibly stupid.

'Look, Chloe, if we're going to carry on, you should know I've changed.'

'In what way?'

'I can express my emotions, for a start.'

'Do I want to hear this?'

'You have no choice. Mum shouted at me the other night and insisted that I told you how unhappy I've been for years because of our unfinished business.'

'What was unfinished, I thought I made things clear at the time? Have you considered your singleness could just be because you're a bit annoying?' She was only rude because of how uncomfortable the conversation was becoming. Her hand was trembling as it rested on the table.

'I never got to tell you in person that you broke my heart, and it took years to recover. Hope you feel properly rubbish now.'

'I am sorry, Joe. I don't know what to say. I needed to break free, however unfair that was. Do you think things happen for a reason? I only met David because he was friendly with Emily but didn't fancy her. Imagine that – they could have hooked up, because she's much prettier than me.'

'I always thought so.'

'Oh, yes, she told me she bumped into you in New York. She

looks great these days, doesn't she? Proves my point about how random things can be.'

'Can we get back to me?' Joe said, keen to change the subject.

'All right, since we've been so honest, let's cut to the chase. The only question for us today is should we do this project together, and based on this conversation, I'm convinced we should. We may not have lasted as a couple, but you must admit, we are quite funny together. So, are we good?'

'At what?'

'Are you OK to work with me?'

'Do you mean, will I stare at you lovingly and try to snog you?'

'Not quite, but OK, will you?'

'You are one hundred per cent safe, I can assure you. What about you? Do you swear you won't flutter your eyelashes at me all day when I'm trying to work?'

'Arguably an outmoded concept of flirtation, Joe, but yes, I'm committed to the kind of non-predatory behaviour that is essential in the modern workplace. Have you got everything off your chest now?' She leant back in her chair, hoping to move on to a safer conversation about the project itself.

'Just one more thing?' Joe replied.

'What's that?'

'I thought I made it clear that I want an apology for the cruel manner in which you walked out.' Joe was enjoying himself and sat back in his chair, folding his arms like a child refusing to eat his supper.

'If I say sorry, can we finally discuss the podcast?'

'On condition you promise never to leave me alone with your agent again.'

'Deal. I am sorry for what I did, and I don't mean introducing you to Mary. I really loved you, and suppose it was too difficult to do anything other than cut all ties when it finished. I'm delighted we have the chance to be friends again. Great friends, and creative partners. How wonderful is that?'

'And for what it's worth, I'm thrilled you've found happiness with David. I hope you can believe that.'

'I do. You'll like him. He's funny, like you, but without all the character defects.'

'I can't wait to meet him. Do you reckon I could take him in a fight?'

'Depends, he often carries a sword. Now, can we get down to business?'

'What, in the middle of the restaurant?' Joe said with an impish grin.

'Oh God, I'm regretting this already,' Chloe said, shaking her head.

Her trepidation was not professional but personal. She had forgotten how much she enjoyed his company.

August 2018

She had promised to be on time for the première. Things unfortunately got off to a bad start when her meticulous planning was scuppered by roadworks on the M4, which delayed her father, who was on babysitting duty as normal. The production company had arranged for someone called Melody to come to Chloe's house to do her hair and make-up. Apparently, she'd worked in Hollywood, including a couple of Batman films, and hopefully she'd make her look like Anne Hathaway's Cat Woman rather than Heath Ledger's Joker. Malcolm's tardiness meant Melody had to contend with Alice as her assistant, passing unwanted lipsticks and make-up brushes like an overzealous nurse in surgery.

There was a temporary but explosive crisis when Alice smudged eyeliner on the magnificent azure-blue cocktail dress hanging on the wardrobe door. The outfit was so expensive that Chloe had raided an ancient savings account to pay for it and her despair at its potential ruin resulted in her screaming at Alice with a fury that she had not expressed since giving birth to her. Her daughter wailed theatrically and curled into a scrunched ball of snivelling misery. Mikey, dressed as a Teenage Mutant Ninja Turtle, then arrived to assess the situation. Seeing his sister crumpled in despair, he expressed his support by hitting her on the head with his plastic shield.

Fortunately, Malcolm had let himself into the house. The shrieking was so loud, he wondered if there was an intruder holding the family hostage and flew up the stairs to confront the commotion. Calm was restored quickly. The twins adored him, and their moods (hysterical sobbing and violent aggression) immediately softened at his arrival. He took their hands and led them away without stopping to find out what had precipitated the chaos.

Chloe's make-up needed touching up from the tears of frustration that had run down her face. More important was the dress. It transpired that Christian Bale had been a messy eater on set and had often spilt lunch down his Batman costume, which was less wipe-clean than you'd think. Consequently, Melody knew a particularly effective hack involving dishwasher detergent, vinegar and her hair dryer, which meant that within fifteen minutes the stain was gone. When Chloe finally tottered down the stairs in her four-inch heels, she had regained her composure, if not her balance.

As ever, Malcolm had the twins engaged in a non-screen-based activity and they were quietly colouring in pictures of animals like a pair of sedated cherubs. Chloe kissed her father an inch from his face to preserve her pristine lipstick. The gesture was so ridiculous that he extended his hand to her as an alternative.

'We can always shake like we're doing business if that feels more comfortable, darling.'

'Don't be sarky, Dad. Do you know what a genius Melody is to make me look presentable?'

'I really am,' Melody replied, putting on her coat. 'This was one of the hardest jobs I've had since the corpses for a zombie movie. You look lovely, darling. Now hurry up and pay me before you smudge something else.'

Chloe handed her a wad of notes and could feel Malcolm's silent disapproval at the cost of her makeover. When the front door slammed, she turned to him defensively.

'I know you hate my extravagance. Come out and say it.'

'It's hard for me to see you spend so much money on something you could do yourself.'

'We live in different worlds, Dad. You do good and help people. I go to parties and try to say pointless things to sound clever.'

Malcolm ignored her, and took a glass from the cupboard and filled it with water. He seemed nervous.

'We may well live in different countries soon, Chloe.'

'What are you talking about?'

Her father's affability was replaced by an anxious expression. She could feel the hairs standing up on her bare arms as a cold, rising fear took hold.

'I'm sorry to spring this on you now, but I can't keep a secret and it's happened so fast.'

'What? Tell me, Dad. You're scaring me.'

'I've proposed to Sally. She's said yes. I'm going to retire.'

Chloe flung her arms around him with a surge of relief.

'That's wonderful, Dad. I'm so pleased for you. No one deserves to be happy as much as you do. High time you left the congregation to fend for themselves. Retirement is wonderful. Have some fun, go travelling. Not too far, though – after all, the twins can't look after themselves.'

Malcolm had his funeral-family sympathy face on now.

'I think you missed the point, my darling. Sally and I have seen a place in the Dordogne we want to buy, to move to France as soon as we can. Start a new life. You have your happy, glamorous world here. I need to spend some time building something different for my dotage. I'm sure God will cut me some slack if I move away for a bit for a new experience. Will you?'

* * *

Distracted by the prospect of her father's emigration, she couldn't concentrate during the film screening. How was she going to get by in the future without Malcolm appearing like the cavalry to rescue her from her insecurities and domestic incompetence?

Their father-daughter bond was atypical, and despite her confident independence, he was the only person whose opinion she would unconditionally follow. She would never be like that in her marriage, no matter how much she loved David.

The film finished with a polite ripple of applause, like an audience of elderly people showing their appreciation at a piano recital. The ensuing party was low key and not as glitzy as Chloe's outfit and hairdo. More a jeans and T-shirt drinks reception than an Elton John bash with a swan made from caviar. It was a shame. She had seen David's recut and reshot version several times and was very proud of him for his tenacity and talent. However, the party reflected Netflix's marketing budget reduction, the death knell for David's expectations of success.

Chicken Wars deserved to do well but the energy in the party suggested otherwise. Unfortunately, the venue had not been changed to reflect the downgraded investment and was therefore too large a space for the sixty or so guests, who stood in small groups metres apart. Conversation was muted and restrained, with discreet whispering about how good the film *could* have been. Chloe held David's hand tightly as she gamely tried to sparkle in front of his creative team and the studio execs, thinking it only a matter of time before someone accidentally said to him, *I'm sorry for your loss.*

A DJ tried to create a party from amid a wake and after an hour or so a few people took the hint at the sudden increase in the volume of the music and began to dance as if they were contractually obliged to do so. Chloe led David to the dance floor and tried to look like she knew how to party. Normally a keen mover with impressive hip action, he shuffled from side to side with the look of a man hoping for a fire drill.

Chloe had drunk without restraint to calm her nerves and realised that three mojitos in an hour, followed by a couple of shots, was a bad idea on an empty stomach. Her gyrations shook up the ill-advised cocktail of cocktails and very quickly she knew she was going to be sick. She made it to the bathroom just in time, although her exit was undignified and involved pushing aside a senior studio executive as she shouted, 'Out the way or I'm going to throw up over you.'

When she returned, there were fewer people in the room and a lot of air-kissing goodbyes. It was only ten thirty and the party was beginning to end. David was making one last effort to be a good host and was the most animated he'd been all evening. As he mingled among people, she wondered if he was imploring them to stay or trying to persuade them to give him and his film a second chance. Chastened by her chundering, she took a few calming breaths and sidled up to his side, once more the supportive wife. He didn't look at her and as she tried to slip her hand in his, he moved his away and turned his back a few degrees. She wondered if he could smell the sour taste in her mouth.

* * *

The cab ride home was initially silent. As they drove through Soho, David stared at the crowds spilling on to the street on a warm summer's evening, drinks in hand, boisterous and carefree. He pushed his face against the car window and wore an expression of sadness, suggesting all he wanted was to hide under his duvet for the next year.

Chloe's stomach lurched under the strain of the alcoholic demands it had suffered and she leant out of an open window, sucking in the grime of the city in search of fresh air that might make her feel better. After about ten minutes, she couldn't take his silent anger any longer. Turning to him, she stroked his face with the sweaty tips of her fingers.

'I'm so sorry, my darling. I let you down big time.'

To her relief, a half-smile replaced his grimace.

'I don't know, you did your best not to be sick on Mark Casey, arguably the most important person there from a perspective of me ever working in film again. Your behaviour may not have been that of a vicar's daughter, but you can certainly run faster than I thought in those heels.'

She put her head on his shoulder and squeezed his arm. What she loved about David was that what she termed his 'moods and broods' never lasted that long. Perhaps now they could analyse the evening together and she might be able to convince him not to get disproportionately miserable because of an atmosphere-less party.

'Was it such a bad evening for you?'

'I don't really know how to judge it. I just get the feeling that I've had my shot at the big time and the people who matter don't think I'm up to the challenge.'

'I don't want to sound like a self-help book, but you do know that creative brilliance can only be built on the foundation of perseverance. That's entry-level wifely wisdom.'

'I do find you particularly sexy when you spout clichés.'

He leant towards her, and they kissed. She was no longer worried about her lipstick, but rather burping a noxious combination of tequila and peanuts in his face. She slid her hand around his neck and they pressed their foreheads together gently. David carried on in a shaky whisper.

'Why don't I just go back into advertising and put plans of another film on hold? I can earn decent money if I swallow my pride, and I'm always getting calls to come back. This isn't going to work, is it? I'm sorry, babe, but we may be done on red carpet events for a while. Not that the *bastards* exactly rolled one out tonight.'

Chloe was relieved, having thought extensively about David's future, concluding it would be better for his well-being to thrive in a familiar environment than struggle in a challenging new one. A bit of security to rebuild his self-esteem and then he could go again.

She wanted to make him feel better about himself and gave it one final go.

'Anyway, we may be judging things prematurely. From my perspective, the film got a lot of laughs.'

He pulled away and a quizzical expression spread across his face.

'Did it? Are you sure, because I sensed your mind was elsewhere. What's going on with you, Chloe? The screen could have caught fire and I'm not sure you'd have noticed.'

She didn't want to cry but suddenly the exertions of the evening caught up with her.

For Chloe, weeping should only occur at funerals and the end of *Armageddon* when Bruce Willis says goodbye to his daughter before sacrificing himself to save the world. How apposite a reference in the context of her father's imminent departure. David wondered if the tears were for him, until she explained.

'My dad's getting married and buggering off to live in France with Sally. They're buying a house in the Dordogne. I'm going to be on my own.'

'You do have a family still, Chloe, or have you forgotten us?'

She was ashamed of how self-pitying she sounded, but her emotions were in complicated free fall. Supporting David at his moment of anxiety was counterbalanced by a selfish need for him to appreciate her sense of loss. There was a further problem rising like an angry kraken out of the sea. Through tears and a runny nose, she was also now thinking about Joe again. He had popped into her head unexpectedly, unwelcomely, and although no longer vomit-inducingly drunk, she was not quite sober. At moments like this, her loquacity could be dangerous.

'I don't want to make this evening about me.'

David arched an eyebrow in disbelief.

'What's happened, Chloe? This can't be just because your dad has decided to build a life away from you. Surely you should be happy for him, by the way?'

His perceptiveness was not helpful, and it was no use holding back. She owed him the truth.

'It's my podcast. There's been a development.'

'What development?'

This was it; she could turn back and make things better. She chose not to.

'Something strange happened after that radio interview I did a few weeks back.'

How she wished he'd bothered to listen at the time. It would have made things much easier.

'You're not going to believe me.'

'Chloe, I always believe your stories, no matter how long they take you to spit them out.'

Yup, he was properly irritated.

'OK, well, by a mad coincidence they had to book a last-minute guest. You'll never guess who?'

'For the love of God, get on with it.'

'Joe.'

'Which Joe? Joe Biden? Joe Pesci? G.I. Joe?'

'Ex-boyfriend Joe.'

David deflated like a punctured balloon in front of her.

'How? And why are you only telling me now?'

'I ... I didn't want to ruin things for you with the film coming out.'

At this point, there were options available that would have minimised her husband's jealousy. The smart thing would have been to be vague and laugh it off. The intelligent response would be to consign the moment to an unlikely but inconsequential coincidence. However, loosened by the cocktails and shots, she couldn't ignore the strange sensation the on-air sparring with her first love had created and her curiosity to revisit the past. The impulse co-existed with her love for her husband and the desire not to upset him.

'Bizarrely, we were bloody funny and rude to one another. The interview sparked loads of interest afterwards. And here's the insane part. Mary invited him to meet me because she thinks we should present the podcast together. She reckons a bit of conflict will make it much better. And he's sort of agreed to do it, subject to the production company agreeing.'

He looked incredulous as she added a postscript.

'Well, what do you think?'

'I think you pick your moments very badly. That's what I think.'

The cab was pulling up to their house as he said this. David mumbled polite thanks to the driver and walked briskly to the front door ahead of her. It was quite an achievement to further ruin an evening that had already been disastrous.

September–October 2018

Joining the podcast was not a foregone conclusion. First, Joe had to be interviewed by Chrissie McCulloch, the founder of its production company, Listen Up. A well-known TV executive, entrepreneurial and tough, she had set the business up in 2015, having realised the potential of this new medium from frequent trips to the US. Joe worried she'd see through his jokes and think him a talentless buffoon, but he managed to pass his audition nevertheless by being witty and insightful, having prepared his answers in advance with Chloe's guidance. Mary had pushed for his inclusion, believing it to be in Chloe's best interests and goading Chrissie with the ferocity of a hungry lioness. Circumspect at the prosect of increasing the budget, however, she had no intention of paying him as much as Chloe. As an unproven late addition, he could share the airtime but not the financial spoils.

Joe's agent, Clive Atkinson, had hoped to dump him from his list. Their fathers were old school friends, but his energies were focused elsewhere. One of his clients had just been short-listed for the Booker Prize and Hollywood had come calling for another of his writers, whose dystopian bestseller was about to go intergalactic. Consequently, he skim-read Joe's proposed contract and, like most people who negotiated with Mary, his primary aim was to minimise the need for a conversation.

When Joe signed his contract, he had no idea if he was being fleeced. He asked Chloe about her own deal and was met with the stammering hesitation of a badly briefed politician at a press conference. He had no choice but to accept his role as junior partner without complaint. After all, he was grateful just to be involved and the fee would increase if the podcast continued after the first series. Money had never been his primary focus, which was why he had very little in his bank account.

Creatively, he was more Chloe's equal. He loved the freedom of their brainstorming sessions. Their initial challenge was to finalise the format, concurrent to recruiting the biggest names for the first series. The podcast had one guiding principle. It would only deal with relationships that had ended. Joe came up with a working tagline for the show – 'A broken heart doesn't mean you can't have a happy ending' – and despite its puerility, it was a useful mantra for developing their ideas.

The podcast would begin with Chloe explaining the relationship of a historical couple (initially from her book) and what it told her about relationships. Joe would also write a short monologue about his own dating failures, of which there were enough for at least seven series. It was scary as he had never produced anything to such a tight deadline before, yet this was what excited him the most. Each episode would revolve around an interview with a couple who had once been together, with five segments: 'How We Met', 'The Good Bits', 'The Not-So-Good Bits', 'The Ending' and finally 'Our Life Lessons'.

Joe loved this new life. Like an intern hyperventilating with enthusiasm, he spent as much time as he could in the Listen Up offices talking to researchers, technicians and the commercial team, trying to understand everything about a podcast.

His most important learning was the crucial role of the producer. He had assumed blithely that the job involved twiddling some knobs, organising the guest list and making sure the carrier pigeon delivered the finished podcast to the right platforms for broadcast. How wrong he was. The producer was the creative energy behind everything: part visionary, scriptwriter, technician, editor, ringmaster, disciplinarian, therapist, cajoler, muse, nurse, publicist, benevolent dictator and loving parent. Poor podcast producers create more unwanted waffle than a second-rate Belgian pancake house and good ones ensure glory that is greater than a Knickerbocker.

Joe and Chloe had been working from the outset with Charlie Rice, who was a pioneer in the medium and had graduated from being a highly respected BBC radio producer to a gun for hire in this brave new world of entertainment. Initially, Joe was cowed by his clear-sighted vision for their show, but as the weeks passed he became aware that Charlie's genius and talent was both God-given and alcoholically lubricated.

What started as a suspicion soon grew to be blatantly obvious as his behaviour became increasingly mercurial. A month before they were launching, he had tried to arm-wrestle Joe after an embarrassing hour of drunken ranting in their status meeting. Joe and Chloe had marched into Chrissie's office to resolve the situation.

To avoid further confrontation, Joe retreated to a meeting room to work on his scripts. At lunchtime, he went to make some toast in the tatty kitchen, which had three days of dirty plates piled up in the sink like a student house after a raucous party. As he pottered around, he realised Chrissie was standing behind him with a quizzical expression.

'You look like you want to shout at the kids about the mess,' he said, unsure if she was looking for him or just a clean cup.

'You're all animals when it comes to keeping this place clean.'

'Don't look at me. I'm tidier than a Swiss railway station.'

She seemed in no mood for humour.

'Can I ask you something, Joe?' she said, without expecting his permission.

'Of course.'

'Are you up to this? This is an investment in our future, and we're about to throw a fortune at your show, not to mention all the favours we've used up to provide you with a stellar guest list. Chloe is fabulous …'

'I'm feeling a "but" coming.'

'You're right. I do have a reservation.'

'Which is?'

'Which is, there's a danger of you coming across as – and I don't know another way to put this – *irritating*.'

'How have you decided this?' Joe asked, completely thrown.

'We did some research on your demo shows. Four focus groups.'

'Were you going to tell us?'

'Don't be paranoid. I'm telling you now. And Chloe already knows.'

'What did it say?'

'Chloe is fabulous. You, less so.'

'Oh,' was the only reply he could muster, his jaw bobbing like a goldfish at feeding time.

'You came across as annoying to some people.'

'Give me their addresses so I can pay them a visit.'

'Listen, and don't make jokes. We all have big hopes for you. You're extremely funny, but you're inexperienced. Can I give you a bit of off-the-record advice?'

'All help gladly received,' he said truthfully.

'Interviewing is like making love. The harder you try, the more unsatisfactory it can become. Chill, relax and enjoy. You're in danger of thrashing around like an over-excited teenager. Bear that in mind, please, when you record the first episode.'

He couldn't think how to reply to this surprisingly old-school analogy. He had assumed he was doing well, only to find out he was being tested behind his back and the feedback was simply 'be a bit less shit'. It was hardly morale-boosting. For weeks, his excitement had grown unchecked. Now, he realised that this was Chloe's show. She was earning more than him and inevitably all the important decisions would eventually be hers. Most worryingly, he was expendable if he didn't perform. It was an experiment to test their chemistry, which, if unsuccessful, would see him being jettisoned without anyone caring too much.

'I won't let you down, Chrissie,' he said, trying not to squeak his insecurity.

'I'm sure you won't,' she replied, not entirely convincingly.

She still hadn't mentioned the earlier incident. With the first show imminent, an inebriated producer throwing up in the recycling bin at ten thirty in the morning was not a good omen. Keen to change the subject, Joe asked the pressing question.

'What are you going to do about Charlie?'

Chrissie replied as if it was an inconvenience updating him.

'He needs to go check himself into rehab. Not my problem though. I fired that drunken fool faster than he could drink a round of shots. You and Chloe are interviewing someone brilliant in an hour. Try not to put him off.'

* * *

This was Kelly Evans' first job interview since arriving in the UK after his new wife made him leave LA to be closer to her family. While London was unfamiliar to him, marriage was not, as she was his third spouse in a twenty-five-year eventful life as a journalist and radio presenter.

Chloe had been taken aback by his appearance. In his early fifties, he looked more the leader of a Californian cult than the serious journalist his CV claimed him to be. His greasy, greying hair was tied in a straggly ponytail, and he sported the sort of goatee you would grow only to raise money for charity. Dressed in tatty bell-bottom jeans with patches and a grungy flak jacket, he must have been the only person in London on that cold autumnal day to be wearing open sandals.

The shabby Listen Up offices reflected that they were not yet profitable, and its two studios had been built so quickly they didn't have time to soundproof them properly.

Consequently, if a recording was going on, the rest of the office had to speak in a whisper. That morning, the over-officious producer of the new sports podcast 'It's Only a Game' had barked that he would fire anyone who ruined the recording of the latest episode. The only meeting room was being used, requiring them to interview Kelly huddled in Studio 2 so close to each other that their knees were touching awkwardly.

Chloe found Joe 2.0 very different from the person she'd walked out on. Through the mist of her own guilt, she remembered him as too passive for her needs. Now, he was brimming with ideas and energy but hid behind the rat-a-tat barrage of his jokes to obscure his personal life. She'd apologised and he had apparently moved on. Surely it was for the best, even if it meant suppressing the unexpected flutters of excitement each time she saw him.

She had enjoyed the last few weeks of preparing the show. They had quickly settled into an effective working partnership and were able to intuit each other's thoughts on most issues. And he really made her laugh. Before Kelly arrived, he had bet her that she couldn't weave a random phrase into the interview without him noticing and she agreed, not wanting to come across as stuffy. However, when he told her to incorporate the made-up cliché *'only in the pond of peace will you find the fish of happiness'*, she knew he'd set her up.

As the interview started, Joe couldn't stop staring at their interviewee's eclectic wardrobe and clearly shared Chloe's reticence.

Nevertheless, Kelly was confident and articulate even if he had clearly ingested significant quantities of therapy, which made his initial answers sound like motivational quotes for greetings cards. He wanted to explore the 'darkness of the soul', 'how trauma transmogrifies into emotional constipation' and the 'sexual conundrum of divergent desire'. They both tried not to giggle.

Beneath this intensity, he also had a clear vision that began to win them over as the conversation evolved. It was no coincidence they were meeting him, and Chrissie must have been planning this interview for a while as he had drafted thoughtful feedback, which couldn't have been done on the fly. He had read both their books, extracting passages that he felt could be used in different episodes and revealing a genuine insight into both of their psyches. He saw Chloe as a person who wanted to be liked and therefore was desperate to understand the alchemy of a successful relationship. Joe evidently had major self-esteem issues that made him torpedo each relationship he had been in to avoid the pain he'd experienced in the past.

'You know how you will make this show work?' Kelly said, interrupting Chloe from the dull questions on her list about his ambitions and greatest weaknesses.

'Tell me?' she asked apprehensively.

'Sparks need to fly between you. The sort that result in out-of-control flames.'

'You bring the kindling, I'll bring the firelighters,' Joe quipped, as if in a bad sitcom.

Kelly ignored him and addressed his next remark to Chloe.

'There must be some danger in how you interact. Like you're going to shout at each other or declare your love for one another. You need to embody the issues that are raised by your interviews in your life as a couple and be prepared to feel exposed in front of your audience. Otherwise, what's the point of having Joe on the show.'

Chloe had agreed to Joe as her co-presenter because they were funny together and believed their shared history should be used for strictly entertainment purposes. Kelly was challenging that assumption, and she understood what he was saying. A degree of intimacy above the verbal jousting was essential. For years, she had written brazenly about her personal life in her newspaper column. The same openness was needed working with Joe now, even if it left her vulnerable to a gnawing worry of how much she liked being around him.

The interview was lurching towards a couples' counselling session. She felt compelled to change the mood and, unable to think of anything else, raised her palm to high-five Kelly. Unprepared as he was for this random gesture, she succeeded in cuffing him lightly across the forehead.

'Sorry, I got a bit carried away because I agree with everything you say. I think you might just be the right person for us.'

Their claustrophobic proximity made her want to escort him immediately to Chrissie, who she assumed had signed a contract with him weeks ago anyway. Joe wasn't finished, however.

'I have one more thing to ask. Why do you want to do this podcast? What's special about it?'

'Those are really good questions, Joe,' Kelly replied earnestly. 'Let me clarify then for you. We're all searching for meaning from encounters that dissolve into despair. I think we could make some real inroads into understanding relationships and how the pain of suffering can build hope? How wonderful it would be if we could adequately explain that famous Emily Dickinson line: "The heart wants what it wants – or else it does not care."'

It sounded profound, although Chloe wasn't entirely sure what he meant. Joe seemed equally bamboozled by the vagueness of the answer. In the ensuing silence, she remembered she hadn't taken up his challenge to introduce the random phrase. She would show him now that nothing embarrassed her. Tilting her head forty-five degrees, she spoke the words with the soothing calm of a yoga teacher.

'Wise words, Kelly. Wise words. After all, *only in the pond of peace will you find the fish of happiness.*'

Kelly's face was a mask of empathy.

'You have kindness in your soul, Chloe. I couldn't have put it better myself.'

* * *

A week later and Joe looked at Chloe in the forlorn hope of support.

'Do I really have to?' he asked in desperation.

'You do, if you want this project to work,' Kelly said firmly.

'Aren't we getting on fine without having to confess our darkest secrets?'

Kelly shook his head.

'As your producer, it's crucial you and Chloe fully trust me. For *Ex-Communicate* to be a proper examination of relationships, we must expose ourselves without fear of consequence.'

'I used to expose myself to Chloe most evenings and look how well that worked out.'

Chloe smiled. They were still in the honeymoon phase of working together and Joe wanted them to avoid personal revelations even though he had written a book about his emotional failings, which he was happy to discuss with anyone else. But Kelly had different ideas and from the moment he took up his role, he dissected their relationship like a corpse in the morgue, explaining that his priority was 'looking for the pain to stimulate your performance passion'.

Kelly had insisted, therefore, that they go to Signora Fraquelli's trattoria in Soho for dinner to answer some probing questions, believing the greater their vulnerability, the more likely they'd make an effective team. Joe considered booking a colonoscopy to give him a credible excuse. It was hardly ideal, conducting a sensitive exercise in a bustling restaurant with waiters constantly interrupting with offers of more Parmesan cheese. The tables were pushed close together, and Joe was uncomfortable that the four young women enjoying a raucous birthday dinner on the next table to them could hear everything.

Kelly had prepared a list of quick-fire questions that he wanted answered without hesitation. So long as they were honest, they could say whatever came into their heads. Chloe had drunk several glasses of wine and was merrily relaxed, whereas the two double whiskies Joe had consumed made him anxious and irritable. As the waiter cleared their main course, Kelly pulled moon-shaped glasses from his ancient leather biker jacket and rummaged in his jeans' pockets for crumpled notes.

'Here we go, team. As I've explained, we're going to bare our souls, no matter how twisted they may be. The questions are going to get more intimate as we go along, and I'll answer them too. Then we're going to discuss it all in detail. Ready?'

'Yes, boss!' Chloe raised her glass with light-headed enthusiasm.

'How much cash would it take to stop this?' Joe implored. 'I have seven pounds in coins and my Oyster card, and I can get more if you want.'

Kelly cleared his throat.

'Right, my first question is easy. *Who was your first love?* Mine was Tamara O'Reilly, who introduced me to sex when I was seventeen and she was twenty-three. What about you, Chloe?'

Joe pointed at himself, but she ignored him.

'Tell us more about Tamara? She sounds much more interesting than my answer.'

'Don't duck the question,' Kelly said to her.

'All right, very dull. It was Joe. He didn't have much competition, unfortunately.'

'For me, it was Margaret Smith when I was in Year 11.'

'Joe, I think the question requires the love to be requited, or at the very least that she knew your name.'

'If you're making me tell the truth, then my first love was indeed you, Chloe. Happy now, Kelly, or do you want diagrams?'

'Don't be gross. You'll make me regurgitate my linguini,' Chloe said, shaking her head.

'From what I remember, it was a beautiful experience for us both. I even gave you a certificate and a proficiency badge afterwards.'

He gave her hand, resting next to his on the table, an affectionate pat and was embarrassed when she recoiled. Kelly banged the table with a salt-cellar gavel to interrupt them.

'Time out, guys. Time out. This energy is too negative. What I want is for you to answer without putting the other down. Do you think you can manage that? It's about being brave enough not to worry about our inner truth.'

'I think I may have left my inner truth at home in a drawer. Are there any other games we could try? What about Fizz Buzz?'

'Come on, Joe,' Chloe barked, 'let's do what he's asking, or we'll never get dessert.'

The women on the next table were now silent and craning towards their table nosily. Joe waited a few seconds to see if Kelly would abandon the game. The ordeal, however, continued.

'Good. Let's go then. *Favourite romantic song*. Mine is "Lay, Lady, Lay", Bob Dylan.'

'Bangles, "Eternal Flame". Joe?'

'"My Humps", Black Eyed Peas. Remember, there are no wrong answers.'

'Favourite love story film. *Betty Blue*.'

'*The Way We Were*.'

'Still? Chloe is the only Streisand fan under forty I know.'

'Don't interrupt and get on with yours.'

'*Harold and Maude.*'

'You made me watch that, I remember. I've seen more romantic funerals.' She kicked him under the table.

Kelly tapped the table again, this time with a little more force.

'Keep on track, you two. *Biggest heartbreak?* Wife two, for me. Constantly unfaithful. Ripped out my heart and put it in the trash.'

'My boyfriend after Joe, Noah Evans. Sorry, matey-boy, you're close second.'

'No close second for me. It was Chloe. Like your second wife, Kelly, only more psycho. Do we have to keep doing this or can I go to the toilet now?'

'No, stay put. *Best sex?* On the beach at sunset in Tahiti on my first honeymoon.'

'What else do you expect me to say to that, other than my husband?'

Joe blurted his answer, knowing it would goad her.

'With Emily, last year.'

'Emily who?'

'Your friend Emily.'

'Shut up, Joe. We're meant to be telling the truth.'

'How do you know I'm not?'

'I know Emily. She's not that desperate.'

'How well do you really know Emily – or me, for that matter? What if we had?'

'You can do what you like as far as I'm concerned, but not with my friends, please. It's just not right.'

Kelly leant back in his chair, defeated by his non-cooperative colleagues, who were killing his idea. Indeed, Joe had no intention of carrying on now that he had an opportunity to make Chloe jealous.

'We had a fling. In New York and here in London. What of it?'

Chloe looked stunned. He had landed his blow.

'I don't believe you.'

'Well, why don't you ask her?'

'What are you, twelve years old? We're not in the playground.'

'Phone her, Chloe. I don't see why it's such a big deal.'

'It's not. I just can't understand why she wouldn't have told me.'

Joe saw the hurt in her eyes and his initial pleasure at her discomfort began to pass. Before he could apologise, Kelly stood up and put on his jacket.

'This hasn't been the evening I'd hoped for. You two are impossible to control and that worries me. I think you should work through why you need to score points like this off each other. I wanted us to be intimate, not unpleasant. For the love of *Jesus*, how hard is it for you to have a proper conversation? I'm done here.'

Joe considered stopping him but the thought of another round of questions about his favourite aphrodisiac held him back. He would make peace with him tomorrow. Now he had to work out what to say to Chloe, who was staring at her phone trying to decide whether to call Emily.

'I'm sorry,' he mumbled, avoiding her gaze.

'For what? You just said you didn't owe me anything.'

* * *

They chatted for hours until the waiters started putting the chairs on the tables, making clear they needed to leave. Joe never drank coffee late at night but chanced his arm with a macchiato after Chloe explained how caffeine worked differently depending on your genetic disposition. He wanted her to think he had the DNA of a Marine.

It was their most personal conversation. He began by telling her about his tryst, defending Emily's behaviour in allowing it to happen. Joe pointed out that there was no code of conduct for going off with the friend of an ex-lover after over ten years and Chloe acknowledged she was being unreasonable, less so when he told her how they had hooked up while Laura was ill in bed. Inevitably, she was outraged at his behaviour towards the woman who had funded his trip to New York. Joe admitted it wasn't his finest moment and she recommended he found someone who saw 'more than a two-week horizon for relationships'.

Joe recalled his relationship with Grace, a caring woman nicer than anyone he'd dated before (and a proper footie fan with a Sky Sports subscription), unable to explain why it failed. He couldn't admit it floundered because she lacked that ephemeral quality of 'Chloeness', and he became wistful when he described her devastation as he moved out of her flat.

What Joe learnt about Chloe's marriage unsettled him further. On the surface, she talked lovingly about David's gentleness, creativity and sense of humour. (Surely he wasn't funnier than him?) He was apparently a great father and made Gordon Ramsay look like a klutz in the kitchen. If a friend was in trouble, he would be straight round to support them. Being with David had cured her restless desire to be the best and brightest person in the room. Several years of therapy had helped her understand that her behaviour was rooted in fear of losing her father and being alone. Her therapist described her search for love as the frantic quest for security of someone in constant fear of an imminent catastrophe. David ended that vulnerability.

She talked openly about her recent frustration. Their careers were not a competition but as David became more professionally unhappy, his resentment grew. When it came to the podcast, he was indifferent about its detail and had reverted to constantly discussing them having another child. She didn't know if this was genuine desire or simply an elaborate ruse to halt her progress. Joe nodded a lot as it seemed the right thing to do, unsure if he should be happier at the evidence of a small marital fissure or the fact that she was confiding in him like a trusted friend.

Later, in the cab home, his brain whirring, Chloe's revelation about David took on a disproportionate significance. *She is not interested in you. She is not interested in you*, he said to himself, like it was his new mantra rather than a summary of his previous dating history.

The bloody coffee kept him up for ages. When he finally dropped into a deep sleep, he was woken minutes later by the shrill beeping of his sadistic alarm clock. Completely disoriented, he tried to piece together the fragments of a vivid dream in which he recalled being astride a giant motorbike on a desert highway. He was sporting a crumpled dinner suit and Chloe was holding on to his waist, riding pillion in a white and billowing wedding dress.

November 2018

She was very nervous conducting her father's marriage service. For a start, she was a terrible ballerina as a child and consequently lacked the posture to keep still. Fidgeting with her notes, she shuffled from side to side, repeatedly touching her glasses to check they were still there. It didn't help that the registrar was a man-mountain who used to be a Royal Marine. Towering over Chloe, he addressed the congregation like he was issuing commands to a bunch of squaddies, and she worried he might make her do press-ups if she didn't fulfil her duties properly.

The setting was an octagon-shaped reception room in a magnificent Georgian house, now an art gallery on the river in Twickenham. The décor exuded a calmness Chloe was struggling to manifest. Doric columns, gilt chandeliers, gold-leaf filigree and elaborate cornicing were brilliantly lit by the shards of winter sunshine streaming through the enormous arch windows. There was a grandeur that belied Malcolm and Sally's desire for a low-key wedding and the small crowd of thirty guests were sitting in chairs spaced far apart.

It was ironic that a retired vicar who had presided over so many weddings, including Chloe's, was having a civil ceremony. Sally's Catholicism, however, made things complicated for them both and such was their desire to be married quicky to begin their new life in France that they opted to eschew religious tradition. Chloe had jokingly asked him if the hasty arrangements were because it was a shotgun wedding. He retorted that despite Abraham becoming a father at a hundred, having her for a daughter had put him off asking for divine help on that front.

Her job was to act as MC for the ceremony, say a few heartfelt words and nod solemnly as the enormous registrar read the legal bits. She stared at her father and Sally in front of her and was overwhelmed with foreboding rather than elation. That she liked her new stepmother was not in doubt; she was a fine woman who clearly loved Chloe's father and would look after him wonderfully. The problem was that Malcolm's new life did not revolve around his dedication to Chloe's well-being. It was going to be filled with local cheese and wine and playing afternoon games of *pétanque* with his new French friends. She would need to get on a plane if she wanted to see him.

Her selfishness contributed to her uneasiness in performing her role. She was ashamed of her need to be the centre of her father's existence. Normally, it was the parent who mourned the loss of a child to a spouse, but for Chloe her sadness was intertwined with the realisation that she would now have to be stronger at dealing with the strains of her family life on her own.

Nevertheless, when it came time for her to address the couple, she steadied herself. After all, she was about to become a podcaster, so it was imperative she could perform under pressure. She smiled at her father, and then glanced at David in the front row with the twins on his lap, imploring them to remain quiet. Trying to sound as natural as possible, she began.

'We're gathered here today not quite in the sight of God because we've given him the day off. Indeed, who would have thought that I'd be officiating at your wedding, Dad, what with you being an actual vicar and me coming from the more heretical wing of the Church of England? Still, it is one of the honours of my life to be able to perform this duty and tell everyone how happy I am for you and Sally. Your relationship is a love story that reminds us of the unexpected but joyous directions our lives can take, and I couldn't be more thrilled for you both to have found each other at this stage of your lives, even if it is a major inconvenience to my babysitting needs.'

The small group of guests laughed with Chloe as she effortlessly told them of her father's foibles and praised his devotion to her over the sometimes troubled years of her adolescence. She painted a comic picture of his meekness in front of Sally, whose former life as a headmistress meant that he was often in detention for some minor infraction of the school rules. It was particularly funny when she read an imaginary school report for Malcolm from Sally with comments like: '*Driving – needs improving. Too middle of the road.*' She threw caution to the wind with the final subject: '*Lovemaking – could try harder.*' While the guests' laughter was spontaneous, and Sally managed to almost smile, Malcolm's horrified look indicated his disappointment at his daughter's lack of judgement.

However, she managed to make amends with her concluding words. Emotion overcame her as she struggled to quell her tears.

'Dad. When we lost Mum, you sacrificed everything for me and hid your grief to allow me to express mine. I've searched for the right words to tell Sally what you've done for me and why she is as lucky to find you as you are her. In the end, all roads lead to our favourite poet, Thomas Hardy, and that volume of poems you gave me when I was eighteen. The closing lines of "On a Midsummer Eve" say it better than I ever could:

> *I lipped rough-rhymes of chance, not choice,*
> *I thought not what my words might be;*
> *There came into my ear a voice*
> *That turned a tenderer verse for me.*

'You are that tender verse for us all, Dad. You make our hearts better. And Sally, you have made Malcolm's heart open and bloom in the autumn sunshine. So may the years that follow be filled with rich fulfilment and the joy of your shared kindness to us all and love for one another. Therefore, it gives me great pleasure now, with the power invested in me today by the giant bloke with the marriage certificate next to me, to pronounce you man and wife.

'You may kiss the bride, but remember all your children and grandchildren are watching.'

* * *

Having met Sally's daughter, Catherine, and her husband, Pedro, a while ago, Chloe had forgotten how hard it was to make conversation with them. She had little in common with these perfectly nice people, who lived a very different life in Valencia. They got together when travelling and Catherine followed him to his hometown in Spain, where he now ran the family construction company, while she had an e-commerce business selling healing crystals.

Their three teenage children were keeping Alice and Mikey amused with a game of musical statues and Chloe found herself trapped in the corner of the room, wondering if she could escape without resorting to the obvious excuses: *Do you want another drink? / I need a poo / Oh, I forgot I left a litter of new puppies in the boot of the car.*

Pedro spoke in heavily accented English about how rising costs were contributing to a tightening of residential construction. Catherine then explained the complex supply chain for her new range of smoky amethyst and quartz crystals from Zimbabwe and tried to sell Chloe one, telling her that amethyst creates a protective shield that keeps negativity at bay while the quartz is a stone for the manifestation of dreams and desires. After five minutes, Chloe's neck ached from all her enthusiastic nodding.

David eventually came to the rescue, appearing with a couple of fresh drinks and a sympathetic smile. As he stood next to Pedro, their physical appearance could not have been more pronounced to Chloe. Pedro was tall and muscular. His pristine white shirt clung tightly to the outline of his sculpted pecs and broad shoulders. He was tanned, even in November, and his hair was thick and curly. He may have had limited conversation, but she could see why Catherine emigrated to be close to him.

For David, the last couple of years of stress had had an impact. A keen tennis player, he hadn't been able to play much recently and did little other exercise. The combination of long hours of filming and lack of physical activity had made him paunchy around the waist and jowly in the face. He was always announcing the start of a new health regime, but the last couple of months had seen him mope more often than going for a jog. Work wasn't forthcoming and his return to advertising had not panned out as he'd hoped, other than some smallish freelance projects.

Frustration made him unkempt. His hair was a mess, and Chloe nagged him to brave the skinhead shaver setting rather than persist with looking like a novice monk. What she had loved the most about his face were his sparkling olive-green eyes, which these days looked permanently sad. Stooped next to matador-attractive Pedro, David seemed to her defeated by recent events.

'What are you guys discussing?' David asked, clinking his champagne glass with Chloe's in a gesture of unconscious solidarity.

'Catherine and Pedro are telling me about their businesses,' she replied, hoping he'd realise she needed rescuing.

'You haven't said what you're up to, Chloe? Mum told me you've written a book. I'm afraid I don't read much.'

'Don't worry, you don't need to. Soon, you'll be able to listen to her accompanying podcast,' David replied on Chloe's behalf.

She hadn't wanted to talk about her work, feeling it would be impossible to explain. As ambitious as she was for recognition, she often found that her esoteric interest in relationships only played well to a like-minded audience and Pedro did not strike her as a big analyser of the vagaries of love.

It was too late. Catherine wanted to know more.

'A podcast sounds amazing. I loved that one from America about the boy who was in prison for killing his girlfriend from high school. I still can't decide if he did it. Is yours about crime?'

'No, it's about what makes for a good relationship,' David interjected.

Why did she keep answering on her behalf and prolonging a subject she didn't want to pursue? Pedro looked as interested as Chloe had when he explained the rising cost of cement.

'Do you know the funny thing?' David continued, 'she's presenting the show with her first ever boyfriend. They were together for seven years, until she left him.'

'Is that weird?' Catherine asked. 'I mean, I don't think Pedro would want me to broadcast with an ex-lover to lots of strangers.'

"It's not about us but what we can learn...'

Chloe's words fizzled out in pursuit of a credible explanation. The manic glee with which he announced this news surprised her. As far as she was concerned, Joe's participation was no longer an issue and David had accepted the logic of the decision. His interest in the pre-production, while at best polite, had not contained any barbs or bitterness, and things seemed calm. So why was he expressing his anger via a casual conversation with strangers?

Catherine put a consoling hand on Chloe's arm and spoke to her like she was a teenager with a broken heart in need of sympathy.

'You're very brave.'

Chloe took a step back to free herself from her new stepsister's unwanted touch, not caring how tetchy she sounded.

'No, of course it's not. He's someone I once knew and a very good broadcaster. Now, let's talk about something else. Maybe we should go find the children.'

About to walk away, she noticed Pedro was wagging his finger in admonishment at David.

'*Es muy malo*, David, *muy malo*. In Spain, we do not allow our wives to spend time with people they used to sleep with.'

'It's lucky we don't live in Spain then, isn't it, *amigo*?'

She spat out her answer with such irritation it was accompanied by an accidental projectile of saliva, which landed on the lapel of his black suit. Pedro was about to respond but thought better of it. The ensuing silence was excruciating and involved much furtive glancing between both couples, trying to work out how to extricate themselves from the awkwardness.

Eventually, Catherine took her husband's hand and gave it a gentle tug.

'Come on, *Mr Possessive*. Let's leave these two to retrieve their children from ours and I can explain to you some of the differences between how couples behave in Valencia and Notting Hill, where they live.'

'It's Chiswick, actually.'

Chloe had no idea why David felt compelled to clarify their home address. It didn't matter anyway as it was addressed to their backs, since they had trotted off as quickly as they could. She suspected there would be very little future contact between them, which was a shame, not because she liked them, but rather to support her father and maintain good relations with his new family.

Chloe turned on David.

'What are you doing? Are you ever going to say something nice about my work, or can't you resist belittling what I do and then having a moan that I'm doing it with Joe?'

David was unapologetic.

'Do you think you might be overreacting? I was just trying to keep the conversation going and thought it might be fun to wind up your new sexist Spanish relations.'

'You can't share my excitement for this project, can you?' she said plaintively.

'What do you mean? I'm very happy for you.'

'Really? You just make jokes every time I tell you something about it. You haven't really said anything other than to tell me when you don't like our choice of guests.'

David put his glass down so that he could gesticulate his defiance freely. Red blotches appeared on his cheeks, a physical response she recognised each time he was stressed.

'I think that's a bit rich. I seem to remember when my film came out, the only reviews you were interested in were the ones for your book.'

'Are you kidding? My recollection is listening as patiently as I could to your agonising about every frame you edited, trying to help make the film better.'

'Well, you did a *shit* job, clearly. Thanks for your contribution. There are more guests at this wedding than people who have watched it.' He folded his arms like a petulant child arguing with a sibling. She saw his hurt and decided to end this argument as gently as she could.

'David, move on, for all our sakes. We're creative people trying to do interesting things. We must deal with disappointment.'

'You're not expecting to be disappointed by your podcast, are you?'

'That's not the point. Whether it works or not, we must support each other through failure, not just success.'

'Excellent, I'll look forward to a big cuddle from you next time I make a crap film.' She sighed and raised a hand in defeat. 'I can't have this conversation again. I want my husband to encourage me, not give me lots of little paper cuts from his snide comments.'

Their slightly raised voices and tense demeanour were beginning to attract attention from the sparse remainder of friends and family. Chloe could not carry on bickering anymore; the day had been overwhelmingly emotional, and she was drained. Fortunately, Malcolm had a sixth sense for his daughter's distress and came marching towards them with a plate of half-eaten cake.

'Hello, you two. Why are you alone, chatting with each other? You have a house for that. Let's get some wedding cake for your feral children before Mikey puts his head in it.'

Chloe knew he had heard part of the conversation and was trying to defuse their frustration, a further reminder of why she couldn't bear him going to France. Who else would protect her from these increasingly frequent altercations with David?

She gathered up her wilting children and got ready to leave. With the first show only days away, positive energy was what she required. She was working so hard with Joe and was adamant that David's irritation would not derail her. If he was going to be jealous of her achievements (not to mention Joe), they would chat it through, and he would have to promise to grow up. But the time was not right for such a discussion. Right now, all that mattered was the podcast. And nothing but the podcast.

'Ex-Communicate'

SEASON 1. EPISODE 1

CHLOE: Welcome to the first episode of this new podcast, *Ex-Communicate*, with me, Chloe Adams, journalist and author.

JOE: And me, Joe Harris, ex stand-up, and writer of jokes of variable quality for other people.

CHLOE: This is a new podcast about relationships, or, more specifically, why they fail and what we can learn from them. We have a basic theory that you can't find happiness in love if you haven't tasted the bitter sting of romantic failure.

JOE: And we should know, given our history.

CHLOE: Indeed, we are perhaps living proof of the concept of romantic failure being the foundation for something better. Joe and I dated many years ago, and now look at us – working happily together without a chaperone. You were my longest relationship before I got married. There are lessons from us that have helped me find the contentment I now have at home. And we want to explore this through the experience of other well-known couples and share their journeys.

JOE: That's right, Chloe was my first serious girlfriend, and when our relationship ended, she never gave me back my spaghetti tongs. Fortunately, it's ancient history and she made amends by offering me this job to co-present with her and I very magnanimously accepted. Turns out, she's a tough boss, so I'd better stick to script.

CHLOE: You're still on probation, matey-boy.

JOE: Right, I'll be on my best behaviour. Anyway, let me explain what's going to happen. Every week, we're going to chat with a former couple who have very graciously agreed to revisit possibly painful memories and uncover what impact they have had on each other's lives. This week should be fascinating, because we are incredibly lucky to be joined by Sir Terence Johnson, former Education and Justice secretary, and Linda Fowler, former Treasury minister, with whom he had a very public, marriage-ending affair. Even more remarkable because he is a stalwart of the Labour party, and she was one of 'Cameron's Babes' (the media's term, not mine) in the Tories. But before we get to them, we'll be starting with Chloe sharing some thoughts with us about a famous romance from the past to examine if there is some relevant insight for us today.

CHLOE: This is where my inner geek gets the better of me and I pretend that you are vaguely interested in my cultural tastes and opinions. And just to say we hope to create a much broader discussion about the subject, so feel free to message us at feedback@excommunicatepodcast.com. Joe has promised to answer every email within a two-hour period.

JOE: Faster if it's a 'yes or no' question.

CHLOE: For this first episode, apologies, but I may be about to ruin a major work of literature for you all. One of my favourite novels is F. Scott Fitzgerald's *Tender is the Night*, published in 1934, which chronicles the collapse of Dick and Nicole Diver's marriage, but in truth is based on the disintegration of Fitzgerald's own marriage to his wife, Zelda.

OK, here's the bit where I skip to its ending, which should not stop you reading the book. Without doubt, the last page is the saddest conclusion of any novel you may read, despite no one dying or any puppies being harmed. It describes Nicole attempting to keep in loose touch with Dick as she lives with her new husband and their children, far away from him. The thing that broke my heart when I first read it is how a passionate, all-consuming love can become reduced to nothing.

It's heartbreaking.

The book begins in the elegant setting of the French Riviera at the zenith of their seemingly flawless marriage and then spends three hundred pages describing its complex unravelling, a result of his alcoholism and her schizophrenia, and mirrors the turbulence of Fitzgerald's own marriage to Zelda.

The Fitzgeralds' volatility can be seen as self-indulgent or suffused with a tragic romanticism. They certainly partied harder than a heavy metal band on tour. There are famous descriptions of them in Jazz Age New York, dancing on the roofs of taxis and getting thrown out of hotels for generally having too much hedonistic fun. I'm not trying to sugar-coat things, of course – Zelda was properly ill and made Fitzgerald's life a fricking nightmare. She once grabbed the steering wheel of the car and tried to crash it, with her own daughter in the back seat. Equally, Scott drank so heavily that his creative output in the last decade of his life was severely diminished, not to mention it making him a horrid person to be around.

So, what I'm wondering is: where does the passion go and what is the point at which life becomes too complicated to sustain the spontaneity of initial infatuation? Why do people give up?

When I was a young woman, I couldn't understand how quickly it was possible for the marriage of Nicole and Dick to become too fragile to be protected from real-life problems.

Perhaps this is the first lesson we all need to consider. Passion is defined in the dictionary as a 'strong and barely controllable emotion', which suggests that it can be wonderfully spontaneous or dangerously unpredictable. What is an acceptable compromise when we've shagged in all the rooms and on all the surfaces and covered all the main conversational topics about our lives and previous histories?

I'm not suggesting we all take up ballroom dancing to reignite some paso doble fireworks. But perhaps those relationships that peter out do so because they fail to find behaviours that are 'barely controllable'. Of course, Scott and Zelda were defeated by mental illness and alcoholism rather than lack of a decent hobby. It was just so sad their union was fictionally portrayed as falling from complex, rich love to Dick's exile from her and his children.

JOE: I don't want to rush you, but we have an interview to do. Let's not lose our audience in our first show just because you want to ruin the ending of every romantic book you've read. I need to get on with introducing our guests since they're putting their coats on and planning where to go for lunch.

CHLOE: Point taken. Go on then.

JOE: In 2004, the nation was shocked when the *Daily Mail* published photos of the Justice secretary, Terence Johnson, kissing fellow MP Linda Fowler outside a hotel in Victoria, with the famous headline 'No Longer in Opposition' reflecting the fact they were from rival parties. The ensuing scandal was enormous and in some ways an era-defining moment, as it raised questions about the nature of true compatibility for a couple with dramatically different outlooks.

The cost to them was enormous. Terence lost his cabinet position and his family in an acrimonious divorce. Linda endured a few years in the political wilderness but became Secretary of State for Work and Pensions from 2010 to 2013. They stayed together for five years, but now Linda is on the back benches and married to someone not connected to politics while Terence has had several relationships, although he tells me he is single these days.

Anyway, we are extremely honoured to have them as our first guests on the show.

CHLOE: Thank you both for joining us. My first question is probably an obvious one, which is: why are you willing to be with us today and give us an intimate insight into your life together? I have to say, when my former editor, Charles, helped broker the conversation for us, I was a bit gobsmacked.

TERENCE: Well, he asked very persistently and promised me a case of wine and a good review for my memoirs, which as you know are coming out next month.

LINDA: Slightly different reasons for me. Since I make up at least three chapters of the book, I want to hear first hand if I'm libelled. These days, I have nothing to hide.

JOE: What is your relationship today? Correct me if I'm wrong, but you haven't been together for about eight years. Are you still friends?

TERENCE: Shall I answer first?

LINDA: You always did. Be my guest.

TERENCE: I'd say we are not friends. That's too difficult. Friends need to be in each other's lives regularly and I'm not sure Linda's husband would welcome my presence given that the nature of our relationship would still attract attention. Frankly, I'm amazed that you two have chosen to work together on this show, but with all due respect to you, Joe, you aren't exactly a household name. However, just because Linda and I aren't friends anymore, it doesn't mean we don't have love for one another. I know I do.

We split because there were too many complications in being together – our careers, our politics, my children – and we couldn't find a *modus vivendi* to deal with them all. And yet, when we were away from those responsibilities, when we found ourselves alone in our flat at the end of the day with a glass of wine, we loved each other's company and laughed continuously. Sadly, we weren't allowed to enjoy intimacy and anonymity concurrently. I couldn't take the scrutiny every time we appeared in public as to whether we were arguing about politics and the economy. It was ridiculous. Do you agree?

LINDA: Well, I'd agree that we can't be friends, that wouldn't work. It's not because my husband would object. And it's certainly not because I'm in any way still attracted to Terence, no disrespect to his trim physique and Hugh Grant floppy hair.

TERENCE: I'm glad you noticed.

LINDA: It's just bloody obvious that as you get older, attraction is not simply physical, and enduring love requires a foundation beyond a relationship's initial combustible passion.

JOE: Are you happy to tell us a little bit about how you got together? Terence, will you give us a teaser from the book if I promise Chloe doesn't spoil its ending on the next show?

LINDA: Well, let me set the record straight before he tarnishes my reputation.

TERENCE: Why would I do that when your government's record can do that much more easily?

CHLOE: Order, order. Will the Right Honourable Gentleman allow the Right Honourable Lady to speak.

LINDA: Thank you. Look, I came on this programme for two reasons. One was to make sure that any future stories about us are ballasted by my version of events. Terry kindly shared the draft of his book with me, and I respect his right to publish his autobiography. He describes the events of our time together accurately – it's just there is always nuance to a story, which is why I'm here. Also, I was taken with the mission of your programme and would like to try and help people emerge from romantic unhappiness with a bit more resilience.

CHLOE: You are the perfect first guest for the show, in that case. I wonder if you can start by telling us how the attraction formed? We all know that love affairs are common in Parliament, but not with such diametrically opposed political backgrounds.

LINDA: We met properly when I chaired a select committee on the future of policing and Terry was giving evidence.

TERENCE: From recollection, she was giving me a very hard time on our policy of reducing the profiling and 'stop and search' powers of the Met Police. She wanted us to go back to something much more brutal and Victorian.

LINDA: Or just try maybe to get a few criminals arrested. Anyway, he irritated the hell out of me, something I told him several hours later in the Commons bar. From memory, it was an unusual evening as the place was quite empty. It's normally very tribal and people stick with their own. Certainly, you don't chat freely with an opposition cabinet minister. Terry was happy to keep on talking after I spent a good hour haranguing him for his policy weaknesses. And after a few drinks, we left politics behind and very quickly began to discuss the complexities of trying to have a life outside of politics. I was single and in my late thirties and had been divorced for ten years from my first husband, who I met at school. Terry, to my amazement, started to talk about his own marriage and how his wife had grown further apart from him the more prominent he had become. She thought she had married a barrister who was going to create a prosperous and private life, and now she was in the public eye and the price she had paid was hardly seeing her husband. Terry suspected she had been involved with someone else and was both heartbroken and terrified that there would be an imminent scandal. He'd had a call from a friend sort of tipping him off that afternoon, so he just wanted someone to talk to. Immediately, I saw him differently, as a lonely man not a rival politician, and his vulnerability was very attractive. Of course, so was he, and there was a moment at the end of the evening when we were silent and stared into each other's eyes and knew that something was going to happen that would be dangerous to us both. It was me who chivvied things on by suggesting we had a nightcap. He was flabbergasted by my forwardness, and I nearly changed my mind when he got all practical about where this would be and how he could get there without his driver knowing. It was a warmish evening, and my flat was only a twenty-minute walk, so we left separately and met on my street corner. The illicitness of what we were doing was an adrenaline rush I'd never known before. By the time we were in my flat, the nightcap was the last thing on our minds. And the rest is not just history but chronicled in Terry's book, available at all good bookshops from next month.

JOE: Wow. That is some story. What were you thinking, Terry?

TERENCE: Very little thinking was involved that evening. I was carried away by the danger of it all and intoxicated by acting without caution for the first time in my life.

CHLOE: And how did that work out for you?

TERENCE: What, apart from my marriage ending, public humiliation in a series of vicious tabloid articles and losing my job in cabinet? Look, we fell in love. We wanted to be together. We thought we could give it a try.

JOE: Was Linda worth sacrificing your political life for?

LINDA: Think carefully, Terry. I could still take out an injunction.

TERRY: It was worth every bloody minute we spent together. Of course it was. Isn't that what people need to realise about why we are here? Just because you're not together doesn't mean you shouldn't celebrate the glory of when you were. It's feasible to have moved on to a new relationship knowing that your happiest moments may have been in the past.

* * *

CHLOE: Thank you both. You've been so open with us for the last half an hour, and with your candour and compassion we couldn't have got off to a better start for this series.

JOE: Agreed, and it's been fascinating to hear how you managed to juggle the confidentiality of your respective jobs while becoming a celebrity couple, and about your shared passion for Manchester United. So, we are left with just one final question, which I'm going to let Chloe ask as she's been desperate to hear your response for weeks now.

CHLOE: It's quite simple. Terry and Linda, you have shared the joy of your passion, the consequences of your actions both professionally and personally, and so what I want to know is what you have learnt about yourselves and how your separation helped you live your best life?

TERENCE: Have you got an easier question for me? I may need to filibuster for a bit until I can think of a decent answer. Linda, you're the happily married one now. Was getting rid of me easy?

LINDA: Hardly. Do you remember when we agreed to part?

TERENCE: Of course I do. The kids had been staying with us and it was an offhand comment from a stranger that sparked everything.

CHLOE: Are you happy to share what that was?

TERENCE: It was all so innocuous. We'd been out for dinner together to our favourite Italian. The kids, who from memory were in their late teens, hated the attention we got in public, which never seemed to diminish. By this stage, I was out of government and on TV the whole time and Linda was very prominent in cabinet. That night, we were at the end of the meal and another diner strode over purposefully and was very rude to Linda, saying something about her government's austerity policies being evil. I asked him to leave us alone and he spat out something horrible on the lines of 'I'm not sure how you can call yourself a socialist and wake up next to a woman who is causing misery to so many people across the country'. Linda, am I telling it correctly?

LINDA: Our evening was ruined. Terry's kids probably agreed with him given they never really liked me and were embarrassed that they had to put up with me as a quasi stepmum. By the time we got home, a gloom had descended over us, and we were all miserable. And it was the venom of the question in the restaurant that got to me. That arsehole had asked Terry what attracted him to someone evil and he hadn't really come up with a good line of defence.

We had navigated such difficult moments, including an election that resulted in Terry losing a job. We told everyone that our love was more important than our political opinions. And do you know, our outlook on the world was much closer than we could ever admit in public. Yet I remember suddenly being exhausted from maintaining these two sides of my life, and I think that was the tipping point for me to say that I wasn't ready to give up my career to ensure some domestic calm. There was much more I wanted to do and if that was the case, then I was always going to be susceptible to these external judgements on my relationship. There you have it. I couldn't bridge the incompatibility of our differences.

TERENCE: I think what Linda is saying is that her love for me was incomplete if it had to exclude another part of her life. Is that correct? What the hell, I've been more open about my feelings than I thought possible. It wasn't the same for me. I was willing to put partying with her ahead of my responsibilities to my party. And I think that what Chloe and Joe want from us is to explain how we have become stronger. I am not. After you left, Linda, I became a less loving person.

LINDA: I'm sorry I did this to you, Terry. For me, it was so different. I ploughed on with my career and found someone who loved me for my politics as much as my in-depth understanding of the offside rule in football. Leaving you made me realise that all that intellectual sparring was best left for the Commons chamber and was too exhausting to make me happy.

CHLOE: Terry, this feels like extremely uncomfortable territory for you now. Do you want to stop?

TERENCE: No, I want to have the last word, even if it's a teary one. Your programme is called *Ex-Communicate*. It's pretty evident what is expected from your guests. I only have one more thing I'd like to say to Linda. She knows I'm happy for her that she has found the stability that was impossible with me. I've revisited our years together and all that I lost.

However painful, I am stronger and wiser. And at the end of the day, I managed not to end up with someone who ended up voting for Brexit, so perhaps there was a silver lining.

* * *

SHOW NOTES – EPISODE 2

This week we talk to the rock legend Nick Sale and his first wife, Maggie, about their ten-year marriage and its influence on Nick's volatile and reckless years as the frontman of the legendary punk band 'The Copiers'. Nick and Maggie met at art college, and he credits her with being 'his creative North Star as well as the only sensible voice in his head' as he was engulfed by the mania of fame, booze and drugs. They tell Joe and Chloe how his numerous affairs (including with their son's primary school teacher) made it impossible for Maggie to continue and how she found contentment in celibacy and sheep farming while Nick is still touring to pay for his subsequent three divorces.

Chloe will also muse about the turbulent four-year relationship of Norwegian painter Edvard Munch and fiancée Tulla Larsen and how its unpredictability (the last time she saw him, she tried to shoot him!) resulted in some of his greatest periods of creativity. Meanwhile, Joe will reveal why his keenness to meet his girlfriends' parents is normally a recipe for disaster.

* * *

SHOW NOTES – EPISODE 3

Jake Wilson and Jazz Green met on the reality show *Opposites Attract* and despite losing in the final, their ensuing relationship made them for a few years the country's favourite celebrity couple as they embraced their fame with refreshing enthusiasm and innocence. Several bad business decisions later (Jake & Jazz's Chicken Grill was closed by hygiene inspectors within a year of opening), they split under the pressure of financial ruin. They will talk about how the quest to become household names has made them both crave anonymity these days, easier for Jake as a newly qualified physiotherapist, less so for Jazz since she married the R&B artist Matty Mooch.

Chloe's 'sermon' is about Woody Allen and why he managed to work effectively with ex-lovers like Diane Keaton, while, for obvious reasons, not with Mia Farrow. Joe looks at the sensitive subject of whether if you have had great sex with an incompatible partner, any future relationship may well be ruined.

* * *

SHOW NOTES – EPISODE 4

Diane Lane and Colin Jameson were briefly the darling couple of British tennis after winning the mixed doubles at the US Open in 1986 aged twenty-two and getting married a year later. Their careers never developed as their early promise suggested and by the mid-nineties they had retired and opened a coaching academy in Brighton and became something of a double act in tennis commentary. After three children and twenty-four years of marriage, they divorced in 2010, and a year later Diane married one of the coaches at their academy. Chloe and Joe discuss with them how they have managed to carry on as business partners despite the personal pain and Colin's realisation that he paid more attention to the business than his wife, even though they worked in it every day together.

Talking of regret, Chloe delves into her favourite novel (and film), *Sense and Sensibility*, to ask the key question we all want answering. Was Willoughby a plonker for dumping Marianne Dashwood in pursuit of a wealthier wife? Joe carries on the theme and tells us some of the occasions when he wishes he'd handled sensitive moments in relationships better.

* * *

SHOW NOTES – EPISODE 5

Tom Hitchburn and Edward Scott met at RADA and made their name in the early nineties as two of the most exciting stage actors of their generation, including their award-winning National Theatre roles as Vladimir and Estragon in *Waiting for Godot*, during which they became a couple. In 2005 they registered a civil partnership and shortly afterwards Tom was cast as Xargon 5 in 'The Last Galaxy Slayer' blockbuster franchise, which rapidly made him a global superstar, while Edward stayed, in his own words, 'a prancing thesp only interested in esoteric roles unlikely to make me a penny'. In 2011, they separated, citing their divergent careers as the principal cause. Tom and Edward tell us why shifting ambitions and commercial needs can sometimes loosen the foundations of a relationship and why being single is something to be celebrated, not feared.

This week, Chloe recounts her trip to see the film *Colette*, the story of how the French writer's first marriage to the uber-controlling Willy liberated her artistic sensibility, and asks if we need to experience unhappiness to become free to pursue our dreams. Joe, as ever, lowers the tone with his thoughts on how and when Viagra should be taken at the early stages of a relationship and how this backfired once when he was too optimistic of success in the middle of a date.

* * *

SHOW NOTES – EPISODE 6

Mia Peel and Jimmy Finley launched their travel website dirtyweekends.com to cater for the millennial and Gen Z market looking for weekends away with a difference. During the mad days of start-up growth, they graduated from business to domestic partners and presided over an empire of 700 people, which they eventually sold for £230m in 2014. Their relationship did not survive the intensity of this sale and shortly after trousering this enormous sum of money, Jimmy left the business. He is now a business guru on the TV programme for wannabe entrepreneurs, *Make Me a Billion*, and Mia runs their original empire. They discuss their tempestuous relationship – from sex on the boardroom table to shouting at one another across it – and why they believe relationships cannot be professional and personal at the same time.

Chloe returns to Paris in the 1920s (where Joe thinks she would have been happiest) to reflect on Ernest Hemingway and his first wife, Hadley, and consider if the distance of time amplifies relationship happiness and blocks out the pain. Joe tells us about his greatest first-date disasters, including accidentally singeing the eyebrows of his date with an ill-advised fondue experiment.

* * *

SHOW NOTES – EPISODE 7

Shalini Joshi is one of the UK's best-loved comediennes, who has sold out the biggest venues and is a constant presence on TV. As a fledgling comic, she was dating her college friend Amy Gladstone, who was training to be a surgeon. She was unable to discuss her relationship with her traditional Hindu family and after four years was given an ultimatum by Amy to commit, which she felt unable to do. Shalini is married now to fellow comic Jason Bingham and Amy has recently separated from her long-term partner, a fellow doctor. They haven't seen each other for over ten years, and they re-examine how difficult it was for Shalini to reconcile her family's pride in her career with their prejudice against a same-sex relationship. The episode examines how we learn that our life choices are sometimes not always in our hands.

Meanwhile, on pretentious planet Chloe we revisit the turbulent relationship of Lord Byron and Caroline Lamb and how their acrimonious break-up hastened his death, thereby denying future generations lots more of his poetry. Joe ('moronic rather than Byronic', according to Chloe) tells us about his thoughts on whether being a tragic romantic figure is sexier than being a nice guy who turns up on time for a date.

* * *

SHOW NOTES – EPISODE 8

A different show this time round in which there are no guests interviewed as Chloe and Joe examine their own relationship. Having separated thirteen years ago, they confront some difficult questions. After all, how can they ask their guests to examine difficult emotional truths if they are not prepared to face their own? Were they incompatible? Did they meet too young? Could Joe have done anything to prevent Chloe leaving and could she have dumped him more humanely? How was her subsequent behaviour shaped by her experience with Joe and why is Joe still single?

* * *

Radio & Podcast Review
The Sunday Times, 6 January 2019
by Graham Russell

EX-COMMUNICATE. A PAINFULLY FUNNY REMINDER OF RELATIONSHIP FAILURE

I must confess I didn't know Chloe Adams when she wrote for this paper, although I'm told that her column about her complex dating life had a cult following. Her new podcast, *Ex-Communicate*, is a magnificent counterweight to this former quest for romantic happiness, exploring the reality that most relationships end in disappointment and if we don't learn from their failure, we will inevitably repeat their mistakes.

She has clearly found herself a tolerant husband these days, because the show's real brilliance is the witty and sometimes caustic badinage between her and co-presenter Joe Harris, her first serious boyfriend, who she left in 2005 when they were both twenty-six after seven years together. We are thus always only a sarcastic put-down away from a reminder of the pain he felt at being dumped and the corresponding release that this parting gave her. What is even more remarkable is the uncomfortable sense that by working together on such a show, a painful scab (certainly for Joe) is being picked open again by sharp nails.

The format is engagingly simple. Chloe gives a short introduction about a literary couple (think the Fitzgeralds or the Hemingways) and what their tempestuous relationship can teach us about our own. (You know, don't be a misogynist, alcoholic, abusive husband – that sort of thing.) This is followed by a much more prosaic and often very funny monologue from Joe on his dating disasters (the story of one girlfriend's mother's attempt to snog him under the Christmas mistletoe is particularly good), to which Chloe adds her observations about his appalling emotional incompetence.

The meat of the show is an interview with a former well-known, now separated, couple about their relationship and the implications of its failure. They have curated a brilliant and varied guest list for their first series and, more impressively, coaxed significant personal revelation from them. For example, listening to former cabinet minister Linda Fowler's account of her early passion for her political opponent Sir Terence Johnson was as excruciating as imagining your parents having sex in public. (Oh damn, I've put the image in my head now.) Comedienne Shalini Joshi explains how being bisexual became a confrontation with her religious family that required dramatic subsequent life choices as well as being a source of great comic material. Legendary hellraiser rock star Nick Sale is particularly moving in recounting the influence of his first wife on providing calmness in the turmoil of his early fame and is candid about never having found such stability thereafter. His ex-wife Maggie, conversely, is much happier now, living her best life on a remote Cornish farm away from the cocaine and groupies.

There may only be a few generic conclusions from heartbreak, but this highly entertaining show proves there are endless narratives to express their impact. I am looking forward to Season 2, in production already, and suspect this show will endure far longer than Chloe and Joe's original romance.

March 2019

What a relief David was so kitchen-competent because Chloe's cooking would give a hospital canteen a run for its money. Sipping from a large glass of wine, she watched him multitask food preparation while taking a work call, staying focused on his conversation as he diced vegetables with metronomic precision. If she gassed on the phone while chopping a carrot, she'd slice off her hand.

There was a reason for her incompetence. As a child, her father's parenting excellence had included preparing impressive dinners, and her memory of their meals together was not just how much they talked, but the deliciousness of his food. It proved a disincentive for her to acquire any skills herself and, before she met David, throwing a dinner party was most definitely not on her bucket list. Indeed, while claiming to be a foodie, she only cared that the conversation sparkled when she went out to eat with friends.

For Chloe, a successful marriage was the balance of complementary skills, and David's culinary prowess was matched by her efficient management of the family's diary. She loved being a mother and, after five years, believed there was an outside chance of a normal upbringing for the twins. She was not perfect. Her ability to produce elaborate dressing-up costumes for school was low (Alice recently attended Victorian Day in a shower cap, which Chloe told her was a bonnet), but she knew that being a good parent required much more than superficial demonstrations of creativity and she managed to prioritise their needs when she was with them. David was equally devoted to the kids but lacked her patience to read and play with them and his energy levels could vary, especially when stressed.

When it came to entertaining guests, he would prepare a complex meal worthy of a Michelin review. It had been quite an education for her. For years, she assumed all that was needed to not starve were plates, bowls, cutlery, dishes and a couple of saucepans. When they moved in together, David brought with him a host of unfamiliar utensils, from ramekins, mason jars and hand blenders to digital thermometers and a blow-torch, which he explained was for crème brûlée rather than spot-welding. His Japanese knives, sheathed in an antique-leather pouch, cost more than her first car.

David had agreed to cook for her dinner party celebrating the fantastic response to the first series of *Ex-Communicate*. She had invited Joe, Mary, Kelly, Nicola the ad manager and their collective boss, Chrissie, as well as their partners. Most significantly, this was going to be the first meeting between her real and work husband, which was why she had poured herself a glass of nerve-calming Chablis before the guests arrived. Perhaps the elaborateness of the menu was David's way of marking his territory to make a point to Joe. It was an odd tactic given alpha males normally beat their chest aggressively to stake their claim to a mate rather than rustling up a spectacular meal of French onion soup, whipped feta dip, tomato galettes and a cheese soufflé followed by chocolate mousse, tarte Tatin and homemade lemon ice cream.

David's work call was not going well. He had interviewed for the role of creative director at an up-and-coming ad agency, and it was clear from his staccato answers that he wasn't getting the job. While he had been doing regular freelance work, he was desperate to get a permanent job, with the stability it would offer. As for his directing, he had recently pitched another idea to Netflix, which they declined after a short meeting attended by a very junior production team.

His disappointment was evidenced by the growing flatness of his tone, and Chloe knew she'd struggle to provide the reassurance he needed. Even worse, he was shortly required to act the charismatic host and toast the success of her creative project. Brilliant reviews had meant that, after nearly three months, Chrissie predicted that the second series of *Ex-Communicate* would be 'game-changing'. Being praised for the quality of his pastry that evening would not diminish his jealousy of her blossoming career.

He finished the call and carried on chopping. She couldn't stay silent.

'I'm sorry, darling, that sounded like bad news.'

His voice wobbled as he spoke.

'Yup. They'd love to work with me but have decided I'm too expensive so have given the job to someone internally. They could have made that decision weeks ago and spared me getting my hopes up.'

Chloe walked towards him to give him a hug, hoping he'd remember to put the knife down. She stopped a few feet away, his demeanour suggesting that he wanted to focus on meal prep rather than being coddled.

'Are you OK with this evening?'

It was a daft thing to say, because if he couldn't carry on there was no way she was going to finish off the soufflé preparation. She hated that he was struggling with his self-esteem in the face of her progress and wanted to support him – after all, they were a team and the sum of their combined professional endeavours. His confidence, however, was now brittle and the more his insecurities grew, the less comfortable he was discussing them. Whenever she tried to ask him what he was thinking, he always replied he wasn't thinking anything. She knew he was lying.

'Let me just get on with finishing the meal, Chloe. It'll be beautiful, and I won't let you down.'

'Thank you. I know this is a hard time. It'll pass, I promise.'

'Why? Did you consult your psychic for me?'

'No, I was visited by the ghost of Christmas Future. He was very explicit. Says this is just a momentary blip on the way to greatness.'

'That's a relief. And here was me thinking I wasn't as talented as I always believed. However, there's just one thing I do need from you today.'

'Anything. Although don't you think we should wait until the guests leave?'

Chloe tried to grab his hand so she could kiss it but he took a step backwards, evidently trying to avoid physical contact.

'What I want is for your friend Joe not to see me in a position of weakness. So, we don't discuss what I'm doing in front of him, OK? You've given him a great job and I'm sure he's loving every minute of being plucked from obscurity by you, but I really don't intend for him to lord it over me if he knows how much I'm struggling.'

She had thought his insecurity about Joe had passed and his vehemence came as a surprise.

'There's nothing to worry about. Joe's not that sort of person and anyway, if you want to know the truth, he's sort of anxious about meeting you.'

'Why?'

'He's a bit in awe. After all, I chose you as my life partner, please don't forget that, and I think he'll be intimidated when he gets to see your wonderfulness. Plus, he can barely boil an egg, so your meal will make him feel completely inadequate.'

She wasn't fibbing, having sensed from a few of Joe's recent comments that he was worried about the meeting too. It was ridiculous. This was a social event, and her husband was meeting her work colleague, who was a friend now. What was the big deal?

Her attempt to assuage David's fears hadn't really had much impact, and he started ferociously chopping a lettuce as if it were his mortal enemy. Intense concentration couldn't mask his thick frown of unhappiness. All she'd wanted was to have a relaxing evening at the end of an intense and highly rewarding period of hard work. Now she was beginning to worry that a fight might break out.

* * *

The evening began awkwardly. Chloe wondered if she had made a mistake inviting partners and her concern seemed well founded when Mary arrived first, half an hour early. Clutching a bottle of supermarket vodka, she introduced a young man called Isaiah, who stood sheepishly behind her at the doorstep. His wispy beard didn't really suit his Old Testament name and he had piercings wherever it was possible to have one. Mary pushed past Chloe into the hall and threw her coat over a chair like a teenager coming back from school, leaving poor Isaiah to nervously follow her in.

'Come on, don't look so fucking terrified,' she shouted. 'You'd better be good company or you're not going to get your end away later.'

Chloe was confused.

'Sorry, are you on a date? I thought you said you were bringing your boyfriend.'

'Dumped him last week. Turned out to be a complete wanking dickhead. Nope, hooked up with Isaiah on Tinder last night and we just met at the station. Thought it would be more fun coming here than having to make small talk in the pub.'

Isaiah had the look of a condemned man in front of a firing squad. Before he could say anything, he was interrupted by Mikey and Alice racing down the stairs to see who'd arrived.

'What's a *wanking dickhead*, Mummy?' Alice asked guilelessly.

Chloe glared at Mary, who was both unrepentant and staring at the twins as if unable to process why they were there.

'Mary, meet Mikey and Alice. I'd really prefer it if you rein it in a bit while you're near them, as their school isn't keen on bad language in Year 1. Isaiah, whoever you are, nice to meet you.'

They moved to the open-plan kitchen-dining area and, to Chloe's amazement, Mary transitioned into a surprisingly adept babysitter, sitting with the twins on her lap and riffing a story about a dress-hating princess who beat up any annoying boy brave enough to challenge her to a wrestling match. Conversation with Isaiah was painfully awkward and after finding out that he was doing a master's in environmental anthropology at UCL, Chloe gave up trying and assisted David with the finishing touches for dinner. Isaiah stared morosely at his phone, still wearing his coat. After twenty minutes of being ignored, he silently got up and walked out of the room. A few seconds later, they heard the front door slam.

'Thank heavens for that, didn't fancy him one bit. Kids, when you grow up, beware of dodgy blokes who don't look like their profile photos.'

Mary turned to her client with a smug smile, as if congratulating herself for not swearing. Chloe wasn't ready to forgive her for making the evening start off so strangely and nodded stiffly in response.

'Are we done now, Mary, or can we expect more random strangers to join us?'

* * *

Kelly's wife, Jasmin, arrived in jeans and an elegant crème blouse with shiny gold buttons, as if invited to a completely different party to her husband. Once again, Kelly had raided his hippie dressing-up box and sported a poncho decorated with embroidered flowers and what appeared to be lilac corduroy chaps, making him look like a rather un-macho cowboy. Jasmin was a successful investment banker at J.P. Morgan and thus Chloe had expected them to be ill-matched, but hadn't realised that she was at least twenty-five years younger than him.

Next, Chrissie tipped up with her husband, Pete, who was at least a foot shorter than his wife. He was very chatty and explained how exciting it was to be in 'a showbiz crowd', in contrast to his everyday life as a GP. Chloe was unsettled by how unlike their partners her colleagues were, an odd reaction given she was building her career as a commentator on the unpredictability of relationships. Surely couples who dressed differently and were born decades apart could still be happy?

David immediately became a polished host, his bonhomie in sharp contrast to the morose moping of earlier. He had always been adept at making conversation with disparate social groups and within minutes was making fun of Chloe while getting everyone to chat freely. When the bell rang again, she opened the door still laughing at something he had said.

Joe was standing with Nicola, holding a large bunch of flowers and a giant chocolate teddy bear wrapped in cellophane.

'We shared a cab because she lives near me. Here, the flowers are for you, and I wanted to buy something for the kids.'

It sounded like he was covering up a crime. Chloe had no idea Joe and Nicola were neighbours and maybe he was just being frugal on travel, having bought such expensive gifts. She wanted her mind not to jump to conclusions and was about to make a joke when Nicola took off her coat to reveal a gorgeous black cocktail dress, stiletto heels, and enough cleavage to stop the conversation of the men in the room mid-sentence. So much for her 'Dress Casual' invitation. She glanced at Joe, whose smile was widening by the second, and fully expected him to start drooling.

'Wow, you look amazing,' Chloe declared, trying not to sound sarcastic.

'Fuck me, are you going on to a party at Annabel's after this?' enquired Mary, having handed the twins to Chloe's sixteen-year-old neighbour who had come to babysit. Her brusqueness stopped the conversation momentarily. Nine people stood in a circle in silence, Nicola blushing that her appearance had prompted so many unsolicited comments.

David offered Joe his hand. Chloe had imagined this showdown for weeks, unsure what would happen. An awkward hug was out of the question, but a simple and limp handshake somehow didn't do justice to the importance of both these men in her life. As their hands clasped, Joe placed his hand firmly on David's shoulder, like a world leader greeting a rival at the airport. David instinctively cupped the underside of Joe's elbow, and they moved their arms up and down, staring intently into each other's eyes.

'So nice to finally meet you, David. Chloe tells me we're in for a real treat tonight. I wish I could cook better.'

'Or at all,' Chloe interrupted.

'So says the self-proclaimed queen of fishfingers.'

'Coming back at you, Just Eat's number-one customer.'

'We're not on air now. You can take it down a notch.'

She hadn't meant to sound rude, it was just that the continual banter with Joe was sometimes hard to avoid.

David seemed nonplussed and started to fill up everyone's glasses with champagne for the first toast of the evening. When he'd finished pouring, he clinked his glass with his index finger, and everyone fell silent.

'It's lovely to meet the team that's kept Chloe busy and happy for the last few months. What an achievement it's been for you all. I for one want to congratulate you all for your brilliance. You're all so talented. Well, maybe not you, Joe. Cheers.'

* * *

They drank many bottles of wine and raucous laughter filled the room. David's meal had been spectacular. To rapturous applause, he'd served the onion soup in multicoloured Le Creuset pots encased in a cheese soufflé. Chrissie took pictures and asked him if he'd gone to a Swiss finishing school, while Mary was so bowled over by his prowess that she savoured every mouthful in silence.

Sitting between Jasmin and Chrissie, Joe launched a barrage of anecdotes, which produced much giggling. Every so often, Chloe caught him glancing furtively at Nicola and wondered if something had begun between them, which was hard to believe given how rude Nicola was about Joe when he wasn't in earshot in the office.

Meanwhile, Chloe struggled to find common ground with Kelly and Pete, the former's liberal outlook clashing with Pete's conservatism, which he revealed through a long exegesis on how 'national productivity can only be enhanced through a commitment to hard work, discipline and, if necessary, compulsory community service'. Sandwiched in the middle, she ignored their angry exchanges and wondered if Joe had been lying to her each week when he explained that he was single and concentrating on his career. And why did it matter anyway?

Dessert was greeted with even more frenzied whoops of delight. David had made individual pots of chocolate mousse in recycled jam jars with redcurrants and a sparkler, and a tarte Tatin that would have graced the Ritz in Paris. Chloe took vicarious pride in her husband's brilliance, as if it somehow reflected well on her. Plates were emptied in moments, all except Jasmin, who picked around the edges of most of the meal with a restraint that suggested an uncomfortable relationship with food.

Chloe served fresh mint tea in ornately decorated glasses bought in the souk in Marrakesh, and Mary, horribly drunk, slumped forward to rest her head in the pastry crumbs on her plate. Soon, she was snoring like a pensioner in no fit state to be bundled home in a taxi. Chloe shuddered at the prospect of her hungover stroppiness at breakfast the following morning. Still, now she was comatose, at least no one could be insulted.

Kelly suggested to the table that it was time to relive the highlights of the first series and, for a few minutes, they shared some of its funnier moments. Chloe congratulated Joe for asking the actor Edward Scott in genuine innocence how he coped with former lover Tom Hitchburn's feature-film success, enquiring, *Has he ever let you hold his Golden Globe?* Tom had replied immediately, *On more than one occasion, and I hope one day he'll buff my Oscar.* The double entendre produced convulsive hysterics from all four of them, which Kelly left in the edit. The subsequent popularity of that moment on social media helped raise significant awareness for the show.

Chloe knew what Joe would pick. When interviewing Maggie Sale in the second episode, she had probed a little too insistently into what it had been like to have a rock-star husband who was unfaithful, sometimes with her friends and family. There had been a long silence before Maggie tetchily replied, *What do you think, you silly girl, it was totally humiliating.* More problematic than the venom of her answer was the fact that she got up to leave, and only the intervention of her ex, Nick, allowed the programme to continue. Thereafter, Joe reminded her before each recording to avoid making the guests walk out.

Nicola gleefully joined in the roast, pointing out that both Joe and Chloe sometimes made her life difficult as unconvincing brand ambassadors for the advertising clients she secured. Joe had revealed his ignorance about personal finance when he asked after recording an ad for an online bank, *Remind me again the difference between direct debits and standing orders?* Chloe refused to laugh when Nicola recounted the moment she told her star that she was *going to have to not worry if her friends mock her for being the spokesperson for incontinence pants.*

The anecdotes, while entertaining for the protagonists, were not that interesting to their partners. Jasmin made little effort to hide her boredom, checking messages on her phone, while Pete's affability was replaced with an aura of general disapproval, the source of which Chloe couldn't understand. Just after midnight, Chrissie explained that they needed to relieve their babysitter and Kelly asked if he could share their cab as they had an early start the following morning. As both couples got ready to go, Chloe managed to gently coax Mary to the sofa, covering her with a blanket and gingerly removing her Doc Martens without her stirring.

Joe and Nicola seemed in no hurry after the two other couples left, so Chloe suggested a nightcap, producing their bottle of special-occasion brandy and four cut-crystal glasses. David was silent now, his earlier ebullience replaced by a look of inscrutability as if planning his next move in an elaborate game of chess. Immediately, she realised she'd made a mistake prolonging the evening. As they all clinked glasses, no one could think of what to say next, until Joe turned to David and asked:

'So, what do you really think of the series? Chloe's very clever, isn't she.'

'Of course I am,' Chloe interrupted, 'I married David.'

Unsure if Joe was being provocative or polite, she wanted to wrest control of the conversation. David swirled his brandy and looked at the tablecloth, refusing to make eye contact.

'You're lucky to be working with her. I'll say that for you, Joe. She's a brilliant broadcaster.'

Joe's hand was now resting millimetres from Nicola's, their little fingers practically intertwined, and Chloe was certain they must be seeing each other. Was Joe trying to prove something to her and if so, why? Even worse, David's graceless comments compared unfavourably with Joe's behaviour, who by contrast had been charming throughout the evening. In fact, she'd been surprised by how relaxed he seemed, and wasn't prepared for his excitement when meeting the twins before bedtime, telling her how perfect and gorgeous they were. She had no idea he even liked children.

'You're right, David. I've struck gold, possibly even platinum, in being given this chance. I always knew Chloe was clever and funny, but I'd forgotten what an articulate presenter she is too. She's up there with the best.'

David nodded slowly. 'She deserves her success. Please don't say anything stupid on air to ruin it for her.'

Chloe's dismay at this oblique threat grew when she saw the corner of Joe's mouth twitch in response, a tic she recognised from first meeting him as a teenager. It signified a minor irritation that could quickly turn into major annoyance. She saw a look of defiance now in his face.

'Oh, and I'm being so rude. I haven't told you how much I enjoyed your film. It was very funny, and I hope you don't mind me saying, inexplicably underrated. That must have been frustrating.'

Chloe's stomach tightened. She was willing to give Joe the benefit of the doubt that he was being genuine, but David grimaced like a man having a surgical procedure without pain relief. He glowered at Joe.

'Yes, I think it was underrated too, and indeed very annoying. Thanks for the reminder.'

Chloe tried smiling at David in a last-ditch attempt to provide reassurance that she was still on his side in a battle being conducted with passive-aggressive jibes. Meanwhile, Nicola's hand was now resting on Joe's thigh in a gesture of either possessiveness or restraint. Chloe couldn't bear the tension any longer. Suddenly sober, her head was awash with dangerous thoughts: jealous of Nicola, embarrassed by David and angry with herself for both emotions.

She needed Joe to leave, any excuse would do. Clapping her hands, she stood up and ended the party without worrying if she was being rude.

'I think we should call it a night, if you don't mind. The twins will be up early, and a hungover Mary is likely to be a monster I need to prepare for. And we have lots of clearing up. Thank you for coming, you've been such great company.'

She sounded unnecessarily formal, like they'd just met for the first time. All she wanted was a deep sleep that would somehow expunge the memory of this bizarre meeting between them, which had been far more excruciating than expected.

Nicola stood up, smoothed her dress and flicked her hair, looking immaculate and full of twenty-seven-year-old energy. The evening had announced her relationship with Joe, and she grabbed his arm proprietorially, beaming.

'Come on, Joe, best not outstay our welcome. Let's leave these two tired parents so they can finish up. It's time for our bed.'

November 2019

Joe hated the small-minded conservatism of the *Daily Mail* and blamed it for most of the country's disasters, from Brexit to Boris Johnson. However, he also understood that its digital alter ego, the *Mail Online*, was a necessary evil to build showbiz careers with its endless coverage of celebrity, no matter how obscure. So, when the photo appeared of him and Nicola at the première of a new Disney film, resplendent in the ridiculously expensive Boss suit she had chosen for him, he was rather pleased with himself.

The overenthusiastic journalist labelled him as 'the relationship guru everyone wants to have a relationship with', a phrase he would never have imagined applicable eighteen months previously, when he would have described himself as only an expert in emotional incompetence. Now he was being photographed with a glamorous girlfriend, sauntering down the red carpet like a former member of a boy band.

Nicola had made upgrading his look her special project. First, she insisted he jettison his loyal barber, Ali, under the railway bridge in Tooting in favour of Gavin, the Covent Garden hairdresser who resembled a Bee Gee. As a result, his bathroom cabinet was now filled with hair products, moisturisers and unfamiliar unguents. Though not quite at David Beckham level, his days of a bar of soap and a squirt of Tesco anti-dandruff shampoo were long gone. His hair, consequently, was 'quite simply lustrous' (according to his proud mother) and touching his shoulders. Not bad for nearly forty, especially as most blokes he knew were considering a trip to Turkey to have the tail of a horse grafted to their balding bonce.

Hatred of clothes shopping was no longer an option. Nicola dragged him from boutique to pop-up to department store concession and insisted that he revamped his wardrobe to accommodate all possible photographable appearances – on air, at a restaurant, a party, or even a trip to the local rubbish dump. She explained that increased fame brought with it the necessity of careful outfit consideration. Before Nicola, what mattered to him was his spiritual worth, not which three clothing items could create a fashion stir. Now that he had a girlfriend who moonlit as both his unofficial publicist and his stylist, he was required not to leave his flat without her formal approval.

The success of *Ex-Communicate* catalysed this shift in fortune and after a three-month gap, the second series had catapulted them to seventh in the UK podcast charts, faster than they could have ever imagined. Joe hadn't expected that he would start to receive attention directly himself, especially as he was supposed to be the junior presenting partner. But suddenly, he was invited on to other people's shows.

He had fired his agent, Clive, on the basis that his consistent indifference was not the support his career needed, and asked Chloe if she minded him switching his representation to Mary. Joe was very grateful when she generously did not object, especially since he knew she was on a better deal and therefore sharing the same negotiating rottweiler could be beneficial.

When Mary wasn't mocking him for 'his fucking ridiculous hair and the dress sense of a nonce', she was laser-focused on his career development. And for Joe, his new-found popularity was staggering. For years, he had struggled to fill comedy venues, toiling to craft his set to generate belly-laughs rather than titters. Now, he found himself on panel shows on smaller TV stations, ad-libbing with much better-known personalities. In less than a year, he had moved from being a no one to being a sort-of-known someone.

This shift in fortune coincided with the unexpected flowering of his relationship with Nicola. Their initial interactions at work had been tetchy and he was sure she thought him at best a harmless idiot. That view ended abruptly late one night when she unexpectedly leant towards him for a lingering kiss as they shared a glass of wine in an empty office. Having never worked in a commercial environment, he was worried when he got home that somehow he had infringed the terms of his contract and would be fired for harassment.

Joe could hardly check in with Chloe for advice and decided his only option was to behave like a Victorian gentleman who had besmirched the reputation of an innocent woman. The following day, he asked Nicola out on a formal date, even arriving at the restaurant with a single red rose, a gesture he had never considered before as worthwhile. To his amazement, it was surprisingly effective, and within six weeks he found himself with more roses in hand when he was invited to her parents' house for lunch. At work, they gave an impeccable performance of two people who seemed not to like each other, so that no one had a clue that they were together until they revealed their coupledom at Chloe's dinner party.

Almost a year on, they were not quite living together, but spent most of their time in his flat, which he'd been able to decorate for the first time. His burgeoning fame suited her sociability, and they were out most evenings with her cohort of young friends, all of whom shared a prodigious thirst for alcohol that he no longer possessed.

It was a strange new existence.

He remembered that when he was Nicola's age, he wanted to stay in quietly with Chloe. Unfortunately, this proved to be a major factor in Chloe's departure, and he never forgot her anguish as she walked out:

'Haven't you guessed, I want to go out, not spend quiet Saturday nights watching a DVD and having a shitty curry?'

The impact of those words made him doubt the right way to behave with a partner whose aspirations may be different. Being with Nicola was ironically a second chance to live the life Chloe had wanted. Yet as the gravitational pull of celebrity drew him closer to its orbit, his confusion grew.

Sitting regularly at a bar after midnight, he often wondered what had happened to his former self, who expected to be pootling along in a suburban house with a brood of kids by this stage. Instead, he was behaving like a Gen Z party animal, shouting over the noise of some late-night DJ's monotonous set instead of getting a good night's sleep. It was hard to decide if he was happy. His carefree girlfriend would normally interrupt these reveries by stroking his Gavin-coiffed hair before pulling him towards her waiting lips, half hopeful of someone recognising him and posting a photo of their very public displays of affection.

* * *

'Hello, "relationship guru". How are things on the red carpet these days?'

He knew that Chloe would have seen the article. Despite being an artsy theatre-loving poetry-reading liberal, she seemed to spend her lunch break poring over the love lives of the reality TV stars in the *Mail Online* rather than reading a proper newspaper.

'Happy to walk down it with you, whenever. It'll make up for never making it down the aisle. Anyway, don't give me a hard time, I'm sure you get many more invitations than me?'

'If only. I need to be home with the kids and don't have time for glamorous nights out. This is a job for me, not some lifestyle choice.'

'Oh, listen to that tiny violin playing in the distance.'

He didn't need the ensuing silence to tell him his sarcasm was misplaced and unwelcome. Chloe, sitting by her desk, swivelled her office chair from side to side as if the motion would diminish her irritation and stared at the script for the afternoon's recording.

'Sorry, that was crass,' he ventured timidly.

'It was, you moronic blunderbuss.'

'I've been called worse, although it would help if I knew what a *blunderbuss* was. Look, I'm embarrassed by the pictures. It's not who I am.'

Chloe shook her head.

'That's rubbish. You're bloody loving the attention. What's got into you? All those new clothes Nicola has picked out. You look like an eighties' pop star – and not one of the cool ones.'

He considered denying being thrilled by having a profile after years of obscure mediocrity. It would be hard to fool her though.

'I think I need to enjoy these opportunities before they disappear.'

'Just don't become a *dickhead*. Do you know what I always said is the nicest thing about you? Your lack of ego. It's what makes you lovely.'

He didn't expect such affection, albeit in the form of a warning.

'Thank you. I will work hard to maintain my man-of-the-people status, even when I'm wearing one of my Italian cashmere jumpers.'

'And anyway, let's not take our early success for granted. We could lose our audience in a flash, especially if they see your next haircut.'

'What are you suggesting?'

'Be selective where you appear. Build a brand for yourself that's true to what you believe.'

Keen for more advice, he pulled up a chair next to her. His knee lightly grazed hers and for a second their legs stayed touching. She shuffled backwards in her chair, as if embarrassed by this contact.

'OK, I'll be more careful accepting invitations. *Yes* to the BRITS and a big fat *no* to compèring the cabaret at the Tory Party

Conference. Enough about me. What's next for brand Chloe? Surely Emily can get you to promote one of her wrinkle creams. You look pretty good for nearly sixty.'

'I don't need to build an image for myself and post ridiculous photos on Instagram like you seem compelled to do these days. I had a profile before this started. I'm a serious journalist and writer with a successful podcast. And while it's nice to see you draped all over Nicola, have you considered you might be a bit old for all of that?'

Now she was being condescending.

'I'm thirty-nine and single, it's not so odd. You're making me sound like Rod Stewart. I'm trying to raise some awareness for our project. God, there was a time you would have loved to be recognised. From memory, it's all you ever wanted. Why are you so reticent to get out there – is David clipping your wings?'

Whoops, his irritation had resulted in him introducing Chloe's marriage into the conversation, which was unwise. For the last few months, they had successfully ensured any reference to her home life was purely functional. Now his attempted joke had obliterated everything.

Chloe jumped to her feet, her face reddening. She took a stride towards him like a football manager about to yell at a below-par player at half-time. He awaited the geyser-like explosion of anger. However, her voice was measured.

'Our relationship is none of your business. I thought I'd made that clear enough for even someone with a low EQ like you to understand. David and I are fine, and in fact he's just had some good news.'

'That's great, tell me more,' he urged, trying to sound sincere.

'If you must know, he's just got a year's contract running the creative department of a large agency in New York and directing most of their commercials.'

That was not what he expected.

'Wow, are you moving to New York? What about the show?'

'No, he's going to commute. And before you say something even more insensitive, yes, it won't be easy, but we'll cope. Don't worry, the podcast is the most important thing in my life and it's business as usual. I'll just have to be even more on top of things at home.'

'I've upset you. That was never my intention.'

She arched her eyebrows, suggesting she was unconvinced.

'I'm sure it wasn't. It's just that your cavalier quest to become some vapid minor celeb because of my podcast *pisses* me off. You need to show some humility.'

He sank further into his chair. Chloe was always able to combine such precise and pointed language when revealing her emotions, yet he suspected her fury was not exclusively directed at him. What had started as her teasing his red carpet walk had become a frustrated admission that she was not as free as she would like to be. Joe looked anxiously around the office to see if her raised voice had attracted attention. A few people were spread sparsely around the open plan and engrossed in their work.

It didn't matter anyway, as Chloe quickly composed herself and was now staring over his shoulder. He turned around to see his mother and her wife, Jane, trotting towards them. Helen opened her arms and wrapped Chloe in their first hug in fifteen years, holding on to her like a mother reluctant to let her child out of her sight.

'It's so good to see you again, Helen. I've really missed you. Let's be honest, you were always more fun than that plonker of a son of yours.'

'You look wonderful, darling. So beautiful. Joe's not so bad, you know. He just struggles not to feel sad when he's with you. You broke his heart into a thousand pieces. And he never had any patience for complicated jigsaws.'

Joe considered sellotaping his mother's mouth shut. What a terrible idea inviting her if she was going to carry on like this, but it was too late, and he could tell Chloe was loving his awkwardness. She pointed to the studio in which the sound technician was fiddling with the placement of microphones, and they walked towards Kelly, who was standing by the door going through his production checklist.

'We can have a drink afterwards and catch up. I'm so excited to get to know Jane. In the meantime, we need to crack on with the show as soon as Michael arrives. Are you ready to record your episode? It's very brave of you to appear with your ex-husband, I must say, and we both really appreciate you doing this.'

* * *

It was Chloe's idea, after the success of the show in the first series when they discussed their own relationship. Bantering and bickering, they shared their recollections of each other's most annoying habits and drew spurious conclusions about what they looked for in subsequent partners. Uncomfortable truths were avoided as they focused on entertaining rather than a painful examination of their shared past. Harmless fun.

However, an hour of listening to his parents discuss the inadequacies of their sex life, couples' therapy, role-playing, new partners and parenting disappointment was for Joe as excruciating a prospect as a rectal examination in public.

Michael must have thought the same because he arrived late with Dull Debbie, muttering to himself and forgetting to shake hands with anyone. Debbie had insisted on chaperoning her fiancé in case the recording would somehow facilitate a return to his former wife. Jane had none of her insecurities and arrived with reams of notes she had drafted about Michael's failings in case Helen dried up with her own anecdotes. A tall woman, she towered over Debbie, greeting her with an affectionate kiss on the top of her head like a kind auntie.

Always courteous with guests, Kelly went into charm overdrive. Before the recording, he took Debbie and Michael aside to explain what was going to happen and was perplexed when Debbie's only question was if it would be possible for Michael to sit as far away from Helen as possible. He tried making her laugh, despite Joe's warning that she had the sense of humour of a pebble. Out of ideas, Kelly resorted to spouting a selection of all-purpose mantras to calm her, taking Debbie's hand between his palms and declaring, 'Sometimes in life you need to find the **cure** to be se**cure**.' Debbie nodded earnestly, as if in the presence of Plato.

Normally, Joe enjoyed the recordings, but this time it was impossible for him to feel relaxed after his mother began the interview by explaining that her twenty-year marriage was a specious act to provide stability for the children and the only way she'd been able to stop her mental disintegration was through a brief addiction to painkillers. Joe had had no idea and couldn't bring himself to look at his father to see if it was news to him as well.

Chloe probed for more detail and Helen admitted that her behaviour hadn't always been kind to the family because of the intensity of her frustration. She likened her marriage to buying your dream house and then finding out that you were under a noisy flight path and your neighbours were satanists in their spare time. She explained that while she loved her children and husband, she couldn't bear the dynamic of the family unit itself. Michael never knew about the passionate relationship she'd had with another woman at university, and years of stoic endurance for the sake of a stable upbringing for the kids did little to camouflage that she was not meant to be with a man. The failure of her marriage was not about a lack of love, it was simply the result of avoiding the truth.

As the conversation evolved, Michael didn't complain about being abandoned as Joe had expected. Rather, through happy tears, he apologised for both lacking the capacity to express his love sufficiently and his patrician attitude to her medical career that required the subjugation of her ambitions to his.

By the end of the interview, Helen and Michael were finishing each other's sentences as they recalled happy family holidays and shared passions rather than the misery they subsequently inflicted on one another. Chloe nudged them towards meaningful conclusions and Helen's reply was carefully considered:

'I know I'm a bit too open about my love for Jane. I mean, Joe has practically had his eyes shut throughout this conversation. The question is, why should they feel this way? I waited until they were adults before I left their father. What I've realised is that imperfect relationships end imperfectly. You can behave with dignity, you can be considerate and show understanding, but there are always unintended consequences of relationship failure. You didn't want to believe, Joe, that we were unhappy, even though the signs were so obvious. It's meant that you've not given yourself fully in any relationship because I suspect you're protecting a memory of your childhood that has been tarnished.'

The speech was met with admiring silence and Kelly announced they had everything they needed, then thanked them both profusely. Joe was dazed by what had just happened. He had listened to his mother blow up his everything with revelations of her unhappiness. Processing trauma was anathema to him, but perhaps his early years were somehow connected to his failure to understand what he wanted.

He had stared throughout the interview at his co-host to avoid his mother's gaze as she revealed yet another toe-curling detail about her life, and Chloe's smile diminished his awkwardness. Afterwards, in the pub where they adjourned for a post-recording drink, Chloe pulled him aside and they stood at the bar alone.

'Was that really hard for you to hear?' she asked sincerely.

'Interviewing my mother about oral sex with her new wife. Have a guess?'

'I think we got a great show.'

'But I'll never live it down at school.'

'Or people will think you have cool parents.'

They clinked their glasses and said nothing as they watched their team and Joe's parents talking animatedly at the long table in front of them. Joe turned to her, his expression one of concern.

'Chloe, can I ask you something?'

'Anything, as long as it's not names of capital cities or dates of battles.'

'Do you find this difficult?'

'Having a conversation with a work colleague?'

'No, I mean working with your ex.'

Her eyebrows arched at the seriousness of his question.

'We're on our third series, isn't it a bit late for misgivings? Most people tell us we work very well together.'

'We do. It's just sometimes, I find it … I don't know how else to say it.'

'Say it, Joe. I can take it.'

'Disconcerting.'

Chloe was about to reply when she was tapped on the arm by Helen, who had come to buy more drinks, and the moment's intensity dissipated. Chloe looked for a second as if she was about to say something, but instead returned to the table to get more drinks orders. Joe stared at the whisky bottles on the top shelf to give the impression he was pondering which single malt to have rather than replaying the conversation he had just had. *Disconcerting* was an insufficient description of how he really felt when he was around her. He was unsettled, excited, frustrated, unnerved, energised and entranced. Perhaps it was best she didn't know the full range of adjectives.

March 2020

'Are you nervous, babe?' Mary asked, taking a large bite of her artisan cheddar and pickle baguette. Chloe was momentarily touched by the unexpected concern but quickly realised her mistake as Mary added, '… Because I didn't have you down as some pussy-whiny actress with stage fright.'

When Norman was her agent, lunch would be in elegant restaurants. Now that she was with Mary and her career flourishing, it was sharing a table in Pret A Manger with a harassed mother and her two recalcitrant toddlers, shivering from being caught in a downpour on the way from the Tube. Mary sat in her zipped-up vintage parka with a giant bull's-eye on her back, a metaphorical challenge to anyone brave enough to take her on.

'You really are such a support at times of stress. You should volunteer in a hospice or a nursing home,' said Chloe, undeterred.

'I'd love that. Telling all those dying *fuckers* there's no God just before they pop their clogs.'

The overwrought mother looked disapprovingly at her, and Chloe remembered it had taken weeks for Mikey and Alice to unlearn the vocabulary they'd been exposed to when they met her.

'Shall we get back to your question of whether I'm nervous?'

'If you like.'

'Well, I am. It's our first live show. Nine hundred people and sold out.'

'You should be ecstatic. I told you this podcast would become something significant. Live events are just the beginning.'

'I'm a writer, not a performer. Joe's the stand-up. What if I dry up in front of an audience?'

'Then you'll look a total numpty. I wouldn't worry, though; I've watched Joe's routines online. You've got no competition.'

'Thus *speaketh* his agent.'

'Well, maybe his agent *loveth* you a bit more. He's driving me mad. The ungrateful bastard wants to renegotiate his contract to be paid the same as you. He should learn his craft and stop photobombing Gary Barlow at parties to get into *OK!* magazine.'

'What did you tell him?'

'I reminded him it's only because of you that he's appearing at the Union Chapel tonight and he's bloody lucky that I get him the odd appearances on UK Gold. Don't be so modest.'

'That's very kind.'

'*Fuck* that, it's the truth. Was he nominated for "Newcomer of the Year" at the National Podcast Awards last month? I think not.'

'I didn't win though.'

'That's not the point. The whole world knows that you're the beauty and the brains behind this show.'

'So, you're saying I have a face for radio?'

She was trying to be funny, but Mary missed the joke.

'And while we're at it, what's happening with the novel I've secured such a massive advance for? When am I going to see the first draft?'

Mary had done a magnificent job on a three-book deal: two novels and a non-fiction about the history of the romcom. Chloe was halfway through the first novel, although not making quick progress. With the working title 'Half Full or Half Empty', it was the story of twin girls – one an optimist but a failure in everything she does, the other a morose pessimist who conversely achieves great success. She was very excited by the project, although daunted by its completion.

'I'm struggling.'

'What do you mean?'

'With David being away, it's hard to make time to write.'

'Diddums. Do you need me to come and babysit?'

'Don't be like that. I love writing it, I wish it was all I did. I want it to be brilliant and I'm scared it's not.'

'Oh, stop being so needy. Why do you need such constant approbation?'

'That's harsh.'

'Well, you don't hear me wanting your validation 24-7.'

'Then let me take the opportunity to say you are not only a fantastically effective agent, but also the most foul-mouthed one I know.'

'*Fuck off*. You love my directness.'

The mother next to them tutted her disapproval for a final time and moved to another table, evidently worried that Mary had exhausted most swear options and was about to unleash the C-word. Chloe waited until she had gone and then looked earnest.

'You know, you can always ask me anything.'

To her surprise, she was not met with derision. Mary looked at her shoes.

'You could help me with something.'

'Of course. Tell me.'

'It's Isaiah.'

Chloe went blank and then remembered the hirsute blind date who Mary had brought to the house for the dinner party.

'He scarpered, didn't he? What about him?'

'The *wanker* has just dumped me.'

'You've been seeing him? For how long?'

'Nearly a year.'

To this point, Chloe would have believed it a biological impossibility for Mary to cry. How wrong she was. Out of nowhere, Mary howled like a wolf with a stubbed toe and buried her head in the crumbs on the table, her shoulders rising and falling with each anguished sob. Chloe tried to console her by stroking her arm across the table, but she didn't want to be touched. Unsure what else to do, Chloe muttered 'There, there' in the voice she used whenever one of the twins fell over, prompting Mary to sit up immediately, wipe the tears away, and shout, 'Is that the best you have to offer? Do you want to hear what happened or not?'

It was more a threat than a question. Chloe willingly gave relationship advice to her friends; however, she feared that the normal principles of empathy didn't apply to Mary, who would prefer instead to discuss how violent to make her retribution.

'What happened?'

'He announced that he didn't love me as much as I loved him.'

'Ouch.'

'Apparently, I'm too full on.'

'I find that hard to believe.'

Mary smiled.

'You think I'm an unmuzzled rottweiler. You should see what I'm like when I'm in love. I wanted the best for him. He's a genius and I told him to do a PhD. We even worked on his proposal.'

'Wasn't he an anthropologist or a sociologist, something like that? One of the subjects that never leads to a job.'

'He was a bit of both. And you'll piss yourself when you hear what he wanted to write.'

'I'll try not to make a puddle.'

'"The evolutionary reasons women fall in love more slowly than men." Ironic, in our case, don't you think?'

'I'm bit lost. What went wrong?'

'Out of the blue, he announced that he's going travelling. Apparently, I behaved like he was my client, not a boyfriend, always telling him what to do. He said our relationship was unbalanced. Total *horseshit*. It was him who treated me like the agent. The tosser gave me no more than fifteen per cent of his emotions on a good day. What should I do?'

She looked wistful, her normal ebullient self-belief obscured by a cloud of self-doubt.

Chloe decided to offer guidance.

'Do you know how many episodes we've recorded so far?'

'About twenty-five? I can check my invoice.'

'Thirty. And do you know what's been true in each one?'

'You've spouted pretentious nonsense about a book you once read because you want to sound like a Cambridge professor?'

'Apart from that.'

'No, what?'

'Every relationship failed because of an imbalance of power. No matter how compatible the couples, there was always someone who had slightly greater control over the other and therefore the ability to bring it to a close.'

'And?'

'And therefore, perhaps you need someone who is your equal to share your ambition and drive. My bet is, Isaiah was scared witless by you. In fact, the bravest thing he's ever done is to tell you his feelings and book a plane ticket.'

'How do you know we can't get back together?'

'I don't. Do you really want him back if he's so intimidated by you? Don't you want someone to love you with the same intensity as you feel?'

'Did you and Joe love each other equally?'

Chloe knew the answer was yes, and it had been her immaturity at twenty-six that made her leave. Not that she was going to admit it to Mary.

'Don't change the subject. This is about you.'

Mary's eyes now sparked with mischievous intent.

'Well, what about David? Where does the power lie in your marriage?'

'Why on earth is that relevant to you? I'm telling you to move on. And who wants to have a boyfriend called Isaiah anyway?'

Despite trying to sound jolly, Chloe's unease grew. How would she have answered Mary's question if she was being honest? David seemed to be loving the life in New York now, no matter how much he missed the kids. They tried to speak every evening, although the time difference meant he was often in meetings and she was too tired to wait up until he finished his working day. He would start each conversation by telling her how much he yearned for her, but when he was home the weekends were so child-focused that it was challenging creating space for their marriage to cope with long-distance separation.

She was terrified the interdependence of their early years was coming away like roof tiles in a storm. He had chosen to work abroad. For now, he had all the power, which was surely risky after what she had told Mary about imbalanced relationships being unlikely to survive. These thoughts distracted her until Mary banged the table with her fist to get her attention.

'*Fuck me*, you're a useless therapist. I might as well talk to my cab driver on the way home. I thought hearing your feelings might help me understand mine. Instead, you've gone into a trance.'

'Sorry. I got lost.'

Mary's demeanour changed, as if the conversation had been inconsequential gossip over coffee with a friend rather than a tortured discussion about the visceral pain of her heartbreak.

'Well, find yourself quickly, you've got a big show, and we'll get a national tour sorted if you do a good job. Focus on being charismatic, there's a good girl. I am so over that *shithead* and hope he goes travelling somewhere dangerous with a high likelihood of being kidnapped. I am a warrior and deserve to be with a prince, not a fucking spear carrier.'

* * *

The Union Chapel in Islington was a unique venue, part concert hall, part church and part homeless drop-in centre. The peeling plaster and musty dampness of its makeshift green room reminded Chloe of the chilly vestry in her father's church. She remembered dark Sunday evenings after her mother died when she pretended to read a book as Malcolm put on his robes for Evensong, consumed with grief while cracking strained jokes to mask his despair.

The rain had been unrelenting all day, biblical and unforgiving, as if the world needed cleansing of its sins. She'd just seen on the BBC that a further eighty-nine cases of this terrifying coronavirus had been announced. So far only one person had died in the UK, but the pictures coming out of Italy were horrific and there were plenty of reasons to be scared, especially with Boris Johnson running the country. He had bumbled his way through a press conference that afternoon talking about a government approach of 'Contain, Delay, Research, Mitigate', based on yoking random words together and hoping it sounded strategic. Like an eccentric Classics teacher at a minor public school, he reminded sixty million people to sing 'happy birthday' twice while washing their hands. The two serious scientists who flanked him at the lectern had the worried look of junior officers who knew that their mad general was about to march them into war completely unprepared.

Chloe was normally phlegmatic about public health warnings but this appeared much more serious than the previous avian and swine flu outbreaks, which had never developed into full-blown crises. She wondered if it was sensible to have so many people crammed together in a poorly ventilated venue – after all, what if a member of the audience already had the virus? It was bad enough being currently trapped in a room full of nervous people before a show, her nausea worsening with each stale crisp she ate from the small bowl the venue had laid out in a measly attempt at hospitality.

Joe sat in the corner with Nicola on his lap, suggesting that their working and personal relationship were now the same thing. Chloe was irritated by this unprofessionalism given Nicola was also hosting a couple of the advertising partners for the evening.

She tried to bond with their guests on the show, the film director Connie Charlton and her former husband, the novelist and scriptwriter Tony Dawson. They had won multiple awards together for their romantic comedy *The Indifferent Suitor*, which had also been the death knell of their fragile marriage when she had a fling with its leading man. This was the first time they had seen each other in years and when Chloe tried to introduce herself to them, she felt as if she was intruding on their reunion. Standing in the corner, their foreheads almost touching, they were oblivious to their surroundings, as if at the start of a relationship not recollecting its demise.

Kelly was not making her feel any calmer. While he had proven himself a brilliant producer, shaping the narrative of each show, he often irritated Chloe with his unsolicited mentoring and coaching advice based on a platitude for every occasion rather than actual insight. Trotting behind her, he reeled off a series of trite messages normally printed on novelty mugs bought from Amazon. She scrunched her eyes more tightly in the forlorn hope he would get the message. Kelly was oblivious to her indifference.

'Tap into the humour of your soul. The more you think it, the less you'll bring it.'

She couldn't listen to any more and snapped.

'What on earth are you talking about? Can you please stop subjecting me to your favourite quotes from *Buddhism for Beginners*?'

Kelly smiled and wagged his finger at her in admonishment. He seemed to think she was being playful.

'Excellent riposte. My work is clearly done and you're in the performance zone. Now, if you'll excuse me, I'm going to do the final sound check. I'm so glad you found my words helpful.'

Before she could contradict him, he skipped off, whistling, and she sensed the room was staring at her as she must have shouted her last comments too loudly. Joe appeared by her side to check what had happened.

'Are you OK? You looked like you were about to punch him, which wouldn't have been helpful. Especially if you want your mic switched on.'

'I'm OK, it's just between Mary's savage advice and Kelly's mad mantras, I'm more terrified than ever.'

'Chill out, the crowd will love you. You're extremely funny, you know.'

'Well, one of us has to be.'

'Ouch. I'll just sit there and look pretty, shall I?'

'You can announce our guests and top up their drinks. That should keep you busy.'

Joe sighed like a child not wanting to play a particularly nasty game anymore.

'You win. You are most definitely the funny one.'

She was embarrassed by her sarcasm. Putting people down and having the last word was such an unattractive trait, but it had become her defence mechanism over the years. If people didn't think she was clever then what kind of opinion of her could they possibly have? Before she could say anything further, Joe grabbed her hand and gave it a squeeze. She held on to his, wanting to absorb its warmth, until she noticed Nicola glaring at them from across the room. His next comment was even more heartfelt.

'This is the best thing to have happened to me, you know, Chloe.'

What did he mean? She assumed he was referring to the podcast, but perhaps it was also a more general statement about their relationship. Her pulse began to race, and her cheeks reddened. She needed to shut out the unwanted thoughts that were flooding her head. Instead of acknowledging the unsettling confection of overwhelming emotions, she gave him a friendly slap on the back, like she was one of the lads.

'Enough sentimental shit. It doesn't suit you. There are nine hundred people waiting to listen to stories about your dating incompetence. Don't go all soppy on me now.'

Disappointment spread across his face as she fled to the safety of the shabby ladies' loos to calm down. It was cowardly to run off after this display of kindness, but there was something in his expression that had completely thrown her. While he may have been declaring feelings she didn't want to hear, she was at the same time intrigued by his openness.

She sat on the freezing toilet seat with her head in her hands, half-heartedly attempting another mindfulness exercise that involved her mumbling vowel sounds. When she looked up, she noticed a tatty and torn flyer for a confidential counselling helpline sellotaped to the back of the cubicle door. Its headline was apposite.

Are you a bit lost and unsure what to do next?

* * *

She was hilarious. Not just witty but laugh-out-loud brilliant. By the time she came off stage, sweaty and euphoric, her worries of the day were long forgotten. Everything she'd prepared had come off. When Joe had attempted to describe in his opening monologue how hard it was for a bloke to choose the right flowers for a girlfriend, she interrupted with a riff about the ineptitude of men at selecting presents for their partners, from buying the wrong perfume to choosing anatomy-defying lingerie. She described how she nearly defenestrated David years ago when he bought her a satnav for her birthday, thereby suggesting she was 'an unsexy dweeb with no sense of direction'. Her ranting went down a storm.

The crowd reaction exceeded her expectations, even if it was accompanied by regular bursts of coughing from around the auditorium, which she worryingly imagined was the new virus being spread indiscriminately. She put the thought to the back of her mind and proved herself an adept host, asking probing questions and commenting on their replies with empathy.

Their charismatic guests were a revelation and did more than just reminisce about their shared past. Connie began by explaining her infidelity and why the actor in question was different to Tony in every way: sport-obsessed, vacuous and materialistic. Tony then apologised for being too immersed in his own writing, which made her susceptible to the attentions of a man 'so vain and superficial that he reckoned his most important asset was his reflection'. They explored the following decade of unsatisfactory new relationships, in Connie's case a brief marriage to said actor, which she ended after six months on the grounds of 'irreconcilable narcissism'.

To the amazement of Chloe, Joe and nine hundred other people, after an hour of musing about what makes people fall in and out of love, Tony announced that they had decided to try again. Their intimate conversation in the green room had somehow revived the muscle memory of the love they once shared and the realisation that it had been in hibernation. Chloe would never have thought it possible that the interview would end with their guests embracing to a standing ovation from the gobsmacked audience.

The show finished with their band, hired for the evening, leading a sing-song. Chloe and Joe had curated a medley of famous break-up songs that meant the feel-good spirit of the evening would be sustained. 'Someone Like You' was followed by 'Don't Leave Me This Way', climaxing with a rousing 'Mr. Brightside'. The energy was incredible, even if it was slightly marred by her decision to throw a few dance moves, in contrast to Joe, who remained seated. As they walked off stage, he whispered to her that she'd looked like she was having a seizure.

Two hours later, in the bar of Soho House, she celebrated with Connie, Tony, Kelly and Joe. For some reason Nicola didn't want to join them, having refused to acknowledge Chloe after the show and clinging to Joe's arm as if she needed help keeping her balance. Surely she wasn't stroppy and sulking because Joe had given Chloe's hand a friendly pre-show squeeze?

She didn't care. The babysitter was sleeping over, and she intended to roll back the years to her partying days. Kelly had ordered a bottle of champagne and a round of shots, and they were consumed with boisterous enthusiasm in minutes. Another bottle quickly followed before the party began to fragment. First, Kelly got a text, which made him scowl and then hastily put on his coat.

'Jasmin is pissed at me for being out. She's been on some mega deal at the bank, and I've hardly seen her. Now she wants me home so that I can indulge her every whim. I'm too old for this crap.'

Chloe, though decidedly tipsy, thought this was not a healthy statement from someone who'd been married for such a short time. Kelly looked dishevelled, gaunt and a lot older than the rest of them, and she worried that he had nothing in common with his wife, which might not be good for him in the long run. Still, consistent marital failure did make him the ideal producer for the show.

Connie and Tony had collapsed into a face-sucking snogging session. Chloe had been a member of Soho House for years and knew that they had strict club rules like no phone calls, photos or ties. She didn't know what the policy for French kissing was, however. To be on the safe side, she tapped on both their shoulders to make them stop. Connie's face had turned a blotchy red, having been scratched by Tony's sandpaper stubble.

'I don't normally say this to our guests, but why don't you get a cab and carry on in the privacy of your own home.'

Tony smiled at Connie and made a thumbs-up gesture that suggested they might not emerge into daylight for several days. They gave Joe and Chloe very quick pecks on the cheek and Connie said, 'And there was me thinking this evening was just publicity for my new film. My mum's going to have a heart attack when I tell her. If this goes wrong again, I'm going to sue you both for all you've got.'

Alone now, Chloe suddenly felt very tired, her post-show buzz dulled by the rapid intake of alcohol. They sat in companionable silence for a few moments, like an old married couple who had run out of conversation. Joe had ordered them both a whisky and she knew that if she drank it too quickly, she would struggle to stay awake. She didn't want the evening to end.

'So, where's your *innamorata* then, Joe?'

'In English, please?'

'Girlfriend. It's a term from the stock characters of lovers in *commedia dell'arte* drama in the seventeenth century.'

Oh God, the drink has made me even more uncontrollably pretentious, she thought.

Joe looked up in agreement.

'Thank you for the explanation, and why use a common word when you can dredge something up from your university dissertation?'

'Sorry. I can't stop my brain whirring. Anyway, answer the question, you philistine. Where's Nicola?'

Despite the fog of alcohol, Chloe could sense Joe's caution in answering. Eventually, he whispered a response.

'She didn't want to come. She's angry.'

'Angry about what? The show went so well.' Chloe knew exactly what had happened.

'She thinks I can't control my feelings for you and that maybe you feel the same too.'

The declaration was uncomfortable to hear. Guilt, confusion and the mixed drinks meant that her nausea of earlier in the evening returned, although this time with the palpable jeopardy of being sick. She took a long drink of water in the hope that it would provide immediate sobriety and mental clarity.

'She has no reason to think that,' she lied.

'I said that too, but she didn't buy it and has gone back to her flat to process everything that's happened.'

'That's so Gen Z. To be triggered and overwhelmed by the slightest thing and then to have to *process* the information like a computer.' Chloe thought it best to deflect from what had in fact happened with a quick rant.

'You're being unfair. We gave her plenty of cause for concern.'

'You don't mean because we held hands for a nano-second while you gave me a pep talk?'

'I think it was more because of how we looked at each other.'

This was becoming dangerously honest.

'I looked at you like a colleague planning an important meeting. Don't flatter yourself, sweetheart. Why, how did you look at me?'

'Much the same. Perhaps with a bit of pity thrown in.'

'Well then, how could she have got the wrong end of the stick?'

The fibs were pouring out. She remembered the tiny flutters of excitement in her stomach and that she hadn't wanted to let go of his hand.

'It's ironic, don't you think?'

'What?'

'That we're having this conversation after Connie and Tony fell in love again in the middle of our show. We've done three series of talking to people about the lessons of their past and then in our first live show, this happens. Do you think it's possible that things are never really over? It's not exactly what we've been telling our listeners.'

Chloe didn't know how to answer. The physical symptoms of fear, excitement and recklessness alternated for her like the changing colours of a traffic light.

'I'm not sure. I think it's dangerous to go back somewhere, no matter how tempting.'

'What if you want to try and prove someone wrong?'

She knew what Joe was asking and wanted to agree with him, succumbing to the temptation. The late-night intensity after such a long, draining day made her desire for affection overwhelming. She moved her chair closer to his and Joe leant forward, placing a hand gently on her shoulder, ready to draw her towards him. Instinctively, she placed her hand on his cheek, where their fingers interlocked. She kissed his palm gently. When their lips touched, it felt familiar and terrifying in equal measure. She shut her eyes and for the flicker of a moment – it could have been minutes – her thoughts dissolved into the blank possibility of a different future.

Not for long. Her mind was still a cauldron of conflict and couldn't quite shut down. There were simple facts she couldn't ignore. She was married. She loved David. She had two children. This was madness, no matter how desirable.

She broke off the kiss abruptly, before the pleasure became irreversible.

'I'm sorry, Joe – we can't do this. Let's not ruin everything. You're my lovely work husband and things are going so well.'

She didn't wait for his reply and headed for the door without looking back, with tears clouding her eyes and a foreboding that everything would be different now. She had to be stronger. For years, she had encased her love for Joe in concrete on which she built the foundation of a new life. It mustn't be allowed to crack.

On the street, the incessant rain had been replaced by sharp gusts of wind, which sobered her up immediately. She needed to speak to David and resume her domestic normality. They'd got caught up in the moment, the show, the emotion of their guests' reunion and the palpable affection they felt for one another. Nothing more.

She was lucky to find a black cab quickly and hoped she would soon be in her bed obliterating the memory of the tender kiss.

'Oh *bollocks*,' she shouted, so loudly that the cabbie half turned his head towards her.

'You all right, love?' he asked, concerned.

'It's nothing, it's just I think I left the bar so quickly I forgot to pay the bill and I'm not sure the bloke I was with will do the right thing.'

PART 4
CONFLICT

May 2020

Pre-lockdown, Joe would oversleep like a morose teenager whenever he needed an early start, but now his painful solitude made him struggle to get six hours' rest. The unusually warm spring weather didn't help. Each morning, an optimistic sunrise would illuminate his bedroom like a floodlit stadium and, despite wearing his black Covid face mask over his eyes, it was impossible to lie in.

Today was a run day; 7km through the deserted streets and an important reminder that the world was bigger than the narrow confines of his claustrophobic flat. He followed this new exercise routine with unfamiliar fervour, having hitherto believed that an endorphin release was something invented by Nike to get you to buy more trainers. Running had become his salvation – an affirmation that he was young, healthy, and unlikely to succumb to the apocalyptic virus.

He had developed a bespoke plan to keep him sane during this awful time. In addition to his four runs a week, he tried to be intellectually stimulated. An attempt, however, to complete the 800-page biography of Churchill on his bedside table was not going well. Three weeks in, and Winston had barely left school. At this rate, it would take him many months to get to the good bit when he saves the world from the Nazis.

Too much of his day was spent watching TV. Not the quality stuff that everyone was recommending online in a 'we're all in this nightmare together' sort of way. He was only interested in series about the drug cartels of Colombia or Mexico and the violent demise of anyone foolish enough to cross them. He had justified his viewing habits to his mother by telling her he was trying to improve his GCSE-level Spanish.

The podcast provided some structure given they were about to start recording a new series the following week. An intense hour or so on Zoom each day with Chloe and Kelly made him focus on being creative and prevented his anguish developing into full-blown despair. A few days before, when audio equipment microphones arrived for him to set up a home studio, he had unpacked the gear with the alacrity of a castaway on a desert island finding a case of rum.

Sitting at his small kitchen table, he poured himself a bowl of cereal and lamented that he was low on provisions, requiring a trip to Sainsburys, a logistical trauma these days with all the awful new shopping rules imposed by the government: wear a mask, stay two metres apart, go to prison if you sneeze twice in an enclosed space with pensioners.

Things could have been very different.

With each bombastic speech from Boris, the country's closing became an ever more terrifying prospect, and he begged Nicola to move in with him so that they could face the uncertainty together. He reasoned that this life-changing experience would establish their future in a way that regular late-night gallivanting in bars could never do. Unfortunately, something had changed after the Union Chapel show and Nicola's suspicion burnt out of control, destroying the equilibrium of her affection. She challenged him repeatedly to explain his true feelings for Chloe, convinced she saw in their interactions an attraction that threatened to dislodge Joe's for her.

Joe responded with partial honesty; after all, there was no way he could confess what happened at the end of the evening. He had not seen Chloe in person afterwards as national panic and the quest for toilet paper interrupted their working life. Not that he would have had the courage to admit that, for him, their brief kiss produced a desire he didn't think possible and a realisation that, for her, it was probably a momentary aberration unlikely to be repeated.

So, he tried to make it work with Nicola, and while his feelings for Chloe were now more confused than ever, he knew she was not going to abandon everything for him on a nostalgic whim. He told Nicola over and over that he loved her, hoping repetition would make it true.

Unconvinced by his declarations, she hid behind the convenient excuse of a global pandemic and decamped to her parents, declaring grandly that she wanted to be near them if the world was about to end. As she lapsed into family life with her two younger siblings, he wondered at quiet moments in the day if he missed her or just company in general. They spoke every day with increasing stiltedness, their enforced separation denuding them of conversational topics other than the incompetence of the government and their exercise routines.

They tried to talk about their future, but Nicola was increasingly vague about what this might look like. Her energetic remodelling of his image and their vibrant social life seemed to belong to pre-war times, when their attitude was more carefree. Within a couple of weeks of being apart, Nicola told him that she was going to leave her job and, to his amazement, declared she wanted to retrain to work in mental health.

Reconnecting with her family had made her realise her values were all wrong, and that included Joe. He had never wanted to be a partying celeb boyfriend – after all, he was a former teacher who, despite wanting to have most of them arrested, really cared about his pupils' well-being. How ironic that his twenty-eight-year-old champagne-swilling girlfriend now saw him as some sort of feckless playboy.

The previous night they'd spoken briefly, and her language unambiguously anticipated their demise when she told him: *I'm going to apply for a master's in counselling and that needs to be my sole focus for the time being.* At forty, he needed to be more than a distraction. They talked loosely about going away somewhere when hotels opened, but he knew that was never going to happen and they would part from one another with amicable indifference, leaving him with a wardrobe of garishly coloured shirts she had chosen for him.

For nearly two years, he'd banged on as a self-appointed expert about failed relationships, while remaining clueless why they never worked for him. Sadly, his options for support were now limited as his close friends were all couples trying to make sense of this unexpected new reality, and his family were even less helpful.

His mother and Jane, for example, were like a pair of newlyweds on an extended honeymoon, calling him on FaceTime from their large brass bed where they seemed to spend most of the day. He would try to ask their advice and would be interrupted by their squeals and giggles, suggesting they weren't paying attention and that something was going on under the duvet that he didn't want to think about. He'd remind her to behave like a grandmother, which only made them laugh at him more.

For his father and Dull Debbie, the pandemic unleashed a fearfulness that precluded meaningful conversation about anything other than their odds of dying. Their home was a hermetically sealed safe space where shopping was delivered at great expense and each item spritzed by Debbie with disinfectant before being brought into the kitchen. They occasionally left the house at night and would walk around the block wearing two masks each and disposable gloves, hiding behind bushes if they saw someone walking on the other side of the road. Every phone call with Michael was a statistical analysis of global infection rates and a risk assessment worthy of a government press conference. The corollary of this paranoia was that Joe couldn't be bothered to explain how lonely he was.

Even his sympathetic sister was too engrossed in her own domestic arrangements to think through what it must be like for him stuck in a second-floor flat in Tooting on his own. They arranged intermittent Zoom chats with a glass of wine, pretending that drinking alcohol on a video conference call was an adequate alternative to genuine human contact. Each of these sessions degenerated into Amy lamenting how hard it was to make a six-year-old learn times tables online when everyone knows that you subcontract that shit to a recently qualified teacher saddled with a class of thirty-five kids. Joe tried to say something helpful, but in truth was consumed with jealousy for the cohesion of her family unit.

What hurt the most was that David and Chloe appeared to have approached lockdown like it was a reset for their relationship. In their daily work calls, Chloe kept mentioning how being sequestered together with constraints was better than the freedom of their family life pre-Covid. There was no mention of what had occurred, and he assumed that she was trying to use the potential obliteration of humankind to refocus her priorities. He was sure she saw what happened between them as a disaster induced by the euphoria of a live show and never to be repeated.

David and Chloe loved being with their children and had created a new routine of walks, elaborately prepared meals, and games. Moreover, the absence of external commitments allowed them to give each other space to write; Chloe was completing her novel and David, in addition to his job in New York, which he was trying to make work remotely, had begun a screenplay that would obliterate the unhappy memory of his first film.

Chloe announced that she was going to learn to bake and every day she would send Joe a picture of another cake she had prepared, complete with an unwanted explanation of its ingredients. In addition to the carrot cakes and lemon tarts, she started producing sourdough bread, which he had never realised was so complicated as, to rise, it required this weird thing called a 'starter', a fermented flour and water mixture that contained yeast and good bacteria. It looked like mouldy plasticine when she showed it to him proudly on one call as if they had just picked up a pedigree puppy from a new litter. Chloe even gave it the name 'Keir' (*'Keir Starter, after the new Labour party leader'*) and within days it had become a much-loved family member that also needed regular feeding.

It was hard for him to sound enthralled when she enthusiastically updated him on the latest batch of bread out of the oven and how she had created an interesting texture by scoring the dough with a razor blade. To his dismay, Chloe's marriage had become its own podcast with a new episode dropped every day, which he was compelled to download even though he desperately wanted to stop subscribing.

It wasn't really that he was lonely. He spoke to people throughout the day and had always been comfortable in his own company. Rather, it was a sense of isolation that caused him a constant low-level pain like a chronic stomach complaint. What he had learnt was that the pandemic had not simply changed the practicalities of daily life but had altered the DNA of most relationships. If there was a stable foundation of love, then the fear of a deadly virus acted like quick-drying glue to ensure fixed happiness, affection and desire. Conversely, as he found with Nicola, if a couple was emotionally incompatible and had muddled along in denial of that fact, lockdown was a turbo-charged catalyst for separation and pain.

* * *

'You look pretty today,' Chloe joked when she appeared on his computer screen later that morning.

Dressed in a very scruffy running T-shirt, his beard was untrimmed and flecked with grey and his overgrown hair held in place by a headband he'd recently bought on Amazon. He looked like a tennis professional who'd fallen on hard times.

'Just because we're all about to die doesn't mean standards should slip.'

'Well, I'd say you are clearly missing Nicola's influence. She must be horrified how you've let yourself go.'

Chloe had no idea what had happened to his relationship, mainly because he'd been unwilling to explain her complicity in its demise. He changed the subject. More than ever, he needed to steer clear of discussing emotions with Chloe because of the fragility of his own.

'Didn't you wear that top yesterday?' he asked.

'Well spotted, Anna Wintour.'

'I suppose you have more stuff to wash than I do.'

'Why are we discussing laundry, Joe?'

'What else do you want to chat about? Do you have an exciting update about your latest Victoria sponge?'

'Don't be like that. I listen to you drone on about your Deliveroo order each night.'

'I thought you were a foodie and would have some insight.'

'Not to questions like *shall I go thin or thick crust?*'

'OK, well, then how's St David today? Any more culinary miracles for his family with the leftover loaves and fishes?'

Even with the low-res video, he could see the irritation spread across Chloe's face.

'He sends his best to you and hopes you're not getting too miserable in your isolation.'

He hadn't meant to reveal his jealousy of David, but her response was nasty. Chloe must have thought this too and blew an unexpected conciliatory kiss into her camera.

'I'm sorry, Joe, that was insensitive. I just find it so much easier to not bring him into a conversation between us. It always goes wrong somehow.'

Joe wasn't sure what she meant and wondered if this suggested the vestiges of confused feelings. He didn't have time to probe because he heard the ping of a text and saw Chloe check her phone and then shake her head furiously.

'Oh no, no, no.'

'What's wrong?'

'It's Kelly. He thinks he's got Covid.'

'Oh *shit*. How is he?'

'Hard to tell. The text says *Feel awful. All the symptoms. Just gone for a test. You may have to fly solo.*'

It was still a shock to hear about people getting ill despite being in a lockdown that was meant to contain the virus. And even worse was the fear that this was not just flu but an illness of ever-shifting symptoms. Boris Johnson had just come out of intensive care, which had shaken the country, although Joe assumed the severity of his illness was because *buffoons* were a vulnerable category alongside asthmatics and the immunosuppressed. Nevertheless, Kelly's news was very close to home for them both and they fell silent for a moment, until Joe spoke.

'Right, the show must go on, or at the very least be recorded. Kelly would want us to get on with things in his absence.'

'At the very least, he'd have a phrase he'd use from his time at the ashram for circumstances like these.'

'*Disease only comes into the body if you allow it in the mind*,' Joe ad-libbed in his best West Coast accent.

'Perfect. I'll text it to him now.'

Chloe started to type a proper reply, which Joe knew would be a compassionate message. Just like her father, she was an instinctively kind person with natural empathy for others, despite the wall of sarcasm she sometimes built around her. He had recognised that from the moment they met as students, and he regretted never really telling her at the time. His thoughts wandered, and Chloe, sensing this distraction, clapped her hands.

'Focus please, Joe. We have a show to sort.'

'Who's going to produce it?' he asked.

'I will. I know exactly what we're doing and if Kelly's still ill, Greg the intern can do all the technical stuff for the recording.'

Greg was only twenty-two, but Joe was in awe of his geekiness. He had helped him set up the recording equipment on a phone call as if it were easier than folding a piece of paper.

'Who will mediate our arguments?'

'We won't have any. I'm in charge as always.'

Her words were not meant seriously; however, they saddened him. Shut off from the world, Joe was reminded that he had no power in this relationship. Because of lockdown, the series was going to adapt its format, and they would interview couples who had not separated but had undergone high-profile moments of relationship distress. The first show featured the well-known retired French footballer Alain Kalzou and his English wife, the singer Madeleine, in which they agreed to discuss the impact of his paparazzi-snapped infidelity at the start of their marriage and how she found it possible to trust him again.

Chloe mapped out the discussion areas and how their role was to give hope to their listeners who were struggling in the current mayhem. They were going to be joined on each show by a different expert who would try and decode the celebrity couple's interview with them at the end of the show. Chloe told Joe she'd had a fascinating briefing earlier in the week with the psychiatrist Gordon Allen, who was joining them for Episode 1. He was a specialist in separation anxiety, which apparently is relevant when analysing a randy footballer playing away from his wife.

Joe let Chloe talk with little interruption. He knew he'd have to prepare properly for each recording and make a significant effort to chip in with insightful questions, but right now he couldn't control the rising tide of his personal gloom. The call lasted about an hour. Kelly texted a couple of times to describe in more detail how frightening it was to feel the shortening of his breath. They parted in sombre professionalism, agreeing what they would finalise when they spoke the next day, their initial carefree banter long forgotten.

Hours later, at sunset, Joe made himself a cup of tea and stared outside the window at the terraced houses that had been his uninspiring view for weeks now. Unloved properties with missing roof tiles and peeling paint were adjoined to recently renovated houses in immaculate condition and Joe reflected how it imitated life, the indiscriminate mingling of contentment and dissatisfaction. Before he could become any more philosophical, he was shaken by the sound of applause and the wild clanging pots and pans from the street. The nation was clapping its gratitude for the bravery of its health workers.

He'd forgotten to join in, too distracted by the thought of the strange late-night call he'd had with Emily the previous evening. She'd moved back to England a year ago, although he hadn't seen her in that time. Chloe had updated him on an unhappy romance she'd had with a recently divorced man who proved unwilling to commit. When the country shut, she hastily moved back to her childhood home in Leamington Spa, a place she hated, to look after her frail mother. Her call was unexpected, and he certainly wasn't prepared for the magnitude of the question she asked.

* * *

'Yes, OK. I'm in,' Joe said, like he was joining a gang.

'You're kidding?' Emily sounded incredulous.

'My sperm is all yours. And you won't even have to sleep with me, although a quick snog on the way to the clinic might be nice.'

'I can't believe it.'

'Why not? Things are so up in the air. Time to be decisive.'

'It's such a big thing I'm asking.'

'I know it is. I want to help you.'

'Are you really sure? There are consequences that will follow you for the rest of your life.' He'd never heard her like this, a mixture of compassion and vulnerability.

'I get it, Emily. We'll be creating a person.'

'And what if you meet someone and want your own family?'

'What if I don't? What if I'm the co-host of a podcast, half in love with Chloe and unable to find someone else?'

'Is that what you think of yourself?'

'Most of the time,' he said forlornly.

And yet, when she'd asked him if he would have a child with her, the decision wasn't difficult. His nihilism needed to be conquered and if he wasn't going to find love with a partner, perhaps a bit of intermittent parenting would make him a better and brighter person.

'That's rubbish. You're special, Joe,' Emily said sweetly.

'Special needs, perhaps. Otherwise, I'm a bloke who has stumbled from one woman to the next and always got it wrong. Perfect father material.'

'You don't have to be involved, you know.'

'I don't think life works like that. There are consequences of every action. Especially jerking off in a test-tube.'

'How nicely put.'

'Well, it's not every day you offer your gene pool to a friend.'

'I shall swim in it wisely.'

'*Euch*. So, what now?'

'I suppose we have to agree some ground rules.'

'I want him brought up an atheist.'

'I mean on how involved you want to be. It's uncharted territory for us both. I always thought that by this age, I'd be living with my husband and more servants than *Downton Abbey*. Now I'm having an inseminated child with a man whose longest relationship seems to be with his postman.'

'Hopefully, if this works, our child may have a slightly higher opinion of me.'

'Of course they will. You're wonderful. I love you for this.'

'Thank you, I appreciate you saying that.'

'But for the avoidance of doubt, I am not in love with you. We're better off as friends with a baby rather than friends with benefits.'

'Can we talk about this more tomorrow? I've had an exhausting day. Lots going on with the podcast.'

'I'll call you. And Joe, please don't tell anyone, especially Chloe. She'll just make it weird.'

'Mum's the word.'

'Indeed it is.'

August 2020

Chloe hated the bureaucracy of the new world order, having endured a ridiculously stressful two hours trying to change her flights. The chaos of travelling abroad during Covid reminded her of a recurring dream in which she would run headlong into a buffeting wind, fleeing some unspecified danger but unable to move forward. The admin was horrific and filling in the online user-unfriendly Passenger Locator Forms required the patience of a particularly patient saint. What should have been a relaxing day by the pool with her father and kids became an anxious vigil on hold to the airline, listening to its excruciating Muzak. She was ready to tell them what she wanted to do to the Girl from Ipanema, but by the time Tracy from Gateshead came on the line, there was no way she was going to risk losing the opportunity to book new tickets for the following day.

She had no choice because the UK government had decided, with little warning, to take France off the small list of countries that didn't require fourteen days of quarantine on return. This meant she would have to curtail her precious time with her father to avoid being locked at home with the twins, an impossibility given her upcoming intense schedule of recordings and meetings. What a year of chaos it had been. First David had only just managed to get out of New York in the nick of time before lockdown and now she and the kids were fleeing on the penultimate flight home like it was the fall of Saigon.

She didn't want to leave her father. It had been so hard to be separated from him since Christmas and, no matter how many Zoom calls they had, not being able to hug him was unbearable.

If only he hadn't built this bucolic new life in Bergerac with Sally. They'd found a six-bedroom house in a quiet spot about a fifteen-minute drive from the town. With a couple of partially renovated outbuildings backing on to an apple orchard and views of the rolling Dordogne countryside, it was all very lovely. After a couple of visits, she too became smitten with the house.

Chloe realised that while Malcolm could no longer be relied on for emergency babysitting, her children were building an incredible relationship with him based on holidays of swimming, walking, reading, and playing all manner of games. Her grandparents had been distant figures in her childhood, while David's parents, divorced and rather selfish, were an intermittent presence for Mikey and Alice. In Malcolm, they were blessed with this wise guide for their early upbringing, who would hopefully stop them becoming drug dealers or investment bankers when they grew up.

David hadn't been able to join them as he was trying to find new work. He'd been very happy at the agency in New York, which he hoped would precipitate the revival of his stalled career. Unfortunately, running a team remotely on a different time zone was not sustainable long term and made worse by the agency's largest clients, an airline and hotel chain, slashing their advertising budgets because of the collapse of global travel. After a few months of lockdown, David needed to find new work again.

Their family cosiness started to dissipate with the socially distanced, mask-wearing uneasiness of a partially opened country. The romantic togetherness of the early days was replaced by the abnormal reality of this new way of life and suddenly Chloe and David had to confront its impact: hyperactive six-year-old twins who needed structure, a podcast now on its fifth series that required constant reinvention, the pre-publication of her novel and the demands of a new weekly column in *The Times*.

Once again, David became the secondary breadwinner in their family, and it rankled. New York had made him independent and validated; now he was forced to find directing projects in the UK in an economically challenged market. He was well respected in the industry but that wasn't enough, and the busier Chloe got, the tetchier he became. During the day, childcare was shared between them, and he grew resentful if he thought the responsibility was not equally divided. They no longer snuggled in bed watching television when the kids were asleep, as he stayed up late drinking whisky and working on his screenplay with increasing diffidence.

The relief for them both was enormous when he was given a week's work on a car insurance commercial on location in Devon. Chloe and the twins headed to France and the week passed in a flash with only intermittent contact with David due to their respective poor phone signals. When they did manage a fifteen-minute conversation, he was preoccupied with the complexity of how to shoot an elaborate line-dancing routine in a barn while socially distancing.

When she was with her father, she never missed David. This holiday had been a particularly wonderful time spent relaxing in the languid August sunshine and doing very little. The kids spent most of the day in the pool or on nature walks with Malcolm and Sally, who were skilled at pointing out the local flora of Etruscan honeysuckle, bird's-nest orchid and wild candytuft and making the names sound funny. Chloe had plenty of time to read and switch off from all the projects she had on the go.

What distressed her the most about leaving suddenly was a foreboding that her life was about to get more complicated. Opportunities presented themselves daily to advance her career in different directions, accompanied by a threat of physical violence from her agent if she refused. Mary was unflinchingly devoted to her, in her own aggressive fashion, and keen to separate her from Joe, having given up any pretence of loyalty to him. She reminded Chloe constantly that if she was wedded to being a double act, she could only ever be as good as his best performance.

Just after she finished re-booking the flights, her phone started pinging with texts from Mary. There were several invitations to appear on high-profile podcasts and she needed to confirm her participation. *À La Carte* was a massive hit hosted by husband-and-wife comedians, who asked their guests to imagine the meal they would serve to their favourite person in history and explain why. Chloe had chosen Jane Austen and was regretting it already because she couldn't think of any funny gags other than something about Colonel Brandon's unique blend of herbs and spices for his fried chicken in *Sense and Sensibility*. She was also being asked on another show called *My Politics*, in which she had to tell a famous political journalist what her manifesto would be if she ran for prime minister.

She wanted to enjoy the last few hours with her family in the sunshine, so didn't want a fractious text conversation with Mary for the rest of the day. It could wait, although Chloe needed to clarify if she was appearing on *À La Carte* with Joe, who she knew loved the show. Mary's response to her innocuous text was brutal:

FFS why would you think that? They want you. Everyone wants you on your own! He's holding you back, in every regard.

* * *

It was a culinary eclectic supper. Sally had prepared vichyssoise followed by her speciality orange chicken, a Spanish recipe with smoked sweet paprika, cumin seeds and orange zest, which she served with a beautiful tomato salad dripping in an olive oil and balsamic glaze dressing and potato wedges in rosemary. The twins inevitably refused to contemplate such exotic food and were allowed the French delicacy of pizza and chips. A giant board of local cheeses for the adults was paired with generous helpings of chocolate ice cream and a token strawberry for the kids. Mikey and Alice drank Diet Cokes while the adults polished off a second bottle of rosé to dull the edges of the children's increasingly manic behaviour.

They sat on the terrace, the heat of the day dissolving into a perfect evening with a crimson sky darkening as the sun disappeared. The air was warm and sweet with the fragrance of jasmine and lavender. Chloe didn't want to go home and confront her workload and the growing tension with David. Plus, there was the wrench of leaving her father, with the prospect of more Covid lockdowns keeping them apart for the foreseeable future.

Her unease was physical, a weight pressing on her chest. The sensation took her back to after her mother had died, when Malcolm sent her to a residential summer camp because he thought it would be good for her. She hated every minute and loneliness clung to her like soggy clothes in the rain. How could she feel sad now when surrounded by so much love?

She held her father's hand in silence as Sally cleared the table and the twins watched cartoons on her iPad. Chloe had grown very fond of her stepmother, not just because of how happy she made her father but also her sensitivity to ensuring their father-daughter bond was unbroken by his happy marriage. Without being asked, Sally shooed the children from the screen and took them upstairs to prepare them for bed, and Chloe wondered if it would be appropriate to tip her.

'You did well, Dad, with that one. She's far classier than those floozies you used to date.'

Malcolm let go of her hand and poured the dregs of the wine into their glasses.

'She's a fine woman and I'm very grateful. Especially as she encouraged me to move abroad to escape you.'

'Seriously though, I really appreciate how happy she makes you. You do know that, don't you?'

'Of course, darling. She adores you. Thinks you're very talented, funny and kind.'

'I don't feel very talented, funny and kind these days.'

Malcolm tilted his head, not so much in sympathy as incredulity.

'I don't want to sour our last evening, but what on earth are you talking about?'

Chloe took a large gulp of the wine, trying to buy time for her response.

'Well, I'm not sure what I'm doing at the moment.'

Malcolm was having none of it.

'Apart from building a very successful career and raising a wonderful family. What else is missing?'

She looked at the floor, avoiding his gaze like a naughty child refusing to own up to a crime.

'Chloe, what's going on? Isn't the podcast going from strength to strength?'

'It is. We're apparently in the top five downloads in the UK.'

'And you seem to get these amazing guests to talk about their most intimate experiences to millions of people. How does that work?'

'I guess it's a combination of their ego to be in the limelight and the catharsis of admitting their mistakes, even to strangers.'

'Somehow, I suspect that's a line you've used before.'

Chloe smiled.

'We may occasionally say it behind our guests' backs.'

'Who have you got coming up?'

'Next up is DJ Biscus, Ibiza's most famous DJ, and his former girlfriend, Catherine Mostyn, who is now married to an earl and writes very successful children's books.'

'Never heard of them.'

'They're both a bit bonkers and it should be fun.'

'Are you allowed to call people bonkers these days?'

'Only if they're mad.'

Malcolm stood up suddenly, his leg having cramped. He stretched it gingerly.

'Are you OK, Dad?'

'My arthritis, nothing more. Let's talk about your book.'

She worried about any aspect of his health, even everyday complaints, wanting him to be immortal. However, she also knew that he hated fuss.

'I'm so glad you liked it.'

'What else do you think I'd say? I know how sensitive you get to criticism.'

'Very funny. You did enjoy it though, didn't you?'

'It's brilliant, honestly. You're a natural storyteller and it's moving and funny.'

'Well, that's the cover quote sorted. I hope you'll take a suitcase full of books and sell them to everyone on Bergerac High Street.'

'Pierre the Boulanger has already pre-ordered his copy. Now, Chloe, I think we're departing from my original question. There is something wrong, you've had an air of sadness. You can tell me, I used to be a big deal in my local church.'

Chloe was relieved to have the opportunity to unburden herself. She'd been in turmoil since her text exchange with Mary.

'I'm confused about my feelings.'

'What feelings?'

'For David and Joe.'

'Ah, those feelings. What's happened?'

'Promise you won't get angry with me.'

'Absolutely not, but go on.'

'Since I've been working with Joe, I've struggled at times to – how shall I put it – not love him a bit.'

'I see. And David?'

'You know I love David. He's a good husband and a great father.'

'Interesting choice of words. Only "good"?'

'No, he's often great. It's just a bit tricky at present. We go in cycles and when I'm having more success, he struggles with his self-esteem.'

'Like you did when I complimented you?'

'No, it's different. His frustration calcifies and he gets angry.'

'Let's come back to Joe. You may not want to answer this, but has something happened?'

Her father-daughter relationship was like no other because she was willing to confess to him without inhibition.

'Yes. I kissed him for about thirty seconds just before lockdown.'

'Did you time it?'

She smiled.

'Of course not. What I'm saying is, it was brief because I realised that it was wrong.'

'Why was it wrong?'

'Have you forgotten the Seventh Commandment?'

'What I mean is, tell me your feelings and why it happened. I was asking rhetorically and no, I haven't forgotten it.'

'My feelings are hard to articulate. I think I still love Joe in some way that I'd forgotten. But why, given he's hopeless? He drifts between a myriad of failed relationships with decent women and never manages to understand their potential or unsuitability. And I'm married to a good man who loves me enormously, even if he sometimes struggles when positive things happen for me. I don't want to disrupt my life and ruin it because of this confused affection I have for Joe because he makes me laugh so much and is rather spectacularly lovely.'

She was silent for a second and then asked the question that she'd been grappling with for months.

'Dad, do you think it's possible to love two people at the same time?'

'I do.'

'And how do you know for sure?'

It was Malcolm's turn to look away.

'Because when your mother died, she was in love with me and someone else.'

* * *

'I always thought you and Mum were the perfect love story?' Chloe asked, trying not to sob. Because of her self-indulgent fantasies about Joe, the narrative of her childhood was about to unravel.

'We were, in the beginning,' Malcolm said wistfully.

They sat alone on the terrace. Sally had gone to bed, aware from their uncomfortable body language that their conversation was not to be interrupted.

'You always told me that you met in the first year at university and it was a *coup de foudre*.'

'It was. Couldn't keep our hands off each other. I was a lot friskier before I found religion.'

'Don't joke, Dad. What happened?'

'It's time you knew. I've put off this conversation for a long time.'

She put her head on his shoulder and whispered, 'Whatever's best for you. I don't want you to be in pain telling me or likewise from holding on to the secret.'

'You should understand what happened, it may explain things. We got married eighteen months after graduating, when we were ambitiously pursuing our careers. As you know, I was a risk analyst for a bank, and it was bloody dull, and your mum worked in marketing for a confectionery company.'

'Did you get lots of free chocolate then?'

'Straight to the heart of the periphery, Chloe. Do you want to hear what happened or not?'

'Sorry, I'm nervous.'

Malcolm took a sip of water and carried on.

'I always had my religious beliefs to fall back on and after a few years of growing increasingly disconnected I sensed there was a higher purpose for me, or certainly one with fewer spreadsheets. By the time I was ordained, you were five, and the reduction in our dual income made your mum even more driven to succeed professionally.'

'Was it hard for you both?'

'Yes, of course. We muddled through, focusing on doing everything we could to look after you, and Alice dutifully supported me as the reluctant wife of an inexperienced vicar. You know what the problem really was, though?'

'I'm guessing not having another child?'

'Yes, and we dealt with it so differently. I leant into my faith, but your mum just worked harder to distract from her sadness. I suppose it was inevitable that as this fissure opened between us, she became susceptible to the flattering approaches of someone at work.'

'Who was it?'

'Some arsehole called James Cartwright, five years younger, unattached, shy, and very good looking.'

'I've never heard you use that word, Dad?'

'Well, sometimes it's important to be precise. Now stop interrupting, this is not an easy story to narrate. So, they'd been seeing each other for nine months, and I was blissfully unaware of the real reason behind the dramatic rise in overnight business trips, when your mum started to feel unwell. It's all a bit of a blur. The leukaemia was quickly diagnosed, with the shocking conclusion that she had very little time left.'

'Oh Dad. I'm so sorry.'

Malcolm spoke very deliberately as he relived his ordeal.

'I suppose she could have taken her secret to the grave. However, as her body weakened, she somehow reconnected with the depth our love once had. Maybe she was just grateful that I'd become a dedicated carer, who also protected you from the impending tragedy. I knew something else was wrong, other than the illness, and a confession was weighing her down, but the shock when she told me was devastating. Her pain relief was so strong it left her feelings unfiltered. She told me everything. When I held her in my arms as she passed, I made a promise to her not to tell you. Am I doing the right thing, breaking it now?'

'I'm glad you have.'

Malcolm hugged her. He was breathing heavily to compose himself.

'You'd better hear the end of the story then. This might surprise you. After Alice died, I reached out to the man who had caused my wife to divide her love between us and invited him to the funeral.'

'You did what?'

'You heard. I'm not sure why. But as you know from your tireless study of the scriptures, the Lord works in mysterious ways. At the wake, I went up to him and wished him the peace to move forward with his life and he broke down. Everyone stared at him as he wept with giant sobs.'

'The big girl's blouse.'

'Exactly. You asked me why the man from Mummy's office was so upset and all I could think to say was that she was very well respected by her colleagues.'

'I don't remember any of this. I just remember feeling alone and no one knowing what to say to me.'

'You won't recall that I had a bit of a breakdown afterwards, and that's why I sent you to that summer camp. It wasn't to enjoy outdoor pursuits in the drizzle of a chilly English summer. I needed to be alone.'

'That's so weird, I was thinking about that summer camp earlier this evening.'

'I had to get my head straight. I got some help, non-divine as it turned out, and vowed that you would never find out. My job was to protect you. I came to realise that despite what happened with Alice, I loved her no less and forgave her. I think I convinced myself that she would have returned to me if she hadn't got ill. That's why it took years for me to trust another person.'

'And there's me thinking you were waiting until I settled down to look for a new partner. You weren't ready to feel vulnerable again.'

'Then I met Sally, and her kindness somehow revived the memory of how being loved could feel.'

'I wish you could have met her earlier.'

'That's not how life works, my love. You live in the present. You must embrace the potential of the future and not regret the events of your past.'

'Did you just make that up?'

'No, I wrote it years ago and shoved it in a sermon every three years or so without anyone realising. But I'm trying to make a point here.'

'Which is?'

'Which is that you keep struggling to move on and always wonder if there's something better than what's in front of you. I understand that you can have conflicted feelings for Joe, but you need to work out what the right answer is and then follow a course of action that brings resolution to you, to David, to Joe, to your kids. I've seen the damage that emotional indecision can bring. It's ugly.'

'So, what's the right answer for me?'

'I am retired. They switch off your direct line to the Almighty when you hand back your dog collar. You'll have to work it out for yourself.'

Malcolm patted her on the shoulder and started to clear the remaining glasses from the table. She sat alone, mulling over what she'd heard. On balance, the revelation of her father's pain generated in Chloe renewed loyalty towards David. Inconvenient feelings for Joe would not disappear quickly, she knew, but they had to be ignored. Her poor father had been hit by the double tragedy of both her mother's death and infidelity. She was not going to cause such pain to her own husband.

As she sat listening to the silence of the night, she tried to contain her emotions and decide what to do on her return. She would pay David more attention, that was a good start. And she would redouble her efforts to praise him whenever she could. As for Joe, that was trickier. She needed to step back and make their relationship purely professional, reducing the many hours they spent together chatting rubbish and laughing. That might be difficult, given the strength of the feelings she was trying to suppress.

Maybe Mary was right, and it was time to go solo.

October 2020

Joe had once done a stand-up routine about the awfulness of British summertime, which concluded: *If we were meant to eat outside, we'd have our own term for 'al fresco' to describe the experience.*

He remembered the joke as he shivered in the chill of an overcast autumnal morning. Buttoning up his denim jacket, he slowly sipped his second espresso and pondered the script he was writing. Dining al fresco was something you did in the sunshine of a Roman piazza with multicoloured bougainvillaea overhanging the balconies of the cafés and restaurants. Today, in pandemic-compliant London, it meant sitting in the road on a folding chair, inhaling traffic fumes and the viral load of the passers-by.

Still, needs must, and Joe couldn't stay cooped up in his flat for another day without resorting to an act of violence on the next Amazon delivery man who rang his bell. The Listen Up offices were not yet open, and Joe was the loser in this recently established 'can't-be-arsed-to-commute' world, consigned to his kitchen table for hours at a time either writing or sitting in Zoom meetings, not really paying attention. All indications suggested the pandemic was not abating, so this new norm threatened to endure.

Worse still, his unwanted isolation was underpinned by a working life consumed with discussing other people's relationships, making the pain of his singledom even more pronounced. He had run dry of dating mishaps to fill his monologue and had now created a regular feature, 'Toxic Relationship of the Week', in which he riffed about a couple in free fall. It took longer each week to find an interesting story, requiring him to scour global news sites and follow weirdos on Twitter who, in his former life, he would have crossed the road to avoid.

After hours of frustrated searching, he had uncovered the story of a local Spanish politician who left his wife for her younger sister. Unfortunately, she was married to his main rival in the regional assembly, resulting in an opposition vote of no confidence and municipal strikes. Joe ruminated in the script on the collateral damage of failed relationships and our responsibility to others when we fall out of love. In this case, because Miguel Ramírez-Sinués couldn't keep *el miembro* in his *pantalones*, the people of Zaragoza now faced the prospect of not having their rubbish collected.

His mind was too distracted by the meeting he'd just had with his financial advisor. New to managing money, Joe had only recently begun the process of squirrelling a fraction of his earnings away for the future. Not that he had much to invest, and their conversation had been particularly depressing that morning. Despite having entered the world of PEPs, ISAs and defined contribution pension schemes, he was not a wealthy man. Marcus, his IFA, explained that the symptoms of Covid were not just a terrible cough and fever, but an annihilation of the global markets. Joe would have to work until he was ninety-seven before considering retirement.

Being single and cash-strapped made him feel completely alone. Relationships were surely about more than sex and friendship, and could be enhanced by a robust dual income.

How would he know? At best, Joe had benefited from the largesse of a wealthy partner like Laura but had never known the comfort of shared mortgage payments with an equal. It would help him now if there were dating apps in which the woman revealed the size of her dowry, not just her favourite pastimes.

Meanwhile, Mary seemed to be his agent in name and verbal abuse only. She got him the occasional appearance on a smaller podcast, but the invitations were drying up in this difficult time of closed entertainment venues. After much cajoling, she secured him a small advance from a second-division publisher for his first novel about the murder of a comedian as he's performing his act. Given he hadn't worked out a plot, the best thing about it was its title, 'The Comedian Who Died on Stage'.

He had become less important to the success of *Ex-Communicate*; another member of the production team churning out twenty-five episodes a year, his role that of Chloe's on-air sidekick. His colleagues listened politely to him in meetings but followed her every utterance like devoted acolytes. While they both delivered monologues in each show, his were sometimes dropped without explanation. The interviews were conducted by Chloe, with contributions limited to when she popped to the loo or got bored with the guests.

Kelly deferred entirely to her in planning the shows and barely spoke to him. Kelly had endured a difficult time over the last few months and Joe guessed his marriage was pretty much over. The clues were not hard to detect: his physical appearance was even more bedraggled than usual, and when he appeared on a Zoom call, he seemed to be living under the stairs, like Harry Potter sitting hunched in the dark. Frequent references to 'that bitch Jasmin' or 'dumb ex-wife number three' were also a bit of a giveaway.

Chloe would often stay on the call at the end of a meeting and had clearly become his confidante. She only had time for one emotionally incompetent friend and, for now, it had become their producer. It wasn't her fault; nevertheless, he missed spending time talking to her, and the rejection stung like salt water. The recent months had been odd. Chloe was always polite but seemed more guarded and he didn't really know what was going on in her life, particularly with David.

Joe considered she might be somehow angry about his IVF treatment with Emily and the possibility that he was going to father her best friend's child. Did she disapprove or was she unconsciously jealous? He'd said nothing to her, but he was sure Emily would have given daily updates on their first cycle of treatment and their combined anxiety as to whether it had worked, which they were going to find out in the next week.

He stared at the paltry three lines of script he'd managed to write in a frustrating hour, hoping he was wrong about being squeezed out. His career had sparked after years of being barely a sputtering flame when the podcast started. Now it had been extinguished by his own mediocrity. Chloe was dumping him, although this time it was a lingering death rather than a single shot to the head.

A fine drizzle turned into proper rain, and he packed up his computer to return home to his empty flat. Walking briskly, pedestrians sidestepped him on the pavement as if he was infectious. After a few minutes of getting increasingly wet in the gathering gloom, he heard an alert on his phone, hoping it was contact from a friendly person. Uneasiness quickly dissolved to fear when he read the message from Chrissie – she wanted to meet him immediately on Zoom. It seemed that these days, even executions were done remotely.

* * *

Harriet the HR consultant didn't smile when she appeared on screen, introducing herself with the enthusiasm of a child being dragged round an art gallery. Joe hadn't met her before, but her presence attested to the rapid growth of the production company and the formalising of its processes. Covid had been great for wine clubs, online therapists and especially podcasts, thus Listen Up had been on a massive recruitment drive and a cohort of new staff had joined remotely.

Chrissie was running late so Joe tried to make small talk, but it was hard work as Harriet didn't want to reveal any personal information or give him the vaguest clue as to why he was there. He'd been on unsuccessful blind dates with more chemistry and his stomach began a nervous cha-cha-cha in anticipation of his inevitable dismissal from the one project in his life that made him proud. A voice in his head declared, *Wait a minute, they can't do this to me, I have a contract*, and he was temporarily buoyed by imagining his lawyer father suing them for millions if they fired him. That Michael made a living as a property conveyancer would not prevent him humiliating Joe's enemies at the high-profile employment tribunal that would ensue.

Five minutes late, Chrissie joined the call looking irritated. She mumbled an insincere apology and explained that Harriet was going to run the meeting to deal with what was a very sensitive issue. On finishing this half-hearted introduction, she got up from her chair and disappeared from the screen. Joe wouldn't have been surprised if she'd popped off to get her knitting to distract from the tedium of him get booted. Instead, she returned with a workbook and a pen.

The opening question from Harriet was not what he expected.

'Tell me, Joe, would you say Chloe is a bully?'

'Well, she tried to steal my lunch money a couple of times.'

Harriet's features froze into a death-mask of contempt.

'This is not a laughing matter.'

'Sorry, go on. Have I done something wrong?'

'Not yet. We need your help with a complaint we've had about Chloe.'

Relief flooded over him as he realised he wasn't being whacked. He tried not to punch the air at the reprieve and his catastrophising of the past hour now seemed ridiculous. In his euphoria, he didn't really process that Chloe might be in trouble. Chrissie looked up from her notes and spoke quietly.

'This is potentially a nasty problem, so please think very carefully about your answers.'

Joe straightened in his chair as Harriet continued.

'What is your relationship with Rick Evans?'

'Our new advertising manager?'

'Yes.'

'Well, we're not dating like I did the last one.'

'For God's sake, Joe, could you possibly act your age for a second.'

Chrissie's patience had vaporised, and he knew that being embarrassed was not an adequate excuse for being an idiot.

Harriet asked the question again, her voice hardening.

'One more time. Please can you tell me about your relationship with Rick.'

'We don't have one. He's been in the business for about two months. We sit in meetings online and I read the scripts he prepares. I've only met him in person twice, I think.'

'Do you remember being in a meeting with him and Chloe to discuss the script for Skin-X beauty products last month?'

'Yes, we struggled to work out how to promote the product. From memory, its ingredients sounded like the fallout from Chernobyl.'

'Did Chloe get angry with Rick?' asked Harriet earnestly.

'I think we both got frustrated because he was being very inflexible.'

'And do you remember her calling him "dim-witted"?'

Of course he did. Rick was a cretin and drove them both mad after he replaced Nicola, who had begun her MA in Family Therapy having adopted a more sober approach to life. Rick was a charmless, rude young man of limited intellect and competence. Chloe struggled to contain her irritation and often gave him short shrift. But there was no way he was going to share this information with Harriet.

'No, I don't remember her saying anything like that. Chloe is always polite to everyone.'

Pinocchio had nothing on him.

'And do you recall her saying to him at the end of that meeting, "come back when you can write in sentences that vaguely correspond to English"?'

'No. Again, that's definitely not language she'd use.'

In truth, he'd thought she'd gone over the top in that meeting, but there were extenuating reasons for her grumpiness: Mikey had been up vomiting the night before and she was exhausted and more stressed than usual. Plus, Rick had an arrogance that got under everyone's skin.

'Do you recall her telling him in a production meeting last week that his script to promote Adriana's Tacos and Tortillas "could have been written by a seven-year-old"?'

'No. No recollection whatsoever.'

Harriet leant forward and paused for dramatic effect.

'Are you aware that Rick is dyslexic?'

'I know nothing about him, other than he once mentioned he lives at home with his mother.'

Chrissie interrupted. 'He's spending more time at home with her now as we've had to sign him off sick with stress.'

Harriet corrected her. 'He has been signed off with stress. He has a *bona fide* medical condition.'

'Has his dyslexia flared up again?'

Joe was beginning to think the conversation daft, but Harriet was in no mood to thaw.

'Rick has made a detailed written complaint about Chloe's behaviour and we're investigating it now. We may have to suspend her.'

'That's ridiculous.'

'That's employment law,' she responded pompously.

By now, Joe realised that Chrissie's ambivalence was not directed at him but at the overzealous woman she had employed to handle

HR, whose attitude suggested she revelled in her own pedantry. He guessed that Chrissie wanted the incident to be forgotten, and he could now do something helpful for Chloe. It was hardly a murder trial, and she didn't deserve to have a tarnished reputation because of one incident of irritability.

'Harriet, let me tell you about Chloe. She is a very considerate person. She loves the team she works with, and she doesn't talk rudely to anyone other than me, which frankly I deserve, as you can probably tell from this conversation.' The declaration was heartfelt, and he intended to be a robust character witness for Chloe. 'She is professional and diligent,' he continued, 'and I'm not sure if Rick is looking to make a fast buck, but either way, he's lying through his teeth.'

He folded his arms and sat back, waiting for some comeback or complaint from Harriet. However, his speech-come-rant had derailed her from her script. She thanked him, explaining that she had everything she needed. If Joe said Rick was lying, then what more could she do? OK, Joe was lying a little, but it was for a noble cause. Besides, while Chloe had been sharp with Rick, Kelly had expressed serious misgivings as to whether he was up to the job in the first place. Joe was acting for the greater good.

Chrissie wrapped up the session and Harriet mumbled an insincere goodbye, looking disgruntled to have been denied the chance of a full-blown trial. When she had gone, Chrissie thanked Joe for his support, grateful he realised it was his job to protect his co-host. Yup, he had behaved like a modern-day Sir Galahad, nobly defending Chloe's honour in a way that only someone who really loves you can. She was bound to be impressed.

* * *

Chloe's wail of pain was so visceral that Joe knew it was more than a reaction to seeing his number flash up on her phone.

'Hello. Are you there?'

'I'm in agony.'

'Aren't we all. It's a cruel world.'

'No, you twat. I've done something to my back. It went into spasm this morning when I was dressing the kids and I've been lying flat on the floor all day. I reached for my phone and set it off again.'

Not the reaction he was expecting, Joe didn't want to be blamed for her pain. He imagined her grimacing on the floor of her bedroom, trying to move gingerly. He, on the other hand, had just come back from a long run and was full of boisterous endorphins. Hearing of her misfortune, he instinctively did a couple more calf stretches, in case talking on the phone increased the risk of pulling a muscle.

'I'm so sorry. I hope the pain passes.'

His attempt at sympathy made him sound like he was working in a care home.

'That's very solicitous. What do you want?'

'Have you spoken to Chrissie today?'

'Yes, she told me everything. It was quite a shock.'

'That I perjured myself for you?'

'I didn't realise you were under oath?'

'I wasn't, but wait till you meet Harriet from HR. She's definitely ex-KGB.'

Chloe let out a shriek.

'Ow, ow ow. Please don't make me laugh.'

'Sorry, it's a gift.'

'Then give it to someone else, I can't take the pain that it brings with it. Anyway, I didn't ask you to lie on my behalf. I need to apologise to Rick if my rudeness has made him ill.'

'Oh, for God's sake, he's fine. He's looking for a pay-off because he can't cope. Bring back Nicola, that's what I say.'

Chloe took a moment before replying.

'Do you mean at work or at home?'

'If I'm honest, perhaps both.'

For a while, he'd been wondering if there was any potential to revive their relationship. He looked out of the window at the coffee shop at the end of the road, succumbing to the nostalgia of their many happy breakfasts there without being able to accurately assess if he truly pined for her now. Joe moved to the sofa and stretched out in sympathy with Chloe lying immobile on the floor.

'Is Covid killing your dating life? It must be hard to meet someone new,' she said sympathetically.

'You know me. I don't really manage to move forward but I'm excellent at travelling sideways.'

'Are you lonely?'

'No, are you?'

'I have David.'

'That doesn't mean you're not lonely. Loneliness in a marriage, it's a dead common problem. Trust me, I podcast about that sort of thing.'

'You're very wise, it's unfathomable that you can't find love.'

'Come on. I risked prison for you this morning. At least tell me how things are going at home.'

'We need a new microwave. What else do you want to know?'

'Who do you love better, me or David?' He said this as a joke, although there was a part of him that thought he might have a chance of winning.

'Really? All right, you asked. David. You're a distant twelfth, behind my dental hygienist.'

'Is he still jealous of your success?'

'David's fine and picking up new commercial work now, plus he's doing a music video next week. It's all good. Stop asking such idiotic questions.'

'You don't sound convinced.'

'What do you want me to say? Since I may never walk again, at least let me be optimistic about my marriage. Why are you fishing around for problems?' Her back pain was now augmented by palpable irritation.

'I don't know, maybe I'm trying to see if things have changed?'

She was right, he was trying to find some small fracture in her love for David that might grow worse with a little pressure from him. Restless, he got up from the sofa and started to pace.

'What things?'

'Can I be honest?'

'It sounds like you've struggled with that today.'

'I think about you all the time.'

After an age, she replied in a whisper.

'I think about you a lot too.'

'Good? Bad?'

'Mainly ugly.'

'What does that mean?'

'Just that these thoughts are not helpful to either of us. This is so messy.'

He was glad they were speaking on the phone and not in the same room, with him desperate to kiss her again. He clenched his fist in frustration, the sudden intimacy of the conversation making him ache for the possibility of what might have been. Despite the strong urge to probe for more affection, the right thing was to give her an opportunity to escape these needy outbursts from him.

'Do you want to stop working together, would that be easier? I've got the impression recently you'd happily go solo. Or is that just Mary trying to dump me?'

Her response was surprisingly vehement.

'No, I don't want that at all. I'd miss you. Besides, you did a lovely thing for me today. It's very chivalric to trash an innocent man's reputation like you did. I owe you at least another series.'

'I need the job, but I don't know how much longer we can go on like this.'

'Let's not have this conversation now. I mean, on the news tonight it says we're going into lockdown again. At this rate, we don't really have to see each other for ages. We're too good working together to stop now. I'll even let you get a word in occasionally.'

'I suppose.'

He tried to sound diffident, but he was overwhelmingly relieved both to still have the job and to not have to exile himself from Chloe. Now it was her turn to be provocative.

'And you'll need the money to support your unborn test-tube baby.'

'Emily told you.'

'Did you doubt she would?'

'No, although she did give me at least three lectures about why I wasn't allowed to say anything. I suppose it's because she was marking her friendship turf. So, what do you think?'

'I think it's none of my business and I'll kill you if I'm not the godmother.'

'Am I mad doing this? What a mess my life is.'

'Not messy, just not that neat.'

'Well, that clarifies things. Now could you give me a concrete opinion?'

'All right. I think concrete is a marvellous building material and I'm happy if Emily is happy.'

'What about me?'

'I think about your happiness all the time.'

Despite them agreeing to avoid personal revelations of their feelings, they seemed to flow spontaneously and uncontrolled in their conversation, as if they were each daring the other to commit to a more definitive declaration. As he toyed with saying something he might regret, Joe could hear the twins now shouting for her with increasing frenzy. Their screams were obscured by the staccato yelps of pain from Chloe as she obviously tried to get up.

Eventually, she managed to speak, her voice an octave higher because of the effort.

'God, it hurts getting up. I know how Paralympians must feel.'

'First the dyslexics and now the disabled. I really should have you cancelled.'

'Where's David? Why isn't he helping you?'

'Downstairs. He's had a difficult day and is a bit low.'

'But he still wants you to deal with the kids when you can't move?'

'It's complicated?'

'No, it's not. What sort of person leaves someone in pain?'

She was now sounding very defensive.

'He's been great. Made me dinner and is bringing me cups of tea. It's just he's had some bad news about his latest writing project.'

'Has he realised that you're more talented than him?'

'Ow, Joe, please stop. It's not like that and you should butt out.'

'All I can say is that if I was your husband, I'd crawl on my hands and knees to stop you crawling around on yours.'

'That doesn't make any sense. Why wouldn't you walk to help me if I couldn't walk?'

'You know what I mean, and he doesn't deserve you if that's how he behaves.'

The conversation had become yet another skirmish in which Joe tried to ascertain Chloe's feelings, groping in the dark of his own confusion. By now he was unable to distinguish between his love for Chloe and his fractured pride at once being rejected, a pain that had worsened as he got to know of David's multiple deficiencies.

Today was not going to be the time for further deliberation, however, because after shouting in pain and anger '*Will you just let it go*', Chloe ended the call, leaving him once more to the silence of a claustrophobic flat. For the next few minutes, he tried not to think about the conversation as he began his post-run ritual of making a protein shake with whatever he could find in his fridge and a huge scoop of peanut butter to mask its taste. When he had drunk it and washed up the detritus of its preparation, he got into the shower and stood for a long time trying to clear his head from the throbbing intensity of a single thought that no amount of amateur meditation could eviscerate.

How on earth could he co-parent a child with Emily and then hope to end up with Chloe. My God, what an idiot!

April 2021

Perched on a stool, Chloe stared into the small mirror and dabbed her cheeks with blusher. Having emerged from another lockdown, the world was in a state of limbo, desperate to return to quasi-normality but unable to do so without lateral flow tests, masks and social distancing. On a film set, that meant there were no make-up artists to help you look good, so she was trying her best to make herself look like a sophisticated broadcaster rather than a frazzled writer who, in truth, often borrowed scrunchies from her seven-year-old daughter.

The uber-keen runner arrived back from Starbucks with her coffee, and Chloe realised that she couldn't quite remember her name. Was it Dakota, Indiana, Chelsea, Rio? It was something geographical.

'Here you go,' the young woman said, handing her a cup and a paper plate with a croissant. Not wanting to be rude, Chloe ventured a guess, thinking it a city in Europe.

'Thank you so much for looking after me, Paris,' she mumbled.

'It's Florence, actually, and it's such a pleasure to be working with you. I can't wait to read your book.'

'That's very kind, and I hope I don't disappoint you.'

'I bet it's brilliant,' Florence said enthusiastically.

Chloe was especially proud of the book and excited for its publication. Unfortunately, Covid made it impossible to have a traditional launch party so her publisher had come up with this elaborate idea to film a message and release it through social media. Her speech was going to be enhanced by a host of well-known personalities giving effusive endorsements for the novel, *Half Full or Half Empty*.

When the idea for a film arose, Chloe volunteered David as director, assuming he'd be delighted to collaborate. He cited the post-production schedule of his latest commercial as a clash and pretended to be mortified at not working with her. His sincerity did not overcome her suspicion that he viewed the project as more akin to a corporate video than a showcase for his talent and, despite his meek apology, was relieved to have a credible excuse.

Coffee in hand, she watched the crew lighting the set, an ultra-modern desk piled with books, notes and an open MacBook, as if recreating her fictitious study. It looked like a page out of the IKEA catalogue for a new range of workspaces with a silly Scandi name like *Flumkst*. At home, she wrote on an antique mahogany table that was rarely used for entertaining. She was a messy worker and the rainbow of Post-it notes stuck on every surface was yet another thing that seemed to irritate David these days.

The winter lockdown had been a struggle. The twins needed the structure of school, so more online classes supervised by resentful parents proved problematic. David and Chloe did their best to take responsibility, but it didn't help that they were both only comfortable supervising English homework. When it came to maths, their teaching methods involved huge amounts of bluffing.

As ever, the tension arose from the conflict of their respective professional ambitions. The momentum of Chloe's success made her much in demand. She now had a support team, including Mary's assistant, Josh, who managed her diary, and Tabitha, a freelance social media consultant, who cajoled her throughout the day to think about how to broadcast compelling content from the minutiae of her life. She hated having to curate this version of herself, but there was little option if she wanted to maintain the trajectory of her career.

Things were also looking up a bit for David, who had several non-advertising projects in different stages of development with resurgent self-belief increasing his unreasonableness. Chloe tried to retain perspective, appreciating their problems were the result of flourishing careers, and this was a blip caused by the pandemic, not their lifestyle. Things would improve when they could find a live-in au pair again.

Besides, their life was not perpetual conflict. Sometimes, at the end of the day, they found space to discuss their work over a nightcap and even make companionable love before falling into exhausted sleep. The following morning, however, the battle for time away from the children would recommence. She knew that all marriages evolved into the complex logistics of shared arrangements. But was the root of her discomfort tiredness, or just plain disappointment?

As the final preparations for shooting were made, she hoped she would come across as an accomplished presenter with her normal crisp, precise diction rather than a novice politician reading the autocue at a party political broadcast. The problem was, she had written her own script and was struggling to sound convincing throughout. One section was proving particularly challenging.

'And to my husband, David, I just want to thank you for the encouragement to bring this idea to life and for giving me the space and time to write it while you patiently looked after the kids and rustled up a cordon bleu dinner with the rotting contents of our fridge.'

Who was she kidding?

* * *

The afternoon filming passed without incident, and she was able to meet Emily in Regent's Park. The friendship was increasingly important to her, even if frantic schedules allowed them to catch up intermittently. Things had been difficult for Chloe, balancing her success with a robust social life. She had a coterie of good mates from her school, university and early working life, but in the nearly ten years of marriage to David, they had struggled to develop a distinct group of shared friends to hang out with together. She couldn't put her finger on why this had happened, given she was an outgoing person who thrived in company. David's old friends were sufficient for him, and so they often socialised separately.

Emily now had a grand title at her cosmetics company that Chloe could not remember but which included words like Executive, Chief, Vice, Senior, President, and was accompanied by an enormous salary that allowed her to live like minor royalty. When they met in their first term at university, Emily boasted an eclectic wardrobe from charity shops and theatrical costumiers. These days, her elegance was intimidating for normal mortals without recourse to a personal stylist.

She got to the café and saw Emily waiting at a table. Conscious that she was late, she opened her arms for an apologetic hug. Emily was not particularly tactile, and Chloe could sense her uneasiness by the little pats she was giving her on the back rather than a full-on embrace. After about thirty seconds, she freed Emily from the burden of being affectionate and plonked herself down on the wooden bench.

'Sorry, Em. Busy day and the shoot overran a bit.'

'You're forgiven. I've known you twenty years and you've only been on time once. And that was by mistake.'

'Punctuality is a bourgeois concept.'

'So is artisanal coffee, but I still bought you one.'

Chloe reached for the large cup and winced as she took a sip.

'What on earth is that?'

'Chai latte. It's mine. This one is yours.'

Emily passed her a smaller cup, with a flat white that had gone cold.

'I don't know how you drink that, Em. It tastes like tepid custard mixed with mayonnaise. Maybe we can walk to the pub to get a proper drink?' Chloe got up and then immediately sat down again. 'Oh, I'm so sorry, what was I thinking. Of course, you're not drinking. Where are you with the latest round?'

Emily shook her head.

'Not this time, I'm afraid.'

Despite her surprise at Emily choosing Joe as her donor, Chloe had desperately wanted them to be successful and this second failure must have been devastating for her. Now she worried that she might say the wrong thing; she had in the past misjudged her friend's emotional distress, assuming her to have a flinty resilience, which wasn't always the case.

'How are you doing?' Chloe asked.

Rummaging in her handbag, Emily produced a pack of cigarettes and a lighter and offered one to Chloe, which she accepted. Emily lit them both and for a second they sat in silence.

'Well, I might as well behave like a kid if I'm not going to be able to have one myself.'

Chloe patted Emily's hand, which was the lowest level of physical contact she thought she could get away with.

'I'm so sorry. It's totally unfair. What are you going to do now?'

'I'm going to give up. Two rounds are enough. It's not the money, it's the whole awful process of appointments, injections and false hope. It's agony.'

'I can only imagine.'

'I'm not sure you can. David smiled at you in the hallway, and you got pregnant. I remember that's how you put it. Well, let me tell you, IVF is so clinical and there's very little to smile about.'

'How did Joe take it?'

At the table behind them, two mothers were jiggling their babies and talking in sing-song voices. She hoped Emily wouldn't turn round and see them. Fortunately, Emily seemed oblivious.

'Ah, Joe. Therein lies a problem.'

'What do you mean?'

'I think he got carried away with the prospect of fatherhood. Maybe I didn't think it through properly, I just wanted a child who was intelligent and had a good sense of humour, so I decided he'd do. He's not exactly mature and my expectations of his involvement were low, which made it seem a good idea and guarantee I'd have the child to myself. Remember, I was locked down in Leamington with my mother, desperate for a new life.'

'And?'

'He surprised me by suddenly becoming the model partner for such an unusual venture. Reliable, attentive and kind. Who knew?'

'I didn't. It was a conversational no-go area for us.'

'Do you know what I think?' Emily took a long drag of her cigarette.

'Tell me.'

'His behaviour was all about you. On the one hand, he wanted to prove that he could start a sort of family of his own. But I also think he was trying to tell you that he'd grown up. That he was somehow a safe bet.'

'What are you saying?' Chloe asked.

'OK, well, since you appear a bit obtuse about affairs of the heart despite your podcast, I'd say that Joe is completely stuck in your orbit. He's like a broken satellite going round in circles.'

'I don't think that's true. He was going to have a baby with you. He wanted to break free.'

'Or by staying connected to me, it meant that he was even more part of your life.'

That was enough self-analysis for one day and Chloe needed to change the subject immediately, especially as Emily's failed IVF was much more important.

'I want to talk about you. Tell me what I can do.'

'There is one thing, come to mention it.'

'Anything. I'll even take your mother out for dinner.'

'I've met someone.'

'What do you mean?'

'It's not that complicated. Boy meets girl. Girl's heart is all a-flutter?'

'You're joking?'

'I'm not a complete sociopath, you know.'

Chloe shook her head.

'We'll agree to disagree. But you've taken me by surprise. How did it happen?'

'It's a very straightforward story. We met online in January during lockdown and dated on Zoom without meeting for weeks.'

'You're kidding?'

'I don't know if you remember, but there were restrictions about meeting strangers, and I was trying to stay Covid-free as part of my IVF.'

'That's so romantic.'

'It was. And I'm normally about as romantic as Darth Vader.'

'So, when did you meet?'

Emily counted her fingers as if it was a complicated answer. Her voice sounded different, and she had the nervous smile of a schoolgirl discussing boys she liked in the playground.

'About four weeks ago, outside at a pub. It was very nerve-racking because we knew each other so well from these incredible conversations but had no idea what the other was like in the flesh. He could have reeked of terrible BO.'

'Did he?'

'No, fortunately he's big on showering.'

'That's amazing.'

'Yes, unexpected, crazy, delirious too. The adjectives are endless, and it certainly softened the IVF disappointment.'

'And how's it going now?'

Emily smiled with evident satisfaction.

'We're talking about moving in together.'

It was hard for Chloe to assimilate so much information – after all, it had only been a few weeks since they last spoke and suddenly her friend's life had changed dramatically.

'"One door closes, another opens",' was the best Chloe could muster in response.

'How beautifully you encapsulate my happiness in a cliché.'

'I'm a writer, words are my arrows. Now, there was a favour you wanted me to do a few minutes ago. What was it?'

'I want you to tell Joe.'

'Tell him what?'

'That his services will no longer be required.'

'You want me to end it with Joe for you?'

'You've got the right experience on your CV.'

'Shouldn't he hear it from you?'

'I will speak to him in time, it's just I think he may be crushed, and I'm not sure I can cope with his disappointment when things are so happy for me.'

'I don't know, Em, if that's fair on me. Things are weird enough with Joe as it is.'

'I've thought about this and here's my logic. When you talk about me, you'll find out how he's feeling about you, I'm sure of it. Sweetheart, you need to make a difficult decision about your future, and this might help. The bloke has never stopped loving you.'

'You think so?'

'Pretty much. And if I'm wrong, you've done me a big favour anyway.'

It was all too much to process, and Chloe got up from the wooden bench thinking a brisk walk and some forward motion would be helpful. She tugged Emily's sleeve to join her, motioning to a path surrounded by flowering camellias.

'I'm definitely going to call you more regularly now, if this is what happens when I don't. Now, get off your arse so you can spend the next hour telling me about this nameless lover who's changed your life and I'll let you know if I'm willing to let you carry on seeing him.'

They linked arms and started to walk.

'Can we not talk about Joe for a while? I'd find that helpful,' Chloe said seriously.

Emily stopped to face her.

'We can give it a go, but you'll last five minutes.'

July 2021

After months of radio silence, Joe texted Nicola to ask if they could meet. She didn't reply for a day and then messaged him back that *your post-lockdown blues are not a good enough reason to go backwards*. Undeterred, he spent half an hour trying to think of something to make her change her mind. He would have preferred a chat on the phone, but Nicola believed it should only be used for speaking in an emergency. In the end, the best he could come up with was a silly message he hoped might make her smile.

Do you know the proverb 'as a dog returns to his vomit, so a fool repeats his folly'? Promise if you come out, I won't throw up ... x

It worked, and a few days later they met for a drink, the long sunlit summer's evening giving their reunion a backdrop of optimism. Sitting in a pub garden, they chatted for hours about his work, her course, friends, and vague hopes for the future.

Nicola had changed since starting her MA in counselling. It wasn't just that her hair was much shorter and a different colour. The ebullience of their former dating had been replaced by an earnestness unseen on their party nights out, when their most serious conversation was whether to get a cab or take the Tube home. She was ensconced in her studies, which involved intense therapy, and this made her question her values and assumptions. She was happy to see Joe but decidedly wary.

He hoped that three years of presenting a show about relationships now made him appear to her wiser and more insightful. Nevertheless, he couldn't bring himself to reveal everything about his life, omitting the bit about being a sperm donor for a former lover and possibly co-parenting a child. There was no need as that chapter was now closed, and he certainly didn't want to revisit his extreme disappointment when Emily called him a few weeks back to say their second round of IVF hadn't worked and she was calling it a day.

He also didn't discuss the excruciating moment a week later when Chloe pulled him into a meeting room at the Listen Up offices to explain that Emily had fallen in love with a mystery man. Unable to provide further information, Chloe had stuttered with embarrassment as she explained the scant details of this unexpected romance. The incident was bizarre. He was irritated that Emily couldn't tell him directly and confused by how inarticulately Chloe was imparting the basic facts.

Their interactions had been more distant for a while now. Since the winter lockdown, he met Chloe mainly in meetings on Zoom and recordings in person, maintaining a distant professionalism and avoiding personal discussion. Having half declared his feelings, Joe assumed Chloe was trying to focus on her marriage and it was therefore best that he sublimated his affection. He knew she had uncomfortable feelings; it was just that her life was not free for him to ruin. It was therefore time to move on from the stasis of the last year and, like a serial offender being released from prison, make yet another fresh start.

When he kissed Nicola by the wheelie bins of her new flat at the end of the evening, she surprised him by suggesting a weekend away as soon as possible, to put things to the test. She wanted to revisit what had attracted them to each other in the first place. As they planned their trip, he began to worry he'd be attending a couples' retreat with therapy sessions rather than a mini-break with lots of time in the spa. Nicola explained that she was unwilling to commit if he was emotionally unavailable. He simply hoped that the sea breeze of a Norfolk beach would be like a jolt from a defibrillator to get things going again.

Something felt awry, however, from the moment they left London. Their car journey to the hotel had been mainly spent in silence listening to music, and an accident on the A1067 outside Norwich made them arrive late. The hotel was half full and socially distanced, its ambience funereal. Guests milled around deserted lounges wondering if their recent third Pfizer jab would keep them safe from the Covid fumes dispersed by the overzealous air-conditioning units, and everyone spoke in a whisper.

Joe regretted his choice as they stood at the empty reception desk. After a couple of minutes waiting, he rang the bell like they were in the lobby of a shabby seaside guest house in 1973 and joked with Nicola that there was a strong possibility the staff had been murdered by zombies. How different from the weekend breaks they had enjoyed in hip boutique hotels in Berlin and Copenhagen before the pandemic, when their relationship was flourishing.

The restaurant in the hotel was understaffed and shoved its unwilling guests on to a bleak terrace in the chill of a blustery July evening. Because they missed their booking time, their meal was heated up in the microwave and thrown at them by a grumpy waitress exhausted from wearing a surgical mask all day and washing her hands each time she had to bring out a plate. The gravy on Joe's chicken main course had congealed like his prospects for the weekend.

Finishing quickly, they adjourned to the empty bar with a second bottle of red wine, the silence of the hotel amplifying their separateness. He reached for Nicola's hand, but she was in no mood for any physical contact.

'What are you thinking?' he asked.

'Other than I never want to have a meal like that again, perhaps this is a mistake.'

'Why is it a mistake? We haven't given it a chance,' he said defiantly.

'You're never going to love me, Joe. We get on well enough, but we won't make each other happy,' she replied, without sounding upset.

'Is it because I'm so much older and you're worried you'll have to look after me when I get dementia?'

Nicola shook her head. 'No, it's not that at all.'

'Is it because you want to marry for money, and you've realised because I booked this shithole that clearly I don't have any?' He wasn't sure why he was being so flippant when Nicola clearly wasn't.

'Joe, please don't make me say it. I don't want to ruin what's been the nicest evening since my granny died.'

The waiter approached their table and asked them if they wanted anything further from the closing bar, as if they were now outstaying their welcome. When he slouched away, Joe tried to sound more serious.

'How can you be sure this can't work between us? We've hardly spoken.'

'Exactly. You've said nothing. Not in the car. Not over dinner. I've tried to get you to talk but apart from wisecracks about this place being like a downmarket Bates Motel, you haven't told me anything.'

'That's unfair. What do you want to know?'

'Oh, for *fuck's* sake, Joe. Do you really want me to explain to you how you're incapable of loving someone new because a piece of you was ripped out by Chloe and you don't work properly?'

'Wow. Where did that come from?' he said, surprised by her vehemence.

'I asked after Chloe in the pub when we met. You said she's fine and looked away. I asked again in the car. You said the same thing. Over dinner, I asked you how Chloe had been, locked down with David, given you always told me he was jealous of her success. Do you remember what you said?'

'I think I said, *how would I know?* Something like that.'

'Exactly, you wouldn't address the situation. Three strikes and you're out, I'm afraid. I needed to understand if your head is clear, and I don't think it is. It's OK that you have confused feelings for her, it's just I need someone who comes with a more open mind.'

'I think you're being unfair,' he replied, knowing that she wasn't.

'I just know, Joe, your heart isn't in this. Love is exciting and enthusiastic. Let's not pretend you are either.'

She was right. It was like being immune to the effect of a drug. He could pretend to be happy being with Nicola but the more he tried to force a reaction, the less forthcoming it was.

Back in their room, they undressed separately in the bathroom. She emerged in heavy pyjamas, as if at a teenage friend's house for a sleepover. The weather had shifted, and rain was now splattering against their window. Like siblings sharing a bed on holiday, they moved as far from each other as they could without falling out. He wasn't angry and he suspected she wasn't disappointed. Switching off the lights, he contemplated giving her a peck on the cheek to remind her he was happy to just be her friend.

Instead, he simply said, 'I checked my app. The forecast is terrible for tomorrow. Storms.'

'I hope you like Scrabble then,' she replied wearily. 'I may also make a start on my next assignment. I brought my coursework with me just in case.'

September 2021

She had been dreading lunch with Mary and Chrissie. While she liked them both, she feared their directness, and after a difficult eighteen months would have preferred to muddle along a bit longer without being forced to decide her professional future with Joe. Arriving early at The Wolseley, she sipped sparkling water and absorbed the lunchtime atmosphere while waiting for the others to arrive. She hadn't been there since that time with Joe three years previously, and nostalgia for that moment of guilty excitement overwhelmed her.

After a few minutes of daydreaming, she saw Mary marching behind a waiter, looking more manic than usual.

'Is everything OK?' Chloe asked, wondering why her agent looked so animated.

'Too right. I am bloody fantastic. I've got major *fucking* news. I've asked Isaiah to marry me, and he's said yes. Not that he had a choice.'

Chloe had given up trying to understand what was going on between the hirsute PhD student and Mary. They seemed to split up at least twice a year. Mary would ring and tell her how her heart was breaking and her plans to murder him. Then, miraculously, they would reunite when Mary threatened to shoot his granny.

'Congrats, my love. I wish you a lifetime of profanity together. Now, I want to hear all the details. Did you get down on one knee? Did he cry? How many carats is his ring? What did his dad say when you rang for permission?'

Mary shook her head angrily as she sat down at the table.

'Honestly, Chloe. Could you try to be happy for me instead of taking the piss?'

Chloe was flabbergasted. She would never want to come across as unkind, especially when discussing anyone's relationship. Mary's typical aggression had made her develop this carapace of sarcasm to protect herself and now her agent was properly riled.

'Just because you make fun of relationships on your podcast,' Mary continued, 'who are you to tell us all what makes a couple work? I mean, your own marriage is unfathomable for a start, and you've never recovered from dumping Joe, as you tell everyone in each episode. So, stop judging me, please.'

Her vehemence rendered them both silent. A waiter arrived to pour water in their glasses, and they stared in different directions. Chloe eventually spoke.

'I'm sorry I upset you, that would never be my intention. I'm very happy for you and Isaiah. Really, I am.'

Mary gave a tiny nod, like she was acknowledging a casual acquaintance she passed on the street. How had she managed to pick a fight with Mary when all she wanted to do was congratulate her?

The froideur was fortunately melted by Chrissie's arrival and several rapidly consumed glasses of champagne. Soon, Mary was regaling them with stories about how she proposed to Isaiah while they were having a shower together, and how she was mandating he took her name. When their starters arrived, Chrissie clapped her hands, signalling that it was time for business.

'Enough small talk. Let's get down to why we're here. What on earth are we going to do with this podcast of ours?'

'I suppose I should say something sensible at this point,' Chloe ventured.

'That would be appreciated,' Mary said, as if still angry with her for her earlier comments.

'I'm well aware you both want me to go solo from now on. I'm just not sure I can do this to Joe. He'd be in dire straits without the podcast and the opportunities it brings.'

'I think you mean the opportunities I bring him. I wouldn't worry, love. There aren't too many of those these days. In fact, this morning I wrote to tell him I was no longer going to represent him. I've given him to my feckless assistant Josh to look after. That should put an end to his career.'

'There's no need to be cruel,' Chloe said defiantly, but she knew she was outflanked.

'Can I say something?' Chrissie interrupted. 'I think we should pause on the podcast after we finish the tour. I fear that the show's strength may also be its long-term limitation.'

'What do you mean?'

'Let's be honest, Chloe, its format needs a major refreshing. You've done an amazing job recruiting so many top-name guests and even better teasing out such intimate revelations. It's just getting harder to find willing volunteers to bare everything for your fans. And it's becoming clear that the show at present is waning in popularity.'

'I feel like you're going to tell me that you still want to be friends and it's you, not me.'

'Far from it. I think we may just need a break and a reset, and …'

'And what?'

'I'm afraid it's *sayonara* Joe.'

'What if I don't want to stop working with him? He makes me better. He's the perfect foil for me and I feel wittier and sharper when I'm next to him.'

'Then fucking marry him, but it's time you go solo. You've outgrown him,' Mary shouted, so loudly that the suited businessmen on the table next to them stopped their conversation and stared at her.

Chloe had a painful flashback to ending her relationship with Joe, when she told him the same thing. She was mortified at the prospect of him feeling this rejection afresh. Chrissie was nodding in agreement.

'She's right. It's not your fault your career is moving faster than his. *Ex-Communicate* is a fantastic property in need of a revamp. You have so many projects on the go, I suggest you have a break, and we work on its evolution. I think it can become even bigger. What if we move away from former romances and feature different relationships that have ended – professional, business, sporting, sibling? Think of the potential.'

Chloe knew these were strong ideas meriting proper consideration, but she wasn't prepared to navigate this change without Joe. Besides, they had a huge tour to get through first. Eight shows in two weeks, it would require a monumental effort from her to perform brilliantly. If that wasn't hard enough, she was committed to delivering the first draft of her next novel to the publisher six weeks later, which would mean writing before and after each show. This was, however, an ultimatum from her team, not a referendum, and there was nothing to be done other than think about what they'd said while hoping that Chrissie and Mary would miraculously change their minds.

Over coffee, Mary raved about the brilliance of Chloe's writing, reminding her that *your fricking book is flying off the shelves like hand sanitiser in the pandemic.* Indeed, its recent launch in the US had exceeded all their expectations and meant that Chloe was now working on the film script too. Her lunch companions didn't notice her turmoil as they plotted her rise and rise. Their voices became like white noise as she drowned in anxiety and silent fear. As Chrissie paid the bill, Chloe turned to her and restated her commitment to Joe.

'I've heard everything you've said, and I know that I have some thinking to do. But what about Joe? What do you expect him to do?'

Chrissie and Mary exchanged indifferent glances. Mary, half-cut and unsteady, spoke for them both.

'Not really our concern. But I suppose he could always go back to teaching. People always need teachers, no matter how miserable they are.'

12.10.2021

From: Joe Harris
To: Johannes Williams

Re: Job Application

Hi Johannes,

    I am delighted to apply for this role as Head of Comedy Faculty at your wonderful College of Live Performance in Melbourne. I have attached my CV and a compilation of some of my stand-up performances as well as examples of my podcast *Ex-Communicate*, which I believe has become quite popular in Australia.

    You have asked for a covering letter that '*makes your case to become head of a faculty that teaches people about laughter*'. Let me answer, therefore, some of your probable questions. (Apart from why I am still single with these incredible cheekbones.)

1. The last three years have been the most successful of my career. When I published my memoir, I thought that might be it for any attention to come my way. My career writing for other comedians was OK, but I had reconciled myself to relative obscurity and a scramble each month to pay the mortgage.
2. A chance encounter with my ex-girlfriend on a radio interview and a few months later I was presenting a podcast about relationships and what we can learn from them. We have done seven series, been a top five podcast and are now about to embark on a big tour for the show. So, you may say the suffering was worth it in the end and being dumped

by Chloe was the making of me, from a broadcasting perspective.

3. The trouble is, she is much better on the programme – a wise and insightful interviewer who doesn't just try to make jokes all the time. I am proud to work alongside her and not competitive, but self-aware that my success has been ignited by her brilliance rather than my intrinsic talent.

4. I think it's time for a change of scenery and a new beginning. Yes, I will be giving up the only creative project that has afforded me positive recognition and a reliable income. We all know that Chloe will be able to cope without me very easily, the show will improve, and no one will mourn my departure, apart from my mother who will say I am an idiot who doesn't grab opportunities for happiness. She tells me this most weeks.

5. Despite revealing my podcasting inferiority complex, I am a good comedian and comedy writer, as you will see from my CV. Having looked at the profiles of your current faculty, I believe I have a wealth of additional experience that will enhance and inspire your students. I am particularly adept at dealing with unpleasant hecklers and have the reflexes of Spiderman when avoiding beer glasses thrown at me, which I bet you don't teach at present.

6. Above all, I have nine years of classroom experience, teaching disinterested teenagers about the Reform Act of 1832. I am sure that a bunch of wannabe Aussie comics will be much more enthusiastic students, even if they aren't as good at irony as some of the fourteen-year-old thugs who ruined my life.

7. This letter is decidedly candid, which may seem odd for a job application. Working with Chloe on the podcast has taught

me that it's best to express your feelings directly to avoid future pain, something I haven't always mastered.
I wasn't looking to move across the world, but now that I have seen this job advertised, I realise it might be the best thing I can do now, personally and professionally.

In conclusion, I hope you agree, having read this note, that we'd be lucky to have each other, and I look forward to speaking.

    Regards,

    Joe Harris

January 2022

Chloe took a long swig from her water bottle to mask her irritation that David had arrived early and caught a glimpse of her puce post-workout face in the mirror. She had hoped after an hour in the gym to enjoy her gorgeous suite in The Lowry Hotel undisturbed. So far, she had been upgraded in each hotel on the tour while Joe had not been afforded the same treatment, texting earlier that his room was 'a laundry cupboard with a bed for a small child'. Instead, David had decided to get an earlier train and was sprawled across the bed in a dressing gown, like a rock star awaiting a groupie. He looked up from his laptop with a mischievous smile.

'Who knew there was an Albert Hall in Manchester? Two thousand, two hundred and ninety of your devoted fans, who will bay for your blood if you aren't hysterical,' he continued. 'I just googled its capacity. Much bigger than St George's in Bristol on Tuesday.'

'Are you here to encourage or terrify me?' she replied sternly. His cavalier welcome made her good mood evaporate and the benefits of the workout disappear. Why would he want to focus on the scale of these live performances, which he knew made her more nervous? While David had joined her for some of her shows, she wished he could show a smidgen of empathy.

They were trying to carve out some time together. The show was the penultimate on the tour and they were staying an extra day at 'The Lowry' to enjoy each other's company. However, a foreboding rose in her that the day would be interrupted by a collective need to distract themselves with their work.

Determined to make an effort, she sat on the edge of the bed, reaching for his hand in an overture of affection. They locked fingers briefly before David closed his laptop and slid over to put it on his bedside table on the other side.

'How were the children when you left?' she asked. 'I had a meeting first thing, so I didn't call them.'

'St Malcolm of Bergerac has everything under control. I think they wouldn't notice if we didn't come back until June.'

'We're lucky to have the help from him.'

The reassurance of Malcolm's presence was tinged with regret that Mikey and Alice, soon to be eight, were increasingly disgruntled about each bedtime she missed. It was such a struggle as she was so behind on her writing and did little else other than record the show and return to her room to finish her book.

Her defensiveness was an instinctive reaction to David, who was courteous to her father but showed him little affection. Having grown up with divorced religion-hating parents, David tolerated his vicar father-in-law but couldn't hide his disdain for Malcolm's faith. Chloe, in turn, would have rather put the kids up for fostering than turn to his selfish parents, who believed grandparenting required their presence no more than three times a year.

'I'm not sure Cristina is that happy to share the house with him while you're gone. You know how inflexible she can be,' David continued.

Their extremely competent new au pair had introduced a military regime to the household, which they were both afraid to challenge. Her father was a major in the Romanian army and Cristina treated their chaotic domestic life as a battle she had to win. Her presence had certainly calmed the simmering tensions of their demanding schedules, but it had also introduced a rigidity to their family interactions.

At the thought of the twins, an idea popped into her head.

'Given how much I've been away, let's book a trip for February half term. What about if we take them on the train to Paris for a few days? We can bore them with stories about why it's the city of love. Although in your case, the city of diarrhoea, if I remember our first time there.'

'That might be tricky. I've got that car shoot at the end of the month. I'll be right in the middle of pre-production. It's a nice idea. Maybe you go with them, and I'll try and join you for a night.'

'That's hardly quality family time though, is it?' she replied, resigned to the failure of yet another attempt to make things better.

David moved next to her and put his arm round her like he was her big brother. For a second, it felt comforting.

'Look, it's a busy time and we're finding our way. Things can't always be perfect. That's just the way it is and sometimes we need to compromise.'

She couldn't think what to say in reply to this barrage of platitudes. Did their life together just revolve around conquering its complex logistics? Wearily, she stood up and gave his cheek a half-hearted stroke before heading to the bathroom to get ready.

* * *

'Compromise is the death of passion. At least, that's what we found at the end of our time together.'

The phrase acted like a post-hypnotic suggestion for Chloe, and the immediate reminder of her unhappy conversation with David rendered her mute. An iridescent spotlight shone into her eyes, her vision blurring as her mind wandered in frustration. Not the ideal time for a loss of speech, with nineteen hundred expectant people (they hadn't quite sold out) waiting for her to say something funny. Words would not, however, form into a coherent sentence.

Sitting at a horseshoe table, their guests were senior doctors who had separated in the middle of Covid, having been together since medical school. The show now began with a chat with 'ordinary people' before the celebs arrived on stage, and Chloe had asked Carol, a forthright Scottish geriatrician, what had been the main cause of the demise of their marriage. Expecting her to say something about the pressures of medical life, she had been shaken by the answer that it ended because of too much compromise.

Silence.

Joe's eyes implored her to say something, but Chloe's mouth moved and nothing came out. For some reason, she remembered the time she forgot her lines in a play at university. Having called to the stage manager for a prompt, it came back so garbled she had to shout *line again please* and she was thereafter mocked incessantly by her friends in the audience that night. She was now experiencing the same paralysing panic, caused by her momentary lapse of concentration.

To her immense relief, Joe started ad-libbing with an effortless fluency.

'Looks like Chloe is having a flashback to when we used to date, and she would never compromise about anything. Back then, we'd only watch subtitled films that were her choice because they were wistful or elegiac and she would never see anything with guns or hand-to-hand combat. She never once came to a Spurs match with me, while she dragged me around art galleries filled with avant-garde installations like the one with a plinth of dog food cans and hoover bags, which she explained to me represented the disintegration of a moral framework in the nuclear family. Don't talk to me about compromise when the home we shared could only contain her pictures and ornaments. I suggested once that I'd like to display my trophy for "Most Improved Player" for the Wandsworth Warriors

Under 11s and she looked at me like I'd asked to put a picture of Mussolini on the wall. By the way, Chloe, your watercolour you insisted on hanging above our bed looked like it was painted for a GCSE project by a blindfolded one-armed child. And when it comes to compromise in a relationship, let me remind our audience that this doesn't mean a couple should visit one parent seven times more often than the other. I mean, I love your dad and all, but sometimes it felt like we were in a throuple.'

The audience whooped and the cheers shook Chloe from her distraction. She stood up as if it was now her turn in an election debate.

'Very amusing, Joe, if conveniently light on the facts. I was the model of conciliation when we were together and could have taught the UN a thing or two about peacekeeping. I tidied up after you and accepted that, for you, neatness was a skill practised by people on the spectrum and Germans. I didn't complain you never cooked for me and lived on your own esoteric diet of scrambled eggs and taramasalata. You left so many pubes in the bath, I could have weaved a wig, and it was irrelevant if you put the toilet seat down or up because you spent most of the time peeing on the floor anyway. I could go on.'

'Perhaps later. We have guests and I think we're being rude.' Joe smiled at Carol and her ex-husband, John, who were slightly bemused that their interview had been hijacked by the tennis-rally banter of their hosts. The audience was cheering, and Chloe made a little bow of acknowledgement before reprising the interview.

'Now, where were we before you were interrupted by my co-host's grandstanding? That's right, you were telling me about why compromise was so problematic.'

'The problem was that politeness prevailed, to the detriment of real emotion. Isn't that right, John?'

'Yup,' her ex-husband replied emphatically, adding the afterthought, 'you know, it's never that sexy if you have to say "please" and "thank you" every time you have a shag.'

Carol turned to Chloe.

'Our love became like a good friendship – we made plans, we were organised, we were punctual. We did everything we could to make the other person happy. But in a state of perpetual accommodation, it becomes harder to remember the unpredictable chemistry and connection that brought you together in the first place.'

The laughter had abated as the discussion grew more earnest. Staring into the audience, she saw David, sitting between Mary and Chrissie in the first row. It was all happening so fast she couldn't be sure, and maybe he was just shuffling in his seat, but it looked to Chloe that he was nodding in agreement.

* * *

It was undoubtedly their best show to date. Their main guests were Andrew Bailey and Leanne Bloch, a couple of actors from a TV cop show whose on-off screen relationship reflected their personal one, and for a while they were rarely out of the tabloids because of their messy domestic arrangements. The spontaneity of a live show and the rowdiness of the audience made for a very sparky dialogue. Chloe's initial introspection was replaced by ebullient self-confidence, which included getting them to confess some torrid stories about on-set lovemaking while both dressed as uniformed police.

Chloe and Joe reached a level of symbiosis they had never managed before. She finished his sentences and set him up with punchlines that he delivered like an old Las Vegas pro at Caesars Palace. Chloe had never experienced a rush like this before. She was not just a writer, she was a magnificent performer, manipulating the emotions of an adoring audience.

The show finished with the three-piece house band belting out their medley of love songs. For the tour, she'd thought it would be fun if she and Joe danced together on stage without looking like infirm pensioners at a family wedding. They'd had three lessons in advance with an instructor so that, for thirty seconds at least, they could look vaguely in time with the music. Joe had been reticent, but his opinion carried little weight, so he dutifully learnt his part and managed to execute a reasonable jive. Chloe was far less of a natural mover and had to count the steps out loud, hoping the audience wouldn't see her lips move. As the house band belted out their version of 'Don't Leave Me This Way', they danced like a couple who were never out of step with one another.

Coming off stage, the guests, crew and production staff were all high-fiving like they'd just won a major sporting event. Joe strode towards Chloe and enfolded her in an enormous hug. His black T-shirt was soaking with perspiration and his hair matted with sweat, but she didn't care as they held each other and rocked from side to side with jubilation and relief.

'You saved my life when I froze,' she said.

'What happened? I've often wished you would shut up, but this was hardly ideal.'

Given her confusion about Joe, she was conflicted about what to tell him. She saw David ensconced in conversation with Mary at the other end of the room. Her agent was aggressively prodding his chest with her forefinger, as if demonstrating a martial art. He saw Chloe and smiled enigmatically.

'Cat got your tongue again?' Joe continued. 'You haven't told me what you were thinking.'

Chloe still couldn't think of an answer. She remembered reading that criminals often confessed crimes because the burden of guilt made the need to be free from their dark thoughts overwhelming. For the last few years, she had camouflaged her feelings for Joe with misdirection and put-downs. Now the vestiges of her on-stage adrenaline overwhelmed her defences, and it was time to tell the truth.

'I dried up because when I'm around you, I wonder if being with David is a compromise.'

'Oh.'

'Oh, indeed.'

'And there's me thinking you were worrying about the weekly shop.'

'I'm sorry. I'm very confused by our chemistry.'

'Do we have chemistry?'

'I think we have more chemistry than a convention of pharmacists.'

They both smiled and Joe instinctively took a step towards her. She kept her hands rigidly by her side in order not to make physical contact of any kind, despite an overwhelming desire to express her affection. Her love.

'This is really not the best place to have this conversation?' Joe's expression was suddenly very serious.

'You did ask why I got stage fright. That's the reason.'

He shook his head as he spoke.

'How on earth could this work? You have a family. We can't go backwards, can we? It's too complicated. I don't know what you are saying.'

'Do you love me, Joe?'

She couldn't believe her bravura, initiating this seismic conversation when they could easily be overheard in the thrum of the post-show party. She didn't care. This moment was the inevitable consequence of her realisation that love doesn't always dissipate with the end of a relationship. Like a cutting from a beautiful flower, theirs had been replanted and was growing once more.

The flushed clamminess from two hours under bright spotlights was replaced by a chill that made her shiver. Why didn't he reply immediately? Joe was looking at his feet, avoiding her gaze, and eventually he spoke, slowly, as if each syllable had a deep meaning.

'Of course I love you. I've never stopped. I adore everything about you and thought I'd made that obvious. Well, I'm glad we got that out in the open. Any suggestions of what happens next?'

Before she could reply, she realised David was walking towards them, having finished his conversation with Mary. Smiling, he was by her side in an instant and slid his hand into hers proprietorially. She steeled herself for the awkwardness of the ensuing interaction and glanced at Joe, who turned his head away, presumably to compose himself.

'You were hysterical tonight, well done, mate.'

'Thanks, David, appreciate it,' Joe replied with a flatness that was obvious to her.

'It's lucky I'm so tolerant of all those gags about when you lived together. Anyone would think it was last week. Spot on, though.'

'How was Mary?' Chloe asked, trying to change the subject away from her and Joe.

'Bloody hell, her unsolicited suggestions on how to improve my script were fierce. Thank God she's not my agent.'

Chloe tried to smile, but the muscles in her mouth had frozen, her heart pounding from the awkwardness of the conversation. There was so much more she needed to say to Joe and now the opportunity had gone. Plus, it wasn't helping her guilty conscience that David, sarcastic and unsupportive before the show, was turning on the charm. After a few seconds in which no one could think what to say, her husband gave her hand a little tug, and he pointed towards the exit with his other one.

'Can we go back to the hotel now, Chloe? I need to get away from this circus. You don't mind loaning my wife back to me, do you, Joe?'

There was no suitable way for her to say goodbye in this situation. Joe forced a pinched smile and tapped David lightly on the arm in a gesture of unconvincing camaraderie. Chloe considered kissing him on the cheek, but that would have been inadequate after their earlier candour. Instead, like a chirpy teenager at the end of a night out, she made the shape of a phone with her thumb and little finger and, placing it to her ear, mouthed the words *call me*. David must have thought she was joking, but then he had no idea that he had interrupted a conversation that might change all their lives.

PART 5
SERIES FINALE

Three days later

Skipping down the steps of the hospital, Joe was delighted his father was coming out and this unpleasant episode was nearly over. The procedure was a success, and it was a relief to see Michael looking so much better, a far cry from the fear he experienced with the early-morning call from Dull Debbie after the Manchester show. Sobbing and struggling for breath, she'd just about managed to say the words 'heart attack' before wailing like a banshee with a migraine.

For a minute or so he'd thought his dad was dead, before she calmed down sufficiently for him to piece together what had happened. It was very scary. Michael had woken up in the middle of the night with sharp chest pains and Debbie had called an ambulance. (They could probably hear her screams across London.) Fortunately, within a couple of hours of arriving at the Chelsea and Westminster Hospital, the excellent emergency team diagnosed his blocked artery and mild heart attack, which required the insertion of a stent to prevent its recurrence the following day.

In those first few hours, as he rushed back to London, Joe tried to focus only on his father's well-being. The day was blustery grey as the train sped through the wintry countryside towards London. Just outside Watford, a fault on the line made them crawl for an hour and Joe texted every few minutes for an update from his sister in A&E, imagining some terrible resuscitation scene from a TV hospital drama with doctors sitting on his dad's chest doing compressions. He was not yet at Euston when Amy messaged her reassuring conversation with the doctor, who explained that everything was going to be fine.

Michael's recovery was quick and for the next couple of days he asked his children to protect him from Debbie, whose catastrophising meant she had probably already ordered her dress for the funeral and chosen a casket. Joe chatted and played cards with his father, while Amy had the much harder job of chaperoning her stepmother. His sister's exasperation grew with each hysterical interaction until she asked Joe if they could borrow a tranquilliser gun from a passing anaesthetist.

He texted Chloe to explain why he wasn't around. While he had been intoxicated by their declarations of love, his father's health scare had sobered him up quickly and the respite was fortuitous as it delayed confronting the many decisions he was facing, in addition to his love life.

The podcast's future was uncertain. Advertising revenue had decreased, and they had dropped out of the top twenty charts for UK downloads amid the competition of a myriad of new shows and formats launched daily. Given the next series was going to be these live shows, there was no new content required for a while. He had worked hard to finish a first draft of his novel but knew that a major rewrite was necessary before anyone was going to take it seriously and he didn't really know where to begin. Josh, his prepubescent agent, was proving ineffective at creating new opportunities; and while he was earning well from the tour, he suspected that his long-term prospects were diminishing and he'd soon need to consider gigs at the local Rotary Club for a bit of extra cash.

It was all serious stuff that would impact the next decade of his life, now made more complicated by the opportunity to be with Chloe. While chaining himself to Michael's bed for three days was one of his better avoidance tactics, time for delay had run out as his father no longer needed him. More importantly, Joe had to prepare for the last show of the tour the following day, their boldest and most ambitious to date. Featuring more guests and a bigger band at a world-famous venue, the Royal Festival Hall. What an appropriate place for him to face the music.

* * *

One of Chloe's happiest memories of her mother was their regular trips to children's concerts at the Royal Festival Hall. The music meant little to her at the time, but the visit to London and the walk along the South Bank took on a disproportionate significance after Alice died. So, when it was confirmed as the venue for the season finale, Chloe convinced herself irrationally that somehow this would make her dead mother proud.

With a day to go until the recording, she was feeling a little more prosaic about the event. Having not spoken to Joe since Manchester, she was uncertain what they would say when they met, let alone how easy it would be to perform together. To make matters more complicated, they had agreed their final monologues would be delivered without the other knowing what it contained. Kelly thought it would be a neat coda to the tour if they each wrote what they'd learnt about relationships and shared any wisdom gleaned from their interviews. Delivering these thoughts on stage without collaborating would supposedly make their insights more real.

Chloe was going to miss Kelly. His divorce from Jasmin was finalised and he was returning to the US much angrier than when he'd arrived. He still peppered his conversation with aphorisms that attested to the power of the human spirit over most forms of adversity, but his short-lived marriage left him harrumphing derisively when anyone made a positive comment in a production meeting about the nature of love.

Her plans now needed adapting after she found herself declaring her love for Joe in a backstage room at the Albert Hall, thirty feet from her husband. The following day, she and David stayed in the hotel, hardly speaking as they sat working at their computers. And it would have been more helpful without Michael's heart attack. When Joe texted to explain that he was not available, she assumed this was his way of finding space. Having not been together for seventeen years, there was clearly a lot to think about and if she was trepidatious at the prospect of throwing her life upside down, perhaps he was also overwhelmed.

Back and forth she went in trying to process what was happening. She thought she still loved David; it's just she had allowed her curiosity about Joe to diminish some of the attributes of their relationship. Maybe she was just like her mother after all, running into the arms of another person to compensate for unhappiness? She didn't believe it was possible to be in love with two people at once, yet here she was, giving a very good impression of someone who was.

The absurdity of being with Joe became clear when she thought about the twins. Raised an only child by a single parent, the moment she became a mother she vowed to create a family life that would cocoon them from the isolation of her own childhood. Pulling them away from their father would surely destroy that notion and create a time bomb of unhappiness that would explode at some point.

She reviewed Joe's attributes while waiting to speak to him. He made her laugh. His face was kind, his crinkly smile cute, and his ever-fluid hairstyles adorable. She admired his unwitting wisdom, insightfulness coupled with a self-deprecation that made him belittle his own creative achievements. She had always loved his mother, a feeling strengthened with time and exposure to David's mum, who was about as warm as a corpse. Chloe recalled her jealousy when he was with Nicola, as well as how the prospect of Joe potentially fathering a child with Emily had gnawed at her soul, which was surely a sign of love in some way.

This went on for days in her head until the necessity of preparing for the Royal Festival Hall required her to draft something. When the children had gone to sleep and David was still out drinking with some friends, Chloe sat in her kitchen to write her monologue.

Outside, the trees swayed angrily in a gusty breeze, and she reflected that in a day's time it would all be over. Filled with love for her children and flummoxed by this rekindled passion for Joe, she started typing.

The next day

Chloe waited for Joe at the stage door, but didn't want a long conversation before the performance. They had plenty of time to talk after the show, given David was away on a location search and Cristina was at home with the kids. Besides, she still wasn't entirely sure what she wanted to say to him. It reminded her of drafting her novel. Loosely plotting its action, she determined her characters' fate progressively with each chapter written.

The early evening was mild for midwinter, but her teeth chattered from nerves as she waited for him. After a few minutes, a frazzled Joe bounded down the stairs from Waterloo Bridge, trying to work out where he was meant to be going. As he neared the bottom, he missed his footing and lurched forward dramatically. Like a duckling learning to fly, he was momentarily airborne, arms flailing unhelpfully, before breaking his fall with his left hand and thigh at least two metres from where he started.

Several passers-by rushed to him, and he sat up slowly, holding his hand as if it was no longer part of his arm. Even in the watery-yellow street lighting, she could see the enormous graze on his hand and the blood that was beginning to seep. Before she could say anything, someone pushed past her and stood in front of her. It was Kelly, who had by coincidence arrived at the same time and witnessed Joe's aeronautical display.

'Easy there, fella. We need you in one piece for this evening. Can you move?'

Joe, still disoriented, carefully got to his feet with Kelly's assistance and for a second tottered giddily.

'Slowly, please,' Joe whispered. 'I feel a bit sick.'

They paused. Joe looked at the ground and took a few rapid breaths to compose himself, and Chloe moved towards him to support him by the other arm. When he realised it was her, his face broke into a thin smile.

'Oh. I assume you clocked that too?'

'Yup, your poor landing means I'm going to have to mark you down on technical, but it's full marks for artistic impression.'

Kelly interrupted her.

'I'm not sure he's ready to joke. We have a couple of hours to fix him up. Try not to distract him.'

'Sorry, you're right. Let's get him inside.'

'Thank you, Mummy, that would be lovely. What time are we going to the zoo?'

Kelly froze.

'Oh my God. He's concussed. We'll need to call an ambulance.'

Chloe knew from his expression that Joe was fine.

'I think he's winding you up. Isn't that right, *Simone Biles*?'

'Maybe a little. I'll be all right, although my leg is hurting so I'd appreciate a bit of proper medical attention if you don't mind. I'm going to need a shit-ton of Nurofen.'

Chloe leant towards him and kissed his cheek. To Kelly, it must have appeared that she was being solicitous, but she hoped Joe appreciated the love contained in that moment.

'I'll get you a horse tranquilliser if it means you don't complain. Now, please will you stop bleeding on my skirt. It's new.'

They were at the stage door and the security guard opened it for them, Joe walking gingerly but unaided. It was not the ideal start, and she hoped the evening would somehow improve.

* * *

He was patched up by Jamal, the venue's First Aid officer, who rubbed in some arnica and handed him two painkillers before resuming his day job as a lighting operator. Joe plonked himself in a dusty armchair in the corner of the reception area to recuperate and sipped a mug of steaming tea. With Chloe perched on a stool by his side, it reminded him of the last few days in hospital with his father.

A steady flow of production staff prevented him milking his accident further. First, Kelly wanted to know if he could walk and Joe demonstrated his mobility by jogging on the spot, despite the purple-black bruise on his thigh that was beginning to throb. Kelly then wanted to check he didn't have a brain injury, firing a series of random mental arithmetic questions at him. Joe was rubbish at all things maths, so convinced his producer he was fine by counting to ten in French and threatening to punch him if he didn't leave him alone.

Even Chrissie stopped by to ask several diffident questions about his well-being. It was galling being treated like his bad fall was the act of a deeply selfish individual and ruining the evening for everyone.

'If I pass out on stage, the show must go on. Please walk over me if necessary,' Joe declared, hoping someone might show a scintilla of sympathy.

Chrissie looked quizzical.

'I just wanted to let you know your fall happened outside the theatre so you can't sue us. But I'm sure some of the guys will set up a "Go Fund Me" page if your injuries are chronic.'

'Nice to know you've got my back, even if you don't care about my hand and leg.'

Satisfied she had fulfilled her management duties, Chrissie trotted off with Kelly without saying goodbye or wishing him luck for the show. Before Joe could say anything about their rudeness, he saw

Nicola walking towards them, clasping the hand of a tall, besuited man. Joe had forgotten he'd invited her. Now, to his surprise, she stood in front of him with a date whose floppy blond hair and piercing blue eyes made Joe instinctively stereotype him as a posh investment banker who chased foxes on a horse at the weekend.

'This is Giles,' Nicola declared.

Joe extended his uninjured hand and Giles squeezed it with such pressure that the pain was now evenly distributed between both.

'We just wanted to wish you luck. I'm so proud of what you've both achieved.' Nicola seemed a little edgy as she spoke, which seemed to Joe unnecessary. He was pleased she was seeing someone, even if the bloke clearly voted Tory and had more than one pair of wellies.

'We couldn't have done it without you finding us haemorrhoid creams and funeral homes to sponsor us,' Chloe interjected.

'Sorry. How rude of me. Giles, this is Chloe,' Nicola said coldly, without looking at her.

'Thank you. I guessed that it was.'

Joe gave a thumbs-up sign.

'It's so nice to meet you, Giles, although if I'd known you were coming, I'd have brought my duelling pistols.'

'Giles is more into kickboxing, so I don't rate your chances,' Nicola replied.

'I'll put a fiver on Giles for a first-round knockout,' Chloe said. Her love of a joke was not that helpful to Joe. He felt awkward enough as it was.

'So how are things going in the confused world of Chloe and Joe?'

Nicola asked the question with an edge that reminded him how difficult it was to sustain a friendship with her because he'd never quite been honest about the ambiguity of his feelings when they were together. Before he could mumble an anodyne reply, they were joined by another unexpected visitor to make their conversation even more complicated.

Emily.

'I know we called the show *Ex-Communicate*, Joe, but perhaps you're taking things a little far by having three of us in one place?' Chloe said, getting up to hug her friend and pat her visible bump.

Having never told Nicola about his relationship with Emily, it was hardly surprising she looked confused by her arrival. He had no choice but to make some introductions.

'Emily, this is Nicola and her boyfriend, Giles. Chloe, you know Emily, I believe. Giles, these are three woman I once dated, in all cases unsuccessfully. I think that just about clarifies everything.'

Nicola was staring at the clearly pregnant Emily as she tried to process what was happening and how it related to her. Sensing her confusion, Emily shook her head.

'Oh, not what you must be thinking? Nothing to do with Joe. My husband's the father. Last thing I heard, Joe was firing blanks.'

'Who would have thought little old me would be lucky enough to have been involved with three such fine women?'

The comment was offhand but true. Each relationship may have been imperfect but there was something beautiful and romantic in the time he had spent with them. Nicola, however, was in no mood to stick around and endure this bizarre encounter. Grabbing Giles's arm for support, she gave a half-hearted wave as she stepped backwards.

'Lovely as it is to be a part of "Ghosts of Joe's Girlfriends Past", we should take our seats. Hope it's a great show. I'm afraid we need to rush off afterwards, so will say goodbye now.'

Seconds later they were gone and Chloe and Emily smiled at one another, enjoying Joe's discomfort.

'Blimey, Joe,' Emily screeched, 'you really are an enemy to womankind.'

'Don't be like that, especially after everything we've been through together.'

'I'm teasing. I'm very grateful to you.'

'There's no need,' Joe replied earnestly. 'It was Covid. We both thought a child together was the answer.'

'That's not what I mean. It was because I tried with you that I became even more unhappy. And that's what helped me meet Lindsey.'

'I think there's a compliment in there somewhere, although I can't be sure. And while we're discussing your husband, you do know he's got a girl's name?'

'I should leave you two to get ready,' Emily said, ignoring him.

'Probably a good idea,' Chloe replied, kissing Emily on each cheek as she prepared to leave.

'You know I love you, Joe, don't you, although Chloe is still my favourite.'

A production assistant tapped his watch and mouthed *ten minutes*, the reality of an awaiting audience intruding with an urgency they couldn't ignore. A year ago, Joe's best chance of a different future had been with Emily and today he was simply a minor character in her unhappy past. God knows where he'd be in twelve months.

Chloe looked beautiful. He drew her into an embrace, and she clung to him.

'You clearly have a lot to say to me,' she whispered.

'I suppose I do.'

There was no time to absorb what was happening. A technician had arrived to fit them with their radio mics. They stepped apart, knowing it was time to concentrate on the show. In the two minutes it took to run wires through their clothing, they stood motionless and silent, interrupted eventually by the sound of an incoming text to Chloe's phone. She grimaced as she read the message, turning the screen to show Joe immediately.

Good luck x

David's supportiveness was not what Joe needed to think about now. He wanted Chloe for himself, and it would have been much easier if the person he needed to dislodge had the moral code of Rasputin. David, however, wasn't a tyrant – just jealous of his wife's success and not that empathetic to her needs.

There were over two thousand people expecting him to be funny and it wasn't going to be easy. The previous night, he'd been up until 3 a.m. writing his script, and the words now seemed inadequate and inappropriate. He had no other choice. He would speak from the heart and hope for the best.

* * *

CHLOE: Thank you to all our guests for making the last two hours so memorable. Special thanks to Molly and Joanna for coming up from the audience to tell us their story on the spur of the moment, which was so emotional. I speak for us all, Molly, when I say that we hope your chemo is successful, and what an amazing way for you to get back together.

A few thanks from me to our incredible team at *Ex-Communicate* and particularly to our producer for the last four years. Kelly, do you want to come and take a bow? Of course you do, put that bottle of tequila down and get on stage. Here you go, everyone, this is Kelly, who you've heard us refer to so many times for the endless advice he gives us. Who needs drugs to cure depression? A twenty-minute pep talk from him and you'll want to break into a rendition of your favourite show tune. Kelly is going back home to the States, and we'll miss him enormously. Our success is largely down to his brilliance, so let's give him a huge round of applause.

At the end of the show, you'll hear our house band 'Split Up' for their final set. You are all invited to stand up and dance. During this tour, you would normally be treated to the excruciating sight of me and Joe demonstrating our three hours of dance training, but Joe decided to maim himself with a nasty fall before the show, so you'll just have to imagine what it would have looked like. I'm a crap dancer, but it's a shame you don't get to see him because he is one of England's finest twerkers.

Well, that brings me to my final words for the evening and indeed this series. We decided we would try and share with our last audience of the tour some of the things we've learnt along the way on this podcast. Eighty-five shows, ladies and gentlemen. One hundred and eighty guests. Fourteen thousand two hundred and eighty-seven pretentious references to films, books, poems, songs from yours truly.

And despite all my unwanted pontificating, our audience has kept growing, which I suspect is because even if you're not a romantic like me, you are still interested in the private lives of the rich and famous. What could be more important than understanding the finer details of these relationships to help realise that we are all the same people making the same mistakes.

When we started this programme, I had a theory that most relationships have at their core a fatal flaw. We all have character blemishes: I can't resist showing off so that people will like me. That's why most of the shows have me explaining something deeply esoteric I once read in the hope that you'll want to be my friend. Joe suffers from being too passive. He lets things happen around him; he doesn't shape his own destiny.

So, based on our experience all those years ago, I believed that if you mixed these flaws together in a relationship, it would be like a slow-release poison that at some point would prove fatal to its well-being. But the last four years have made me think differently.

Think of what some of our guests have told us. They often still love each other years after separating. They may be married, celibate or have changed gender, we've heard it all on this show. But love does not disappear. It's just covered over by experience with someone else. I don't believe any more that relationships are doomed by the character traits of its protagonists. I believe that we're often in love with people, irrespective of whether we're still with them.

Love does not disappear. It may be obscured by the passage of time, or you may never see one another again. However, if some strange turn of events reunites you years later, the experiences you have since accumulated may help you realise what you have lost.

So, dear Festival Hall audience, that's it from me for this series and for the next few months as we're going to have a bit of a break. No more Shakespeare quotes or Thomas Hardy poems. Simply remember to never take for granted the depth of love you feel for your partner. If you remember why you love them, you will love them forever, regardless.

Joe, I'm letting you have the last word. Make it quick. This lot want to go home.

* * *

JOE: Thanks, Chloe. And thank you again from me to our lovely guests for agreeing to appear with us. You clearly have high thresholds of pain. To Kelly, who is leaving the show to go home to the US – just to reassure you that it wasn't me who reported you to the visa people at the Home Office.

I have good news for you all. I had prepared my own in-depth analysis of every person we've interviewed and what it taught us.

But bugger that. I'm going to speak off cuff. Maybe even off my sleeves too.

I want to tell Chloe how much I love her and how grateful I am for everything she's done for me over the last nearly five years. She's given me a chance to rebuild my career and helped me regain some self-belief. I am immensely proud of what we have created together, and have learnt so much from her – and I don't just mean the essential life skill of how to analyse eighteenth-century love poetry.

She has helped me understand the elements of a successful relationship and how a failed one can be the foundation for personal growth. Thank you, Chloe, for making me realise what I need to do to be happy. That is the real gift of this podcast.

Now, I too have an announcement to make.

I think this show, when it continues, will benefit from some fresh energy and a different perspective. I think Chloe will be better off without me. I've felt this for a while, but tonight I realised it properly. Today, I was offered the job as Head of Comedy Faculty at the wonderful College of Live Performance in Melbourne. Yes, it's a real job at a real performing arts university, which will suit me as I used to be a teacher and my pupils were always laughing at me. I need to reset.

Tomorrow, I will accept the role. They want me to start in April. Does anyone want to rent a flat in Tooting?

* * *

From the moment Joe announced he was moving to Australia, Chloe worried she might faint like the heroine in a Victorian melodrama. During the musical finale, she remained seated as the entire crew and their guests ran on for an impromptu disco. She jiggled a bit in her chair, glancing furtively at Joe, who was standing on the other side of the stage staring blankly at the audience, unable to look in her direction.

When it was over, she joined the backstage mêlée of production team, advertisers, guests and fans, greeting everyone with sufficient professionalism not to draw attention to herself. There was no after-party so she didn't have to be polite for long and she wondered if they could see her disappointment and distraction. Eventually, Joe sidled up to her sheepishly and for a second they stood among the chaos, neither knowing what to say, until Joe asked if they could go for a walk.

Silently, she put on her coat, and they exited the stage door without speaking and went up the steps on to Waterloo Bridge. Joe guided her lightly by the elbow and they crossed the road and walked for a few seconds until Joe stopped by the railing. They stared downriver at skyscrapers shaped like cheese graters and walkie-talkies next to the illuminated dome of St Paul's. Thick, moonless cloud muted the view.

'Well, isn't this a clichéd setting for our denouement,' Chloe said eventually.

'It's my favourite spot in London,' he replied.

'It's everyone's favourite spot in London, you plonker.'

'And there's me thinking I was the only one who knew this bridge was here.'

She stared ahead of her, unwilling to look at him directly.

'I assume you've arranged for a boat to pass by with an orchestra?' she whispered.

'No, but the firework display should be starting any second now. Would you like me to sing to you while we're waiting?'

'No. I want you to talk to me. Properly.'

'Are you angry?'

'Yes. Disappointed too. When were you going to tell me? And are you such a coward you had to do it on stage?'

'Believe it or not, that wasn't my plan at the start of the evening.'

'You must have nailed that job in Australia quickly then.'

'I need to start walking, I'm afraid.'

'To Australia? There are easier ways to get there, you know.'

'No, my thigh is throbbing from the fall. I need to keep moving,' Joe said, stroking his leg and wincing.

They walked down the stairs by the front of the National Theatre. Chloe was holding his arm tightly now as they ambled in silence, putting distance between them and the show. After a few minutes they arrived at Gabriel's Wharf, its restaurants and bars now shut. Joe led them to a bench facing the river and they stared at the unlit dredgers and party boats bobbing on the oil-black Thames. He put his arm across her shoulders and she nuzzled into its crook, absorbing his warmth in the quiet of the night.

It was eerily deserted. A couple passed them, walking their dog. Three teenagers performed casual pirouettes on their scooters in their vicinity before disappearing, and a man in a hoodie shuffled by talking to himself, a pungent vapour trail of weed following on after. Minutes passed before Joe eventually spoke.

'I wasn't going to accept the job. I applied ages ago and heard nothing. They sent an email in the morning with the offer, and I intended to turn them down.'

'Then why didn't you?'

'Because I realised, tonight, I needed to leave.'

'You decided on the spot?'

Joe reflected.

'Hasty, I know. I certainly should have told my family first. My mother is furious, you should see the texts. Thank God Dad wasn't there, he'd have had another heart attack.'

Chloe didn't smile and Joe knew her scrunched features well enough to understand she was processing.

'I thought you loved me and wanted to be with me? I wanted us to try and make this work.'

'Do you know how much I love you, Chloe? How I've never stopped loving you?' Even in the gloom, he saw the tears on her cheek.

'I love you too. I think from the moment we met again, something happened. It's terrible, but it took me over. I just want to be with you. I arrived tonight ready to leave David and be with you.'

'Don't do that.'

'Are you listening? I want to be with you. Don't you want to be with me?'

'Since about 2001. I've spent the whole day imagining how we would find a way to live together, but then realised tonight it would be wrong.'

'What are you talking about?'

'I was so anxious not to be late for you, I fell over, and then you sat with me like you were afraid to let me out of your sight.'

'What's wrong with that?'

'Nothing at all. It was when Nicola and Emily arrived that suddenly I felt like the most pathetic bloke on earth.'

'You're wonderful. Maybe you don't realise it,' she said despondently.

'I can't do it, Chloe. I can't.'

'Do what?'

'Risk getting it wrong. Risk hurting you. I've been such a failure in my relationships. I'm holding you back on the show, that's clear, and I can't afford to make a mistake when the person affected is you. You're better off without me.'

He exhaled deeply.

'I want to be with you,' Chloe said with increasing desperation.

'And I feel the same, but how can I be sure it's the right thing? You've surrounded me with all these stories of other people's relationships and their pain. And what have I learnt? That I never managed to find happiness because of the giant shadow you've cast over me. I failed to be with someone, have a family. Be normal. You have a decent husband, who I've been hoping would leave you for a twenty-five-year-old actress so we could properly hate him. Maybe you can make it better with him? What if you give up everything for me and, like the show, I'm the inferior partner?'

'Don't say that, it's not true. I should never have let you go.'

'I agree, but you did, and now you have children who don't need me in their life. I can't do it. I *can't* do it. I love you too much to ruin everything for you.'

Joe held up his hand to suggest he had nothing more to say and they stared at one another, exhausted and despairing. Chloe wiped her cheeks, moist and puffy with emotion.

'I don't suppose you want to kiss me?' she asked forlornly.

'Much more than I want to go live in Melbourne.'

He cupped her face in his cold hands, and she shivered at the touch. They kissed briefly, but it was too cold now and Joe needed to stand up again to alleviate the ache in his thigh.

'This isn't really working as a farewell, is it?' she said, trying to smile.

'Not really. I'd hoped for a less painful evening in all respects.'

Chloe supported him and he hobbled alongside her. Eventually, she spoke.

'What were you going to say before you decided to change the script and emigrate in front of a live audience?'

He turned towards her and kissed her lips one more time with the love that had lived within him for so long.

'I'd written some nonsense about how love never dies, it just adapts.'

'You'd have ruined the show.'

'And that's why, my darling, you are so much better off without me.'

* * *

She got in a cab, leaving Joe to limp home on the Northern Line, and returned to a cold, silent house. David was not due back from his recce for another day and she sat in the kitchen staring at the clock, willing it to be morning. She was starving and queasy at the same time, but didn't have the energy to eat anything other than a handful of almonds.

Sleep was impossible and after hours of staring at the ceiling, she turned on the radio and listened to *Farming Today*. Pork production was 5 per cent up on the previous year and she listened to a farmer explain how a brave new world for bacon manufacture made a mockery of the theory we would all soon be vegans. Focusing on his soft West Country burr, she tried not to think about how empty she felt now that both the podcast and her relationship with Joe were over.

The *Today* programme was reporting on the clamour in the Tory party for Boris Johnson to resign when the twins ran into her room and threw themselves on the bed. Using all her acting skills to be the perfect mother, she showered them with affection getting them ready for school. It was drizzling as she walked them to the gates, and she trudged home damp and melancholic.

Writing her novel would be impossible and she desperately wanted to send an SOS for her father, despite knowing she had to get through this herself. What had happened with Joe had made her feel foolish, sad, confused, angry, self-pitying, despondent, and completely alone. She couldn't possibly inflict that on Malcolm again after all the support he'd given her over the years.

The morning dragged like an interminable long-haul flight. Chloe wandered from room to room, trying to find a place to rest where she was comfortable. Her mind wouldn't calm and all she could see on the horizon was hard work, frustration and regret. Lying on a sofa under a blanket, she heard David enter the house at lunchtime. She didn't call out and waited for him to find her in their living room.

'I didn't think you were coming home until this evening,' she said flatly. There was something odd about his expression. Like he had bad news he didn't quite know how to share.

'We finished early.' He sat down next to her and then added as an afterthought, 'How was the show?'

'Pretty good, but I haven't got the energy to relive it, if that's OK.'

'Fine by me.'

They lapsed into a silence, as if they had just met in the waiting room of their local dentist.

'Is there something wrong? You seem out of sorts.'

David shook his head and stood up from the sofa. A brief panic that he knew what had happened was quickly replaced by incredulity when he spoke.

'I'm so unhappy. Surely you must be? I'm sorry, Chloe, but we've become more distant from one another than I ever thought possible. Maybe we just don't work anymore? I think I should move out for a while.'

April 2023

As the queue shuffled along, Joe stared at the floor, wondering if it was a good idea to be there. This was not how he'd imagined spending his evening when the day began at the Cool Beans Coffee Shop next door to his South Yarra apartment. Every morning, Shaggy Sean the barista would make him an impeccable flat white with a milky design that was like an inkblot test, and today it had been a large heart with an arrow. Joe hadn't thought much about its significance, enjoying instead the cobalt-blue sky and warm autumn sunshine.

His year in Melbourne had been everything he had hoped – informal, cool, and buzzing with unflustered energy. He didn't miss the podcast and was enjoying his new role teaching comedy to a group of enthusiastic young people with very different senses of humour. His reputation had spread like bushfire ('*wildfire*' was what you got in Europe) and with each workshop or seminar, he attracted more attendees. The faculty were delighted with him, and this success had prompted him to start performing a few gigs, which had gone surprisingly well.

If he said so himself, he'd never looked better. A new exercise routine included the gym, five-a-side football, and a myriad of scenic routes for long runs. Most importantly, he wasn't lonely, having curated a circle of friends who knew little about his past life and didn't judge him for being single in his early forties. Although dating wasn't a priority, he'd even managed a harmless and enjoyable relationship with a lawyer called Cassie, which ended amicably when she moved back to Sydney.

He did miss his family and kept in regular contact on scheduled Zoom calls. His father was healthy and flourishing, having just returned from a holiday in Mauritius where, unbeknown to his children, he married Dull Debbie on the beach. Joe now had three very different mums: Helen and Jane, who gave Joe unsolicited updates on their passionate marriage, and Dull Debbie, living proof that charisma was optional in the pursuit of happiness.

As he sat eating his granola breakfast, he felt grateful to live in the moment and not worry about his direction of travel. The moment, however, didn't last long when he received a rare message from his agent, Josh. It wasn't an update on the search for a publisher for his novel, but rather a surprising invitation to an event at Dymocks bookshop later that evening.

Ten hours later, he stood in line like a condemned man. Inching his way forward, he tried to look inconspicuous among the mainly female crowd by covering his mouth with his hand. Somehow, she didn't spot him as he edged closer, focusing instead on writing warm messages in the books of her loyal fans. For hours, he'd rehearsed pithy one-liners that now seemed inadequate. Instead, he handed Chloe his newly purchased copy and said quietly,

'Can you sign it to *Joe* and write something funny.'

Her body jolted in shock when she saw him. On the cusp of saying something, she composed herself quickly, unwilling to betray emotions in front of the large cohort of her readers who had come to hear her speak. Without looking at him again, she signed the book, and then turned to the teenager waiting patiently next to him like she was a long-lost friend. The coldness of the encounter confused him but when he opened the book, its inscription made him laugh out loud.

Please can we go for a drink as soon as I'm finished. And your flies are undone x

* * *

'Don't get crumbs everywhere. I only change the bedding every other month.'

Chloe sipped her coffee and then took a defiant bite of the croissant, so that flakes of pastry landed on the crumpled sheets. It had been so many years since he'd shared a bed with her, and she looked lovely in his frayed Edinburgh Festival T-shirt. Thrilled with her proximity, he couldn't stop stroking her face.

'Are you going to manhandle me all day?' she asked, kissing him slowly on the lips.

'I'm game, if you are.'

'We'll see. Last night was special though, wasn't it?'

He nodded in enthusiastic agreement. 'Is this what usually happens on this book tour?' he asked.

'Normally, I just get requests from writers for advice. Old saddos like you never get past security.'

'I suppose I'm just a little distraction as you breeze through town. Oh, I feel so cheap now.'

Joe's heart was beating like he had run for hours. He assumed it was fear she would leave and not return.

'I wasn't sure you'd come to the show,' she said.

'Are you kidding? I love your books. You should keep going with them, you might do quite well one day.'

'You know that's not what I meant.' She kissed him again. Even the sour taste of coffee on her breath was enticing. 'I wanted you there so much, it was hard to focus.'

He paused to absorb the compliment and then kissed her eyelids.

'Can I ask how on earth you managed to get a book published so quickly with everything that's happened to you?'

'Writing was my refuge from the nightmare of couples' therapy, mediation and divorce lawyers.'

'I am sorry, I feel responsible for all this shit.'

Chloe took his hand and kissed it before placing it against her cheek.

'Don't be. It turns out David wasn't just jealous of you but didn't like me anymore, which was a much bigger problem. It took two excruciating months with Bethany from the Choice & Resolution therapy practice in Camden Town to find out. How weird – we paid her a fortune just as we were about to split our money in half.'

'Are you done now?'

'Nearly. Let's just say, it's messy when the wife is the bigger earner and the husband has self-esteem issues. The decree absolute is still a few months off, so I'm not quite "middle-aged, free and single".'

'Maybe not single, now?'

He regretted his presumption, but hoped he was right. He'd gone to her event expecting at best to have an awkward reminisce and believing it would be too complicated for her to consider even a long-distance friendship with him. But from the moment they adjourned to a quiet bar, he could tell that little had changed in her heart since their conversation on the South Bank. They talked mainly about his work and new life, and she said very little. As soon as they were seated with their drinks, it was obvious there was only one place they wanted to be. They guzzled down their G&Ts and within minutes were kissing in the back of an Uber, like they'd just been informed of an imminent armageddon.

'Can we just enjoy the morning and being together?'

'I'm sorry, it's hard to know how to behave when all you've ever wanted falls in your lap. And then on top too, about half an hour later.'

'Very droll, Benny Hill.'

He drew her into an embrace, and they stayed motionless. Flyaway strands of her long hair got caught in his mouth, and he removed it like dental floss.

'If you want a memento, I can cut you a lock without you pulling it out with your teeth,' she said, disentangling her hair. 'And I don't suppose you have a scrunchie lying about the flat from one of your previous conquests?'

'I think last week's may have left some string under the sink, if that helps.'

'I'm having my hair straightened before the next show. You'll just have to take me frizzy this morning.'

'Honestly, Chloe, right now I wouldn't care if you were bald.'

'That's the most beautiful thing any man has ever said to me.'

Unable to think of a riposte, Joe kissed the top of her head, and then realised this was more the gesture of a parent blessing a child than a would-be new lover.

'There's so much I need to know,' he continued. 'Most importantly, how are the kids?'

She leant back against the headboard and sighed.

'All things considered, OK. We're trying to do lots as a family still and David only lives five minutes away, which means he can pop in whenever he wants. It's chilly between us, but we've promised we'll do everything to not be idiots in front of them. My lawyer is annoyed because she says I'm blurring boundaries and making it harder to come to an agreement.'

'It must be hard,' Joe said, ashamed for contributing to this mess, but not enough to dampen his jubilation that Chloe was now husband-free.

'I wouldn't wish this on anyone,' Chloe said wistfully. 'Families are meant to be a safe unit, not two selfish individuals traumatising their poor children. Ask me in a year how much damage we've done.'

'And David?' His interest was disingenuous. He needed to know Chloe would never go back to him.

'Angry. Not just with me, but with the world for his professional misfortune.'

'Hollywood lost his number then?' Joe said, immediately regretting the barb.

'Don't be horrid. His film producer has dropped him from his latest project, so he's still having to make German air freshener commercials.'

'I am sorry. I think I'm just anxious and don't want to do anything wrong.'

'You'll be even happier to know then that he poses no threat to you whatsoever, given he's dating like crazy. My loss is Tinder's gain.'

'How do you know?'

'Emily bumped into him when she was walking the baby, and he confessed. I don't really want to talk about him anymore, if that's OK?'

He'd waited forever for this moment and was happy to change the subject from a discussion about David. She leant into him and rested her head on his shoulder.

'Tell me about all your work projects. We didn't get far last night before you threw yourself at me,' he said.

'And as a result, I'm filled with self-loathing and remorse. Now, what do you want to know?'

Joe had forgotten how much sharper she was than him. He knew she wasn't being serious, but he didn't like hearing her use the word 'remorse', even in jest.

'For a start, how's the podcast without me?'

'You really don't mind that I've started again on my own?'

'Are you kidding, I think it's much better with just you. You always were the proper interviewer. I was just the bloke that shouts *Heeeeere's Johnny* before the guests arrive.'

'That's rubbish,' she replied, shaking her head instinctively.

'No, it's not. You didn't need a sidekick, the ideas were all yours. Your new format works much better with you not being interrupted by yet another bad joke from me.'

'You were my partner, Joe. *Ex-Communicate* was successful because of the both of us.'

'I'm just proud of you. Unlike your ex-husband, I'm not intimidated by your talent. It's rather sexy, as talents go.'

'Maybe one day we could think of a way of bringing back our double act?' He knew she was being serious. For some reason, she still had a higher professional opinion of his abilities than he did.

'Chrissie would never want that.'

'It's not up to her anymore. I make my own choices these days when it comes to the future of the podcast.'

'What do you mean?'

'It's confidential.'

Joe looked around the bedroom, furtively.

'Who am I going to tell? We're in Australia. They've only just discovered mobile phones.'

'I'm serious. We're just in the middle of negotiations with Spotify. Mary would kill me. Well, she'd kill you, in truth.'

'And take great pleasure in it.'

'Anyway, she's been amazing and has got an awesome deal on the table.'

'Does that mean I can stay home and look pretty for you while you go to work?'

'It's a distinct possibility, but you'll need some Botox and filler to keep me interested.'

Joe flexed a bicep.

'I think these babies should do the trick.'

'Mary's been amazing,' Chloe said, ignoring him. 'She gives me so much self-belief. It was her idea that I come on a book tour to Australia.'

'I did wonder why you've come so far. Is it worth it?'

'It is now.'

Their legs were intertwined like the roots of an ancient oak.

'I'm not following you,' Joe said, with a growing sense that their reunion wasn't accidental. 'Wasn't it your publisher who sent you?'

'Not really, they initially refused and needed a lot of persuading. Mary probably used her friends in the criminal underworld to get them to change their minds.'

'But you have loads of fans over here?'

'Even so, the cost of this trip almost outweighs its commercial benefit. Come on, Einstein, must I spell it out? "*Cupid, draw back your bow*", "*Matchmaker, Matchmaker, make me a match*". Do you need any more song lyrics to help you get the picture?'

Then he understood.

He'd never have taken Mary to be such a romantic, but there had clearly been a careful choreography to arrive at this moment. A book tour of indeterminate value as a means of engineering their reunion? Quite a risky strategy if he'd said no to Josh's invitation. The timing and wording of the text must have been planned with military precision. He could not contain his elation.

'I love you so much, Chloe. I love you so much. I've waited the last six years to say that without fear of losing you or my job on the podcast. In case you haven't guessed, I've never stopped loving you and I'm not going to let you leave again. I mean, of course you can go home and see your children, I don't want to come across unreasonable, but we need to plan a life together. What do you say to that then?'

'*I do love nothing in the world so well as you, is not that strange?*'

He frowned.

'Quoting *Much Ado*. Really, *now*? We're not recording an episode and I'd rather hear it in your own words, if that's OK.'

'Sorry. It's just, I've always wanted to use that line in real life. You understand that it's a declaration of deep love after a period of intense stress, so it seemed kind of the right time to bring it out of the locker.'

'All right, clever clogs, then tell me what we're going to do now. I know it's only been twenty-four hours, but I feel that we've wasted enough time getting to this point.'

She looked at him seriously, and twizzled loose strands of her hair between her thumb and forefinger like she was playing with worry beads. Eventually, she replied.

'It's not going to be easy, what with you living nine thousand miles away. You can hardly pop in for coffee. And you love your job. How will I introduce you to the kids? Plus, it's not that likely we'll have our own, is it, and maybe that's a problem. Since you ask, I haven't got a clue what'll happen. Does that matter?'

Joe shook his head, unwilling to undermine this hard-earned happiness by discussing it further.

'No. We'll work something out and I'll make every effort to learn from my inadequacies first time round. I'm sure there are some inner-city delinquents I can find to teach back in London.'

'And I promise that from now on, I'll celebrate my good fortune loving you rather than trying to make my luck elsewhere. You have a deal. Where do I sign?'

She held out her hand to shake his and he pulled her towards him. They kissed for a long time, until a thought struck him.

'One more question, please.'

'OMG, how much more do you want to analyse this situation? I'm beginning to hanker for gormless Joe.'

'It's just, I forgot to ask about Malcolm. Given his importance, how will he react to this news?'

'*Duh!* Who do you think I'll be texting as soon as you have a shower and who do you think drove me to the airport to make sure I got on the plane without changing my mind? He made quite the speech in the car. I can't remember the exact words, but the gist of it was that he had listened to all our shows and had come to an important conclusion.'

She paused like a TV host about to announce the result of a reality show.

'Which was?'

'That our banal observations provided no insight into relationships, and it was a miracle anyone listened to us. Really, he thinks a podcast focused on the relentless pursuit of emotional truths is the height of self-indulgence. You should find someone you love and just get on with building a life together. But none of that mattered. He always really liked you and thinks if we get back together, he'll have a much quieter life.'

Acknowledgements

It may not mean much to Robert Redford or Barbra Streisand that I am thanking them now for their performances in *The Way We Were*, but they have a lot to answer for.

To those not familiar with the 1973 Sydney Pollack film with its famous Marvin Hamlisch theme song, let me explain. I first saw this schmalz-laden weepy in 1982 when I was an impressionable seventeen-year-old, wondering what romantic escapades would come my way. (Previous fumbles at the school disco were hardly worth writing a sonnet about.) And I loved it so much that I watched and re-watched its ending to try and understand what had gone wrong for its protagonists.

The use of '*were*' in the film's title is a massive plot-spoiler as to the outcome of their relationship. Nevertheless, I urge anyone with a love of an old-fashioned romance to watch it, if only for its moving denouement in Central Park in the Autumn sunshine. They clearly love each other, but their clashing personalities makes it impossible for them to stay together. Oh, did I also mention that they split just after they have had a baby, making it even sadder?

By the time I had watched it for the twentieth time, my romantic purview was blurred by the realisation that love and desire were apparently no guarantee for eternal happiness. From then on, I was hooked on all literature and art that had the narrative of a complex relationship, ideally accompanied by some pain and suffering. I was fascinated by what makes them work, how they come apart and how they survive the vicissitudes of everyday life.

So circuitously, this is why I wanted to write a love story grounded in a world in which relationships, fictional or real, are endlessly discussed and dissected. This book is my outlet for those curated romantic associations and thus contains references to all the films, books, songs and places that have helped me become the soppy old bloke, about to get his free bus pass, that I am today.

Pretty ironic, given my astonishingly happy love affair (now in its thirty-seventh year) with my wife, best mate and business partner Hannah. We are opposites in many ways, which is why we are so content. For example, I cry at the drop of a hat, and she tells me to man up and pick up the hat. We do however, both love a romcom and frequently pepper our conversations with quotes from our favourite films. ('*Six years later you find yourself singing "Surrey with a fringe on top" in front of Ira*'.)

This book is only possible because of her unstinting love and support; she knows that Chloe's need to be liked and Joe's attempts to be funny are the twin facets of my personality, and she provides the reassurance and laughter to satisfy both cravings. I am forever grateful to her for her patience, wisdom and kindness.

To John Bond, Julia Koppitz and the team at Whitefox Publishing, thank you for working on our third book together and always being so supportive and encouraging. My thanks to Shaun Patchett, with whom I have worked for twenty years, who designed the wonderful cover. And to Laura Lees, the nicest publicist in the world, my gratitude for all her calm advice, guidance and connections.

Finally, thank you to my children Sophie, Matthew and Jake, who remind me every hour of every day that the greatest joy of a happy relationship is a loving family, even if they point-blank refuse to watch *The Way We Were* and the other cultural masterpieces I recommend.

April 2025